WAR
AND
CRAFT

TOR BOOKS BY TOM DOYLE

American Craftsmen

The Left-Hand Way

War and Craft

WAR AND CRAFT

BOOK THREE *of the*
AMERICAN CRAFT SERIES

TOM DOYLE

TOR

A TOM DOHERTY ASSOCIATES BOOK

NEW YORK

WAR AND CRAFT

Copyright © 2017 by Tom Doyle

A Tor Book
Published by Tom Doherty Associates
175 Fifth Avenue
New York, NY 10010

www.tor-forge.com

Tor® is a registered trademark of Macmillan Publishing Group, LLC.

The Library of Congress Cataloging-in-Publication Data is available upon request.

ISBN 978-0-7653-3753-5 (hardcover)
ISBN 978-1-4668-3459-0 (ebook)

Our books may be purchased in bulk for promotional, educational, or business use. Please contact your local bookseller or the Macmillan Corporate and Premium Sales Department at 1-800-221-7945, extension 5442, or by email atMacmillanSpecialMarkets@macmillan.com.

First Edition: September 2017

Printed in the United States of America

0 9 8 7 6 5 4 3 2 1

TO MOM

I once again want to show you a craft that I've made.

ACKNOWLEDGMENTS

The American Craft series and this book in particular would not have been possible without the support of many people, some of whom are specifically thanked below:

Editor Claire Eddy, whose patience during my recent tribulations gave me the time and confidence to write this novel properly.

Editorial assistants Bess Cozby and Kristin Temple for going pirate hunting with me.

Agent Robert Thixton for continuing to persevere.

Dominick Saponaro, Irene Gallo, and Peter Lutjen for the joy of seeing such wonderful cover illustrations and designs for my work.

Copy editors Anna Chang, Ivy McFadden, and Debbie Friedman for their obsession for detail.

The members of the Writers Group from Hell for journeying for a year with me from one chunk of text to the next, for the third time.

My brother Bill Doyle, whose research on climbing above twenty thousand feet was very important (so many ways to fail!).

My partner, Beth Delaney, who kept me alive so I could finish this trilogy.

Moira Fitzgibbons, who helped again with Latin, and who also advised on the appropriate handling of old manuscripts.

Colleen Cahill and the Library of Congress for the use of their map collection.

Robert O'Donoghue, Shannon McRae, and Angie Greene for their assistance with the prologue.

Tom Zanol for a helpful bit of Italian, and for lending me his name for the first book.

All the indie book bloggers who mentioned my work or allowed me to be their guest.

Among the many references I used, I'm particularly indebted to Lawrence Sutin's *Do What Thou Wilt: A Life of Aleister Crowley* (St. Martin's Press, 2000).

Most of all, I'm grateful to the readers who've followed my craftspeople through these three books.

Thank you!

WAR
AND
CRAFT

THE CRAFTPERSONS FILE

(WHAT HAS GONE BEFORE)

STOP! If you are not cleared for documents classified TOP SECRET EX-22, return this file to the office of Director J. Edgar Edwards <u>immediately</u>. Anyone reading further without such clearance is subject to instant sanction.

TOP SECRET//EX-22/CRAFTPRO/FOUO/NOFORN/ORGCON
ORDERS
From: Eddy Edwards, Director, Special Surveillance Service, CIA
To: Inductees; Morton/Endicott Farsight Analysis Team
Re: <u>Background of Certain AWOL Practitioners and Their Associates; Order Regarding Same</u>

Some of you receiving this memorandum and order are currently being read into the craft secrets: the covert history and activities of magician-soldiers and psychic spies at home and abroad. You have waived your right to due process of law and your related constitutional rights in the event you disclose any of this material.

How will we know if you've disclosed? If you've heard whispers about "The Peepshow," that's us. Our intelligence service is responsible for viewing events and persons in the future or at a distance. If you disclose anything, we will know it, perhaps in advance, and we will find you and kill you. My apologies, but absolute clarity on this point is more important than sugarcoating the message.

What follows is the necessary background for understanding the recent activities of Major Dale Morton, Major Michael G. Endicott, and Lieutenant Scherezade Rezvani, all absent without leave and in the company of Royal Navy Commander Grace Marlow in Tokyo, Japan (collectively, the "AWOL practitioners").

I. THE MORTON AND REZVANI FAMILIES

The Mortons are descendants of Thomas Morton of the Merry Mount settlement. Many of the Mortons are excellent weathermen (controllers of local weather). They often can see a person's "sins" (either committed or intended) in the form of glowing letters. They also may have forebodings of their imminent deaths. The Mortons have a mutual-protection compact with the American Sanctuary, and Dale Morton was able to obtain temporary asylum there during his self-initiated mission to uncover the Left-Hand cabal in the Pentagon's craft service section, "H-ring."

The orthodox branch of the Morton Family has saved the armed forces of the United States on several occasions. But the Left-Hand branch of the Mortons once led the craft world in the forbidden practices of life extension, psychic vampirism, and possession, with an accompaniment of mass murder.

A. The Left-Hand Twins: Roderick and Madeline.

1. Madeline Ligeia Morton. Deceased. Madeline's ghost is currently the leading voice in the Left-Hand Morton collective spiritual entity. During the later part of Madeline's centuries-long life, she was one of the leaders of the Left-Hand cabal within H-ring. She practiced the art of life extension through possession of a series of young bodies; the last living body she fully possessed was of a Gideon special ops tracker, code name Sakakawea (Captain Shannon McRae).

In death, Madeline has shown an unexpected protectiveness toward her living family, particularly toward Dale Morton's spouse, Scherie Rezvani. We cannot determine the ultimate goal of this strategy. Attempts to foresee Madeline's actions induce headaches, nausea, and PTSD. She is at least as dangerous in death as she was in life.

2. Roderick Morton, aka "The Red Death." Deceased, spirit presumed destroyed. In the early 1800s, he led the Left-Hand cause until the orthodox Mortons and the other craft Families defeated him. He survived as a decomposing head subject to the will of his twin sister Madeline and her lover Abram Endicott, and he only recently gained his freedom during that H-ring cabal's downfall.

With a new body and a new home in Kiev, Roderick attempted to suborn the craft services of the major powers and gain godlike power for himself. In a secret craft bunker in Virginia, he accessed the magic of one of the dead alternative Earths, or "hellworlds," but the AWOL practitioners defeated him and cast his spirit into the hellworld. Farsight gives a probability of greater than five sigma of his destruction by the demonic entity of that world's collective dead.

B. Major Dale Morton.

Major Morton is the last craft-practicing scion of his family, and the most powerful living weatherman. He has a remarkable record of countercraft assassinations, but his mission to kill a Persian sorcerer (Operation Butterfly) has left him with a residual curse, and it remains unclear whether he could face a Muslim practitioner in combat. His efforts to find the traitor who set him up in Operation Butterfly led to the uncovering of the Left-Hand cabal within H-ring.

Major Morton's father, grandfather, and biological mother are all deceased.

- His father discovered the possibility of the Left Hand tapping into a hellworld, but he drove himself insane during this investigation.
- His grandfather acted as Major Morton's sole parent (living or dead) for most of his childhood.

• Morton's biological mother was code name Sphinx, aka Dare Smith, former Director of the Special Surveillance Service. This family connection to one of the greatest oracles of all time makes Morton and his close associates extremely difficult to track psychically.

While the prejudice against the orthodox Morton line has been completely unjustified, the continued proximity of Dale Morton to Left-Hand influences and the Left Hand's interest in him bears further observation.

C. *Lieutenant Scherezade "Scherie" Rezvani.*

She is the most powerful exorcist in the world, which given the use of spiritual possession and necromancy by Left-Hand practitioners makes her an essential asset. She is also a skilled healer. Dale Morton is her spouse. Up until Lt. Rezvani's emergence as a practitioner, her family was mundane, with any practice of craft falling below service jurisdiction. She was instrumental both in the inadvertent liberation of Roderick and in his eventual casting out from this world. She uses an inordinate amount of profanity to focus her emotions while working her exorcisms and dispellations.

Farsight and mundane reports indicate that Lt. Rezvani may be pregnant. If so, the sex (and therefore probable powers) of the child remain unknown.

II. THE ENDICOTT AND MARLOW FAMILIES

The Endicotts are descendants of John Endicott of Salem. Their spiritual gifts often include an exceptional power of command or suasion. With a few notorious exceptions, they have remained faithful to the beliefs and morals of their Puritan ancestors. The long-standing feud between the Endicotts and Mortons appears to have ended with the friendship of Dale Morton and Michael Endicott.

A. Major Michael G. Endicott.

By rank and consensus, Major Endicott is the leader of the AWOL practitioners. He has recently acquired the so-called transnational power—that is, an ability to replenish and draw on craft power in any country, whether friendly or hostile. His power of command, formerly normal for someone of his Family, has also expanded greatly. Unchecked by self or others, he could become a new conqueror on the order of an Alexander or Caesar.

While fleeing the UK through the Chunnel, Endicott was seriously wounded, and recovered only through an injection of the Left-Hand nanite serum. In a second attempt to kill him, this time by the *Oikumene*, Endicott lost an eye and some brain tissue, and he avoided death only through the synergy of the Left-Hand serum and his transnational power. During his fight with Roderick in the Virginia bunker, he lost half of his foot. But that which could not kill him has apparently only made him stronger.

Although Endicott's loyalty to country and antipathy toward the Left-Hand way are as close to certainties as farsight determination allows, others (particularly the *Oikumene*) believe his exposure to the Left-Hand serum and his transnational power make him an imminent global threat.

Endicott's father, General Oliver C. Endicott, died during the fight with the H-ring cabal. His spirit is in command of security at Arlington National Cemetery.

B. Abram Endicott.

Deceased, spirit presumed departed. With his lover Madeline Morton, Abram headed the Left-Hand cabal within H-ring.

C. Royal Navy Commander Grace Marlow.

Two of Commander Marlow's earliest known practitioner ancestors were playwright and spy Christopher Marlowe and Tituba of Salem witch-hunt fame. Commander Marlow's skills include stealth, theft, seduction, the detection and deployment of deception, and combat of all kinds. She has repeatedly saved Major Endicott's life and was an essential part of Roderick's defeat.

Major Endicott and Commander Marlow will be marrying soon in Japan. *[Handwritten note in margin: "Tell them to stop asking what the hell she sees in Endicott. They may have the security clearance, but they clearly do not have a need to know."]* H-ring is sending Captain Katrina Hutchinson of their PRECOG section as the U.S. witness of their wedding. Captain Hutchinson is married to the current commander of countercraft operations, General Calvin Attucks, and is a family friend of both the Endicotts and Mortons through her cousin, the late Colonel Elizabeth Hutchinson. This makes her acceptable to all parties as a witness.

Below, I note some security concerns regarding the AWOL practitioners and their wedding.

III. FOREIGN PRACTITIONERS OF CONCERN

A. "Mr. Cushlee" Renfield.

We have determined that this particular Renfield was responsible for several attempts on Major Endicott's and Commander Marlow's lives. He also violated Arlington National Cemetery in order to obtain the spirits of the unknown and forgotten dead for Roderick's plans. We are near certain that this Renfield survived his involvement with Roderick; surviving such schemes is what his Family does best.

B. Vasilisa.

Cryptonym of the only survivor of the Russian *Spetsnaz Magi* assault on Roderick at Chernobyl, where she was likely used as bait due to her general resemblance to Madeline. She aided Dale Morton's escape from Moscow, and she'll be attending the Endicott/Marlow wedding.

C. Miki Kaguya.

An agent of Japan's craft service, she was instrumental in obtaining a provisional asylum for Morton, Rezvani, Endicott, and Marlow. She has a previous professional and personal connection with Dale Morton. She also has some association with Japan's craft black-ops group, aka the ninjas. (Yes, they're real. You can tell that to anyone you'd like; the ninjas don't seem to mind.)

D. The Oikumene.

An international craft organization, they have opposed the Left Hand since the dawn of history. Their leader holds the office of Pythia. Fearing Major Endicott's transnational power of command and his exposure to Left-Hand craft, the *Oikumene* attempted his assassination, leaving him with the damage described above. On the other hand, they've shown some concern for Lt. Rezvani's wellbeing.

IV. STATUS OF AWOL PRACTITIONERS, THREATS, AND RESPONSE

You may be aware that, as a result of Roderick Morton's infiltration of the major craft services, many of your fellow practitioners here and abroad are now subject to house arrest or other restrictions. Apparently, our four AWOL practitioners had advance knowledge of the repercussions of Roderick's subversive activities and, after defeating him, fled in a government supersonic aircraft to their present residence in Tokyo.

Farsight reveals intense worldwide focus on our AWOL practitioners and the upcoming Endicott-Marlow wedding. Motives for possible hostile action include but are not limited to:

- Denying the United States and Great Britain these assets
- Revenge for their anti-Left-Hand activities
- Concern about possible offspring from an international craft marriage (not everyone wants another Churchill)
- Obtaining certain intelligence information
- Continued concern from the *Oikumene* regarding Endicott's power and intentions
- An outstanding Renfield contract for the murder of one or more of the AWOL practitioners

Together these four AWOL practitioners destroyed the most powerful mage in history. While they remain difficult to track in farsight, we can foresee that their survival is of central importance to U.S. and global security. They should also be regarded as extremely dangerous.

Therefore, all intelligence, farsight or otherwise, regarding the AWOL practitioners shall be sent directly to me and not shared with any other person or authority within or outside this service, and no action shall be taken regarding the AWOL practitioners without my express order.

By Order of the Director, Special Surveillance Service:
/s/
Eddy Edwards

Addendum to Memorandum re: AWOL Practitioners

I thought this went without saying, but again for absolute clarity, do not attempt to leave the country without my express order. The AWOL Practitioners could get away with it; you can't. The recent surge in the number of identified practitioners does not mean that any particular absence will go unnoticed. If we can't keep you, it's EX-22: "Thou shalt not suffer a witch to live."

/s/
EE

Classified by: J. Edgar Edwards
Reason: 1.5(c)(X1)
Declassify on: Not Applicable

PROLOGUE

TERRIBLE BEAUTIES ARE BORN

Too long a sacrifice
Can make a stone of the heart.

—W. B. Yeats

All was quiet on New Year's Day before dawn. Near Galway, below a thatched cottage like they kept for the tourists, the quiet old man called Oz came suddenly awake in his cave, as if the lack of noise had startled his sleep. He got up from his warm cavern bed and rubbed his gray stubble, cross with the world. He hadn't had a foreboding since the peace in the North, except for the gentle one that came to all the old and told him that he must pass on his gifts soon, lest they be lost.

No use complaining. In the dark, Oz put on his worn white Aran sweater and one of the fancy fiber macintoshes the young ones preferred. He slung his rifle over his shoulder and, every joint hurting, climbed up the ladder to his cottage home.

He stepped outside. Beyond his yard's low wall of rounded stone, the ground was flat and exposed. There'd be no surprises today. He made a sign of the cross in the air, and walked toward the town. They'd be coming from there, rested and ready.

He walked stiffly, as if he'd ridden a horse for a few centuries like his ancestor of honored memory. He wouldn't have to walk far. He whistled a traditional reel, then hummed something by the Pogues. A mist blew silently in from the west, chilling, but well above freezing. Good on you, Gulf Stream, but couldn't you do better? But no, it was warmer these days, and snow wasn't as general over Ireland, thank ya, climate change. Let the Yank weathermen try playing against that for a while.

The foreboding that had woken him capped a week of his personal warning signs. A photographer with long hair and etched face, like David Warner in *The Omen,* boarding the ferry for Inis Mór. A pale young woman in colorless clothes, like one of the hard ones he'd known in the Provisionals, drinking steaming coffee out of doors in the gray weather. A dog growling at Oz's shadow.

With the mundane peace, the signs he'd seen about town could only mean one thing. They were again coming for him, coming for his gifts. Not that he cared to keep such things, but they wouldn't be coming for the right reasons. They were coming for the worst reasons in the world.

The worst reason they'd want his gifts would be to open a way to hell. He knew that from another sign: a phantom pain from his index finger's missing tip, which he'd lost poking like an eejit at a hellworld's portal. Same as the ache in his joints foretold rain, that finger pain told him another portal would be opening soon, if it hadn't already.

Ahead, three faint shadows moved toward him from the glow of the town. Oz looked about him. This field, never plowed, was the place.

The three would be Cúchulainns, Hounds of Ulster. Tough bastards, but some had anger management issues. He didn't need to discern the blond hair of a deliberately bad dye job and the pair of eyes of different colors, one green, one gray, to know who their young leader was.

"Fergus," he called. "What business has you out on this fine morning?"

Fergus raised a hand, and his two companions, a man and a woman, halted. "We'll have them, Ossian MacCool. The flail and the sand and you. All the gifts."

"Ah, lad," said Oz. "I can understand working for the Left Hand. But the Sasanach too?"

"Albion is divided," said Fergus. "It's an opportunity."

"Albion can go feck itself by itself," said Oz. "You brought three against one? You're treating me like Roderick Morton."

The Hounds drew weapons and panned the countryside, looking for others. Damn his loquacious habits. Oz had gone too far, and the Hounds must have heard the deception. He whistled, and his own young (or at least younger) ones sprang up from their craft-camouflaged positions, a matching man and woman for Fergus's, weapons at ready.

Fergus gave a grim chuckle. "We have a fair fight."

"We have a standoff," said Oz, waving his hand back toward Galway. "So stand off."

"No," said Fergus. "We have a duel."

Now that was a surprise. Oz considered. His commission was important—more important now than ever—but he was one of the *filí* to the bone, and he could not decline another craft poet's challenge even to keep the gifts safe. "Fair enough. A duel then."

Their companions drew back, lest some shrapnelled syllables hit them. A modern Irish duel of craft poets did not require original composition; it was improvisational pastiche, deadly riffs on the nation's verse and song, which already had all the magical words one could desire. Each duelist would find the words that had both power and hard truths to sing against their opponent. After a few rounds of verses, the damage to body and spirit would tell, and one of the poets would fall. Any outside interference during the duel would draw the wrath of all the *filí*.

With an indulgence ill-befitting the seriousness of the conflict, Oz nodded at Fergus to begin. The challenger would go first.

In a quavering voice like the lead singer of the Undertones, Fergus sang:

> *You are stretched in your grave*
> *You shall rot there forever*

You shall smell of the dirt
You'll be worn by the weather.

The red craft of each word bit into Oz like bullets, and he saw himself crawling back to his cave, and the earth folding in on him, finally giving him peace. Fergus leered at him. Stupid boy—nobody won a major duel with one round of verse. Oz shook off the bits of death and launched his own words in return, matching the craft of his challenger in a fine Irish tenor, so unlike his old and gravelly speaking voice.

The night is long
And no day shall come;
I promise that
You're the dying one.
Being what you are,
You could never learn:
Like another Troy,
I shall make you burn.

Fergus flinched away like a scalded cat from the fire in the words. But Fergus did not pause to collect himself, replying with an instant growl as if hoping to catch Oz off guard with haste and simple malice:

You Left-Handed maggot
You're weak and you're haggard
This Solstice past
Shall be your last.

Oz's nose began to bleed. The words had wounded because they were true. Like many others, Oz had pulled some Left-Handed tricks during the Troubles, and he felt sin on his soul that no confession could remove. This year was certainly his last on earth. But, perhaps because Oz accepted their truth, the words did not carry immediate death.

Anyway, Oz could play on past sins as well as Fergus:

Like all the tea in China, dog,
The sins you cannot leave behind,
They boil inside your mental fog,
They tear in two your greedy mind.

Fergus's hands went to his head, clutching it as if it buzzed with bees instead of crimes. But he recovered himself. "Still wide awake and sweet as honey," he said, spitting blood onto the grass like a boxer. For this round, he gave himself more time, no doubt to think more carefully about his words. In their weakened state, they both knew that any verse now could be their last.

You change, change utterly:
Your heart is turned to stone.
Your center cannot hold:
Slouch off to die alone.

The bitter words burned like cold iron. They tore at Oz's heart and drove him to his hands and knees. Just one more word, the right syllable, would have quartered him along mystic dotted lines. Like sharks smelling blood in the water, the other Hounds inched toward him.

But Oz didn't leave the living stream. Painfully, he rose up on his stiff knees. "My death is too soon for you to trouble me with it." Time to give Fergus the bad news about their relative power; time to end this. But he would not take Fergus's life, not today. One thing he'd learned from this exchange: he'd killed enough. He didn't want more blood staining his karmic ledger now, and dead craftsmen aplenty would be coming soon.

In the east, the sun was rising. With his best full-throated voice, Oz sang:

Who will drive for Fergus now
When all his light has gone to shade?
Why lift his tender eyelids now
When his bright eyes forever fade?

The words flew from Oz like knives into Fergus's face. With audible pops, Fergus's eyes burst from his sockets.

Fergus screamed like a snapper; his fingers went to his bleeding eye holes. "You bastard!" he howled. Fergus wouldn't understand this grace—his whole generation refused to understand such cold grace. Cut off from sight and the active service of the Left Hand, Fergus might yet become the greatest of the *filí* and another Turlough O'Carolan of craft song, while Oz would be moldering in the grave.

The other Hounds stared at Oz, hands ready to bring weapons to bear. Oz dismissed them with a wave of his arm. "Take him away before I give you the same." With reluctant slowness, they led away their blind leader as he wept blood.

One of Oz's guards, a dead ringer for Maureen O'Hara at fifty except for the shorter hair and grimmer mouth, said, "They'll be back with more."

"So they will. Give them something to remember us, *macushla*." But Oz wouldn't be here. He was packed and ready. He'd go to Shannon Airport and pass through the flow of returning dead from the diaspora and the ghost guards. And go on to where? He'd need more of one of the gifts, but he wouldn't fly to Italy directly. First, he'd go on to somewhere they wouldn't immediately follow; somewhere he could feel for the coming portal. Into the west? Maybe, but he wouldn't think about it; he didn't want any farsight tracking his movements until it was too late.

Had the time truly come to use *all* the gifts? Fergus and his friends seemed to think so, though their uses would be different from his. In the first light of dawn, Oz looked about at his country, and the dear sight of it brought him another foreboding, and a few tears. After today, he'd never see his home again.

PART I

BY THE WATERS OF BABYLON

Like a picture it seemed of the primitive, pastoral ages,
Fresh with the youth of the world, and recalling Rebecca and Isaac,
Old and yet ever new, and simple and beautiful always,
Love immortal and young in the endless succession of lovers.
                                        —Henry Wadsworth Longfellow

Joyance is come, dispelling cark and care;
We are united, enviers may despair . . .
One hour of joyance made us both forget
What from excess of terror grey'd our hair.
                              —from Richard Burton's translation of
                                        One Thousand and One Nights

cras amet qui numquam amavit
quique amavit cras amet

                                        —"The Vigil of Venus"

CHAPTER

ONE

My name is Scherezade Rezvani, Lieutenant, U.S. Army, and craftsperson. Like my namesake, I have a story to tell. Unlike hers, my story ends with a funeral.

But like my namesake's, my story begins with a wedding, the marriage of craftpersons Major Michael Endicott, U.S. Army, and Commander Grace Marlow, Royal Navy. Endicott had met Marlow while we'd been fighting the evil Roderick Morton. My husband, Dale of the not-evil Mortons, was Michael's best man. Just a couple of years before, that friendship would have been unimaginable.

Endicott and Marlow planned on marrying in a small church in Yokohama. We three Americans were stuck in Japan because, in his fall, Roderick had managed to pull down with him a good section of the craft world, so in the U.S. we would at best have been under house arrest along with many other practitioners in the service. Marlow's situation was more ambiguous. MI13 wanted someone minding us, and she gave them reports to keep them content.

Before the wedding, I'd dismantled a doomsday machine at the Yasukuni Shrine and dispelled the Japanese war dead. As a *domo arigato*, the Japanese craft servicepeople had ceased shadowing us around Tokyo, so as far as they were concerned we could stay or leave Japan as we chose. On the one hand, I felt pretty pleased with myself for having done what no one else in the world could do. On the other, I was homesick and exhausted, and yet I still had more work.

What work? I was Marlow's matron of honor (well, matron of "honour," as Grace's invites had that Brit spelling). In the craft world, my role wasn't just organizing the bachelorette party. Maid or matron of honor meant security.

I couldn't complain. All my life I'd been a fan of science fiction and fantasy, and now I was part of something that was like both. But bodyguard at a wedding wasn't in the usual epic job descriptions. My pregnancy didn't grant me leave from this or combat. According to Dale's lore, "Nature likes to take care of her craft children so much that you'll be tougher to kill now more than ever." But he added, "Please be careful anyway."

So, as part of security, I took the subway to Shinjuku to scope out the honeymoon accommodations. Shinjuku Station was the world's busiest, and the first to have the official packers to push people in, so for comfort I waited until after the evening rush.

I loved my friends, but I really wished they could have put off their happy event. The timing wasn't their fault. Here was our sitrep: Dale had recently discovered that his real mother was Sphinx, one of the greatest oracles ever. This meant Dale gave us a bit of screening when we were with him, which was how we'd been able to avoid the farsight of Roderick and others.

However, from the moment Michael and Grace had gotten engaged, it'd been like we had precog RFID chips implanted. A craft wedding was always significant, but a union across borders of two major Families was far too important for Dale's presence to confuse the farseers. Wherever we went, they would see Endicott's and Marlow's trajectories toward their marriage, and they could pinpoint us for attack. This was bad now, and potentially fatal when we had to leave Japan.

That left another possibility: why not go into a bunker somewhere? A secure undisclosed location wasn't the most romantic destination wedding or honeymoon, but the security sure would be easier.

The answer came mostly from our old frenemy, Eddy Edwards, director of the Peepshow at Langley. When he hadn't been putting us in harm's way, Eddy had helped us survive and had made our escape to Japan possible. A few weeks ago, he'd managed to send us his files on prospective guests along with a message: "Bunker strategy has greater than 90 percent chance of failure." He hadn't said why. Perhaps, even given recent events, practitioners wouldn't try anything as outrageously magical in public as they would against an isolated place. Or maybe a bunker just lengthened the period of vulnerability to when the couple exited their concrete honeymoon suite.

Or maybe, and most dangerously, we could no longer trust some of our Japanese hosts, and the more isolated our position, the more easily they'd be able to betray us.

In any case, this wedding had to be open to craft witnesses because an attempt (like Dale's father's) to hide the lineage and likely powers of prospective offspring was frowned upon, often with extreme prejudice. All those stories about inviting the bad witch to the ritual were a bit of Emily Post for the magical world.

For Dale and my wedding, it'd been enough to notify H-ring, though we also had General Attucks as a witness. But this international wedding across two different services had to be open to all craft witnesses, potential enemies too, or its closed doors would be considered a diplomatic affront and a license to mischief. It seemed the whole craft world was planning to show, though most would only attend the reception.

This openness went with a traditional truce for the duration of the ceremony and reception. This truce would expire—I had trouble wrapping my brain around this—at the moment of consummation during the wedding night. Sure, Endicott and Grace had done the deed, but they hadn't formally consummated as spouses. Unpleasant prior experiences helped enforce the truce. From the night before the wedding until formal consummation, the karmic penalty of killing either spouse would be particularly severe, probably involving impotence and chronic repulsive illness. Dale said this was just an evolutionary feature of the craft, while Endicott and Marlow seemed to regard it as a sign of the divine.

But the moment after consummation, the newlyweds were fair game. A lot of farsight would be focused on that moment, so we couldn't do much to conceal the site. If we were in the home country of the bride or groom, the wedding night might be in their Family house. Here, we could only work on our defense and hope that it would be enough.

Also, despite tradition and curses, we still couldn't rely on the peace holding during the ceremony and reception. Too many people had reasons to harm those at the altar, and the unusual number and importance of the guests would attract persons and governments with scores to settle. We would have ninja ushers and body armor for all.

Shinjuku was pretty cool. It was the only part of Tokyo that fully met my William Gibson and *Blade Runner*–induced expectations of what an Asian City of the Future should be like, with the appropriate skyscrapers to go with the giant electronic billboards. Earthquakes kept the rest of Tokyo's skyline smaller, with more open and green spaces, but Shinjuku had solid bedrock beneath it to build up on. Maybe Shanghai did the sci-fi cityscape better, but I doubted I'd ever see it in person—China was not safe for American craftspeople.

From the subway station, I walked into the district called Kabukicho. I could have read a book by the brightly lit signs. All the urban entertainments were here, though like too many things in Japan, they favored the boys. But pachinko didn't favor gender. The rattle, roar, and lightning of a pachinko parlor competed with some looping musical track that sounded like an interrupted dance. Pachinko was pinball without any control and played for money, only I felt and saw that some people with very weak craft were trying to skew in their favor the random movements of the balls. The craft radiated out and made me a little tipsy.

I passed bars, some of which I couldn't see into from the street, but I could hear them. Since my supposedly delicate condition began, my senses had been doing odd, sensitive, and synesthetic things, and I was hearing as much craft as I saw. These Kabukicho bars had a song like a siren's call, a craft that fed on alcoholism, and their cute beckoning porcelain cats seemed evil. I didn't have any trouble resisting. *Should I thank an Islamic upbringing or the bun in the oven for that?*

Mundane noises behind me—a pair of drunken Japanese men were trailing and making offers with an edge of threat. "You come with us," they said. So gross. Not sure if this was bad English or just the way they did pick-ups around here. Their hands reached out to grab me.

"No," I said. "If you bother me anymore, I will hurt you."

The men scrammed for easier prey. Such threats might not work on a rapey American, but they sometimes did wonders in Tokyo.

In the narrow street, the ridiculous Cadillacs of Yakuza were completely illegally parked. A woman in chilly-looking Japanese schoolgirl fetishwear ran giggling down an alley. Few people, but the way was thick with ghosts: women and men killed in sexual violence or fire-bombed people with their burning houses. As I approached, most of the ghosts parted and fled, sensing what I was. Some lingered, a question on their faces, perhaps longing to leave this plane. I considered dispelling them. This wasn't my country, and I was still tired from the dispellations at Yasukuni and Roderick's bunker in Virginia, but it might be a good deed.

Still thinking on it, I turned right, and I felt a flash of warmth in my belly. In the middle of the narrow street, oblivious to the foot and other traffic, a dog faced me—I mean a literal dog, and not some Japanese mercenary equivalent of a Gideon. The animal looked distinctly Japanese in the way a canine in their comic books would, don't ask me to explain how. I think it was at least part Akita, but crossed with bigger breeds, with a red-on-white coat and perfect erect triangle ears—all the way forward and ready for action. The beast growled at me through bared teeth, like I was a terminator. Even in the wonderful world of craft, this was weird. Other dogs liked me fine, and there weren't many homeless animals or people in this part of Tokyo.

"I'm not going to eat you," I said.

The dog turned and loped away. But I didn't think I'd persuaded it. I walked on.

A presence, behind me—I turned to face the new threat. Two women stood there, each wearing a bodycon dress more appropriate for this party district than my urban combat leather, though a bit chilly for the street. I recognized one of them—just my luck. "Kaguya-san," I said. She'd been the perfect hostess during our stay in her country, even inviting me to train with her ninja friends, but I couldn't warm to her. I'd never been jealous before in my life, but Dale's history with her had gotten under my skin.

"*Konbanwa*, Rezvani-san."

Other presences were here, unseen, but I felt them anyway. "I thought watching us was going to be difficult, *ne*?"

Kaguya-san had a pained expression. *Oh my, I've forced her to be direct.*

"Our position towards your government regarding your departure—that will be soon, eh?"

"Yes, soon," I said. The honeymoon would indeed be over.

"Our position on your departure has nothing to do with your security while you are here. This wedding is important, and everyone will be watching, including us."

"Fine. Could I have some time alone with the site? All your ninjas make it difficult to see."

To her credit, Kaguya-san didn't act surprised by my observation or try to deny it. She simply made a small gesture, and I felt the ninja presences fade. The other woman drew closer to Kaguya-san and whispered into her ear. Except, no, it was a man. Or again, maybe not. Ninjas had always been a bit flexible on gender.

Kaguya-san's gaze returned to me. "You spoke to the dog?"

"Yes. What's its problem?"

"Cemetery dog," she said. "Stay away from him."

"OK," I said, though I didn't understand.

Kaguya-san gestured at her colleague. "This is my friend. You may call her Mama Suji. She is known here and in Shinjuku Ni-chome." That was the neighboring district that catered to LGBT Tokyo. "So she'll be on duty for the wedding night. You may trust her. Good night, Rezvani-san."

A tickle at the back of my mind. "Wait," I said. Dale had told me to listen carefully when Japanese craftspeople spoke and hear all the things they weren't saying. "Do you mean there are some I shouldn't trust?"

Kaguya-san smiled sadly and nodded. "I may have been mistaken in trying to speak for all in my nation's service. Your husband will understand. Good night, Rezvani-san."

In a blink, she and Mama Suji were gone. No smoke or other mundane ninja tricks, just gone. Good. I'd heard what I'd needed and really dreaded to know: a faction in Kaguya-san's organization was hostile to us.

In another blink, another presence: Madeline, robed like the bodhisattva of mercilessness, eyes with the slightest hint of the Japanese. She was part of the Left-Hand Morton collective spiritual entity, but I still considered her as an individual and very much in charge of that mass of ghosts.

She said, "You could, you know."

I bit. "I could what?"

"Kill her. She seems tough, but you could take her. We could help."

Remembering some Morton history, I said, "You were never good about the host and guest relationship, were you?"

"We're Mortons," she spat. "Not *Oikumene*." She faded back into the ether.

This was the typical Madeline mix of helpful cruelty, aristocratic pride, and modern language. I sometimes forgot that she wasn't like Roderick had been; since her birth in the late 1700s, she'd been in many bodies and many roles, and she'd always kept contemporary enough in speech and manner not to draw suspicion. She also seemed to enjoy her own code-switching.

Her more evil twin Roderick hadn't had as much opportunity to adapt. Like a Left-Hand cautionary tale, he'd been stuck to his own flesh for two centuries, and most of that as a rotting head, until I'd fucked up and freed his spirit to cause global mischief. I'd made up for my mistake by assisting in his exorcism and banishment to some hellworld, where no solitary spirit could survive the all-consuming, demonic mass-consciousness of the dead. Always cheered me up to think of that.

I strode on through Kabukicho, and in a few steps I could see the love hotel, the one with "*Supai*" or "Spy" in incongruous flashing neon on a long sign running up the side of the building. The love hotel had been Dale's idea, but I'd agreed. He'd said that it wasn't just a place for the illicit, but for anyone seeking a romantic getaway in space-starved Tokyo. Like many love hotels, this one had rooms with individual themes, but here all the themes related to spies. A ninja suite, a Mata Hari boudoir, a Casanova room with a view, an Austin Powers groove pad, and three different James Bond options. We got them the Fleming. It came with many devices that would have made Q blush.

Given what Marlow had told me about her family history, the Bond connection was a little creepy, and I'd said so. But Dale had said, "Grace will love it, and Mike will be too nervous to complain." I agreed about Endicott's nerves. He was a tough veteran of many craft fights, but his Puritan background and dedication to duty hadn't allowed for much romance in his life.

The problem with hotel rooms was that they usually didn't allow for much defense in depth. A typical room had only one entrance—good—but that was the only exit as well—bad. The Fleming room however had a "secret" door which connected it to the Austin Powers room, for those who wanted their spies swinging. That wouldn't be us for all sorts of personal, professional, and supernatural reasons, but it was ideal for our defensive strategy.

We had already scoped out some of the physical issues; I was here for the metaphysical. Dale hadn't been wild about me coming here alone, but having him around might distract me while I was using my new sensitivity. "OK, see what you can see," he'd said. I took the elevator up and stood in the hallway outside the rooms. I closed my eyes, and opened my senses.

First, I heard the buzz of Kabukicho's magic in full. So much wanting, so many wills trying to bend reality their way without inhibition. Though mundanes might only have fleeting sparks of craft, a little craft multiplied by such numbers has an impressive force.

I tasted the radiant infrared of the district's sex magic, the by-product of more immediate heat, synergistically shared. My little bite wasn't a Left-Hand action, because the energy was freely given. It made me slightly horny.

But only slightly, because beyond Kabukicho was a colder craft. I felt their eyes upon the spot where I stood. Minute by minute, the strength of their regard grew—not one craftsperson or even one service, but too many farsights for me to count. They were looking here and ahead to the moment of consummation, when a blast of sex energy would radiate out from Michael and Grace, when all those watchers could smite or witness the smiting. In my warm coat, I shivered as if naked and alone. "*Enough*," I said, and I opened my eyes.

The wedding was days away, but I had to tell myself to keep calm as I left the Spy Hotel.

Above me in the narrow space between Shinjuku's buildings, the starless dark beyond reminded me of horrors past. Still shivering from the stress of the world's regard, I went back to my husband.

With our short lease up in Moto-Akasaka, we'd all moved into the Okura, a grand hotel from the build-up for the 1964 Olympics. The place had an odd institutional feel, with corridors that never seemed well-lit and an expensive restaurant dominated by the strange, flat taste of Japanese-Italian dishes. Dale could afford it; he used one of the Family overseas accounts for us, and I assumed Marlow or Endicott was doing something similar. Nobody was making serious efforts to cut off our cash. The Pentagon's lips said they wanted us back home ASAP, but their actions suggested otherwise. By staying here, we kept things simple for H-ring.

But I was homesick for the States. While Dale was out on a much needed run to "work off some stress," I called my parents on Skype, hoping for comfort. I was badly mistaken. My parents' eyes had the tired and hard look they used to get when I broke curfew as a teenager. As with high school, they immediately started in with questions: "Why are you still in Japan?"

"I'm fine, thanks, how are you?"

But they didn't let up. More questions, like why was I letting my hair grow out? (That one was easy—I didn't want to deal with a foreign hair stylist.) But the others involved craft secrets that they could never know. Dale and my friends came from practitioner Families that went back hundreds of years; I was the first craftsperson in my line (though my mom's sense of when I was trying to hide stuff from her seemed a little uncanny). H-ring was insanely protective of the craft secrets, and telling my parents anything about magic might put my life and theirs at risk.

Only one way I could think of to make my parents stop their inquisition: "I'm pregnant."

As if I'd worked some mind-controlling craft on them, they became perfectly happy idiots. More annoying questions followed, but at least I could answer them honestly. Yes, Dale was thrilled. No, we couldn't come home yet; we were staying for our friend Michael's wedding.

"Wedding?" That brought on a renewed inquisition, though less frenzied. Good thing they didn't know too many details. While in Ukraine, Endicott had lost an eye and had basically risen from the dead. So in Islamic apocalyptic thinking, by working with Endicott, it might appear I was serving the Dajjal, our one-eyed equivalent of the Antichrist. What would my family make of that?

"Come home soon," said my parents, bringing me around full circle. What could I say? We couldn't go home yet, and we weren't sure where we could go next. But we didn't need Kaguya-san's warning to know that we had to go anyway, and soon. With the possible exception of Endicott, in Japan we couldn't replace as much craft as was seeping out of us, and we were slowly but steadily losing our internal reserves of power. We'd already been here too long.

I had time for one more ninja sparring session before the wedding. Kaguya-san showed, and I tried being friendly as I worked through my forms. "So, what are your books?"

"My books?" she asked.

"You know—Dale and Michael have their Poe and Hawthorne. Grace cuts a rainbow-colored swath through Brit lit. You?"

"Our training tries to silence the words in our heads, bad or good."

"Aw, come on."

She nodded, relenting. "Not books, but plays. Plays of magic, ghosts, and revenge."

Great. I'd seen some of those plays, and they were bloodier than Hamlet with half the sense. But now for my more immediate question. I stopped wheeling my arms and legs about. "You haven't told us your plan yet to secure the sites. We need to know."

She smiled the way the Japanese do when they're about to tell you something unpleasant. "We will secure all entrances and approaches. Beyond that, I will not tell you any plans. When the time comes, we will communicate; we will improvise. I have at least five scenarios in my head, and I won't discuss any of them. I advise you to do the same, *ne?*"

Not this BS again. "That'll just confuse us, and it won't stop the hostile farsight."

"You've felt it, eh? Every eye in the world is on the picture of the honeymoon. The only way to win is to draw a master's stroke of uncertainty across it. You did it before against better oracles. Do it once more."

Easy for her to say. We had payment due on those runs of the table, and the house would always win in the end.

CHAPTER

TWO

As Dale and I dressed on the big day, I made gallows chatter to cover my concern. "Ever notice how in the stories, someone always dies right before their wedding, like in that *Star Trek* episode?"

"Hey," he said, looking very serious, "that really happens." Then the laughter burst out of him. "To complete assholes!" But he again went somber. "Usually."

I helped the bride dress and prepare, but Marlow had more experience with fancy clothes and looking good in them than I ever would, so mostly I just said the ritual bridesmaid things about how great she looked in her gown, which happened to be the God's honest truth.

The Japanese had promised "acceptable" local weather for Yokohama Christ Church, and they delivered. Outside, Mount Fuji was ghostly white against a sky as blue as a dead computer's screen. Inside, the sunlit Christian iconography wasn't my thing, but the whole space was inimical to Madeline, and that was A-OK. She'd been a bit smother-hover with my pregnancy, which had made me wonder about her ulterior motives.

"Don't worry," she'd said. "I wouldn't take an infant. I'd be too vulnerable."

So she could do it, but restrained herself. "That's not very reassuring," I'd said.

"How's this then: a healer like you won't have much morning sickness."

"How would you know?" I'd asked.

A moment's pause. "I've worn many bodies," she'd said. And one of those she'd possessed had been pregnant? Again, not very reassuring. But she'd been right; I was in the last bit of my first trimester, and I'd had no problems with sickness.

Though fewer guests would attend the ceremony than the reception, the church was small and narrow, so the space would be packed. At the church entrance I was giving each guest a really good look while Dale checked their metaphysical rap sheets. Vasilisa from Russia, a nervous kitty on a hot craft roof, came close and whispered to me. "He's really gone?" I didn't need to ask whom she meant.

"Yes," I assured her. "He's gone." I'd helped kill Roderick myself, though I could understand her nerves about him with her Madeline-style looks.

A ninja usher in his salaryman suit interrupted us. "Bride or groom?"

Then came Captain Hutchinson, here on duty as the mutually acceptable American craft observer. "How are Tom and Huck?" she asked, meaning Dale and Endicott, though I wasn't sure who was who.

I nodded at my husband. "Dale's looking pretty hunky in his tux," I said in a low voice, though it seemed like he might hulk out and burst. "And I thought Major Endicott in formal wear would just be stiffer than usual, but he's a bit goofy and more than a little nervous today."

I didn't get into how we were really doing; she'd just have to report it back home to her husband General Attucks. Besides, I was busy thinking about other entrances and choke points and kill zones. One major area made me sweat: we'd all be concentrated at the altar for a good long time. *Ave, ave, the gang's all here.*

Due to our AWOL circumstances, we had to drop some traditions. No dress uniforms for the bride and groom, and no arch of swords—the only sword we allowed in was the one Endicott kept at his side. Still, it didn't need the costuming to feel very military, this vow to a service within the service.

The ceremony was timed so the vows would be at noon. The matri-archal-looking Anglican bishop was a friend of Grace's family. The bishop read in her Oxbridge accent from some old and crafty iteration of the Book of Common Prayer that Grace had insisted on, sexist language and all. As I scanned the congregation for ill-intent, we came to the part of the service made infamous in *Jane Eyre* and other novels:

"Therefore if any man can shew any just cause, why they may not lawfully be joined together, let him now speak, or else hereafter for ever hold his peace."

In that silence, it was as if I could hear the congregants prepare their spells, like the small noises of small arms being readied to gun down anyone so rude as to interrupt the proceedings. A bad precedent hung over our heads—"for ever hold his peace" had been the signal for the first attack on Grace's ancestor, Edward Marlow.

A stirring at the back of the nave as, with excruciating slowness, a very old man stood—the Aboriginal Australian practitioner known only as "Dude," dressed in perfectly tailored tux with a black head-band restraining his long gray hair. He had no spells radiating readi-ness, but the craft ambience of the room was going ugly fast, providing excellent cover for anyone who'd strike the bride and groom.

Shit, what should I do? Taking down an old man didn't seem smart, nor did my impulse to tackle the groom and cover him. I looked to Endicott for a signal, but the bastard smiled with the resigned calm of someone who'd expected this moment. "Honored guest," he said, in an officer's projecting tone. "You wish to say something?"

"I do," said Dude. His public voice had the same Oxbridge accent as Marlow's and the bishop's. "I speak for those who will not. A great fear lives in this room. We fear that you have become one of those against the land. We require some sign that you are not one of the so-called Left Hand."

Everyone seemed to hold their breath. There it was—all the suspi-cion about Endicott's use of Roderick's serum, his resurrection, and his possession of another body, out in the open. Endicott turned to squarely face the guests. "Here then is your sign. I vow to let myself die at three score and ten, whatever my condition."

I wanted to protest. Seventy was a long ways off, but it wasn't that old these days.

But Dude's concern lay elsewhere. "And who shall enforce this vow?"

Endicott nodded. "If I should break this vow, may the Furies . . ." A hiss from the crowd and Marlow interrupted him with some whispered advice.

"May the Kindly Ones," he continued, "render their full judgment upon me and all those who assist such an oath-breaking. So help me God."

Dude sat down, and Endicott calmly turned back to face Marlow. The ambient craft faded even as the collective whispers of the crowd grew. The bishop let out her held breath, loosened her grip on her crozier, and said, "To continue," to silence the crowd. Then she spoke to Michael and Grace. "I require and charge you both, as ye will answer at the dreadful day of judgement when the secrets of all hearts shall be disclosed, that if either of you know any impediment, why ye may not be lawfully joined together in Matrimony, ye do now confess it."

Dreadful day of judgement—that might be sooner than the bishop thought. It had come close enough already in that bunker in Virginia.

But not just now, not before my friends said their vows and happily kissed. All felt tremendously right with the world as they went down the aisle to the exit. "*Dry eyes, dry eyes,*" I said, using some of my healing craft. Stupid pregger hormones. Not that I was a big crier, but I couldn't afford the blurry vision.

F or the reception we limo'ed from the old but Western-looking neighborhood of the church to a restaurant in Yokohama's Chinatown. As we entered the large event space, we passed an indoor rock fountain, and in front of it a man was playing "Bibbidi-Bobbidi-Boo" from *Cinderella* on a guzheng.

That made me laugh, but this gathering of covert power seemed more like the wedding at the beginning of *The Godfather* than *Cinderella*. What would be our *Godfather* theme? Something grander and sadder.

While on watch, I didn't get to eat much. Bizarrely, what I craved most was healthy food, and plenty of it, but a little more of this Chinese meal, even when blandified for this restaurant's Japanese clientele, would have been awesome.

People had traveled far and dressed fashion forward for this show. The craft had so few opportunities for international gatherings that this reception became a sort of unofficial peace conference. The attendees would be those whom their governments thought reliable enough to be given this leash. Despite their smiles, many guests also had a hollow look in their eyes. They were worried about what their leaders would do next; they wondered whether they would be spared.

The recent threats of Roderick, global Left-Hand activity, and craft security breaches had triggered confinement or house arrest of practitioners considered unreliable, and close surveillance of the rest. Some had been "disappeared" or even gunned down in the public street. The U.S. was only marginally better than many other parts of the world in how it was treating its craftspeople. Despite what we'd done against Roderick, our exposure to him, Dale's Morton name, and the concerns raised at the wedding about Endicott meant that we'd all be firmly in the "unreliable" category if we went back to the States. But some of our guests might return to their countries to face a bullet they couldn't skew.

When not dreading their own fate, our guests also may have wondered where some of their fellow practitioners had gone. Both Left- and Right-Hand craftspeople had been vanishing from their countries in substantial numbers well beyond those likely "disappeared" by their own governments. If anyone here knew where these people had run off to, they weren't talking to me about it.

On the other side of the room, the gorgeously tall Jessica Mwangi of Kenya, the distinguished David Cheong from Malaysia, the short, smiling Omar Khan of Pakistan, and the oath-demanding Dude had practically queued up to confer with Dale, as if he were the bride and groom. The politeness was straining him.

No one seemed to be paying much attention to me. That was good, because I wasn't going to rely on the ninjas to keep an eye on things.

Then, the VIP from China strode over in my direction. Zhuge Wu was descended from Zhuge Liang, the master tactician who could also summon the winds. The Zhuge with us was the eldest son of the secret head of the Shaolin-trained craftspeople of the People's Liberation Army. He had dyed his hair gray to look older than his black-haired inner party peers with lined faces. Out of uniform here, he was dapper in his Hong Kong–tailored suit. His frequent smiles were divorced from his dark, intelligent eyes that took in much and gave away little. He wasn't here on his government's leash; he was one of those who held the leash.

I also recalled that he'd selected the vegetarian option instead of the Peking duck—I may have overstudied some of our guests' details.

We introduced ourselves and exchanged some pleasantries about the wedding. "It is such a great pleasure to finally meet you," said Zhuge, laying it on a little thick. "Which makes me wonder more at the attention your husband is receiving. Why do you suppose so many wish to speak with him?"

I had to be very careful in my responses to such fishing. Many of those here in the room were very good at detecting deceit, and a lie might reveal as much as the truth. But for this question I had no difficulty with the honest answer. "I think those guests might like us to come work for their countries." They would want us for the same reason the Red Sox often bought a player—to keep us from the Yankees. Though Dude might just want to chat.

But I had missed Zhuge's point. "Why then are they not speaking with you," he said. "Or the bride and groom?"

It was true: they were paying particular attention to Dale. That could mean only one thing: they wanted Dale's supposed Left-Hand expertise.

"He doesn't have the knowledge they want," I said, perhaps too quickly.

His eyes went up and down as if reading my soul in Chinese. "Loyalty is a great virtue in a spouse. The only deceit I detect is of yourself."

"Then please, you should feel free to ask him," I said.

"I may do so," he said.

"Or perhaps you're just trying to sow doubt among the enemy?" That had a vague *Art of War* sound, and I smiled to take the sting from it.

"Always," he said. "And among such lovely friends as well." With that, he returned to his table. Charming, but I wasn't feeling it. China's obsession with Dale's Left-Hand knowledge had already been a problem; their weathermen had tried to crash Dale's plane during his flight over their country toward his rendezvous with Roderick in Kiev. But would the Chinese dare move against us in Japan, where the craft response to them would be particularly vehement?

No one approached me to ask if we could help with the current Left-Hand crisis and craft civil wars. If it was the same for the others, then so much for Endicott's ideas about our mission, at least for the moment.

To stay sharp, I forgot all about the wedding truce. I had to protect all the guests, and that meant I had to assume an attack could come at any time. But this room was full of the craftiest bastards in the world, and they were scarfing down their Peking duck entrees with evident confidence about their future health. All farsighted eyes were on the wedding night and the newlyweds.

Under this overhanging, voyeuristic threat, I briefly wondered if Endicott would experience performance anxiety. Then, I tried to assess which of these gorging guests would be involved in the attack. But this worrying bunch finally seemed to be relaxing, talking, and laughing—really enjoying themselves, as if they'd left their assassin hats at home.

Standing near the cake (mmm, cake), I took a break from craft pro-filing to watch the newlyweds' first dance. Endicott had been trained old school, when officers were expected to be adept at all the formal arts, including dancing. But this was beyond all expectation. He took off one of his shoes, and the chrome of his prosthetic foot gleamed, creating its own disco ball effect in the light. The metal of his toes clicked in time with the music, like flamenco, growing in speed and intensity. Strictly ballroom, but full of craft. He was glowing in com-plex colors, and I finally understood what Grace might see in him as she twirled around him and moved in close, tango style. Focusing in, I heard Endicott whisper in her ear: "Wouldn't trade this for anything. Not for all the kingdoms of the world in a moment of time."

"A delightful couple." A slightly accented male voice just behind me—how had he gotten so close?

I turned to blink-assess him, then made sure no one else was out of place before giving him another look. The man had the white collar and black shirt of a priest, his dark hair trimmed to perfect edges above a tanned and lined face. A bit of illicit frosting at the corner of his mouth, he smiled, thin-lipped and beatific, like some Renaissance painting's martyr before his grisly end. I knew him and his file of course: Monsignor Cornaro, here representing the Vatican.

"Good day, Monsignor. I'm a little busy." I scanned the crowd again.

"No need to face me or stop what you do."

But there was a good reason. Cornaro was a craftsman of the Dominican Order, one of the "hounds of the Lord." Regarding him head on, I said, "I've had some bad experiences with hounds."

"Yet I think you may have less prejudice against us than your colleagues."

OK, Endicott wanted us to find the next fight. "Please, go on."

He sighed. "We have some concern. Some very old lines of farsight predict that this will be the last pope before the end of the world. We suspect that this farseen end is not the glorious one of the second coming of Christ, but some catastrophe brought on by the Left Hand."

"Do you know about our recent travels?" Just months before, we had prevented Roderick from ending the world.

"We are aware, and we are grateful, but this evil line of time is more, ah, resilient?" He made it a question, as if uncertain of the word.

"You would like our help?" I asked. "None of us are Catholic."

He waved this away with his hand. "We must accept whatever help we can find. The Church does not recruit so many as we did when we were the guardian of the common magi against the aristocratic craft."

"The craft—you acknowledge it?"

Both hands were up now, emphasizing his words. "Of course. We practically invented some of its terms." He lowered his voice. "Such as exorcist."

Now he had my complete attention.

"We have considerable writings on exorcism," he continued. "Whatever you decide, they are available to you, at your convenience."

A snarling voice to my left. "Why should we care?" Madeline had manifested and was having some heated words with the craftswoman from India, Colonel Madhuri Pandava. But Dale was nearby and waving me off.

"Poor creature," said Cornaro, nodding at Madeline. "Why don't you give her peace?"

Dispel Madeline? "It's complicated," I said. And none of his business.

"Do you trust her?" he asked.

"That's part of the problem. She has done some good things. She helped save the world."

"I see. But you know she is not good."

"I know," I said. Then, to end the discussion, "We'll talk soon about the other matter."

"Until then," he said, passing me his card. Then in a blink, he slipped away into the crowd. Another charmer, but I still didn't like the hounds.

A flash of movement at the entrance. I yelled in panglossic, "Everybody take cover." I was there just as two of Kaguya-san's ninjas were tightening their grips on an innocuous-looking little girl, pig-tailed and bug-eyed with fear. In her shaking hands was a box wrapped with exquisite paper and technique as only the Japanese can.

"Who is that from?" I asked.

She looked up at me, uncomprehending despite my panglossic, eyes filling with tears. The woman ninja holding her said something in Japanese, and the girl pursed her lips. "Pit-tia," she said. *Pythia*.

The *Oikumene*, the Pythia's international cabal of anti-Left-Hand zealots, had sent a gift. We had a gathering of magi in winter, so of course we had gifts. Usually, no one gave magical items—too rare and double-edged. But magic radiated out of this box from an organization that had already once tried to kill the groom. When Endicott had first displayed his transnational power of command, the *Oikumene* had shot him rather than risk a modern Caesar.

Despite sharp intakes of breath by disapproving ninjas, I took the gift from the girl and opened it. Inside was a small bronze figurine of a man on horseback, and a slip of paper describing it as an uncatalogued piece from the recently discovered tomb at Amphipolis. The figurine had the same vibe coming off it as the Serpent Column in Istanbul. This was one of the *Oikumene*'s communication devices. Could they be trying to track us? Could they really believe we'd want to talk? I had nothing more to say to them.

"Put it with the other gifts. Let me know if anyone tries to touch it."

I looked around, and if anyone had actually listened to me and taken cover, they had resumed normal partying by now. Grace swayed up to me, still glowing from the dance. "Tonight, I am going to cripple him," she said impishly, ignoring both Endicott's foot issues and their need for post-coital combat readiness. "He shan't be able to walk for a week."

I was no prude, but my face felt a sudden blush-heat. "Excellent," I said, and walked away as if still on patrol. But with no further threats, I allowed myself a moment to look at the reception as a participant instead of a guard. Above us the stars were aligning, and the celestial spheres were falling into place like tumblers on a lock. Here below, this happy conjunction of love and craft fellowship was someplace we wouldn't visit again soon.

A growing murmur of discontent pulled me back into wariness. *Shit.* Despite all our detailed planning and explicit warnings to the restaurant, they were serving fortune cookies. A couple of guests threw their cookies back at the waiters, another backed away from his like it might explode. All went uneaten, as trivializing oracles was very bad practice.

A ninja chauffeur appeared at the entrance, a silent signal that the limo had arrived. The reception was over, and with their security again their own responsibility, the guests exited with seemly haste.

In the limo, Dale rode up front with the driver, while I sat in the back with the newlyweds. The way they were touching each other, I wanted to tell them to just do it now and get it over with, whatever the embarrassment to me. Only some instinct stopped me, some feeling that, when the consummation happened, a moving vehicle would be too easy a target.

Not that we had too long to wait. As if traffic had been deliberately cleared, we drove speedily and with few stops to Kabukicho.

Dale and I waited in the Austin Powers love suite, fully dressed and no shagging allowed while I kept watch with my heightened senses. The room reeked of patchouli air freshener; the bedspread had a leopard-skin pattern. We were still in our clothes from the wedding, though I had combat-ready shoes. Dale sat back in the zebra-patterned beanbag chair, bowtie hanging loose, a katana across his knees. "I'll show Endicott something about swords," he drawled. He seemed relaxed enough to sleep through the building's collapse.

We all had earpieces to talk to each other and Kaguya-san. Whatever else they were doing, the newlyweds better have kept theirs at ready. Kaguya-san had promised that her people guarded the entry points, but that just sounded like an oracular epitaph. Our room's TV was wired into the hotel's own security cameras in the doorway, lobby, and hallways, but I didn't trust those either.

The moment approached. The oppressive eye of global farsight that I'd felt before was strengthening. Next door, a Tantric engine ignited, stroke by stroke, then burned and boiled like a steam locomotive as it rode the kabbalistic rails up my spine from Malkuth to Kether and back again. The milder energy of other rooms, other stations, fell unconsciously into the same rhythm. The chaotic noise of all of Kabukicho danced with them.

Dale whispered conspiratorially. "Do you think they're enjoying themselves?"

"Shut up, trying to listen," I said.

I was irritated by Dale, by horniness, by wanting to lie down in the goofy Austin bed. Someone else might have given in to all the ambient pleasure, but not me. I wanted a bigger rush, but first I had to have quiet. Defying the rhythm next door, I counted as I breathed in and out, in and out. I didn't quiet the noise; I absorbed it. The rhythm mixed and resonated with my very bones. I slowly spread out my arms. I was here; I was not here.

Between breaths, a swarm of insects crawled on onion skin paper. Though they were as quiet as ninjas and invisible to the cameras, I felt the intruders enter.

"They're here," I whispered to Dale. "In the building."

CHAPTER

THREE

How did they get through so easily?" asked Dale.

How indeed, Kaguya-san? But I was already out the door and into the corridor. To my left was the elevator. We'd broken its button for this floor, but mostly to keep out the innocent, as that wouldn't stop the serious. The elevator alone would be a bad choke point for them—small, so at most only three at once. To my right, though, was the stairwell, and they could make as long a line there as they liked.

I felt at least twenty in the building. Our plan was intended for a stealthy handful, not this insane overkill. Perhaps I could pause things, set up a better defense . . .

Just then, the first rush of heat of the consummation hit me, followed by wave upon wave of aftershocks. Too late.

I said "Kaguya-san" to my earpiece to connect me to her. Got a damned recorded message in Japanese. "Improvise!" I yelled.

The elevator chimed like the timer in an oven when dinner was ready. Stealth foregone, footsteps were now pounding up the stairwell. Dale was out in the corridor with me. Ignoring rank, I told him, "Cover the elevator." I pounded the newlyweds' door. "Major, Commander. Time to go."

The elevator door remained shut. I sensed people in there, so it wasn't just a bomb. They must be waiting for the other prong of the attack up the stairwell. We could take the elevator first, but then what?

Endicott and Marlow burst out of their room in their hotel yukata robes, and nothing else. Endicott had his sword at ready and was roaring in his own weird panglossic: "*In God's name, get the hell out of here!*"

But I could still feel them coming up the stairwell, if a notch slower. "That didn't work, Major."

My earpiece twittered. "Don't kill her."

"Kill who?" we all said.

Opposite our rooms, a door opened, a door we had all ignored, and that meant serious stealth. Mama Suji stood before us in an androgynous kimono. She looked as post-coital as the newlyweds, though no one else was immediately visible.

"*In Jesus's name . . .*" Endicott was still trying his power of command.

"Save your shouting for later," said Mama Suji, scolding like a parent. "They are North Korean and Shaolin."

That explained it. North Koreans were bound to only one command by decades of craft conditioning. They didn't need Stonewall chips, and (unless he planned on taking over the world) Endicott's restrained power would bounce off them. The Koreans would be the proxies for the more skilled Shaolin agents of China, who'd have enough concentration to simply un-hear most of what Endicott said.

"Out here!" Mama Suji pointed to the open window in her room, and I dashed forward to recon. Outside the window was a tiny pseudo-balcony that could maybe hold a Japanese Juliet, but that was it. "The sign," said Mama Suji, pointing up to the left. Did she mean some oracular nonsense? Of course—the sign for the hotel. Tall and thin, it ran the vertical length of several floors along this wall, attached with horizontal pipes at various points like a trellis for a desperate Romeo. In full combat mode for strength and acceleration, we scampered onto the balcony and up the sign like monkeys. Another of Suji's colleagues in the schoolgirl fetishwear and smeared makeup was waiting to help us onto the roof.

A nice improvisation, but a very temporary solution. "What now?" I asked.

The sound of a helicopter answered: we were to be evacuated by air. "OK, now we're talking," said Dale.

Mama Suji was waving the copter in. Endicott and Grace were quiet, as if still trying to shift from love to combat. Even with the glow of the city lights, the copter's windscreen was like an obsidian shell. I strained to see the pilot's face.

Instead, I saw glowing red letters, two capital *B*s pulsing like neon signs from the cockpit. With them came a whisper in my own voice that tingled my bones like a forgotten nursery rhyme. *B is for Betrayal.*

Kaguya-san's warning about the Japanese craft service came back to me. Betrayal was how the intruders had gotten into the hotel so easily. "Dale, stop them," I said. "Bring them down."

Dale's lips moved as he reached out his hand, and a gale-force wind plowed into the copter, driving it back.

"What are you doing?" said Mama Suji. But the copter opened up with guns blazing, and we went for cover behind the air conditioner unit as we skewed their shots.

Or mostly skewed. Suji's colleague fell, multiple rounds through her chest. Suji's lips quavered like the brief flutter of a moth, but then her face went as implacable as a Noh mask.

"I saw their sins," I said. "They're traitors."

"I couldn't . . ." said Dale, sounding a little awed. We could both guess what this might mean. I might be carrying a Morton boy, a very powerful Morton boy.

"They've got weathermen," continued Dale. "That's as far as I can push the copter."

Whatever Suji had arranged to block their path, the ones below us would be here soon. We were eight stories up. Sure, with some tricks and Dale's command of the air we could survive the fall, but not without significant injury, which would make us dead meat anyway. Despite nature's enhanced protection, I also worried about the baby.

Could we make it over to a neighboring building? It would be a long jump just to face the same problems. The nearby power lines criss-crossed in crazy Tokyo fashion—could we use them somehow?

"Down!" yelled Mama Suji. A shot right where Grace had been crouching dented the air fan housing. The round seemed to come from a construction crane two blocks away. We could skew those shots too, but that would only work so long. We'd blown it. I'd blown it. I hadn't foreseen this scenario.

"We jump," said Mama Suji.

Dale looked disgusted. "We can't fly."

He was answered by the sound of tires squealing on a tight turn. I crawled to the edge of the roof and peered below. A mini-truck came barreling down the street towing a large flopping plastic mass of . . . something. Brakes ground to a sharp stop, and the plastic mass piled up almost vertically against the truck before settling down. It was nearly right below me.

"There's a stunt bag down there," I said.

Shots continued to try to find us on the roof.

"No time," said Mama Suji. She sprang up and leapt backward over the edge, down toward the plastic. In pairs, we followed her, counting to ten in between.

"Oh shit," I said, as we went off the roof and into midair. Dale did what he could to slow us down, and landing backward was best for both me and the baby. On impact, the bag punched the air out from me as it made a deflating fart. Baby sitrep: A-OK.

Dale and I rolled off the bag immediately. It was stuffed with in-flated male and female sex dolls, their features hyper-accurate in shape and exaggerated in size. Some were deflated slightly from our impacts. Perhaps Kaguya-san had hoped for some unconscious modesty to cause the enemy farsight to blink at this, and perhaps it had.

The hotel shadowed us from the crane's sniper, but our opponents would be down here with us soon. The utility-uniformed truck driver was ignoring us as he set up a movie camera with a more modest and realistic-looking mannequin standing behind it. I guessed this would be the legend to keep this excessive display of craft contained: we were making a movie, a martial arts film no doubt, with some fantasy elements.

The driver fled the scene as shots started to pop the dolls we were using for cover. "Into the truck," said Suji, as she unhooked the improvised stunt bag from the vehicle. Dale and I climbed into the back and lay low in the small open bed. Mama Suji crammed into the front with Marlow and Endicott and took over as driver. She put the truck into gear and took off. But at the same moment, tires squealed and an engine revved as one of the Yakuza's big Cadillacs came straight at us.

"*Shimatta!*" said Mama Suji. But the Caddy wasn't playing chicken. It pulled up in a tail spin and blocked the way forward with its street-spanning length. Unmistakable in their sunglasses and tacky suits, Yakuza muscle and practitioners emerged from their car and, taking cover to the sides, raised their knives and sited their guns on us.

With gears grinding, Mama Suji reversed, swerving onto the curb to get by our stunt bag and nearly hitting the first of the hostiles to cross the street from the Spy Hotel. But even as we swerved back into the center of the road, another big Caddy moved in to block that direction as well. The streets to left and right were plugged too.

So, our opponents had Yakuza along with their North Koreans, Shaolin, and treacherous ninjas, and they had prepared for our exit on the street. Move, countermove. *Our turn, Kaguya-san.*

But it was the opposition that moved again, pouring out from the Spy Hotel's entrance and fire exit. What else could we do? We got out of the truck and faced the four quadrants, with Mama Suji in the middle conversing rapidly in Japanese.

Why the hell were so many practitioners here and gunning for Endicott and Marlow? My friends had done nothing to deserve such extreme adverse attention.

I crossed my arms against the big beat of my heart and readied my mind and craft. Here it was, the real rush. I wasn't a sociopath. I loved Dale, my family, my friends, my country. I loved my unborn child. I just didn't mind killing people very much. I didn't seek it out—had plenty of opportunities on the job.

Our opponents surrounded us, but did not yet charge. Instead, two North Koreans dressed all in black aimed handguns at us.

They must have been test subjects. "*No guns on this ground*," said Mama Suji. She stomped her foot. Red glowing craft leapt up from the street. Flesh sizzled as the North Koreans dropped their weapons. This land didn't like guns.

This was the only signal our opponents needed. They came at us in a charging mass of dark business suits like salarymen gone wild, and we fought. Except against Roderick, we'd often had reasons for restraint in combat, but tonight we had none—the only way out was to cripple and kill, again and again.

With my pregnant sensitivity, I felt or heard with sonar-like detail what I couldn't see of my comrades fighting. Dale's katana flashed up and down, slashed side to side. Like Jackson Pollock as samurai, he splattered blood everywhere. The copter tried an overflight, but Dale shook it with wind until it backed off.

Endicott was using his commands again, now that he could make hesitation a fatal flaw. Endicott's blade was economical; when his craft-commanded opponent paused, it struck, then parried the next opponent while Endicott readied another prayer for death. Whenever some mundane showed themselves, Endicott managed a "*For God's sake, get back inside and stay there.*"

But it was Grace's fighting that stunned me. She glowed like a furnace in craftsight as she executed combinations and snapped her opponent's bones—not with the smoothness of a dance, but in the fractal patterns of chaos. She purred her Latin craft like a phone-sex operator. Sexual energy had always been intimate with her craft, and Kabukicho had all the energy she could want. Two bodies and their swords lay still at her feet. When her attackers paused in fear and frustration, she baited them: "You came for us here? Better the Marlow House itself than here!"

Little ol' me? Of course, I'd brought my knives, long and short. Our attackers' points of vulnerability called to me like mewling kittens, and I hit them with all of my new maternal strength.

Still, as we were, we couldn't win. We were badly outnumbered. The Shaolin were masters, and their North Korean proxies were not mere zombies. The treacherous ninjas were as skilled as their loyal colleagues. Our energy came from our bodies, our focus was tied to our minds, and use of both was exhausting. They were landing blows, they were making cuts. I was bleeding from gashes as I struggled to heal more serious internal damage and to keep my baby from harm.

Worse, something was wrong with Dale. He seemed to be tiring more rapidly than the rest of us, and that was very unlike him. One way or another, this would end soon.

We weren't completely engaged though. Since she'd disabled the guns, Mama Suji had done nothing but talk on her earpiece. "A little help?" I suggested, as I jabbed at two encroaching Shaolin.

"Agreed." Mama Suji raised a hand, and up and down the street the lights and neon went dead, and no emergency lights came on. The electricity was cut off.

Our opponents slackened their blows, uncertain. Then, glowing in craftsight, they came. From the love hotels, nightclubs, and hostess bars emerged the women in schoolgirl fetishwear, in sailor shirts and skirts, the men in glam Elvis garb, and the transgendered in colorful combat kimonos. In command of them all, Kaguya-san, dressed in naval officer whites. She and her loyal ninjas had at last entered the ring. I finally understood: to avoid any more surprises, she had waited for the enemy to commit everything before going all in herself. Like the 47 Ronin, her loyalists must have been actually engaged in all the activities of the pleasure district to fool farsight.

It looked like we might win.

Then I saw what had been happening to Dale. A North Korean attacked him—not with particular skill or hope of success. Dale slashed his neck, and he went down. But in my craftsight, I saw Dale's energy bleed off with the spirit of the departing North Korean. Dale's already low lifeforce was now at its limit.

Another Korean was approaching. Fuck no. "Dale, wait! I'm coming."

One of the Shaolins yelled something, and all the enemy shifted. Like basketball players, they were setting picks on us, containing me and everyone else from reaching Dale. "Dale, fall back!"

But either he didn't hear me, or just didn't listen. He swung the light katana around as if it were as heavy as a broadsword, but it did the job. The North Korean fell next to his comrades.

Dale, his lifeforce draining away, toppled to the ground. With their preternatural swiftness, two Shaolin swooped in, lifted Dale's body, and bore him away at a sprint.

Our other opponents were falling back. They didn't care about Endicott and Grace. Though I'm not sure I knew that when I ran after Dale.

He's not dead yet. He'd tell me if he were. I sprinted down the street. Daggers and throwing stars passed through places I'd been and places I might be but never found me where I was. Monk after monk tried to interfere, and I cut them down for slowing me.

Ahead at the Cadillac barricade, a Yakuza held up a hand to the two Shaolin carrying Dale and three comrades who'd joined them. "*Matte!*" said the Yakuza. Apparently this Chinese move wasn't part of their plan. But the Shaolin knew how to improvise too. With only two blows, they cracked the Yakuza's skull. Then they took his electric car key, opened the doors, and shoved Dale into the backseat.

I was slashing the carotid of somebody who'd gotten in front of me as the car started to pull away. With a last preternatural burst of speed, I ran up to it and leapt. I landed a foot on the bumper and pushed forward. Coming down on all fours on the trunk, I scurried over the rear windshield before the Shaolin could draw a bead on me, and then surfed on the car's roof as it sped forward.

Not much time before they would eliminate me up here and speed away onto the thoroughfare. I would have known where to strike even without amplified perception, but now I could be absolutely precise. *Shatter and die.* I dropped to my knees, and with the full arc of my body and arm, I brought my blade around, punching through the front windshield and through the eye of the driver.

The car swerved and ground itself like a dull knife against the wall of a building. Sparks flew as I gripped the edge of the roof with my left hand, my right being a glassy, bloody mess.

The car lurched to a stop, and I slid off the roof and fell into a combat stance. All that power I'd used to get here had drained me. Worse, as the four Shaolin in the car scrambled out, another five Shaolin arrived on the scene. With them was Zhuge Wu. He had pulled the strings and sacrificed so many for this result.

Something in me snapped, and I rushed him. Without craft energy, I fought mundane good, but not magus good. In seconds I was pinned, tied with zip tie cuffs, and hauled up seated against the rear tire of the Cadillac.

Zhuge waved his hand. The world went fish-eyed. We were in a stealth bubble, which would delay our being found.

They hauled Dale out and sat him up just a little ways away. His eyes fluttered open, and the fingers on his bound right hand sought something on his left forearm. In a blur, Zhuge ripped away part of the fabric of Dale's shirt and snatched something away from Dale's fingers. His suicide needle. So that was one reason that they hadn't tried for Endicott: Michael could more easily kill himself.

I finally got it: this whole attack hadn't been about Endicott and Marlow at all. They'd wanted Dale, and our friends' wedding night had been Zhuge's last chance to know exactly where Dale would be in advance—on guard duty.

Zhuge contemplated Dale's suicide needle, then tossed it aside and brought out a KA-BAR-style blade. "The Left-Hand secret—now! Or I kill your wife and your child."

I shook my head. "I told you. He doesn't know."

Dale nodded, drunkenly. "I've never known it."

Oh God, no. The red *L* was glowing like a lighthouse. Dale was lying. He knew.

Apparently, Zhuge saw the deception too. "You're a terrible liar!"

"Don't tell them," I said. "Not worth it." A hundred Rodericks? The world couldn't survive it.

"So brave," said Zhuge. "Maybe I cut her down to size first."

"No," said Dale. But he didn't say anything else. Good, he wasn't going to be stupid. Bad for me though.

"Yes," said Zhuge, as he aligned his knife with my nose.

None of us saw the cemetery dog. He charged out of thin air. His jaw snapped on the Shaolin leader's gripping hand and, with one shake of his head, worried the knife out of it.

Zhuge brought his foot around to kick the beast, but the dog had backed off. My craftsight went strange, and instead of an Akita's face, the dog had the head of a jackal. I'd never seen any animal show up in craftsight except with the black light of Left-Hand mutation.

Zhuge said something angry in Chinese, and the other Shaolin went for the dog while he knelt for the knife. But the dog had already picked the weakest in their herd and leapt for him, snapping jaws seeking his throat.

Zhuge had found his knife again. He was rattled now. The shouts of martial combat echoed down the narrow street. I was cold and bleeding through the remnants of my bridesmaid's dress. I was useless.

"One last chance, Major," said Zhuge. "I succeed either way."

"How dare you attack our Family!" yelled Madeline, as she manifested in ectoplasmic flames and windblown robes and hair, like a temple's guardian demon. Shit, but she was terrible to behold— practically solid and incarnate next to Zhuge, focused completely in a way she hadn't been since Roderick had tried to bind her to the House.

Zhuge stepped back from her and me. "The stories were true." But something was wrong. He wasn't afraid. He was smiling as he pointed at her with his left hand. Madeline screamed, but the sound cut off as she disappeared, leaving only another echo in the dark streets.

Zhuge laughed in satisfaction. He stepped toward me, knife raised. In desperation, Dale rasped, *"Now I am become Death, destroyer of worlds,"* but instead of a Jovian lightning bolt, I only felt a little shock of static electricity. He and I were drained.

"Ha, ha—" A blast of gunfire, and Zhuge toppled over. The other Shaolin were already running away as fetish-dressed ninjas overran the car and our position. But I didn't see a handgun among them. The bullet hadn't skewed an inch, so the gunman must be very close. Sure enough, Monsignor Cornaro stepped out of the shadows, the whiff of gunshot preceding him like the devil's perfume. We were outside the perimeter of Suji's craft, so a gun was just the thing.

His *K* for killing Zhuge glowed recent and red, but I saw no impending sins, so I trusted him when he retrieved Zhuge's knife. He cut me out of my restraints. I looked down at the dead Shaolin. A red wound like a third eye on his forehead, a pool of blood on the ground from his blown-out skull. "Nice shooting," I said.

"Te Deum laudamus," said Cornaro, helping Dale out of his bonds.

"Where's Madeline?" I said. Only great power could have dispelled her when she'd been so completely present.

"I do not sense her," said Cornaro. He dropped the gun onto the still chest of Zhuge—the eldest son of the head of the Chinese craft service. "Our hosts will find this very . . . difficult. I think I must leave now." In a blink, Cornaro was gone.

A cold misty rain began to fall. In another moment, Kaguya-san and Mama Suji were on the scene, looking for someone else to hurt. I was in the surreal place between waking and passing out—not a safe state of mind for a craftsperson. I croaked out questions. "Endicott? Marlow?"

"We had to restrain them," said Kaguya-san. "They were in no condition to help you."

Mama Suji sniffed the air, and said something in Japanese. "Who else was here?" said Kaguya-san.

He'd said his involvement would cause difficulty, but I was too tired to even consider deception. "The priest, Cornaro."

Mama Suji sucked in air at the name. "We didn't see that he would be here," said Kaguya-san.

"We didn't expect it either," I said. Then, concerned Hutchinson, frantic Vasilisa, and calmly smiling Dude arrived. They helped us up.

"Time for you to go," said Hutchinson.

"Sure," I slurred. "We'll just rest first . . ."

"You have been declared personae non gratae," said Kaguya-san.

That slapped me to attention. Her government wanted us gone immediately? "Since when?" I asked.

"When the attack began," said Kaguya-san.

Hutchinson had my arm draped over her shoulder, while the elderly Dude was somehow supporting my bobble-headed husband as he stumbled around Zhuge's corpse. "Dale," I said. No answer. "Major Morton."

His head snapped up. "What?"

"Where the fuck is Madeline?" My profanity glitch was on, betraying a concern I didn't want to admit.

"Auntie," he said. "Don't make me summon you." A so vain threat—he could barely stand. But no manifestation.

Then, bits of shadow like eye floaters coalesced in an amorphous blot on my vision—the Left-Hand spirits. Instead of an answer, they echoed my question. "Where is she?" they moaned. These revenants of psychic vampires, mind-raping possessors, and power-mad world threateners had degenerated into the multi-voiced and pathetic thing they'd been when I'd first seen them, before Madeline. "Give her back to us!" Like spiritual smoke lost in a breeze, they drifted out of sight, their collective wail like a departing train.

I felt the wet of rain, sweat, and tears on my cheeks. *Can't be gone. She's mine to dismiss. She saved our lives, again.*

A black sedan pulled up. Our ride? Men got out. All men. Something about that cut through my haze. It definitely bothered Mama Suji. Between heartbeats, she was gone. But her boss, Kaguya-san, stood absolutely still, arms outstretched in submission to possible handcuffs, eyes closed in submission to any craft. "Do nothing," she said.

Very deliberately in our plain view, the men grabbed Kaguya-san. They cuffed her, arms behind her back, and her eyes sprung open in seeming surprise at the excess of it. As they dragged her into the car, her face had a feral, angry pride I hadn't seen before. "Fucking worth it!" she shouted in English, straining her head back around toward us, toward me.

"*Domo arigato gozaimashita*," I mouthed, and bowed unsteadily as they slammed the door behind her. In seconds, they had quietly sped away. Kaguya-san had pulled off a magnificent game of chess against a farseeing opponent, yet she could not save herself. No, she had chosen not to; instead, she had saved us. Dale had said that craft makes strange enemies but stranger friends. Venting my anger, I spoke a thought aloud: "One day I will do something about this." Just words, useless words.

Dale seemed in total shock, but part of him must've still been assessing our position. He whispered between ragged breaths: "Personae non gratae. Not a threat. A warning. Real consensus against us soon."

"We need to be long gone by then," I said.

"Is stupid," agreed Vasilisa.

Another car pulled up—the wedding limo. More of Kaguya-san's male colleagues coming for us this time?

The door opened and revealed Endicott and Marlow leaning into each other under a quilt with a kimono-like pattern of flowers. Endicott's metal foot protruded from under the cover, bent up and covered with dirty gore.

The limo driver took us to Haneda Airport in Tokyo proper. Kaguya-san had our plane moved there in case we needed a quicker getaway than Narita. Like everything else, she'd seen to it. Damn her for being that good and gone beyond thanks.

Our baggage and gifts were thoughtfully ready, but not so thoughtfully on the wet tarmac. With the gifts was the *Oikumene*'s statuette. I flipped a mental coin. "Bring it," I said.

We'd gotten enough of our wind back during the drive to help load up with trudging mundane strength. Now the land wasn't merely stingy with its power; it felt actively hostile and draining.

As I was about to close the cabin door and shake the dirt of this country from my shoes, I heard something like a sharp cough by someone rudely interrupting. There, at the bottom of the airstairs, sat the cemetery dog, his ear raggedly cut, his muzzle and paws bloody. He barked again, and looked up at me, not with puppy-dog big eyes, but a defiant stare, as if saying "Make up your mind. I haven't got all day."

"Kaguya-san said to leave you alone." But Kaguya-san was gone. "*Irrashaimase*," I said, as if I were welcoming him to a restaurant.

The dog limped up, bringing wet dog smell with him. Dale, Michael, and Grace gaped at him with dazed horror and amusement.

"Can we keep him?" I said.

One problem prevented our immediate takeoff: where could we go? Kaguya-san had arranged carte blanche on our flight plan, but that window was closing, and we needed a compass direction at least. Our options were extremely limited. Back in the States, we still faced house arrest or worse.

We sat together in the passenger cabin. Marlow was helping Endicott clean his foot. I was checking Dale's injuries and he checked mine. I couldn't do any healing yet. "We have an offer from the Vatican," I said. "No strings attached. Well, no Left-Hand strings. They want our help with the end of the world."

Endicott frowned, angrier than I'd ever seen him without something Left-Hand in the room. "Endicotts don't treat with the pope," he growled.

Despite his pain, Dale chuckled. "Think they're going to massacre us in our sleep, Major Puritan?" But he raised his hands at Endicott's glare. "Not that I trust them either."

Marlow shook her head as she tinkered with a metal foot joint. "Rome is too far. We have an eight thousand kilometer range. At minimum we need someplace we can refuel first. Even the overflight countries on a direct flight path will be problematic."

"It'll be Lubyanka next time Russia gets its claws on me," said Dale.

"And we've seen China's position," said Endicott.

China reminded me of Madeline, and what they'd done to her. Evil Madeline who'd saved my life again. I nearly felt her all-consuming rage at this. That anger made me think of Madeline at the reception. "Madeline was shouting at the Indian representative."

Dale took a moment to switch gears. "Madeline shouting isn't that unusual." He was still using the present tense for her.

"She said . . ." What had she said, exactly? "She said, 'Why should we care?' What did Pandava tell Madeline that pissed her off?"

"I heard that part," said Dale. "Pandava was saying something about their homes for spirits. Madeline called them hospices for the already dead."

If I were Madeline, what would enrage me about this, besides Pandava presuming to speak with me, or even being capable of speaking to me? I said, "Auntie must have seen it as an offer—a rude one." So India had an offer for Madeline. "They might not know that she's gone. So they might let us stop there on the mistaken assumption that Madeline would be keeping close to us."

Marlow held up a single finger. "India? I love you all dearly, but you have no bloody idea what you'd be getting into. The Families there have traditions going back into mythical times. To them, we're all spiritual parvenus. They aren't terribly concerned about our Left- and Right-Hand distinctions." She paused, considering. "My Family's history during the Raj might also be a problem."

Endicott straightened up. Time for a command decision. "Any other options?" He looked at each of us, Marlow last.

Marlow said, "Let's not stay long."

A s our best deceiver, and as someone who'd worked with them before, Marlow called the Indian craft service, the Special Research and Analysis Wing, or SPRAW. She informed them that we were coming, leaving them to interpret what that might mean regarding Madeline. Even if Pandava had left immediately after the reception, our supersonic jet would probably beat her back to her country, though we didn't know whether this would help or hurt us. "We're being less than candid," said Marlow. "And the Pandavas are extremely proud."

Gazes shifted toward Endicott. "Yes, beyond Michael," said Marlow, "believe it or not."

"I don't," said Endicott, actually smiling at the joke at his expense.

"No other craft Family has continued so long," said Marlow. "The Endicotts have been in the craft for four hundred years. Multiply that pride tenfold. Also, do not make the mistake of confusing her Family's beliefs with the ascetic ideals of Hinduism. Her Family has always believed in the dharma of action in the world, not withdrawal from it."

"What are Colonel Pandava's talents?" I asked. Her file had been vague on that point.

"Uncertain," said Marlow. "The founders of her Family had a wide variety of powers, and she may have a variety all by herself."

Marlow had to fly the plane as primary pilot, popping amphetamines, so she and Endicott wouldn't get any more honeymooning during the flight. I think Dale and I passed out for a bit. Otherwise, we rested and repaired, and I had a little craft back for healing.

I checked again on the baby, and all seemed well. My damage was mostly cuts, and I had a lot of them, such as from my fun with the car windshield. Dale helped me clean and bandage those. So, having some magic to spare, I laid my hands on Dale. I gave him some of the life energy he'd lost, doing deliberately what I'd done unconsciously while on the run with him from H-ring, back before I'd known what I was.

Even international air space felt more generous with power than Japan had been at the end. Eight thousand kilometers meant about five thousand standard miles in range, and we would need most of it to reach New Delhi, as we would skirt around Chinese airspace. We could have tried for India's Andaman Islands, which were closer for us, but that would have looked strange to our hosts and would have left too much distance on the other end to get to Rome in one hop.

If we could get to Rome at all. The others weren't wild about it, and the Italian craft service might not be as obliging as the Vatican and Cornaro seemed to be. Also, India might be easier to enter than exit.

After we'd finished patching each other up, I cleaned and examined the dog. Japan was an orderly place, and even occult street animals had collars and tags. Endicott read the characters. "*Hachiko no Rabu*. Love of Hachiko. Let's call him Rabu." Rabu barked.

"Private Rabu," I said, just to make sure he knew who was in charge.

"Cemetery dog," said Dale. "Makes sense now." He started into professorial mode about Hachiko, the dog who had waited every day at Shibuya Station for his beloved master to return from work, not realizing that his master had died.

"I know that story," I said. "It's like the dog in *Futurama*."

"But that's not the full story," said Dale.

"Oh," I said, anticipating him. "The ghost."

"The ghosts," corrected Dale. "First, just the master's. Then, others. Following their old work routines, and then returning at night to Shibuya Station and the comforting presence of an animal that could see them."

He paused, eyebrows furrowing. "Still, given my family's bad history with pets and ghosts, I'm not sure why Rabu here wants to follow us."

Particularly as we already have someone for his job. I knew a word for what Hachiko had done, for what Rabu probably did, because I did it too. We were psychopomps, guiders of souls, on patrol on the border between life and death, sometimes shepherding them as sheep, sometimes driving them out as wolves.

Sometimes, we failed. "What's wrong?" Dale asked.

"Besides the obvious?" I asked. "Madeline. I think I'm going to miss her."

I tried smiling, but Dale responded with the tone he reserved for all things serious and Left-Hand. "I have trouble mourning her. She was either already dead or . . ."

Or she still wasn't. The relationship of the Left-Hand Mortons with death was always ambiguous. But I saw no reason for such hope or fear; even in international airspace, she remained AWOL. That meant permanent dispellation. "There was nothing in Zhuge's file about exorcism," I said.

"Then maybe one of those with him did it?"

"Maybe."

"You saw some sins," said Dale.

"Yeah," I said, suddenly self-conscious at this change of topic.

But he didn't ask about the baby. "Did you see any weird sins for Cornaro?"

"No."

"Me neither," he said. "Just the usual small letters."

"Would dispelling Madeline have been a sin?" I asked.

"Good point," said Dale. "But deceiving us would have been a sin, particularly when he'd just been our guest. He should have glowed with the lie or the betrayal if he'd been involved in any way."

"He said you and the others were prejudiced against him."

"Not him personally. But the craft has a long unhappy history with his church. Sure, for centuries it provided cover for craft outcasts and kept them hidden, but that just made it all the more vicious in attacking rogue craftspeople to reassure the public."

But even as I was going to ask more about Catholics and craft, I heard the dog sniffing at the kitchenette and making a sound more like a low hum than a growl. I felt around, and found a hidden compartment in the cabinet. I expected drugs, but instead found cans of dog food and two metal dog dishes.

Without a word, I took out a can, popped the top, and served it to Rabu, then filled the other bowl with water. Dale stared on, scowling in something between anger and horror. Whether it was Kaguya-san's people or Eddy, pet supplies were just one anticipatory step too many, even for this farsight-shocked crew.

Endicott slept, leaving only Rabu and his big dog eyes attentive to us, ears up and head tracking. Dale and I shared a privacy that we might not have again for days. We had something important to discuss—the truth he couldn't conceal from Zhuge or me.

I wasn't truly angry with him; I hadn't felt that sort of rage since I dragged him out from the destruction of the House, when I'd thought he had used me in the worst way. But I was definitely upset, and the more I thought about it, the worse it got. Still, I kept my voice as low and controlled as I could. "You know the secret," I said. The Left-Hand way of immortality, and he hadn't told me.

He shook his head and held a finger to his lips. "Can't speak of it."

Oh, no, you don't. "We have to speak of it."

He held up his hands. "Fine. Whatever you want to know." He sounded angry at my demand, but his hands were shaking, as if talking were the most fearful thing in the world. I reached out and touched his shoulder. He flinched, and then, though I had no reassuring craft, his hands stilled, and so did some of my own anger. We had time enough to go at this gradually. "Who else knows?"

"No one else. No one living. Roderick is gone. Madeline too, now."

I wasn't sure about any of that. "Endicott knows."

He smiled grimly. "Endicott can do the tricks. But it's mostly the nano-craft inside him that has the know-how. He doesn't know how he does the tricks, and he can do them clean."

"Do your father and grandfather know?"

"We don't talk about it," he said. "No one could make them talk anyway." I loved Dale's dad and granddad, but they were long dead and very stubborn besides, so no one was likely to compel their spirits to do anything they didn't want to.

"OK," I said. "What do you know, exactly?" His eyes went wide with terror. I held up both hands. "Not how you'd do it. I never want to know that. But what do you know how to do?"

"All of it. How to rip a soul from its body. How to take a body, and how to keep the flesh going even as it decays. How to feed on the power of those around me. How to slowly destroy a soul."

"How can you know?"

"Ever since we took down Roderick, the Left-Hand part of my brain, it's gotten louder. It's not telling me to kill anyone anymore. It just recites the Left-Hand way, like a catechism, like a damned cookbook, over and over."

"Some craft to make you forget?" I suggested.

"I've tried every trick to not know, and then unknow it. I'd end up erasing the rest of me first." Another shudder ran through him, as if the terrible knowledge were seeking a way out. Something so many were willing to kill for, and he was tearing himself up inside not to know it.

"At least Zhuge is dead," I said. "We won't tell the others. Won't lie, but won't tell."

Dale shook his head. "Makes no difference tactically."

"It makes a difference to me."

"Everyone thinks I know anyway," said Dale. "They won't bother to try to capture Michael and Grace alive. He can kill himself, and she can deceive unto death. I need a better suicide method."

"Not this shit again!" I said, anger returning all over.

"Keep it down," he mouthed.

I took a breath. I couldn't blame him for not confiding in me; he was as always just trying to protect me. But that pointed to the real problem. "There's something you need to understand. You can't ever use it to save me, or our child. Not even to save the world."

"Endicott . . ."

"Endicott can walk that line. I can't, and neither can you."

"You didn't say don't use it for myself."

I stared at him, incredulous. Did I have to say it? "Ah, love, I know you wouldn't. That's not your weakness. You could resist Zhuge because you knew that talking about it wouldn't do us any good, and even if Left-Hand craft could have helped, you were too exhausted to use it. So that won't be the situation."

I felt the tingling certainty of it run down my spine. Was this some new oracular power or the Morton foreboding that the unborn kid was giving me?

"Try not to put yourself in that situation," he said.

"Right," I said. Because it was bullshit. Perverse irony was the staple of armed service, and the probability skews of craft service just made the ironies more real. Sooner or later, the poetically bad thing was bound to happen.

Hearing nothing more of interest, Rabu laid his head on his paws and closed his eyes, perhaps to dream of lost ghosts.

On our arrival at Indira Gandhi International Airport, it was still the middle of the night. India felt electric after Japan, and not just because it was a notch warmer. It was generous with magic, though Marlow had hinted that it could be heartless in many other ways.

We landed without incident, but when I opened the door and airstairs, we faced lots of guns, probably Tavor assault rifles by the look of them, the weapon of choice for many special forces units around the world. Viewing the tarmac in craftsight, some of the rifles were aimed by mages who wouldn't allow much probability skew. My heartbeat surprised me with its steadiness. I was getting used to this shit.

The only soldier without a Tavor, an officer with a close-trimmed beard and mustache, stepped forward. He appeared to have seniority and a more colorful assortment of sins over his colleagues. "Welcome to India," he said. "You will kindly follow us to the transit waiting area. Major Endicott, please be careful with your choice of words. We have precautions in place."

So they knew about Endicott's power of command. Were the precautions remote? Automated? If our hosts were smart, they'd be redundant several times over.

"Thank you for your welcome," said Endicott. "Why are we going to the waiting area?"

The officer looked dumbfounded. "To wait, of course." *Oh Michael, you just couldn't help yourself, could you?*

Rabu poked his head out of the cabin and leapt down onto the tarmac. Surprised, the officer considered him a moment, then yelled at us, "You cannot enter the country with that animal!" He sounded fearful and outraged.

Marlow started into a polite objection, but I knew a better response. "Come on, Rabu." I turned around and, without seeing if my friends were following, stepped back onto the airstairs with Rabu. Those little noises again, this time of both craft and rifles being readied. I heard Endicott say, "Lieutenant," with some sharpness, but it sounded like he was following me, as was Dale. That we had no fuel to go anywhere else didn't matter.

"Wait!" called the officer. "Please stay. My apologies. Loyalty to a craft animal is an ancient test, and not foolproof, but it is shocking the number of times Left-Hand foreigners fail it. This way please."

"Shall we, Lieutenant?" said Endicott, a little pointedly. Being right didn't always mean much with superiors.

On the way to the holding area, Marlow asked, "The Mahabharata?"

"*Twilight Zone?*" asked Dale.

They wanted to know my source for my response to the test. I scratched Rabu's head and smiled at my own fangirl triumph in their magic book world. "Both," I said.[1]

The "waiting area" was an old building of decaying handmade bricks and metal roofing, untouched by all the recent construction and expansion of the airport. According to Marlow, holding those in transit in India had been a Cold War tradition of the British Magic Circus. Her mentor, the Left-Hand traitor Christopher Dee, had played against the Russians here.

The uneven wooden chairs seemed as old as the cramped, airless room. The others found ways to rest, and Rabu lay on the floor, head on paws, sleeping. After a couple of hours of this, I didn't care anymore about looking inexperienced. "What are they waiting for?" I asked.

"I expect they're waiting for Colonel Pandava," said Marlow, politely covering a brief yawn. She used Pandava's title to be respectful, assuming that everything we said at this point was closely monitored.

I was more than willing to wait for Pandava. She might know something about Madeline. If she were in any way responsible, I'd find a way to make her pay.

Either it was just a coincidence or our words were a cue, because without a knock the door opened and in came Pandava. She wore her hair in a non-regulation long braid, which her file speculated was justified by her undercover work, though she might just prefer it that way. Her complexion was darker than what a Delhi matchmaker would like, but that would be the matchmaker's loss. Her accent with English was similar to Grace's, with just a tinge more tonality. She'd left her reception dress behind for a short-sleeved army uniform and

---

1. See Appendix, Part 1: The Dog Who Was Dharma

beret. Gone also was the smiling, cordial woman of the reception. Without introduction or apology, she demanded, "Where is your Family's spirit?"

"Colonel Pandava." Marlow again tried to be the pleasant negotiator. "We're sorry, but we came here without her. We would like to refuel, and then we'll be off."

"I'll ask once more," said Pandava. "Where is your Family's spirit?" She wasn't looking at Marlow; she was staring at me with a gaze that had some craft behind it.

"She's gone," I said. "She—"

"Exorcist!" Pandava practically spat the interruption. "Only one person in the world could have permanently dispelled Madeline Morton." She pointed a finger at me, accusing. "If you've destroyed her, we shall all suffer the consequences."

"Colonel Pandava," said Marlow, trying to redirect our angry host's attention.

"You aren't going anywhere, Commander, until I know exactly what happened to Madeline Morton."

I glanced at Marlow. Her mouth had frozen into a neutral line, but her eyes had the same annoyed narrowness they got when Endicott did something foolish despite her warning. She had been more right than she'd known: we hadn't realized what we were getting into, and getting out again might be a problem.

The office of Cardinal Nettesheim, the head of the Vatican Department of Spiritual Gifts, was a terribly cramped room in the lower, secret levels of the Library. A small desk for the cardinal, an uncomfortable wooden chair for his current guest and subordinate, Monsignor Cornaro, and a few crucial volumes sequestered from the Library were the sole adornments. At this, the center of Roman Catholicism, space was at a drastic premium. Deceived by the Vatican's small size, some people viewed its separate nationhood as a quaint technicality, but for the craft, it was anything but. The whole point of the craft arm of the Church was that it didn't depend on blood lineage (a fact of which the Grail conspiracists were fortunately ignorant), but it still needed a land, and the Vatican's tiny state was ancient, full of history, ghosts (not always holy), and power.

The Catholic craft's geopolitical operations were few, but in conjunction with other powers its force could tip the balance, as it had during the Cold War. Its main operations were against Evil, which in these modern times wasn't merely some difference in theology. For the Catholic craft, Evil particularly meant the so-called Left Hand and the malevolent dead spirits that emerged from its practices.

Nettesheim wore the black garb of a simple priest. Of course, he held his appointment as cardinal secretly, *in pectore*. If anyone asked, he was just Monsignor Nettesheim, scholar of Church history. The old man rose to the head of the order after the John Paul I fiasco, when in the prime of his powers. The future Pope Benedict had been one of his German associates.

Cornaro was two decades Nettesheim's junior. He came from a craft Family, but one where the craft skipped a generation. This happened all too often in ancient Families losing their gifts. Cornaro had been an altar boy in '68, when an explosion of craft entered the mundane world. Many thought that was a sign of the millennium, and maybe it had been, though a failed one. But Cornaro had found his calling.

"You were correct, Your Eminence," said Cornaro. "Pandava was at the wedding, trying to make a deal for the Hindus. We got the revenant just in time."

"You could have let the Americans die," noted Nettesheim. "That would have solved the problem of the Left-Hand secret completely."

"I had no orders for that action." Probably just an oversight of the cardinal's (he'd been making a lot of those lately), but plenty of cover for Cornaro's killing Zhuge in time to prevent Rezvani's and Morton's deaths. "It seemed like one sin too many."

"The Chinese are not happy with us," noted the cardinal.

"The Chinese never have been. They should not have presumed that an operative of the Church would be so easily suborned to follow their plans for the Mortons, whether those Mortons were living or dead." That was a good one—invoking Church pride always went over well.

The cardinal took off his glasses and rubbed his tired eyes. "She's truly gone then?"

"As thoroughly as the Georgetown demon," said Cornaro, with a grim smile at this inside joke. "She won't be telling her Family's secrets to anyone else."

After a pause, Cornaro came to the important part. "Your Eminence, I would like some time to renew my spirit before my next assignment."

The cardinal frowned, and raised a finger as if to protest. Did he suspect something?

"Your request is . . . granted, of course." The cardinal smiled and nodded at his own little joke. "Your work has been exemplary, but I can well appreciate the amount of energy such an exorcism required. Take the rest of the month. Maybe visit your family home?"

"Yes, Your Eminence," said Cornaro, trying to sound embarrassed about his intention to return to his family's luxurious villa. The old dog must have thought he was being sly with that dig, but he really didn't know how sly.

The cardinal dismissed him with a blessing and "Go in peace." Cornaro reflected on their meeting as he went up into the more public part of the Library, where the compasses of Freemasonry were painted on a high lintel for all to see—odd to find that symbol here in the heart of Catholicism, but not to those with knowledge. *Nettesheim is definitely too old for his position.* Such bald-faced deceptions and obfuscations would have never worked on him as a younger man. Alzheimer's or any dementia was dangerous in craft—he'd have to be replaced soon. But such a poor watchdog was convenient now, leaving Cornaro free to put his plans in motion.

Like the sower of the parable, Cornaro didn't know whether the other seeds he'd planted would come to helpful fruition. Anonymously, through intermediaries in Goa and Japan, he'd made sure that India's SPRAW was aware of certain details of Rezvani's case file: how Rezvani had previously, if temporarily, dispelled Madeline, and how she'd threatened to do so again. He'd also leaked the stories of various attempts by the *Oikumene*, the Church, and other powers to permanently dispel Madeline and of their failure, and some of these stories were even true. Should SPRAW continue to be interested in Madeline's fate, this would leave one and only one suspect for her disappearance.

Gilding the lily? Perhaps, but Cornaro didn't want foreign watchdogs either. He would be busy during his holiday; he was taking his work home with him, and that work would not be pleased.

PART II

ROMAN HOLIDAY AND LOST HORIZON

Life never gives us what we want at the moment that we consider
appropriate. Adventures do occur, but not punctually.

—E. M. Forster

But I didn't take no interest in the place, because there could be ghosts
there, of course; not fresh ones, but I don't like no kind.

—Mark Twain

Notes on the Witch of Endor story found in the House of Morton:

Lesson one: when the times are good, the witches, wizards, and
necromancers are hunted down and exiled or killed, because the state
doesn't like other sources of power and authority besides the
sanctioned religion.
Lesson two: when the chips are down, the orthodox religion may desert
the state, even go over to the enemies of the state.
Lesson three: even when they believe in our power, governments try
to lie to us, to manipulate us into doing what they want.
Lesson four: don't trust the rulers to keep their promises even when
you've kept yours.
Lesson five (the hardest lesson of all): we have to be decent to individuals
even when they're part of a system that tries to kill us.

In an office near the waiting area, Colonel Madhuri Pandava of the Indian Army and SPRAW meditated, concentrating her whole being on her Family's mantra, "On the field of dharma." After a moment, she stood within a simulacrum of a chariot from India's age of heroes, incandescent with synaptic fire, with four white horses that seemed to tint with other hues from green to gray to golden. The chariot was inside her own mind, and she was in that chariot as an avatar of her own consciousness.

This is not going to be pleasant, thought Pandava. *But no use in delay.* She would again invite the spirit that called itself Prithvi to join her in the chariot. Here was a craft secret hidden in the Mahabharata: without harm to themselves or their riders, the Pandavas could be excellent vehicles for powerful spirits.

Prithvi was also the name of the Hindu earth goddess, and Pandava forgave this presumptive attempt to fit with Indian culture. As the Pandavas knew all too well as "chariots of the avatars," even the greatest spirits on this plane of existence had begun as human beings. Despite Prithvi's long existence and tremendous power as the directing will for the magical order of all the Earth's lands, she was in the end merely a mortal's ghost.

Pandava and Prithvi had been aiding each other because of the imminent end of the world as they knew it. Another of the Pandava Family secrets was the timing of the end of the Kali Yuga, when the worst of ages would flame out in apocalyptic struggle, taking much of the globe with it. Such hidden knowledge was an advantage of having so long a magical lineage. Pandava's ancestors had fought in the Armageddon that brought an end to the last age: the Kurukshetra War of the Mahabharata. The next transition wasn't a precisely known point; it could happen any time after 2014. Perhaps it had begun. The gathering of craftspeople in the mountains was certainly a preliminary sign.

Naturally, Prithvi seemed very anxious to save what she could of the world. Pandava was particularly concerned to save the Indian part of it, and perhaps come out better than all other lands in this change of ages. Pandavas didn't like to lose.

"*Prithvi*," she called. "*Please come.*"

Prithvi appeared next to her in the chariot, dressed in a traditional blue sari and with a face that resembled that of Pandava's mother. This manifestation was more comfortable for the colonel than the strange, dimension-defying form that Prithvi had assumed in her earlier visits.

"Well, daughter," said Prithvi, "where is Madeline Morton?"

"She appears to be gone."

"Gone?" said Prithvi, voice rising. "What do you mean?"

"Madeline's family has come here to India, and they say she may have vanished from this plane of existence."

"Are the Mortons responsible? Did Rezvani dispel her?"

"Uncertain. I've been questioning the Mortons and their friends individually. They deny responsibility, but I don't know of anyone living besides Rezvani who could have permanently dispelled Madeline."

"Madeline Morton is essential to my plans. Essential to the world. You have to find her!"

Synaptic lightnings flashed around them. In the outside world, Pandava's physical body twitched uncontrollably. Then, an awkward silence. Finally, after Prithvi seemed calmer, Pandava asked, "What if she really is gone?"

Prithvi sighed. "You mentioned the friends of the Mortons. Who exactly is here?"

Pandava didn't understand this lack of knowledge. "They are all in the room next door."

"I do not wish my presence to be noticed just yet."

Pandava listed the four names. "Perhaps something can be done," said Prithvi. "I've given Endicott a channel to Earth's power, though he is only vaguely aware of me. But the Mortons . . ." Prithvi shook her head. "Here's what you should do. Question the Mortons one final time, but both together. I shall stay within you for the interrogation. The Mortons have the power to see murderous intention, and right now I can provide you with plenty of that. Perhaps that will frighten them sufficiently to reveal what has become of Madeline."

"And if their denials continue?"

"If their denials continue, we may have to do something that we shall probably both regret."

I tried a breathing technique to relax as Pandava started yet another round of questioning. Pandava might have hoped to break us, but Dale and I were a synergistic team of exasperation, and I was beginning to think Pandava would break first. That could be bad news, as she might kill us from frustration. A faint letter *M* was getting more intense. She very much wanted to murder somebody, and we weren't helping.

"Let's go over this one more time," said Pandava. "You think Zhuge dispelled Madeline."

"He was there," I said, trying to keep to the facts and only the facts.

"He pointed his finger," said Dale, demonstrating with his waggling left hand.

"There's no evidence that he or anyone in his Family has ever had that sort of power," said Pandava.

"I know," I said.

"Then someone else must have done it," she said.

"Perhaps," I agreed.

"At the time, everyone seemed more concerned with killing us," said Dale.

"Major," I said, a warning in my tone.

"Only trying to help," said Dale, eyes still on Pandava. "Look, don't you have someone who could detect deceit?"

The way she glared at Dale, I thought we were dead right then and there. "I assume the colonel can do that herself," I said quickly, hoping to keep her calm.

"And she's not detecting any," said Dale.

"She's just being thorough," I said. "We're scary Mortons. We might be good at deceit."

"Ahem," said Pandava, her *M* really bright now.

"Right," I said. "You're the interrogator. Please continue."

"Please continue?" said Dale, incredulous. "We didn't do anything. End of story."

"But that's not possible," said Pandava, emphasizing every word. "Only one person had means, motive, and opportunity."

"Who told you that?" asked Dale, face scrunched as if he'd tasted something unpleasant.

"I admit I had means and opportunity," I said. "But I kind of liked Madeline, and that was not the time to dispel her."

"Even to keep her from the Chinese?"

"That hadn't even occurred to me," I said. "My husband was my only concern. As for being the only person capable, I have no idea. It's a big world, and I'm still new at this. Monsignor Cornaro said the Vatican has all sorts of writings about . . . dispellation." I didn't use the word "exorcists," as Pandava seemed not to like it.

"Cornaro discussed exorcism with you?" she said.

Shit, I'd opened up another line of inquiry. "You might as well tell her that story too," said Dale, rolling his eyes in an annoying way.

"We were on our way to the Vatican when you stopped us," I said, still trying to keep it simple and straightforward.

"And you stopped here, in India," said Pandava, her *M* flashing with her incredulity. "Right into my hands," she added, gripping them tightly together to illustrate.

She paused, nodding slowly at her own words, then sat down heavily and closed her eyes. As if speaking to herself, she said, "Madeline is really gone."

"We can't reach her," I said.

Pandava was massaging her temples. "I am seriously going to regret this," she said, again more to herself than us. The *M* didn't vanish, but grew less urgent, making it unlikely that murder was what she was thinking of now.

"Regret what?" I prompted.

"This is a bit awkward," said Pandava. "We could use your help."

I wanted to tell Pandava that she could find help someplace in a Hindu hell, but one look from Dale reminded me that Endicott and Marlow weren't with us here, and we weren't yet free.

We were brought back together with our friends and Rabu at India's Ministry of Defence, located not very far from the airport in a huge, Raj-era building with a central dome that was an odd mix of Western classical and South Asian motifs. The structure seemed too heavy for a warm country.

We walked through the main entranceway and were waved through security. In the long corridor, Pandava returned salutes or otherwise acknowledged persons who were clearly mundanes—she was obviously well known. Rabu strode with us as if he'd been a military K-9 his whole life. We went into a conference room that was directly off the main corridor. This was way too normal. Pandava didn't seem to worry about keeping herself or craft ops sequestered in any direct physical way from her colleagues and their ops. If this was true for all craft officers, a lot more people must be aware of craft ops in India than in the United States, and yet nothing bad seemed to be happening here. Weird.

We sat down, Rabu at attention on the floor, ready for the sales pitch. Endicott had taken Pandava's change of course as if we'd been greeted like friends from the start. He wore that smug look that still irritated me and nearly drove Dale to violence, though this time it seemed to say that everything was going not just his way, but all of ours. The turn of events flowed over him, like water over a shark, and at the wedding even the black of his eye patch and the gleam of his prosthetic foot had seemed more like future iconography than the marks of past damage.

A wall screen showed us the skewed diamond shape of India and its immediate neighbors. Pandava directed her interactive pointer along its northern borders in a sweeping gesture. "We have the usual sorts of forces on our border—patrol ghosts in threes, a few craft troops sprinkled in, farsight always focused against new incursions by our neighbors. As you know, the high ground is different for craft, and this is the highest ground in the world."

All I knew was that I'd never liked high mountains, though I had no problem with tall buildings or bridges.

The pointer's red dot came to rest, not on the bold line marking India's border, but instead where three dotted lines came together. "Here, in Kashmir, near the Indira Col in the Karakoram Mountains, is the tripoint of effective control of India, Pakistan, and China. My government does not recognize this border, but our troops do."

Some instinct for Dale's moods made me glance at him next to me. He'd shifted his posture into ramrod attention mode. Below the table out of Pandava's view, his fists clenched once, twice. It was a tell of his when he was worried about something.

Pandava clicked and clicked again, giving us a succession of images. First was a fuzzy aerial view, probably a sat photo, of a larger building shaped like an upside down T with smaller structures in front of it, on a plateau set in a frame of rough terrain. Then a plateau-level view, distant and again hazy. The haziness might have been a subtle stealth, like a magic heat mirage, obscuring the buildings.

The smug little smile left Endicott's face. "The Sanctuarium Mundi?" he asked.

Pandava nodded, saying something that sounded Hindi or Sanskrit.

"Oh, great," Endicott muttered, but I was hearing every word, even the subvocals. "New Age nonsense on a global scale. This will be twice as much fun as the American one."

Sitting next to Endicott, Marlow could also hear him. "Self-pity is not your most attractive feature, dear."

I could feel Dale's craft shifting toward red alert mode. What about this had him so edgy?

Pandava clicked several times, and we got an artist's renderings of a series of structures. "The Monastery," she said. She pointed at the largest structure. "The monastic hall." The design and curved roofs of the front of the hall looked Chinese or Japanese to me, while the outer buildings were a cultural hodgepodge, as if architects from different places and times had designed them. Another drawing showed the high plateau as a whole more clearly; it appeared unnaturally flat for this environment.

Next, an overhead schematic. Three approaches to the Sanctuary's plateau, about 120 degrees apart, were represented as long stairways ending in outward pointing arrows marked India, Pakistan, and China.

Dale had recovered himself enough to ask a question. "Floor plans?" *The Mortons and their craft buildings.*

"Later," said Pandava. "They're mostly guesswork anyway. No one farsees into there, and few living or dead have reported back."

"Are any of the structures sentient?" asked Endicott.

Pandava seemed surprised as the rest of us that he'd been the one to ask. "There's consciousness everywhere, but we don't know whether the monastic hall or other buildings have achieved awareness equivalent to the House of Morton. But please, may I continue?"

Everyone nodded except for Dale. "It isn't big enough," he said. "Where's the rest of it?"

The plateau and its stairways seemed huge to me, but then I remembered the American Sanctuary, and scaled it up.

Pandava gave an Indian head shake. "To enter a Sanctuary, there is always a crossing point. But within the World Sanctuary, we believe the Monastery holds a second gateway to a greater, inner Sanctuary."

Dale nodded like he'd already expected this answer. As if to shake such complacency, Pandava said, "You may have some incorrect notions about the World Sanctuary and its Monastery. Yes, it is the probable inspiration for Shangri-la, and only the approach of global war explains why the British let that book out." She looked down her nose at Marlow as if she were personally responsible. "But this place is no utopia. The name Monastery also makes it sound more religious than it is, though it is very spiritual in the practical, craft nature of that term. It's a collection of monks and nuns working on non-Left-Hand life extension."

Dale raised a finger. Pandava shook her head. "Major, you're going to ask how that's possible. We know little for certain, but we believe it can be done, and that they are doing it—but at a price. They spend ninety-nine percent of every twenty-four hours focused on their life extension techniques. That means constant meditation, extreme fasting, and all the other methods of harsh asceticism. We speculate that their subjective time sense is in a perpetual state of combat mode, with even seconds seeming like eternity." She paused, as if extemporizing. "I find it helpful to view it as a very slow form of time travel into the future and not as a truly longer life. Their amount of effective action, of real living, remains a constant that they are stretching out to fill the span of years."

Pandava couldn't hide her disdain for this life choice. From Marlow's description of her active-in-the-world Family, this reaction made sense.

"What about the rumors that they are the secret masters of the craft?" asked Marlow.

"They are not the bloody masters of anything," said Pandava. "Not even their own hyper-extended lives. Though these practitioners can be very powerful if the need arises. And they do represent a problem of another sort of power."

She clicked to another slide, this one showing black-and-white photos from the early twentieth century of men and women from around the world. "As with any Sanctuary, the population of the Monastery has traditionally consisted of those who've wandered into it and some few who've deliberately sought it out. In peaceful times, perhaps one person in a decade would disappear into there; in times of serious trouble, as many as four might make it there at once."

Pandava paused, then said, "In the past three months, we know of two dozen people that have eluded the nearby troops and made it to the Monastery. We believe that the true total may be much higher. And farsight indicates that many more are on their way."

"Who are they?" asked Endicott. It was a craft elitist question, but one we were all thinking.

"Those we know about are all practitioners. You may not have noticed, but there has been an uptick in new practitioners and craft activity." I wondered if that included me, but I wasn't as new as all that. "It's at least as extreme as the late 1960s, though less publicly visible. Some of these new practitioners are coming here, and some veterans with them."

"Can't you stop them?" asked Endicott.

"Perhaps. But wouldn't it be wise to first consider whether we should? And how important is it that we do so?" She was dissing the usual American approach to foreign policy, but we ignored it.

"So where do we come in?" asked Endicott.

"We want you to go up there and claim asylum. The other parties may try something similar. We don't want or expect a fight, but we want the information."

"You could do that yourselves," said Endicott.

As if he knew the answer to that, Dale again squeezed his fists. But it was Pandava who spoke. "The modus vivendi is that no craft-militant incursion is allowed in that area. If we send in an Indian squad, the other parties will get upset." Which in the past in this region had meant fighting with very high casualty rates.

Dale closed his eyes. "Why don't you tell them the rest?" he said.

Pandava regarded him for a moment. "Very well. Like most Sanctuaries, this one moves and hides from would-be intruders. Not everyone who goes up there is capable of finding it. Even someone who has found it once may not find it again. But someone from a Family with a covenant with another Sanctuary might do better."

That meant a Family like the Mortons. Dale and his Family had a mutual-protection compact with the American Sanctuary, that preserve of the lost and the craft dead. A Morton could find that Sanctuary at will. Dale nodded. "That's the nice reason."

Pandava grimaced. "Yes, quite. The other reason is that previous attempts to attack the Sanctuary have gone seriously awry. These attacks failed due to three factors: the inability to pin the Sanctuary's location, its enormous ability to skew ballistics and bombs of all sorts, and its own force of response. But these factors point toward a fourth: extremely good, superpower-grade farsight. No one intending damage on the ground gets close enough."

"Why do you think we can avoid that?" asked Marlow, revealing as little as possible.

"There have been speculations about how you managed to defeat Roderick," said Pandava. "But one explanation is in your arrival here—no one saw you coming."

Endicott had regained some of his smugness. "We want to be helpful to everyone. Help keep the peace. But this really isn't our mission."

"We can offer you a base for your operations until your home countries return to normal. As you must have felt by now, you'll have no problems here with craft power."

"What we'd get out of this," said Endicott, "isn't the point."

"I was told you'd say something like that. There's nothing more that I can offer. But what about all the practitioners disappearing into the Sanctuary?"

Endicott was about to reply, but Dale interrupted. "Perhaps we should confer for a moment."

Pandava agreed and left the room. "Let's sit closer together," said Marlow. She mumbled some words in Latin, and the room distorted around us. "They shouldn't be able to hear much except my great-grandfather's favorite drink recipe."

"Why did you stop me, Major?" said Endicott. "She's not telling us everything."

"I know," said Dale. "But she wasn't really trying to hide that. I don't think she can tell us everything. Probably under orders not to."

"What makes you think so?" said Endicott, more interested.

"Because it concerns something not currently healthy to speak of. When I first found out what my father had asked the shrine in Japan, the Sanctuarium Mundi was where I was going to go next. Roderick interrupted my plan. But that place has always had too much power. Mere meditation and force from the land can't account for it. It's the Omphalos, the navel of the world. It marks the border of borders, and maybe not just borders in our world."

"You think some other place is leaking through," I said.

"Something is. Doesn't seem to have been bad before, but times have changed. I think we need to balance the craft books of the Sanctuary, both Right-Hand and other." Even with the stealth, he was reluctant to say Left-Hand.

"It's still winter up there," said Grace.

"I hope that's our biggest worry," said Dale.

"It's right on the border," I noted. "What if the Chinese try to grab us again?"

"In that area's conditions? If they can find us, they're more likely to kill us," said Endicott.

Then, a penny dropped, and I remembered the name of the region where we'd be going. "Kashmir!" I sang a brief but famous musical riff. It was greeted with stony silence. "Come on," I said. "No Led Zeppelin?" Dale always with a quip, Grace probably a fan? But no, they all frowned at me, even Rabu.

"Not funny," Endicott said.

"Aleister Crowley by any name is never funny," said Grace.[2]

So, a simple mission: go up, take a look around, find out what's happening to all those practitioners, make sure the monks and nuns are happily sitting and starving themselves in order to live for centuries and not summoning some dead world's demon, report back. But not so simple for me. "Before we say yes, I have some other questions."

"Keep it brief, Lieutenant," said Endicott.

I had an interest distinct from our leader's. So when Grace dropped the stealth and Pandava returned, I said, "Colonel, before we take this mission, I need to know: what did you want with Madeline?"

"It's not related," said Pandava. But she was no Marlow at deceit, and the oracular irony dripped in every word.

"Humor me."

Pandava let a little anger into her voice. "What does it matter, now that she's gone? I saw Madeline. If she's dispelled, no one else but you could have done it."

"We've been down that road," I said, getting a little heated myself. "Please answer my question."

"She was becoming something different," said Pandava. "We offered her a place."

---

2. See Appendix, Part 2: The Crowley Sanction.

"She had a place," I said. "She had the whole world. She had us. You're still not telling me something."

"Need to know." Then, maybe seeing my reaction, she pursed her lips and furrowed her brow, and for a moment closed her eyes. "And you need to know. Let me show you." She held up a hand and added, "Just you."

"Why?" We were all finally together again after the interrogations, and Pandava's latest abrupt change of direction made me look for an earbud or a spirit—was she getting orders from someone else?

"We'll be back within two hours," said Pandava. "The rest of you need to rest and prepare."

And I didn't? But though Dale gave me his worried smile that said *please stay*, he only shrugged with fatigue. In verbal echo of Dale's gestures, Endicott said, "Your choice, Lieutenant." The reasoning of trust was simple: if she wanted us separated, we would still be so, and if she wanted us dead, we'd be dead.

"I'm going," I said. I looked around for the dog. Shit, where had he run to? "Someone find Rabu while I'm gone."

Pandava and I left the building, but instead of the car we'd taken from the airport, Pandava commandeered a messenger's scooter. "Hop on," she said. I sat behind her, and she took off. It was early evening now, with lots of traffic on the roads and diesel fumes and dust in the air. Pandava drove like suicide would be fun. Maybe she was so desperate to get rid of me that she would kill us both and the baby too.

We were going back in the direction of the airport. I'd seen pictures of India's cities remade by growth in the south, but from what I could see from the scooter, this part of New Delhi was still mostly older buildings. I again felt the healthy paranoia that Pandava might be dividing me from the others to ship me off somewhere or hold me hostage.

But it was just her alone with me. I remembered Madeline's voice: "You could take her." Again, I was missing Madeline.

More parks and green space were out here than I expected in such a populous country, though it was the dry and fragile green of northern California rather than a tropical lushness. We passed a sign for Nehru University, and then sped along the bumpy park path, branches threatening. Approaching a low rise of tan and gray rock, Pandava abruptly braked, skidding us through a line of stealth craft that hung over the area like a veil.

The entrance to a cave was now visible—rough walled, about three feet wide and five feet high. "This better not be the *Star Wars* cave where I see myself," I said, "because that would be—"

"Lame," said Pandava, completing my sentence. "No, this is distinctly not you, and it's no joking matter. Understand this: no matter what you see, if you use your exorcist power, I will kill you."

You can try, I thought. But she seemed awfully confident in her threat.

Pandava took out a candle and lit it, as if modern light would insult the place, and we went inside this wound in the earth, walking at a crouch to avoid hitting our heads. Within a few yards, candlelight was the only illumination, and daylight seemed miles away. Our steps echoed with the sharp quick vibration of striking a tight metal cable.

We entered a chamber about twenty feet in diameter. Its curved rock wall had a smooth, polished-looking surface that reflected the candle and our own distorted images. In the wall were dozens of carved niches holding a variety of cubes and stones, none much bigger than a softball. The cubes were silver, gold, copper, or steel, and they were covered with fine lines and engraved letters. The plain rocks, colored crystals, and sparkling gems were shaped, faceted, or etched with lines in an odd and often asymmetric manner that seemed occult rather than aesthetic. Two cubes or stones might share a single niche. Above the niches were miniature paintings, similar in style to Persian ones I'd seen, of people with traditional Indian dress and oversized eyes like anime, male and female, and some that were a bit of both.

These little, alien-looking paintings, these precious cubes and stones—they struck me dumb and breathless with terror. When Dale had taken me into the subbasement, I hadn't known about craft or the Left Hand, but I had felt the weight and menace of the place. Now I knew more, and I had the sense to be far more scared. The very air seemed to wrap around my chest and constrict like a python. My hands went to my navel, as if I could physically intervene against this threat to my child. I wanted to swear at this threat, dispel it forever.

Pandava seemed to read my mind. "Not one bloody dispelling word. Your first profanity will be your last."

Instead of speaking, I let out a breath and drew in another, deeper. My mind cleared enough to make distinctions. This feeling was different; this power, as tremendous as the subbasement's, was unchained, flowing.

"Is this a temple?"

"Not a temple," said Pandava, "for these are not gods. But they are like gods in some ways."

Shadows flickered against the walls. The arms of the shadows moved in a retinal afterimage, silent-film stutter that appeared to multiply the limbs, like beings in other dimensions caught in a succession of snapshots in our meager 3-D, then reduced to the two of the wall.

"What are they?"

"The objects are spirit houses," said Pandava.

"They're so small."

Her resonating voice had gone inhuman and cold, like the dead. "You give your ghosts your homes, but the head of a pin would be infinite space for them, if that head were properly designed. We gathered them from all over India to save them, brought them out of Pakistan before the partition."

Before the partition? "How old are these?"

"Some are over five hundred years old."

I had no polite way of expressing my skepticism, so I just asked, "How?"

"Part of spirit survival is some enduring point of physical connection.

Still, they are fading. They are all from before the Raj. None has arisen to replace these."

A childhood image surfaced. "They're like jinn in bottles," I whispered in awe.

A windless rustle disturbed the chamber, as if, during a party, I had yelled something obscene, and the penalty might be death. I felt a sensation like an insect crawling up my leg.

"The cruelest thing you could imagine would be to seal one of these," said Pandava. "Your Sulayman was a monster." Solomon had supposedly kept many such spirits.

"We set Madeline free," I said, in response to an unspoken accusation.

"Yes," said Pandava, "houses can also be traps. As long as she had any tie to your home, she was subject to the whims of your family. The physical node is their strength and their vulnerability. We have a reputation going back thousands of years for better treatment."

"You offered this to Madeline, even though she was Left-Hand? The worst of the Left Hand?"

"Some of these came to be here by Left-Hand means. We do not care. The Rakshasa, our demons, have always been our own dead."

My skin was now crawling all over with ghostly cockroaches, a spiritual infestation. "OK. I get it. Are we done?"

"No," she said. "You need to understand about the Lords of the High Places."

The hell with the high places, these things right here and now were reaching for me with their many shadowy arms. Reaching for my child, as if to take his growing body for their own. Against this, an explosion was building inside me. In another second, I'd go nuclear against these spirits.

Not trusting my words, I ran into the darkness, I stumbled against one rough wall of the tunnel, then the other. I bumped my head against the low, uneven ceiling, and then sprinted into sunlight.

I hugged myself. Had this hurt my baby? How could I forgive myself if it had?

Pandava emerged, unrushed and unsolicitous. I yelled at her. "You brought me in there, pregnant! What the fuck were you trying to pull?"

"You are quite right," she said. "I was making a point, and I find that demonstrations are more convincing than explanations."

So, she had known I was pregnant, and she didn't care. "Explain. Now."

"A great many persons of spiritual power have, over the millennia, gone up into the Himalayas and Karakorams to meditate. They forsook family and all attachments. They forsook their very selves."

Oh, no. I could see where this was going.

"The mountain elements are harsh to the living, but conducive to spirits," she said. "The Karakorams have some of the most powerful independent spirits in the world."

Pandava pointed back to the cave. "The spirits in there are domesticated. The wild Rakshasa, the so-called Lords of the High Places, are not. They particularly hate exorcists. If they came at you and your child in force, do you think you could dispel every one of them? Could you be on guard every moment? What would happen when you slept? If they merely possessed your child, what would happen when you fought them for it?"

"There must be a way," I protested.

Pandava held up her hand and shook her head no in the Indian fashion. "If your colleagues go on this mission, you cannot go with them."

Without warning, a flurry of motion in the underbrush, and Rabu leapt out, landing close enough to go for our throats next. His fur was up, and he was barking and baring his teeth—at both of us. I got over my initial surprise enough to resent this.

Pandava had her hand on her gun. "Call off your dog," she said.

"You don't take criticism well," I said. Then, to Rabu, "Sorry to scare you. I was scared too." He calmed down into a low growl.

"I see," said Pandava, taking her hand from her weapon. "The dog is a psychopomp."

"Your stunt seemed to threaten some very important spirits," I said. But Rabu's response also answered a question I hadn't yet asked. Like Pandava, he was more concerned about protecting spirits than protecting me. I could not rely on him to help me in the mountains.

P andava had her own non-canine backup on hand, and though they had missed Rabu's infiltration, they were useful now. She gave the scooter to one of the craft muscle duo, and the other would drive us back in their car.

As we went back toward the city center, I considered my options. I believed Pandava. My friends and I could resist possession, and my craft could perhaps handle the problems of high altitude for a growing fetus, but I could not repel these Lords of the High Places from my child around the clock. Could not, unless I had more power that I could better use.

I had a bitter thought: Madeline could have protected my child. But now I'd have to protect him myself. I needed more and better power as an exorcist. Then I realized where I might find that, and maybe some better answers about Madeline's fate. I would talk to Monsignor Cornaro.

Monsignor Cornaro drove his old tiny Fiat up from Rome to his family's home in rural Tuscany. Despite not having taken an oath of poverty, in Rome he kept up a frugal appearance. But his home belied the crappy car. Though not enormous, his Renaissance villa was extremely graceful. The fields of brown stubble, the twisted bare branches of the vineyards, and the rich soil of the garden were all still winter fallow, waiting patiently for spring. Snow on the higher hills framed the exterior classical symmetry of the home. In his designs, the architect had been influenced by Palladio, as well as by certain occult ideas. The house had three visible floors; its main entrance was a two-story, columned portico-loggia at the top of a stairway that bypassed the former service rooms of the ground floor. The columns were long and austerely white.

Cornaro spun the wheel of his car and turned from the narrow road on a right-angled dime into the cramped garage. This move always terrified his rare passengers.

He brought his black leather briefcase in from the car and went first to the kitchen on the ground floor. He opened a window, and breathed in the cool clean smell of the hills, so pleasant after the dank odors of Roman decay and pollution. His housekeeper had left him fresh mozzarella with tomatoes and basil from the greenhouse. Simple and perfect.

The house was called Villa Alighieri due to some odd features of its history and design, though there were legends about some more direct connection with Dante's family. It might have been called Villa Boccaccio, but that history and legend had been successfully suppressed. It was one of the two true sites where ten upper-class youths had gone to flee the plague and tell stories, thus inspiring *The Decameron*. But what happened to the youths afterwards was another story, darker than any of Boccaccio's tales.

In the 1500s, the villa had been completely rebuilt by the Timpanos, then later sold to the Cornaros. His Family had made some dubious remodeling choices over the years, but now the house was restored to its sixteenth-century beauty.

After Monsignor Cornaro had eaten, he went up to the second, main floor with its high ceilings and better views. The proportions of the rooms on each floor roughly followed the golden ratio, like a pair of nautilus shells, breaking with classical symmetry and creating the sense either of growing compartments, or a shrinking trap, though many of the rooms were only divided by decorative hanging textiles, as had been the way five centuries ago. The light and dark pattern of floor tiles gave a sense of movement in the static space; statues of formerly revered Timpano family members populated the six large interior niches.

Through the back entrance was a courtyard lawn defined by tall hornbeams within a high wall. A warded and locked iron gate did not keep out all intruders. Just before his trip to Japan, he'd had to dispose of a small craft animal that had squeezed through the bars and wards, nosing into his business. Fortunately, his own spiritual power gave him some protection against such creatures.

On each floor, the fireplaces were working—a rare thing in a historic villa because of the risk, but Cornaro had occult precautions against both flame and soot damage. Near this floor's fireplace, a brand was mixed in with the pokers. He really should put that away when he wasn't using it.

A book cabinet, the one for public display, held early printed editions of Petrarch, Dante, and Boccaccio mixed with Church histories. A more private shelf held his esoterica on Hermeticism and the Renaissance occult—so-called white magic, or now just craft. He also had the writings of Joachim of Fiore and his followers, which were surprisingly useful in parsing apocalypses.

The villa had sparse decoration and furniture, because that was the way in the late sixteenth century, and because the frescoes on the walls were meant to be seen. The frescoes were not the usual attempts at false windows on a pretty painted nature. Illustrations of scenes from the nicer parts of Dante had given the place its name, but the villa's frescoes also included copies of those in Orvieto's cathedral which depicted the end of the world.

In one of the Orvieto copies, the Antichrist (a rougher-looking version of Jesus) stood on a pedestal in the middle of a forum, speaking to a crowd. The Devil stood intimately naked behind him, whispering in his ear. The Devil's arm passed through the Antichrist's sleeve and emerged as the Antichrist's own hand, representing the Antichrist as Satan's life-sized meat puppet.

The image reminded Cornaro of Left-Hand evil. Perhaps these were not the sort of decorations to have in a home with children. They'd haunted him all his life.

As a boy, he'd been convinced that the Church held all the secrets. He wanted that learning in order to fight against the end of all things that stared at him from his home's walls. But he'd seen the heart of the Church's craft militant, and they didn't know the secrets. They very deliberately didn't know them.

Cornaro did not believe God's instrument of the end times was the Left Hand, so he could fight it without defying God. But he would have to fight alone for now. The Church's craft militant was willing to decline in power and employ the secular craft Families of many nations for its work. Cornaro had glimpsed the future, and this would not suffice. Victory down that path would require sacrifices no sane person would make.

Now, he was going to get the secrets, all the arcana. He could do it without an unforgivable sin against a human soul, which was also a sin against the Holy Spirit. He could even do it without murdering anyone. That was one reason he'd saved the Mortons; that, and if his plan failed for some reason, he'd need them alive for their information. He'd seen Dale Morton's deception: Morton knew the Left-Hand secrets.

But Cornaro sincerely prayed that it would not come to that. For his plan, all he needed was one spirit, already damned, and whatever he did to it would be less punishment than it deserved, far less than it would ultimately receive from God in the true afterlife.

Cornaro climbed up the spiral staircase to his bedroom and knelt before a mirror, his old knees against the hard floor. He said his confession. "Lord, I killed a man, Zhuge, in the line of duty. I also deceived my hosts and betrayed their trust in me, however inappropriate the subject of that trust was." And so on, through the many, forgivable sins he'd committed. He had prayed in advance for absolution for his deceit, which had been enough to hide it from the Mortons, but it was best to also confess after the commission of the sin.

In Catholic teaching, confession to a priest led to the forgiveness of sins. Cornaro's solo confession had another purpose. *"Lord, wash away my iniquity and cleanse me from my sin,"* he prayed, invoking one of his spiritual gifts. Like a Morton, Cornaro could see his own sins in the mirror, and he could now see them fade to small, trivial-looking things. Whether they were truly gone or merely hidden wasn't something he liked to consider for long; it only mattered that practitioners like the Mortons wouldn't know what he'd been up to.

He went back downstairs to retrieve his briefcase. From it, he removed an intricately carved hardwood box. Some of the details were only visible through a microscope. Within the patterns some small circles stood out. Four circles in the rough shape of a Y were on one side of the box. One dot each marked the sides to the left and right of the Y, and one larger circle dominated the side below it.

He took the box and went to the smallest chamber on the ground floor. Unlike most of the house, a door with several locks separated this room from the others. With several keys, he opened the door and clicked on the light. The room was dominated by an opening in the floor. Within the opening was a folding ladder of the type used for attics, though it descended down into the dark cellar.

He went down the ladder, then lit a candle and set it at his feet on the floor of polished stones. He folded up the ladder to close up the opening in the ceiling; also, the ladder interfered with the visual component of the prison. The room was hexagonal, with floor-to-ceiling mirrors on each of the six walls, like a cell from a hive of narcissistic bees. The repeating images of the flickering candle flame receded in all six directions.

Human bones were embedded in the stones of the floor, like an ossuary, and the stones hummed with the vestigial madness of his previous guests—another necessary part of the prison. He had used this space many times, seeking the secrets of the lesser dead, refining his techniques for this moment. In the center of the chamber was an old rolling stool, like from a doctor's office that hadn't discovered anesthetics. He sat down on the stool and began to work.

In one of the six corners where he'd left it, Cornaro found the wooden puppet-like thing that he'd made. It had no legs or arms, just a head and trunk, so no strings, but not free. In gold letters, he'd drawn the Kabbalistic Tree of Life of the ten sephirot, or points of power, upon the trunk and head, with the name of each sephirah in Hebrew letters. He'd placed the five-pointed Seal of Solomon at both ends of the tree, drawn around the letters for Kether on the crown of the head and Malkuth on the base of the trunk. He'd marked one point of each star as oriented toward the divine. The people of nearby Collodi had once used such techniques to animate puppets with their own dead children, until the Department of Spiritual Gifts had put a stop to it.

The thing's head had shallow semispherical hollows for eyes, nose, mouth, and ears. In the back of the head was a panel. Cornaro slid it out, revealing a cubical hole. He pushed the box into the hole. It was a tight fit, but it was important that the circles on the box had good contact with the sense points in the wooden body. The lower large circle's connection with the neck allowed the sense of touch and some minimal motion. No, sense of touch was a euphemism, and he mustn't allow self-deception at this stage. Sense of pain was what the connection to the trunk allowed.

He was ready. He spoke to the wooden head. "*Buongiorno, signora. I have some questions.*"

It took a while for the screaming to stop.

In 1794, when they were six, Madeline and Roderick's father, Curwen, took them to live in the House of Morton, which had finally come into his hands. Mother was already dead; women had a difficult time on the Left-Hand side of the family. But the House was kind to her and Roderick. They were children, and the House loved Morton children.

Father invited all the Left-Hand dead to come and dwell there. Madeline spoke to them, and Roderick did too. Their conversations were different; Roderick's never sounded friendly. Roderick would often eat her food, saying that she shouldn't get fat, even as he bloated like a tick.

Father raised his children, to the extent he raised them at all, with the expectation of eventual incest. Unlike some of the Left Hand though, Father didn't try to take her himself. He said he didn't want to get between her and Roderick's alchemical union. "It's you two, or nobody," Father said. "You'll produce the child who'll lead us to the land of promise. You'll beget the one who'll lead us all to godhood." Perhaps he was also a little scared of what Roderick would do to an interloper.

Father went to work on the subbasement. He built the great chamber and the altar. Other Family members came and collaborated. His work and his experiments would inspire Lovecraft generations later.

Unfortunately for Father, the idea of preserving oneself through a sort of dehydration process with certain alchemical salts was a literal dead end. But his end wasn't like the stories—the good guys never got him. Roderick killed him, and when Roderick wanted somebody dead, they stayed dead.

It happened when Roderick reached the age of legal majority in 1809. He trapped Father and ran the process on him, then dissolved the salts in the sea. "Now we can be alone together," said Roderick.

She and Roderick were married in the craft and they had physical relations. Lots and lots of physical relations. Despite Roderick's unkindnesses, she enjoyed the sensations. But Roderick no longer cared for his Father's plan or for progeny generally. He assumed children would do unto him as he had done unto Father. Also, he thought he could fulfill the Left Hand's destiny without any further help.

Then, something happened that she would have trouble remembering later, something that made Roderick very angry. But he wasn't angry very long. He took something from her, then said he'd taken care of it. This had made her sad.

Roderick didn't like her sad, yet he didn't want the bad thing to happen again, so he drugged her and put her in a coffin. She screamed and tore at the lid, losing her fingernails and bits of finger too. Then, she gave up, and she left her body. Her spirit floated out and found the space waiting for it. Insistent on life, she took over the new flesh.

Roderick was very happy about this. He kept her first body "as a reminder," but he would dispose of the later bodies.

"Never do that again," she said. But Roderick just smiled.

Madeline wasn't happy or sad. She felt confused and empty, and gross in this physical form. She ate little, but seemed to take strength from the very air. She feared Roderick would put her in the box again.

But Roderick didn't have to do anything except say, "You're growing stout. *Please deal with it.*"

So she did, and Roderick observed and planned his own form of flesh-bound immortality.

They needed a great deal of power for Roderick's experiments on them both, and that meant killing many craftspeople and many more mundanes. She had thought she wouldn't enjoy killing, but their energy made her feel so good that she found she not only liked it, but that she needed it. Roderick kept her starved of that energy too.

Closing in on immortality, Roderick also became obsessed with otherworldly power. The House turned ugly and mean, but did as it was bid. The Left-Hand spirits began to eat away at a border between the worlds.

At some point, she couldn't later remember just when, Poe visited the House, being drawn to it, being able to see the House despite its stealth. Amused, Roderick put on his creepy show, displaying objects that Poe had seen in dreams, then sending him away, troubled.

Roderick collected the author's stories, and for a long time she didn't even look at them. But when she heard Poe had died under strange circumstances, she finally read his tales. *These aren't the way it happened*, she thought.

That led to the next thought: *Well, how did it happen?* Her insides shifted, and she saw everything that had occurred, everything that Roderick had done to her, in its proper place.

She couldn't kill him directly; even corpse-like on the slab in the subbasement, he was always stronger than she was. So she spurred him to excess. When the orthodox Morton patriarch Elijah visited, offering peace, Madeline tempted Roderick to kill him.

The wrath of the Families was more terrible and swift than she could have hoped. Only when they'd already laid siege to the House did she realize that she didn't want to die along with Roderick. As the besiegers prepared for a final assault, she prayed. "House, save me."

For the first time in years, the House spoke directly to her. *Go,* it said.

No, not it—*she*. House spoke with the gentleness of a tired mother to her sad child. *Mausoleum,* she said. *Keep you hidden.*

"But Roderick. You will let them in?"

Let in. Joshua.

"Good-bye, House." Madeline went through the subbasement route to the family mausoleum without Roderick seeing her, and from there she escaped out into the world. That should have been the end of it. She was free, and no one would recognize her in this body.

But even when she'd learned that the siege was done and the Families scattered, she'd also felt that Roderick remained in the world. She tracked him, thinking she'd find him with Joshua. But his head was with an Endicott—old Abram himself.

She knew what to do to an Endicott. To her great and pleasant surprise, she also enjoyed it.

In all her years thereafter, Madeline lived a great deal and died a great deal. She did much evil and a little good. But she never forgot the horror of being entombed alive for the first time.

Now, despite her tremendous power and her guardianship of her family, she was alone and in the box again, and this time she had no escape.

Madeline let out the stored-up screams from the return of the old nightmare, an animal howl because her words and mind were lost. Though she no longer needed to breathe, she had been slowly and spiritually suffocating. The return of light had only partially relieved her terrible, justified fear of being buried alive.

"Shhh," said Cornaro. "Everything is going to be fine." He had picked her up and was cradling her with impossible ease. What sort of body was she in—an infant's? Oh gods, not that.

He held her up and turned her about to see the walls. The small chamber was like a fun house, completely mirrored. In the multiple reflections she saw Cornaro holding a crude wooden doll, like a log with a head. That was her. The despair renewed her struggle to break out, but it was as if she'd never escaped a body before. She searched the mirror-image of the kabbalistic design on her prison for a flaw she could exploit, and found none.

Her first words were obvious. "Release me. Now!"

Cornaro took out the blade, an antique stiletto, and held it before her vision. "This will make my initial point." He jabbed it into one of the sephirot—Tiphereth—and spasmodic flame filled her stomach. She screamed again, shocked at the carnality of the wound. She had not felt physical pain since dying, and the sensation had never been so pure since her first body.

With the hurt still echoing through her, he was talking again in the singsong Italian accent that even permeated the panglossic. "I will explain this to you. In interrogation, confusion and disorientation are the usual tactics, but in this instance, they would waste more time than they would save." He tapped her with the length of the stiletto, and she flinched inside. "So, you are held in a specially faceted and finely etched gem set within a wooden box that has been designed as a multidimensional labyrinth, in which the exits curve back in on themselves. I have placed the box within a wooden mannequin without limbs. As you can see, the Tree of Life further contains you. But the bars of your wooden prison allow for certain sensations to pass through, including pain."

She again found her voice. "What is it with you Catholics and pain?"

Cornaro ignored her. "My reason for this is simple. I need the power to hurt you in order to make you talk. So I have incarnated your revenant in this poppet. The Morton taphephobia is a fortunate coincidence." He didn't insult her by saying he was sorry. "You may know that the Church has held many spirits; none could escape this. While you lived, you learned the secrets of the Left-Hand path and other mysteries of power. Now, you know even more. Very soon, you will tell all your secrets to me, and I will free you from this thing."

Very soon. He had made a mistake. He had implied that time mattered to him.

But like an actor in a play performed many times, he knew the exact next lines to kill her hope. "As you well know, torture is a game of time. All prisoners break, but will you break soon enough? You think no. What you do not understand is, powerful as you are, you are merely the reflection, the recording, of a soul, and not the soul itself. As with any recording, you may be slowed down. So even as your box is infinite space, an hour can be infinite time."

He whispered something in some unknown tongue, then jabbed the wood again. The pain went on and on. In the howling madness of it, she stared death at Cornaro. But he seemed to remain absolutely impassive, not blinking. Not breathing.

Then, after a seeming eternity of hurt, Cornaro withdrew the blade, and the world resumed its motions.

"That was as quick as I could stab you. How long did it seem to you?"

The ectoplasmic bile in her throat burned with fleshy reality. But she put on that old submissive, baby-talk voice. "Incarnate me in a real body, and I shall serve you and initiate you myself."

"Even as you served Abram Endicott?"

"Yes," she said, sincerely eager as he seemed to take the bait. "I will do anything you ask."

"No," he said. He smiled with the sad gentleness of a doctor about to do something awful. "I would fall as he did, and be damned for it."

Her rage redoubled, both at her failure and her betrayal of herself. She would not do that again. Escape, destruction, or eternal damnation, she would go as herself.

"*Die*," she said, putting all her strength into that word.

"I am afraid that your curses, your blessings, your screams can no longer reach anything. Nothing of you can escape this place." He held up a finger. "I will leave you for a moment. I'm going to have a coffee. Even for me, this may be a long night. But consider—you can end this at any time."

He placed her gently on the stool. He blew out the candle, climbed the ladder, and turned off the light upstairs.

With darkness and silence, the terrible sense of live burial returned, a breathless panic that craved space and light. She wanted to pound her fists against the coffin lid, to tear out her fingernails scratching for air, but her new limbless wooden body was itself the coffin. If she tried to disengage and move her spirit, it was worse—like falling backward in a tumbling cage down a dark void without bottom.

Eventually, the terror settled into a dizziness and she could think again. *Always the box*, she thought. *Even if it means my destruction, never again.*

As Cornaro had said, torture was familiar to her, though mostly from doing it to others. Roderick had usually led, but not always. She had tortured for energy, for information, for fun. She did not believe in justice, but the craft did have a karma to it, the Law of Return. Craft karma was as twisty as craft oracles, but also as inevitable. Useless to her now.

She had already screamed as loud as she could, so no one outside must be able to hear. That left a possible ally, the same sort of being that had saved her before. Perhaps, like the House of Morton, the villa would hear her pleas and intervene. "House, can you hear me?"

But instead of help, she heard a rustling, like rats' feet over shattered glass in a barren subbasement. Below her were other spirits. They laughed and cried and made other nonverbal noises, unpleasantly insane and broken. Cornaro must have held them here before her, no doubt imprisoned in other boxes. He had not freed them; instead, he'd used them to help seal her in.

She knew herself, and knew that she was not sane in any sense the modern living world would understand. But she was far from the state of these creatures, and she could dread their fate.

She called out for the villa again, but whatever spirit it had must have been dark and heartless, for it did not respond. Stripped of the rest of the Left-Hand spirits, sealed away in a box within a box, she was utterly alone.

The light came back on, and she was drawn back into the external world. Cornaro returned bearing an old black leather bag of the type that doctors and priests used to carry. "Will you talk?"

Nothing for him. She remained silent.

He sighed, seeming sincerely sad. This annoyed Madeline. He opened the bag, and as she had done herself, he made the traditional display of the instruments to the prospective victim. These ones were only remarkable for their simplicity: pins, needles, knives, the standard tools for poppet magic. But he also displayed craft-infused holy water that would inflict spiritual suffering. Because he had trapped her so completely in this form, he could augment her pain with words of exorcism that would not dispel but only torment her.

He spoke his temporal craft, and time slowed again to the crawl of near eternity. She then endured what no living person could: subjective years of continual torture, with a few brief minutes of breaks for the questions. Mostly, he was using a regular, inexpensive Swiss Army knife. The stiletto had been effective for a brief demonstration, but now each wounding blow carved a little more from her body. The blows weren't random; they followed the geometric lines of the Tree of Life drawn on the wood like a fabric pattern. When he reached each intersection of the lines at a sephirah, he drove a needle into the center, and smaller pins around it in the direction of each line.

As the design went from drawing to graven image, it seemed also to tighten around her like the coils in the Laocoön, slowly strangling her being. The holy water dripped from her like blood.

She sought some escape within. Most effective meditations involved having a body—counting its breaths, controlling its movements. She could not do that. Instead, she concentrated on the flame. At her current stretching of time, each slight flicker was a distinct event, like the slow inhalation and exhalation of a sleeper. She focused her whole being on the subtle change, and counted each cycle, one through ten, then began again. As she became more absorbed in concentration, something like breath moved through her. When her focus lapsed, she tried to recall every scene of her life, again and again. Some moments still eluded her in the blazing agony, and she could not see the thing Roderick had taken from her original, saddened self.

All techniques failed against the timeless hurt. Though she tried to make herself one with the pain, it was still destroying her. She would talk soon. Just not now. And not now. And not now.

And now she was breaking. She'd seen how this would go. She would babble something true soon, and then she wouldn't be able to stop. She sought one more motivation to resist. From the candle's height, she guessed the real-world time. If her family was coming, how soon could they be here? If her family wasn't coming, when would she be certain of it?

A low tone like Tibetan throat singing sped up, the world moved again. A phone was ringing.

She saw Cornaro's expression in the mirrors before he could hide it: the face of a husband receiving a call from the other woman. With craft speed, he let her drop to the floor as he pulled down the ladder to scurry up and take the call. *They are coming for me! She is coming. She isn't terrible enough for him, but I will be.*

In no apparent haste, Cornaro returned down the ladder. "You have perhaps guessed who that was. You think they are coming. Yes, yes, she is, though she is not coming for you. You will talk or I will hurt her. Or I will simply hold her and force her husband to follow, then hurt them both. You can stop it. Tell me all, and I won't invite her to stay here."

Madeline stared at her ugly wooden form in the mirror. In all her endless time of pain, she had not allowed herself to foresee Cornaro's use of her family, because she would have faced just one solution. Only now did she begin to consider ways to destroy herself, once and for all.

CHAPTER

SEVEN

We reached the Connaught Place business hotel where the Indian government would be hosting us. I had to clear my plan with Pandava; they'd know when I tried to contact someone. "I'm calling Cornaro," I said. "I'm going to get him to send me the Vatican's information on exorcism. How much can I tell him?"

"If you must . . ."

"I must," I said.

"Then tell him nothing," she said. "I say that for the safety of your husband and colleagues, whether you go or not. Other powers will be looking for them, and Cornaro simply doesn't need to know."

I dialed the number Cornaro had given me. The phone rang ten times, then rolled me into voice mail in Italian. I shouldn't have been surprised; he might be in transit back to Italy or elsewhere. "Monsignor, it's Scherie. Thank you for your help." That was weak for what he'd done for us in Tokyo, but it was as much detail as I'd give over the phone. "Please call me. It's urgent."

Perhaps the delay was for the best. I was exhausted and would not be studying arcane texts effectively without some more rest.

Rabu came with me to our room, and no one at the hotel objected. Dale had the shades pulled and was sprawled out face-down on the bed. I put my phone on the nightstand for when Cornaro called. I was so wound up, I thought I'd never sleep, but I coaxed a muttering Dale to give me some room anyway and spooned myself into him. He and Rabu both fell into lightly snoring a lullaby. Soaking up the shockingly generous local energy, I fell asleep.

When I awoke, Endicott and Marlow were already in the room, talking around the little table with Dale about the challenges of the mountains, unconcerned that I was largely undressed. Modesty and military didn't mix. I checked my phone; Cornaro hadn't called.

So, while putting on some cleaner clothes, I told everyone the situation and my plan. "I'm not just waiting here." But Dale in particular seemed more relieved than upset at the possibility that I might not join them in the Karakorams.

I tried Cornaro again. It was four and a half hours earlier in Italy, so I thought I'd just be leaving another message, but on the tenth ring, he picked up. "Signora Rezvani! So good to hear from you."

"Sorry to wake you," I said, though he sounded wide awake.

"You and your colleagues are well?" he asked.

"Yes. I didn't have a chance to thank you."

"It was nothing," he said. "My duty."

"Did you get my message?"

"No," he said. "You left a message? *Ecco*, now I see it. What was it?"

I heard no deceit, but I wondered what could be keeping a priest so distracted, and the communication failure was reminiscent of Roderick's manipulation of our phones. I'd deal with it later. "I was calling about your offer. The writings you mentioned—could you send them to me?"

He sighed. "They may not be scanned. The head of my order . . . ehm, even before Roderick's dominance of the electronic world, he did not trust the copying of certain documents. Now, it would be impossible."

"Could you read them to me?"

"Again, that would create an electronic, audio version. But even if it were permitted, the central teachings are kabbalistic, which means the words have a power as written, and the adept must take their images into her mind."

"I really need them."

He paused. "Could you not come here? Our invitation remains open."

My first thought was no way, it would take too long. But I wasn't thinking supersonically. I ran the times in my head. Four hours to fly there, four hours back . . . but he might expect some service in exchange. "I couldn't stay long," I said.

"As you would say, no strings attached. Your need is great, and your goodwill is worth much to us."

I would need to study the texts with panglossic craft. "How long would it take to read them?"

"For a particular need?" he said.

"Yes."

"A day will suffice, whatever the need."

"Thank you. I'll let you know when I get there." I was going to hang up, then remembered another problem. "To get to the Vatican I have to go through Italy." NATO ally Italy might have a different attitude about my presence.

"Easily arranged. You'll be greeted before customs. You'll be designated as Vatican diplomatic personnel."

"I'm a Muslim."

"Details," he said, and I could imagine his hand waving in dismissal. Then, sotto voce, "You're the one they're not worried about."

A bit of an insult, but I couldn't object too much, as it would work for me. "Please have the texts ready." *And also some answers, gentle priest—in particular, about Madeline.*

I laid out my intent to the others. "I need Cornaro's crash course in exorcism. I can be there and back in two days, tops. You'll need more than that to prep for the op anyway. If some dead or possessing spirit is involved, I'll be ready for it."

Endicott said, "Sounds like a plan, Lieutenant. But don't be late in returning."

"I'll keep the team posted," I said. They gave me doubtful looks, and I remembered Istanbul. "Not that I'll ever fully trust my phone again."

"Wait a minute," Dale said, open hand trying to tap down this plan. "I'll come with you."

"Sir," I said, reverting to military ranks on the assumption we were bugged. "I don't think so. The Italians don't care about me and my exorcist talent, but the rest of you worry them. Powers of stealth or command would be scary enough. A Morton by blood would be worse."

Dale looked pointedly at my going-to-bump-soon belly. "Ah, come on, sir," I said. "You know what I mean."

Endicott came to my aid. "I agree with the lieutenant. If something goes wrong in Italy, better to have a larger force here for the rescue." Or revenge, I supposed.

Endicott's quick support should have worried me, but he'd been our friend for so long that I'd forgotten some things about him, like what an asshole he could be, so at the time I didn't even notice it. Marlow's silence should have concerned me too.

Dale, the love of my life, only said, "I'll help you get ready." Maybe I'd come on too strong in my demand that he never use his forbidden knowledge to help me, but that was no excuse for what he'd be doing soon. Anyway, we weren't in the realm of legal orders anymore—anything he did was by his own free will.

Rabu's eyes were tracking me, his ears up at attention. His going to the mountains would be a bad idea. I remembered Dale with the House of Morton, and how just because we could give a nonhuman sentient orders didn't mean we should.

"Rabu, stay?" I asked.

He stepped up to me, turned around, and pressed his flank against my leg. "With me then," I said.

We returned to the airport. Pandava had found one of her relatives to fly the plane. "My Family is good with transport," she said, confirming what Marlow had told us about a variety of talents, but not revealing anything about her personal powers.

When I hugged Dale good-bye on the tarmac, I felt something like a Morton foreboding. It wasn't a feeling that this would be the last time I'd see Dale, Michael, or Grace. It was the near certainty that when I saw them next, we wouldn't be the same.

But like a child indicating his age, Dale made a three sign with his fingers. Me, him, and the baby—our trinity, and his way of saying everything would be OK.

D ale watched Scherie's plane disappear into the sky. "We're not waiting for her, right?"

"No," said Endicott. "Pandava's had everything ready to go for months. She just needed the team. We'll head out in an hour."

"Your wife will hate us for the rest of our short lives for this," said Marlow.

"Yeah," said Dale, with a small cough to clear his throat. "She can tell our kid about it." He didn't need to add, "when I'm gone." He was a Morton, so the casual cynicism was assumed.

A s the plane took off, and with the pilot in the cockpit, I realized that I was truly alone for the first time in months. Well, except for the dog. The *Oikumene* statuette was also joining me on this Roman holiday. In the rush to depart, I'd forgotten about all of Michael and Grace's wedding gifts, including that one. Probably for the best to keep it away from Endicott anyway; even if it wasn't booby-trapped, neither he nor the *Oikumene* needed any reminders of reasons to kill each other.

I slept most of the four hours. I'd already recharged a bit in India, but some more rack time in the air also helped.

After we landed and taxied to the private business jet area, I told the pilot to wait a moment before opening the cabin door, and I brought out the statuette's box. It was pulsing craft at me, like a damned Batphone. But without Endicott around, it seemed safe to answer the call from my former allies. I touched the statuette with my bare hand, and tried to restrain myself from all the profanity I wanted to pile on the *Oikumene*. "What do you want, Pythia?"

The Pythia's familiar voice responded: "Lieutenant Rezvani! We're having difficulty seeing you." That must have been the Morton powers of the child again, this time obscuring farsight.

I did something kind of stupid: I told them the truth, some of it anyway. "I'm in Italy," I said. "Stuff I need to learn."

"You're pregnant," said the Pythia. "You mustn't risk yourself. We can guard you."

"You tried to kill Major Endicott."

"That doesn't matter now," she said. "Nothing else matters. Your child is all important."

That explained a lot. "I'll keep you posted. Ciao." I snatched my hand off the statuette like it was a hot coal. I couldn't help but feel a little insulted. Everything they'd done for me had apparently been for my baby. Sure, the reasonable thing would have been to hear them out on why the baby was so important, but when I couldn't trust anything they said, only dangerous manipulation would result from that.

As the pilot opened the door, I reminded her that I expected to return within twenty-four hours. She acknowledged this without enthusiasm, and despite having her contact number I didn't get the feeling she'd be very supportive if things went sideways. I left the *Oikumene*'s statuette in the plane—they already knew enough about my location, and it was probably contraband besides.

The Vatican's representative got me through the business jet area's customs and took me, Rabu, and my bag to a waiting limousine with black-tinted windows. I opened a window a couple of inches for Rabu, and he stuck his snout out to enjoy the air. Ah Roma—I was getting more romantic world travel without Dale.

But as we drove along, it became clear that we weren't heading into scenic Rome and the Vatican. Instead, we were on our way toward Firenze—Florence. I called the driver on the limo's intercom. "Where are we going?"

"The Monsignor's home in Tuscany," he said. "The Villa Alighieri."

Oh kay. First, I dialed Cornaro to confirm. "Yes, yes, I'm inviting you to my family's villa. The texts you want are all here." It would sound petty to complain, but these would be additional hours there and back again. "The driver says you are bringing a dog?"

"Yes," I said. "The dog from Tokyo."

"Oh, of course," said Cornaro. "A noble animal. I will see you soon."

Now for the other precaution: I sent texts to my team, and additionally called Dale and left him a voice message. No response though. Maybe this time it wasn't interference like Roderick's. Maybe life was all rainbows and unicorns too.

We arrived at the villa. The driver agreed to return for me at dawn, then helped me with my bag up the stairs to the main entrance; a necessary convenience, as I wanted my hands free in case anything was fishy. As always, I had my knives.

Out came Cornaro into the cool Tuscan air. "*Benvenuta*," he said, smiling with beatific warmness—was that something old priests practiced, or did it just come naturally? He patted Rabu's head. "Good dog. Very good dog. We've had such guests before. I'll have my housekeeper give him some food."

We went inside, and Cornaro introduced me to his housekeeper, an older woman who frowned at me as the driver handed off my bag to her and exited. "She will take care of you until she leaves this evening."

We passed through a large central room on the entrance floor, then went to the right and up a spiral staircase to the upper floor. Some of the frescos I saw made me worried about Cornaro. It couldn't be healthy to live with the end of the world 24/7. One wall had the woman clothed with the sun and the great red dragon. This Renaissance piece was nothing like the William Blake version, but it bothered me— wasn't the woman supposed to be pregnant?

Another fresco showed the damned being hustled into hell. *Villa Alighieri indeed.* But the entrance to hell wasn't like a fortress gate. It was the fanged maw of some great motionless beast, forever gaping, eternally hungry.

But, even with the creepy frescoes, the little I saw of the house was enough to impress me. My family came from wealth, but they'd lost it. I'd married into money, but normally we wouldn't spend it. This villa was the sort of place used for movies.

Cornaro showed me and Rabu to the guest room on the upper floor, then to an adjoining smaller room with an antique desk and a sturdy-looking table. The table was already piled with ancient-looking tomes, but they were well preserved and not dusty.

"Rabu?" I was going to tell him to stay in the other room, but he'd already sat down at the threshold, sniffing the air.

"Before we commence," said Cornaro, "will you have some of the house prosecco with me?"

"No, thank you." I didn't need to offer pregnancy as the reason. He knew I was in a hurry.

"How is your husband?"

"Fine." I remembered what Pandava said, and kept further information to myself. Instead of gabbing, I thought, *Show me his sins.* My new craft worked, and the letters of his faults glowed before me. Then I said, "I need to ask you something. What happened to Madeline in Tokyo? Is she really gone?"

"I saw what happened," he said, nodding gravely. "I don't believe it was a final dispellation either. I can help you find her."

I had asked him in person to see if there was any deception or other sins in his response. I saw no new scarlet letters after he spoke, but the sins I'd seen initially seemed slightly different from those I'd seen in Tokyo. They weren't altered enough to make him a possessed person— some small new letters had appeared, and some other sins had faded. It was hard to remember details from the heat of battle, and whatever the changes, they didn't seem relevant to what concerned me.

"Madeline will have to wait," I said, reluctantly. "So, what in these books will help me keep spirits away from me and my child?"

Cornaro cocked his head, birdlike. "What sort of spirits?"

"Mountain spirits."

"Lords of the High Places."

"Yes." I didn't like that this disclosed where I was going next, but I needed the right answers quickly.

"*Primo*, we wash hands." A small closet of a space held a half bath with sink. To demonstrate, he thoroughly cleaned and dried his own hands. I followed suit, while he selected a dozen volumes of various sizes from the table and placed them on the desk, some in piles, and some singly. He placed each book in turn on a set of foam wedges designed to keep any strain off the binding. With each opened book, he marked one or more pages with strips of cloth, then returned it to its position on the desk. "I mark only the beginning of what may be useful. You should read much farther, until it no longer helps you."

I hesitated, nervous to handle such rare materials. He chuckled. "Are you thinking of *The Name of the Rose*? Don't stick your fingers in your mouth to turn the pages! Spit is not so good for either vellum or paper."

His joke put me at ease. I adjusted the wedges as I'd seen him do, placed a volume on them, and turned to the first marked page, holding it down with weighted "snakes" for that purpose. Having watched me, he nodded his approval. "*Bene*. I also have urgent business, and my boss, though forgiving, is very demanding." His eyes turned up to heaven, and I laughed at his church humor. "I will leave you alone with my best friends. Your dog, would he like to go out into the courtyard?"

I nodded at Rabu and, still sniffing like a blood hound, he followed Cornaro downstairs. I wondered what spirits he'd find on this old ground. I sat down at the desk, summoned the panglossic craft for reading, and began to study. Without craft, I would have had trouble with the ancient handwritten pages in English, but Latin, Hebrew, or other? Forget it. I was rushed, but I was also happy. I was a science fiction and fantasy fan, and that meant that I also loved books. The only thing better than books about obscure old tomes were the old tomes themselves. I could have stayed here for weeks, but I only had a day.

She is here," Cornaro told Madeline. "It is time for you to decide. It is already after noon. If I do not know everything when my housekeeper leaves at eight this evening, I will begin my work on Signora Rezvani."

Rabu dashed out into the courtyard with the unfeigned eagerness of an outdoor animal. He let loose his fight or flight responses and ran about so he could be a good dog later. Panting in the cold, he found a suitable bush and relieved himself without any delusion that he was marking territory. His territory was mostly not of this world, and definitely not this place marked "Cornaro."

Rabu growled low at this thought. He was a shepherd of souls, and Cornaro was another human who interfered with Rabu's nature. Scherie, the interfering woman he was guarding, was more acceptable. Despite the threats she posed, she smelled right, like a sunny field of tall grass. Perhaps she could be properly trained. Cornaro's scent was wrong; it had changed since Japan, and was changing still, like a sick animal. Rabu knew better than to bark at someone in their own territory. He would have to warn Scherie and everyone else of the danger some other way.

The sick man wanted him outside, but that was where Rabu wanted to be too. Sure, the priest had many interesting things to track indoors, but Rabu's best senses didn't need line of sight. He would save time if he first hunted clues without anyone watching him and then got a report from the local authorities.

More relaxed, Rabu snuffled the air, and smelled the ghosts of many things. This place was old, and some of its scents were very faint. On summer evenings, people had danced in this courtyard, leaving behind the last lingering perfume of their sweet sweat. More recently, the essence of a large family pervaded all, but standing apart was the hard-scrubbed odor of a serious boy who would later become the owner, Cornaro.

Rabu paced along the back of the house as if he simply wanted to get back indoors, then put his nose right up against the cracks in the wall where the lowest visible floor met the ground. He recoiled at the bitter tang of tattered spirits, unsavable by any power. *Bad place.* Blank, still air beyond those shattered souls pointed to stealth of some kind; he would have to dig that out too. He relieved himself some more to mark the spot for later. He crisscrossed the lawn, and found a patch that remained a healthy green even in this season. With a small anticipatory whine, he put his nose to the grass. A dog, not long dead, buried here by the villa's owner. *Bad place, bad man.*

Time to call in the locals. The courtyard had a tall back gate onto a dirt road that led through the dead fields. The gate's wards smelled like ozone; he wouldn't be leaving this way. With a touch of craft, Rabu barked three times and waited. No one appeared, but he scented that someone was close. He barked again, more insistently.

A older female Maremma scent hound skulked up to the other

side of the gate. Her wolf aspect flickered into view for just a moment, like a countersign to his call. She had either foreseen his coming or had been on patrol. She might be top dog around here, but Rabu's line had a global recognition, so he wouldn't assert dominance, but wouldn't go beta either—just friendly, like one big happy psychopompic litter.

She was shivering as they sniffed at each other, noses not crossing the line of the gate. The shivers weren't from the cold. No wonder she'd hesitated to approach. A dog's universe was smell, and Rabu smelled fear, hers and the dead dog's before her.

The two communicated through a sort of panglossic not available to humans. The complex minds of human practitioners had evolved away from sharing thoughts as a sort of self-protection. Dogs had simpler, less protected minds, so those with craft could share images and basic concepts with only the sounds of a low bark, growl, or whine.

Her name was, naturally, Lupa. Lupa quickly confirmed what Rabu had already guessed: creatures like themselves were in danger here. That meant danger for Scherie too. But he also found out why Lupa and the dead dog in the courtyard had been sticking their noses into this villa. In the short gap between his car and house, Cornaro had been sensed carrying trapped spirits inside, spirits which were never again sensed except as the tattered things of the lower levels. He'd just added one to his collection recently.

Very bad man. Cornaro was now a trespasser in Rabu's territory. But how could he punish the man and help Scherie against the threat? Pulling her by his teeth out of the villa would probably not work; Cornaro would be on them before they could escape. Even if they eluded Cornaro, something was rotten in that house, and it still smelled wrong from outside. Why didn't Scherie sense it?

Perhaps fearing that Rabu would request help, Lupa turned tail and darted off. Rabu growled epithetically. *Some she-wolf.* Then he lay down, head on his paws, to consider his options.

PART III

SONG OF SCHEREZADE

Blessed are the weak who think that they are good because they have no claws.

—Baruch Spinoza

What are men to rocks and mountains?

—Jane Austen

It's easier to ask forgiveness than it is to get permission.

—Rear Admiral Grace Hopper

And it shall come to pass afterward, that I will pour out my spirit upon all flesh; and your sons and your daughters shall prophesy, your old men shall dream dreams, your young men shall see visions.

—Joel 2:28 (KJV)

CHAPTER

EIGHT

Dale, Endicott, and Marlow would fly north toward Leh Air Force Base with Colonel Pandava in a G100 Astra reconnaissance plane. Before takeoff, Dale watched as Marlow brought out a package wrapped with Japanese fineness. She unwrapped it herself. Like a prince before Cinderella, Marlow knelt before Endicott and offered him the contents. "As I suppose this is our wedding vacation, here is your honeymoon present."

It was a new prosthetic foot, but as marvelous as a glass slipper. Unlike the flashing chrome of his current model, the chameleon adaptive camo changed colors as Endicott turned it in his hand. It had specialized attachments, and with a double tap of the little toe, blades sprang from where the toe nails should be.

"It's beautiful," said Endicott. He sounded choked up, which still made Dale uncomfortable. *I was once ready to kill this man for his name alone.*

After takeoff, they all moved to a set of seats configured around a table for an officer discussion. Any gear that required sizing was being readied for them; the rest would already be packed and ready: ice axes, glacier glasses, camo tents, and enough climbing line to make a hobbit weep.

"One thing you will not be bringing into the Sanctuary: mundane weapons," said Pandava.

"And you waited until now to tell us this?" said Dale. "Nothing against suicide missions, but I've got a kid on the way."

"Mundane weapons are suicide there," said Pandava. "Modern

rifles, explosives—and yes, Major Endicott, swords—always trigger an attack by the Sanctuary when crossing its boundary, sometimes even before. Once you find the way in, you must leave all weapons behind and rely on your craft."

"Good to know," said Endicott.

"As long as it's a level playing field," said Marlow dryly, as the Karakorams certainly weren't that.

Dale wasn't happy. The American Sanctuary was tetchy about many things, but not weapons. But he didn't complain further, as he wasn't going to drop out of the mission in any case.

They looked over a topographic map of the target area. The tripoint lay between the local low 5,800-meter elevation of the Indira Col and the top of the 7,400-meter Sia Kangri, around where the Sia Group made a T with the Karakorams. The Siachen Glacier area had been called the Third Pole for its extreme cold and harsh conditions.

"From Leh base," said Pandava, "a helicopter will take you as close as it can to the tripoint."

"Pretty high ground for a copter," said Dale.

"It's our Dhruv Mark III helicopter with the new Shakti engine," said Pandava. "The helicopter is unarmed, as the Sanctuary is particularly sensitive to the approach of motorized threats. Allowing for this, the pilot will approach as close as possible to the Sanctuary, though the helicopter will not be able to enter. The special engine means that the target is within the Dhruv's ceiling, but it is just as well that Lieutenant Rezvani isn't with you, as weight will be at a premium."

This was small consolation. Endicott changed the subject. "Besides the Sanctuary, who's the opposition?"

"Pakistan and China have patrols," said Pandava, "and some of those are practitioners."

"What kind of practitioners?" asked Endicott.

Dale knew, but Pandava said it. "Snowmen. They aren't very respectful of the lines of control. Some of our casualties due to Siachen's 'conditions' are from them."

Marlow and Endicott grimaced, and Dale wasn't happy either. Snowmen and snowwomen had inspired the stories about Yetis. They were fully human, but able to do tricks of air and warmth, and to do them longer than other craftspeople. This allowed them to live almost year-round at elevations that slowly degenerated and killed others.

The snowpeople weren't significantly hairier than other humans, but they preferred wearing furs to modern synthetics due to the nature of their craft. Some of them had naturally darkened skin to deal with the high-altitude sun, while others used craft to raise their pigment protection. They also had a combination of craft and natural protections against snow blindness. Over the long term, they were vulnerable to heart disease, as they carried above-average body fat for warmth and the long stretches without supplies.

Dale and his friends had trained for mountain special ops. Their craft could compensate for their lack of altitude conditioning, allowing them to instantly adapt to the elevation and still be preternaturally skilled at combat. Also, one thing that a craft mission could do to avoid attention was something no sane mundane climber would attempt in these conditions: they would climb at night.

But the snowpeople working for Pakistan or China would have a significant home-field advantage. They lived and fought in those conditions on a daily basis. The best strategy was to avoid them.

Even as he and his friends prepared for the mission, Dale circled two loops in his mind like an infinity sign. He'd betrayed his wife's trust. His rushing the mountain mission was for her and the baby's protection, but that didn't make him feel much better about it. He wouldn't change his mind now. Arguing with her beforehand would have been useless; none of them had any authority over the others except by consent. Better to beg for forgiveness after the fact.

The other set of his obsessive thoughts circled the droning catechism of the Left-Hand way in his head. "*First, in the ancient tongue, say . . .*" and so on, over and over. Sharing that secret with Scherie had helped for a while, but Scherie was gone now.

I should only be thinking about the mountains. Think of anything else, and the mountains would kill you.

They landed. The airbase at Leh was on a high flat plain, light brown and desolate, surrounded by tall snow-capped peaks. While the Dhruv was loaded, Pandava finalized communication arrangements with them. Pandava repeated the biggest problem with staying in contact: "This Sanctuary interferes with all electromagnetics—radio, sat-phones, Wi-Fi, lasers, everything."

"Right," said Marlow. "We will test radio immediately on drop-off and establish rendezvous coordinates. You will have the copter return to seek radio or visual contact daily starting at forty-eight hours after insert until one week passes with no contact." Because if they weren't in touch within a week, they were captured or killed, and something else would have to to be done.

"You'll also need this," said Pandava. She held out a chronometer wristwatch. "This watch is in sympathy with a clock in my office in Delhi. In the Sanctuary, you may find that time passes at a slower or faster rate."

"That isn't the case in the American Sanctuary," said Dale. "At least not when outsiders are there."

"The World Sanctuary is different from those of individual na-tions," said Pandava, "though our reports are far from clear on the precise temporal distortion."

"As our Sanctuary expert, Major Morton should take it," said Mar-low, passing Dale the watch to put on.

Pandava told them that their pilot would be a weatherman code name Hima who regularly ran the missions to the Siachen helipad, the highest in the world at 6,400 meters.

"How good is he with the weather?" asked Dale bluntly.

Pandava responded with equal bluntness. "Two years ago, an ava-lanche fell on the local Pakistani military headquarters, killing over a hundred people."

"That was Hima, alone?" said Dale.

"Correct," said Pandava. Up here, away from the eyes of the mundane world, they could get away with that kind of craft.

By sunset, all their gear was ready and loaded. In snow camo and armed for the approach to the Sanctuary, Dale, Endicott, and Marlow took off with Hima.

Colonel Pandava watched the Dhruv depart from Leh, then returned to her guest office to sip tea. With the Anglo-Americans all gone, it was like the quiet after the departure of children. Perhaps she shouldn't have thought of them that way, but it had made it easier not to tell them every small detail, such as her communications with Prithvi and the imminence of the end of the world.

The colonel's Family may have been the oldest continuous craft lineage in the world, dating back to the Mahabharata and beyond. This lengthy history marked her for envy and gentle mocking. Her colleagues called her the Pandava of the Kali Yuga as a kind of joke. Not so funny anymore, with the actual end of the age threatening.

Pandava called up the photos of her five partners on her phone—two men, two women, and the polygendered Purusha. It was not a truly polyamorous group; they were all with her, but only with each other in her presence. This was the legacy of her ancestor Draupadi, who had been the wife of all five Pandava brothers. But the colonel's lovers weren't like her ancestors; they were not practitioners.

The number five was important, as the Americans with their usual vulgarity announced from the Pentagon. If she joined with the Americans, their four would become five. They probably saw themselves as being like her ancestors: noble exiles from their kingdom preparing for the great battle against evil. But they were no family of hers, and now they couldn't be a five. Rezvani was in Italy. Cornaro had tried to feel Pandava out about the impending end of the world. That had been suspicious, but Rezvani could keep him occupied.

As for the other three, she and Prithvi would use them and let them go to their fate. When this one-way mission forced the true threat to reveal itself, she would commit India's mundane and magical forces for the decisive battle. Maybe an age hence, she would be remembered alongside her Mahabharata ancestors.

Why then did this mission bother her? Perhaps it was because these Westerners had repeatedly defied farsight, and that meant they wouldn't be her or Prithvi's or anybody else's tools. Perhaps it was the insane part of herself that was telling her how glorious it would be to fight and die with these foreigners at the end of the age. But she had served her country well by controlling that voice, and she wouldn't give in to it now with the world at stake.

Madeline had often imagined destroying herself. In her mass funeral-pyre dream, her beauty had been terrible to behold, and everyone had witnessed. But with the moment arrived, she was just an ugly log in an old man's lap. Did some afterlife await, or were Roderick and the Endicotts right, and whatever part of her was an eternal soul had gone on already to dissolution or judgment?

Fuck them. She now had all the reality she'd ever felt in the flesh, and this cell already had every necessary feature of Hell. *Let's get on with it.* When Roderick first put her in a coffin, her spirit had gripped life like a fist of bone around a little girl's throat. With lightning-quick will to keep Cornaro and herself from stopping it, she let life go. She echoed Rezvani's words. *Poor thing, you're already dead. Go.* And added, *This time forever.*

A flash of craft within her. Nothing happened. *Gods, no, still here— take me into your many ancient arms and dissolve me in your madness, but don't leave me here, Old Ones!*

Cornaro gave his sad smile. "You thought the Left-Hand way made you special. But if spirits could escape through self-dispellation or any craft, this would be useless. The wood that contains you is as eternal as the trees that hold the suicides in the inferno."

She didn't scream—she was screamed out. How could this little man with his puny sins . . . ? *Puny sins.* The Morton ability to see sins wasn't active craft; it was integral to their nature. Ever so slightly, Cornaro's sins had changed. So that was how he had hidden his nature from her family. Perhaps she could make him share some of her despair.

"Nice trick with your sins," she said. "But I hope you don't think you are really forgiven for what you're doing here."

Cornaro's face went as impassive as a bust of Caesar. "You're not even a true soul," he said. "Just a recording."

"Adjust your theology, shaman," she said. They hated it when you called them something they considered primitive.

But Cornaro's damned smile returned. "Nothing wrong with a shaman," he said.

She wouldn't let go. "My reality is beside the point. Your intentions are too. The Left-Hand way is the gateway to all sin. Even my branch of the family didn't start out by thinking, 'Hey, let's kill and torture lots of people.'"

Even as she said these words, she was struck with their truth. A melancholy revelation, and centuries too late to do anyone any good.

"It won't just stop with you, either," she added. "It likes to spread."

"Enough," said Cornaro, raising a blade to recommence carving her.

"Don't," said Madeline. "I will tell you everything."

And she would. Madeline would tell Cornaro absolutely everything to delay him from harming Rezvani. She started with the Left-Hand tactics of H-ring's black-ops section—trivial material. It was like a child's catechism, so deeply ingrained that she could think up a way to communicate with Scherie as she recited the dark teachings. She found it harder to plan in Cornaro's slowed-down hell-mode than to think while talking.

Why was he hiding now? Rezvani must be able to see sins. The child's powers were active, and working through her.

One power in particular might help Madeline now, but how to let Rezvani know? If she was seeing sins, Rezvani might not even guess that she had an amplification of this other power, because she'd be confused about the child's gender. First, Madeline needed to know precisely where Rezvani was and what she was doing. Only now with time to scheme did Madeline notice how narrow her reincarnated senses were. The stealth that shielded this space didn't explain it: stealth only worked in one direction or it would be dysfunctional. For years, Madeline had lived in the subverted body of a former Gideon craftswoman, codenamed Sakakawea. The Gideons were called hounds for good reason; their enhanced senses were akin to those of dogs. Where were those transhuman sounds and smells now?

Stupid for not realizing it before—being out of practice with her physical senses was no excuse. If she could have loathed herself more for this additional failure, she would have.

Madeline tried to recall the Gideon portion of her patchwork spirit, and instead she found a blind spot, an event horizon of alien horror within Madeline's own darkness, barring her way. Perhaps she could bridge it with the power of names—Sakakawea's real name. Something Celtic, wasn't it? She ran through associations: rivers, Mac-somethings, ginger hair in the sunshine.

Captain Shannon McRae. Madeline gave a name back, like a password, to this consumed person. *Shannon, give your senses again to me.*

As if being consumed for the first time, her Gideon-self resisted, but with a difference: this time, Madeline felt no joy at having to break this small bit of spirit all over again. Not that it was wrong. It was just beneath her.

At that thought, Madeline felt an inner lurch, and her Gideon-self gave way. Madeline's narrow world widened.

She strained to hear anything, but heard only the priest's heartbeat as he became excited, then frustrated, with her revelations. She tried another sense. Her cell wasn't air-locked, and a Gideon's sense of smell was no more tied to normal physics than was farsight. With pure will alone she sniffed the air. She detected Scherie, familiar, with the new hormonal *eau de femme enceinte*. No waft of fear—Scherie was safe, for now.

Farther out but strong, Madeline smelled a dog's piss. Not just any dog, but a dog that still had Japan and the scent of graveyards in its bodily fluids. That damned hound from Tokyo was still with Scherie.

Cornaro had left her capable of screaming, perhaps only so she could hear herself. He seemed confident that his craft would prevent ordinary sounds from leaking out to any person who could respond. But a dog could hear higher sounds than a human, and Cornaro was unlikely to have shielded the full spectrum of vibrations associated with sound—that would be a more serious drain on his energy, even at home. If she could make such sounds, the old man wouldn't hear or otherwise detect them.

As with smell, she had to remember that her current physical limits weren't organic. She pursed her virtual lips to create the smallest of holes, and drove the ether that she used for words through it with in-human energy. Between each sentence of her confession to Cornaro, Madeline whistled to the dog. She chose a cheery little tune. Given the animal's smell, it should recognize it.

Rabu's ears shot up of their own accord. A whistle sound, in the range meant for him. Friend or foe, friend or foe?

The whistle was a song, higher than human normal, with long gaps between sets of notes, but he knew the tune. It was the music most familiar to his breed, funeral music, not Japanese, but he still recognized it. It came from that area of the house he could not smell. A spirit was in there, a spirit who knew him.

In Tokyo, Rabu had been fighting when the Morton spirit-monster had been ripped in two, and the part called Madeline had disappeared. He hadn't gotten a good scent of it, and Left-Hand monsters weren't usually in Rabu's territory, but he had wondered who had done it. Cornaro and Scherie had both been there, and now he knew Cornaro was the bad one. Lupa had sensed a spirit coming in recently, though difficult to say when. A psychopomp dog's sense of time was not precise—almost a requirement for the job. Still, likely it was Madeline.

Rabu's nature wasn't commanding him to save the bad Madeline, but she might be a helpful part of the pack, if Cornaro didn't put her down first. How to connect Madeline and Scherie? Rabu whined. This was going to be unpleasant.

Then, the woman who smelled of garlic and ammonia opened the door. Should he dash in? No, she was putting out the promised food for him. Now things were smelling interesting. He was so hungry.

Cornaro's housekeeper left me food and drink in the other room, and towels for rewashing my hands before handling the books again. I ignored the food; my hands felt a little greasy and smelled like shoe leather from handling the vellum, which wasn't great for my appetite. Instead, I tried my phone, but this time I got no bars. Best just to hurry and be done.

I didn't hear anything more from the courtyard. Rabu would certainly let me know if he were unhappy. Cornaro had been oddly obliging regarding the dog, maybe because he could see he was special, or maybe because he agreed with the Indians that hostility to animals was a Left-Hand tic.

It didn't take much reading to realize that no one spell would be the answer, no wizarding *"exorciamus!"* and be done with it. I wrote notes to help me focus. As I read, I felt something shifting inside me, as if the writing were unlocking certain doors in my mind. Words had always been intimately linked with craft, giving spells direction, but these books seem to point to the hidden skeleton, the root of that connection.

Certain texts read like the memory of dreams. A volume with burned edges held an exegesis of Jesus expelling the Left-Hand spirits of Legion into the swine, with an odd, hastily scrawled annotation: "We are all pigs." An account of Islamic exorcism read like the Zensunnism of *Dune*. And one crucial story was buried in a *Thousand and One Nights*–style fairy tale: Solomon, or Sulayman, under constant threat from the jinn during his campaign against them, turned himself into a living, inviolable pentacle. It could work for me. But such a transformation seemed to have hidden implications. Also, like pre-twenty-first century everything, it didn't take into account a woman's issues such as pregnancy. How would such transformative craft affect my child?

I hadn't found the Sulayman story until after hours of study. Why hadn't Cornaro highlighted this obvious one for me? Still, I'd gotten to it eventually, so he was being helpful. And I had hours to find the rest of what I needed before I had to head back. Hours, and hours . . .

My tired mind fell into crazy craft dreamland. As if carried by a moving walkway, I was approaching a cemetery. I think it was the pseudo-Etruscan cemetery in the first *Omen* film. On my left, Rabu was keeping pace, body low to the ground with fear. On my right . . . on my right was a small child, fuzzy, more like the possibility of a child than a reality.

At the wrought iron gate stood that damned traitor, Abram Endicott, beckoning me to come in. I could read black metal words in its arch. "*Lasciate ogni speranza, o voi ch'intrate.*" I was still in panglossic reading mode, so I didn't have to know Dante's Tuscan to recognize the words: "Abandon all hope, you who enter here."

Yeah, Christian hell—so what? If I had to spend eternity with Saladin, so be it.

But then the gate began growing teeth, long white fangs dropping down from the arch and springing up from the ground below. Coming

together like the columns of the villa's portico, and me moving between them, then trapped within the cemetery, with the dog barking
and Abram leering at me.

I sprang awake, heart pounding. Just a dream in a cat nap. No, I'd
never had such a vivid dream before in my life. It was too like something Dale had described—how he'd known the Left Hand was coming for him before his retirement party. Through my child, I'd gained
another Morton power: foreboding. I'd been warned of imminent
death.

I thought it through. From the foreboding's symbols, Cornaro
might or might not be the problem, but this place, this Villa Alighieri,
certainly was.

But I was so fucking close to the answer on how to keep the mountain spirits away. What could this place do to me? It didn't even feel
sentient. I just needed a few more minutes. The answer was there, right
in front of me, just out of reach, dangling . . .

Like bait. Suddenly, everything about this—the invitation, the
arrangement of the books—looked like cheese, and I was the mouse.
I felt as paranoid as any tin-hatted basket weaver. I felt very right.

I was desperately trying to get knowledge to accompany Dale and
my friends on a mission and to help keep them safe. But staying here
and risking death wouldn't help anyone.

I stood up. Despite the adrenalin of the foreboding, I was tired,
probably from all the travel and being preggers. I emptied my small bag
and shoved some of the remaining books into it. Whether I was bor-
rowing or stealing, I didn't care. If I didn't find the answer, well, tough
shit. Life and the craft seldom provided ready-made solutions to hard
problems; I would have to improvise.

I tried my phone again, but still no reception in this place. I also saw
that the battery had gone from near full charge to dangerously low.
Weird. I would try it again outside; I'd have to make it count.

Outside—that reminded me. I had to retrieve Rabu.

Leaving my little work area, spiraling back into the main room, I found dark in the house, and dark outside the windows. My fancy watch said 8:30, but it had stopped. That seemed another bad sign. I went down a floor and to the main back entrance overlooking the courtyard. Faint night lights illuminated the walls and the ghastly images of the end of all things.

I opened the back glass-paned door. An empty stainless steel dog dish at my feet. The smell of dog's piss assaulted my nose—the preggers thing again. "Rabu," I whispered stagily. Nothing.

"*See better*," I said. There, in the dark at the foot of the stairs, lay Rabu, frozen still, not as if sleeping, but as if he'd collapsed where he stood. The empty dish—oh God, poison, they'd killed him. *My fault.*

I looked again at Rabu, switching from amplified vision to craft-sight to confirm that his spirit was gone. Instead, I saw his jackal head's eye, open and looking back up at me.

I signaled with rapid movements of my arm. *Get up here, you're not fooling anyone.* Of course Rabu would know how to play dead. I'd kill him for it later. What had he done with the food? Was it really poisoned? Questions that would have to wait.

I reassessed my position. Did I need to subdue Cornaro? I was a powerful exorcist, but I wasn't world class in other areas, and I was in his house, with no idea where he was or what weapons he could pull. What chances would I give an intruder in the House of Morton? No, we were leaving.

I looked again at my phone—still no bars. Very suspicious. OK, we'd walk, run, or hitchhike; anything was better than staying. Rabu seemed in full agreement.

No longer concerned about appearances, I drew the long knife from my boot and held it at ready in my free hand. Delicately, worried about every noise, I crossed the main room and tried the front door. It was locked. I clicked the bolt back and forth. Still locked by some force. Rabu snuffled it, and turned away. Craft radiated from it. Alarm wards guarded the windows. Even if I could open them, or break through them, Cornaro would know.

I pointed back to the courtyard. "Out?" Rabu shook his head and stared up at me with his big dog's eyes, scary because more desperate than vicious. Then, he trotted off for the stairway down.

We descended to the ground level and found the modern kitchen and casual dining area, marble and stone scrubbed to ancient cleanliness by the housekeeper. My weird new senses could hear the insects, but no sign of Cornaro. The small kitchen door and windows to the outside were also locked and craft warded. "This isn't working," I hissed. How stupid was I to follow a dog.

But with the stiffness of a pointer, Rabu stood at a shut door that led into one of the wings. Above the lintel was a fresco with a cutaway view of a buried coffin containing a fresh-looking corpse. This seemed a grim and unappetizing image so close to the kitchen. Trouble would be in that direction. I left my bag on the kitchen counter that divided the room—being caught in a fight weighed down with books would be worse than losing them. I opened the lever-handled door and we went into a smaller room, with another door at right angles to the entrance. The pattern was the same as the top floor where I'd been working. Above that door was another cutaway fresco; in the coffin, the corpse had gone green, and the flesh had sunk on the bones.

This went on for three more rooms, each halving in size and spiraling inward, each with its fresco of a corpse's progressive decay. Above the fourth door, the corpse in the coffin was nothing but bone, and when the painting was in the corner of my eye, something else seemed to stare out from that dark, buried space.

If it followed the upstairs pattern, this would be the final room. The close space reeked with rot, but not animal—more like water damage. Did Cornaro know his villa had problems?

I turned to Rabu. He sniffed the last door and shook his head. Then he pissed against the wall.

I resisted the urge to call him a bad dog, giving him a look instead. But I had a flashback, complete with a tang of post-trauma—Dale pissing on someone else's car to distract a Gideon. Rabu's urine would draw a Gideon's attention here. Would that be Cornaro? No, that wouldn't make sense—Rabu could just bark for him. Who was the Gideon then, and why was Rabu trying to get their attention?

Then, I felt the vibrations through my feet. I pressed my ear to the ground. *Hear better*, I thought.

A deafening whine like guitar feedback hurt my ear, then voices. They were hard to recognize—the tones weren't like anything human; they were some sort of harmony of ultralow and ultrahigh. But the words identified the speakers as surely as their voices could have, though I'd thought one of them was far away from this place and plane.

Beyond all my hope and fear, Madeline was here.

Enough trivia," said Cornaro. "You must tell me the most important secrets now."

"The secrets build," said Madeline. "One upon another." *Not a lie, not really.*

"Do not try to cheat a cheat. This is what I have done with Signora Rezvani, delay her with trifles."

What to tell him? As if in answer, Madeline smelled a new waft of dog urine. Beneath it were other scents: deodorant, and the human odors it hid. *Scherie.* Scherie and the dog were right above her. Madeline was surprised at such competent assistance from an animal; Left-Hand minions had a history of disappointment. For just a moment, she regretted all those dogs she and Roderick had experimented on. But she didn't regret the cats, never the cats.

Time to return the favor of helpful competence. Pregnancy had am-plified the strength and range of Scherie's senses, so perhaps Made-line could give her intel. She didn't consider how she knew this about Scherie; what mattered was that a male priest wouldn't think of a mother's ability. When Madeline spoke next, she would add harmon-ics above and a new fundamental below the range of normal hearing. Then when Cornaro spoke, she would echo his words with these tones. The lower frequencies would also vibrate the walls. One way or an-other, Scherie could hear her, if she knew what to do. Madeline would have to drop some clues to her and Cornaro's identities though; they wouldn't sound like themselves.

"You're a little old to fight Rezvani alone," said Madeline.

"I am not alone," said Cornaro.

"So you'd use the house against her. She's already as much the villa's prisoner as I am, and doesn't know it. It sounds like the house Roderick and I grew up in."

"Not quite," said Cornaro. "This villa is not sentient—but you already knew that, didn't you? It had a sentience, but no soul, so my grandparents, they had the skill of killing a house's mind. They decapitated it."

"Very nice," said Madeline, sincerely. "What's left, some form of probability defense?"

"Something more active," said Cornaro. "The house is still alive, and nocturnal. At night, it feeds. It consumes Rezvani now. She will not notice it. It starts with her electrical devices, then her craft energy, then her life. It is slow, but inexorable. By the morning . . . pfff." He waved a hand in dismissal.

"It doesn't like your taste, shaman?" asked Madeline.

"This room is safe, and I am safe. However, you should be quick with your knowledge, or Rezvani and her child will die. I have already killed her dog."

No, you haven't, my dear, dear, idiot priest, thought Madeline. Centuries later and a subjective eternity of torture, and Madeline still took such joy in male hubris.

"Very well," said Madeline. "Here is your damnation. Here is the summit of the Left-Hand way."

No," I whispered against the floor, hoping Madeline would somehow hear and not talk.

"I will tell it to you," said Madeline, "and then you must go and release her. Immediately."

"No," I whispered again. *Don't you know that I'm right here, above you?* But she must have known.

"*Sì*," said Cornaro, too eager to negotiate.

Madeline then recited one of the darkest secrets of the Left Hand. I will not repeat her instructions here or anywhere else. It was not one of the ways of immortality: the preservation of the flesh or the transfer of the spirit. It was the secret of creating human vessels. She told him how to master and suborn another soul and how to drive a spirit out of its native body. She told him the way to destroy a spirit such that it was never seen again.

I should have stood up, stopped my ears with my hands, and run away to some far corner of the villa. But I stayed, because Madeline wanted me to know this. She was sending me a terrible message.

As if to confirm this fear, Madeline spoke with a casual smile in her voice that promised cruelty to the unwary. "For an average practitioner, the process of destruction takes time, days if completely under physical control."

Cornaro took the bait. "What about for an exorcist?"

"Perhaps . . . perhaps not so long," said Madeline, as if she hadn't been thinking of just this point. "They are related powers. At some point the power of exorcism becomes the power of final death."

"Very good," said Cornaro.

"More than one powerful exorcist working very, very closely together could do it faster still."

"Why do you think I'd want to know that?"

"Apologies. You're right, it's not an immediate consideration for you, lonely shaman."

But for me it was? Then, it fell into place. Despite all the Morton powers I was acquiring, my child would be a powerful exorcist, and that power would pass in the female line. My hand went to my mouth—no, I had to hold my feelings in a little longer. But her meaning was clear. Like an evil fairy godmother, Madeline had just been the first to tell me: I was going to have a daughter.

Madeline interrupted my maternal moment. "What time is it? I smell nighttime, and I don't smell your damned housekeeper anymore."

"You can smell that far?" said Cornaro. "That is a flaw I should repair."

"You'll have to cut off my nose to spite me later," said Madeline. Could Cornaro hear the recklessness of endgame in her taunt? "Not another word until Rezvani is gone," she continued. "Have her return in the morning as insurance. You'll want to repair your new nasty sins anyway."

The creak of wood and the twang of springs signaled me to get up and prepare an ambush, but I was slow, which in this instance was good, because Madeline spoke again. "You expect to need that gun?"

Cornaro didn't deign to reply. I stood up, and for a moment the room went tilty. The villa's drain on me was particularly nasty here. Rabu and I swiftly backtracked through the spiral of rooms into the dining area and kitchen, and I shut each door behind us as it had been. Still a bit dizzy, I thought I could just go back up to the room and pretend I was still immersed in reading, and Cornaro would never know. Maybe he would really let me go, or maybe I could try to escape again after he'd seen me still at work, but before his villa could complete its meal of me.

Rabu tugged my sleeve with his mouth. OK, the dog's survival would be difficult to explain, but not fatal. But Rabu tugged again, and stood with a pointer's attention toward the door where Cornaro would come.

"We have to fight?" I said.

Rabu growled in response. Perhaps he smelled something about Cornaro; perhaps he knew what Cornaro intended with that gun. The dog had been right so far; Cornaro could probably dispose of me and convince Madeline that I was safely gone.

I took a deep breath. "OK," I said. As best I could, I readied myself for combat. I took an ambush position beside the doorway to the spiritual prison wing. I was surprised at my own steadiness in the face of being slowly digested. But my increasing weakness had shown itself in dizziness, fuzzy thinking, and a dangerous longing for sleep. *Better get him right away or I'm done.*

In this fight for me and my child, I would use surprise and any other trick to win, no matter how low. But I would not, could not use the terrible knowledge Madeline had given me.

I looked for Rabu to order him to a favorable position. But the dog had disappeared. Oh, he had stealth; that fit what he'd done in Tokyo and Delhi.

I went into accelerated mode, and waited in that slower world. It would only be objective seconds now.

Behind the door came Cornaro's voice: *"Sono io la casa. Io la stringo."* Arms of force gripped me. The handle of the door moved. When Cornaro came through, he'd see me and kill me.

The door opened. But even as Cornaro was clearing the corners and lining up his Beretta pistol on me, Rabu sprang out of thin air and leapt toward the priest's throat.

Cornaro may have had more grace and power than those Rabu had faced in Tokyo, but perhaps Rabu knew this, because he shifted in midair and went for the pistol instead. Cornaro fired, hitting nothing, and the Beretta flew out of his hands. Rabu bounced off him and hit the ground rolling, then dashed after the sliding pistol.

All this had broken Cornaro's concentration. I was free. Without a telegraphing thought, I stabbed at his heart with my knife.

In a flash, Cornaro parried. He had brought a knife too, an antique-looking dagger. Like his blade, Cornaro's age belied his speed, strength, and skill. He could draw on the power of his home place. I was in trouble.

At least fighting him seemed to be enough of a distraction so that he didn't try again to use the villa actively against me.

While we fought and maneuvered, Rabu retrieved the pistol and brought it to me. *Good boy.* Still waving the knife defensively with my other hand, I felt the slobber on the grip as I raised the gun to shoot.

Cornaro hadn't exerted himself to interfere with this, and I soon saw why: the pistol was Stonewall chipped.

As if in response to my frustration, Rabu again charged at Cornaro before I could coordinate our attacks. This time, I saw Cornaro's craft; he had some protection against dogs or animals. Rabu seemed to slide off to Cornaro's side without leaving a mark, yelping when Cornaro gave the dog a nick with his dagger. Rabu wouldn't be able to get in a serious strike.

Cornaro's defensive power was paired with one for attack. An old sin involving cruelty to animals was glowing brighter; Cornaro was readying some deadly craft against Rabu.

"Rabu," I said, between striking at Cornaro to try to keep the priest from executing his spell. "Fetch Madeline." A lot of assumptions there: that Madeline was fetchable, and that Rabu could work the lever-handled doors and whatever other mechanisms that led to her. But if the dog was a psychopomp, these challenges wouldn't mean much. The dog himself didn't hesitate; he was off.

I dodged Cornaro's next strike, stepping back toward the small dining table and tucking the gun away—didn't want Cornaro to get it back. Then, with a few quick thrusts, I made Cornaro respect my reach, and I drew the small blade from my thigh strap. I threw it at him, but even at such a close distance, he skewed it away. I drew my other small blade.

In answer, Cornaro made two crossing sweeps with his single blade; I went for an ambidextrous pair of pointed thrusts. Right now, I just wanted some time for Rabu to return. Using my sensitivity to judge the distance without looking, I sprang backward onto the dining table, continued into a roll, and landed on the floor on the other side. Childhood gymnastics were good for something. "You've heard enough," I told Cornaro. "Give me Madeline and let us go."

"You have heard too much," he said, moving cautiously around the table. "Will you stay silent?"

I doubted I could deceive such a practitioner. "Depends," I said, honestly. "You're a fucking priest. Why the hell do you want physical immortality?"

"I don't," he said. "You don't understand." He was still edging toward me. With my strength going, he would want to close with me.

Quicker than I'd thought possible, Rabu returned, a hunk of wood in his mouth. "Keep your distance, Rabu," I said.

Rabu dropped the wood and stayed out of Cornaro's line of sight.

"Scherie, what are you doing?" The wood was talking to me with Madeline's voice. It bore the hack marks of crude carving. I thought of Cornaro's knife. He'd put Madeline into this thing. *The cruelest thing you could imagine would be to seal one of these.*

Suddenly, negotiations no longer seemed such a hot idea. I was so shocked, Cornaro was able to lunge and nick me with his pass, ripping my blouse and drawing a line of blood.

"The deal stands, shaman," said Madeline, as if responding to my display of vulnerability. "I'll tell you the rest, just let her go."

"No deal," I said, counterattacking Cornaro and sounding already winded. "You don't get to keep her in that thing."

"Silence, Rezvani!" Despite her current form, Madeline had assumed her old imperious tone, though tinged with a little desperation.

Didn't matter. Cornaro's sins were flashing all wrong. "Doesn't look like he's in the mood for deals, Auntie," I said.

Cornaro and I went at each other again between the table and the kitchen counter, trading attacks and drawing new lines of blood, while Madeline started singing craftless words in a guttural language I didn't know and in a new, vaguely familiar voice. Then, recognition hit: the voice was mine. She was pretending to be me.

Rabu was barking and running about, keeping his distance from Cornaro. Tattered bits of spirit, worse than the ghost I'd seen at Roderick's in Kiev, were dancing about him like insects, every now and then trying to sting him, but he was herding them.

I didn't know what the hell they were doing, but it sure wasn't hurting Cornaro or helping me. But Cornaro wasn't the entity they were trying to distract and fool. They were drawing the villa's instinctual hunger to themselves alone. The mindlessly evil thing's weight lightened, and I felt the land's power and the revulsion of the very soil at this place.

Madeline spoke again in the strange hi-low tones from before that only I and maybe Rabu could hear: "Scherie, we can't distract it from you for long. You must act now."

No, had to be another way. "Why this?" I asked Cornaro, double-stepping in retreat.

"If I don't do this," he said, "the world ends."

"Better the world ends," I said, remembering what I told Dale.

"And every soul destroyed?"

Maybe just one. But no, couldn't even think that. "Must be another way."

"Yes, a fate worse than the final death. No one will do it."

His own words seemed to decide him. I felt the pilot fire in the kitchen range resonate in anticipation of some Dominican craft. I saw the unmitigated sin of his intent glowing. Summoning all his strength and the villa's, he intended to kill me and my child.

I wish I could say I hesitated, even for a second, but I didn't. Everything I'd told Dale about not using the Left-Hand way was gone in a flash of rage. All I could think was of the two necessary images of the craft—Cornaro's soul present, Cornaro's soul destroyed. I pointed the knife in my left hand at the spot between his eyes, uttered the words, and poured my remaining power and life out in a roaring spiritual flame.

Nothing was truly instantaneous, not in the accelerated mode of craft combat. There was time enough for him to realize what I had done and what it meant. Time for his eyes to show his horror at me and terror for himself. Time for a single word, "Jesus."

Then, the blast took him. His body fell, but he was gone before it hit the floor. I'd seen many deaths, and each one had been marked by the spirit's departure. No spirit left Cornaro's corpse. I'd killed him absolutely.

I folded to the ground. Perhaps I would have stayed there until the morning, but Rabu barked at me, and Madeline sounded as shrill as I felt. "Scherie. We can't distract the house anymore. And it's pissed."

The villa was still alive, the death of its master only unleashing its hunger. I got to my knees and tried my new Left-Hand craft on the house, but either I was too weak or whatever sort of spirit powered it didn't have the part that those words could destroy.

So fucking weak. I got up, and with the handles of my knives, I tried to break a window near the door to the outside; it had earlier seemed warded only with an alarm. Nothing.

"Lift me up there," said Madeline. "Hold my head right next to the glass." I tucked my small knife away so I could do what she said. Her wooden head had very little movement, but she banged it against the glass, faster and faster, like the blur of a jackhammer. Surely either her head or the glass must break. But with a cry of rage, she stopped, and I sat back hard on the ground. All that, and only the smallest of cracks in one small pane.

Rabu was manically battling the physical villa itself. He was pissing everywhere, scratching at frescoes, and barking for help. But he was slowing, limping, halting.

I crawled to the door and started hacking at it with my long knife. It was like the door in Roderick's bunker that never gave way no matter what we did to it, only the whole house was that way.

I looked about. My bag with the books and my notes was still on the counter. I could write a letter to explain. I crawled toward it and reached up for the strap, and saw that my hand was shaking wildly. It was no good. So I and my daughter would die, and Dale would never know why. Perhaps I deserved death for what I'd just done. But not my baby, dammit.

Madeline was where I'd left her on the ground, softly sobbing, like a child's crying doll. I wouldn't have thought her capable of such sorrow. With my last energy I pulled myself across the ground toward her, then reached out and rolled her closer to me, my trembling hand resting on her wooden form. Rabu scooted over, joining our Pompeian duo.

"Can I free you from this thing?" I asked.

In answer, Madeline just sobbed more.

"I'm . . ." I coughed. Consoling Madeline while dying myself seemed ridiculous. "I'm sorry I couldn't save us."

"That's not it," she said. "No deal. You told him, 'No deal.' You wouldn't have left me in this, forever, even to save yourself and your little girl."

"Goddamn it, Madeline." She had no right to break my heart here at the end. Did she think everyone else was a monster too? What had Roderick and her family done to her?

"You and House let me go when you needed me," she said. "This was different. This was . . ." She paused, as if searching for the right word.

In the distance, an owl hooted, the faint sound leaking through the window cracks in synesthetic colors. Like some siren of Hell, Madeline answered it with a scream. The force of it rattled the door and vibrated the ground. My ears rang between each outburst, and Rabu whined.

"Madeline . . . Madeline . . ." I wanted to interrupt her, to ask why the fuck she was bothering to scream now. But I was so tired, and even her weapons-grade noise couldn't keep me from falling into darkness.

TEN

Before they boarded the helicopter, Endicott was watching Morton—something had been up with him. Was it Rezvani's absence? No, Endicott felt a strange resonance in his bones around Morton, and that was bad, because his bones were filled with some serious Left-Hand serum. After all they'd been through, was Dale finally turning toward the darkness? But Morton looked back at him, grinning, and the sense of evil passed.

That would have been it, except Endicott noticed that Grace seemed to be watching both him and Morton with some concern. *Probably a good idea,* he thought. *I might try to take over the world, and Dale might sacrifice us to demons.* The absurdity of it made him feel better.

Their ride started bumpy, and got worse. Bad weather assailed the copter. Hima guided and shaped this thinner, untamed air, but only just enough to ensure progress, not comfort. Endicott had never fully appreciated the Morton skill at managing air travel. Sitting up front as copilot, Dale was otherwise occupied, letting himself go as he felt for the way in the dark to the Sanctuary, opening himself to the particular vector they needed to travel. "Easier to do it at night," he'd said. "Fewer distractions." Morton would save his weather talents for the climb.

Though generous India gave more power than Japan, it was still not like home ground for Morton or Grace. But for Endicott, everywhere could feel like a fount of energy, if he let it. It would be dangerous to immerse himself too far in any power.

Grace was sitting next to Endicott, but like Morton her attention was also elsewhere. She was trying desperately to keep them off radar, but they were under so much hostile focus here.

On one mission or another, they'd all been here before, coming in stealthy on a copter to a place of occult danger. But none of them had ever had such a high-altitude destination.

Endicott didn't need night vision or special equipment to follow their progress up the run of the glacier. His one eye could see so much that it was disturbing—he often willed it to see less. They flew over an ice field that transitioned from a rubbly mix of frozen mud to the pristine white of snow, toward the spot between Indira Col and Sia Kangri where three nations came together. India and Pakistan had fought at Siachen for decades. A truce had been in place for the last decade, but casualties happened just by being present. Weather and conditions had killed more on the glacier than the enemy ever had. India's throwing away its own soldiers' lives up here wasn't a good sign for an operation with foreigners.

The name of the area was another dubious omen. The Karakorams meant "Black Mountains." Sounded like a fantasy name, like Mountains of Madness, like something Scherie would have gotten a kick out of. Dear God, she was going to be pissed at Dale, at all of them.

Grace's hands went to her head. "It's beginning," she said, off phones to him alone. "Like a probability defense with malice. It wants to swat us. But not yet."

Another minor lurch shook them. Abruptly, Hima's voice, spiky with nerves, spoke into their headphones. "We've got to turn around."

Endicott couldn't be sure, but Hima's words seemed more like a response to external psych suasion than to realities. As such, Hima was already being manipulated by craft, so Endicott countered with his own: "*Keep going, Captain.*" *In Jesus's name*, he added to himself. No need to double the offense by throwing religion in Hima's face, whether he respected Jesus as an avatar of Vishnu or not.

If Hima felt the compulsion, he didn't object, and Grace didn't call Endicott on this use of his power. But he still worried, because he felt the temptation to keep commanding, even up here with so little to command.

After a few more minutes. Endicott guessed from the rough look of the terrain and their speed that they should be near the T where Sia Group met the main range and very close to their destination. As if in answer to this thought, Grace spoke into their phones. "Now we have to stop."

"Still a ways to go," said Morton, coming back to the mundane plane.

"No choice," said Grace.

"Hima, take us down," said Endicott.

The snowy, icy incline would not support a landing, so they fast-roped themselves and their gear down into the darkness and onto a relatively gentle portion of the slope. Radio communication with Hima at this range from the Sanctuary worked, and they set their extraction point half a klick to the southeast to avoid going out the same way they came in. Hima didn't wait after that for good-byes—without Grace on board, he was more vulnerable than ever. With the copter gone, they were alone on the roof of the world.

Please God, a little warmth! If the center of Hell were indeed cold (no basis in scripture, but Dante had some spiritual connections), this place was its high-altitude equivalent. The wind stabbed at him, searching out any vulnerable point from which to steal heat. The climbers had no exposed skin; it would freeze here in just minutes. Even with spiritual power and the best mountain gear, they had to be extremely careful about hypoxia and frostbite.

They immediately readied weapons, specialized for extreme cold with special lubricants. Craft could help keep their bodies from freezing, but best to rely on chemistry for their rifles. Their snow camo would be redundant with the darkness and spiritual stealth, but one slip, and one of the party could fall outside Grace's range, or Grace's control could go wobbly for some reason.

To complement their craftsight, Grace and Morton wore night vision goggles adapted for high-altitude conditions. Endicott just wore clear ski goggles against the polar cold, and his remaining eye pierced the darkness and saw whatever he focused on with daylight detail.

They roped together, Morton to Grace to Endicott to allow Grace to keep them all under stealth, though the distance was a strain on her ability. The combination of a stealth bubble and Morton's concentration of the air around them produced an odder distortion than the usual fish-eye effect, with the cold stars not just twinkling more, but shifting and jumping about in all directions. None of this would stop projectiles though, if someone was able to draw a bead on them.

The terrain was tactically dangerous. Endicott had an instinctual hunger for the high ground, but the top of the ridge would be worse for covert movement because it was right on the Chinese line of control, and stealth wouldn't hide their silhouette of distortion against the night sky. Here on the lower ground they'd have no good cover if someone farther up could spot them, and return fire against an elevated covered position would be difficult. Though this would have been decisive for mundanes, a spiritual advantage was always the best ground. Whether or not his team had such an edge, Endicott hoped to find no hostile patrols as he surveyed his surroundings.

Balanced against these problems of terrain and crazy bitter cold, their combat craft and prayers meant that they'd probably avoid altitude sickness or cerebral and pulmonary edemas. In the two-edged category was the loneliness of these mountains. The general public wouldn't see them, so they could unleash their full abilities, as could their enemies.

They climbed along the Indian side of the ridge toward the high peak of Sia Kangri, a shadow against the stars. They were in a combat mode that wasn't so much accelerated as very present in the moment. Dale led them, still following that feeling that guided him to the ever-uncertain location of a Sanctuary. He moved with a goatlike sureness, and seemed to use his ice axe not so much to test the snow and ice as to confirm what he already knew. Endicott was convinced that alone, Dale might have moved at a near run. But this was better. Even a thin layer of snow could hide crevasses, and defensive craft might fool Dale.

With no spiritual skills to assist his team's climb, Endicott was well suited for the rearguard and for attending to their defense. The team wore communication headsets with craft encryption, but they observed silence, so no noise but the steady rhythm of their crampons with each kick, step, rest, repeat. For once, Endicott appreciated the lack of feeling in his prosthetic toes; even with boots, good to have fewer extremities to be running spiritual heat through.

Endicott scanned for traps, and searched for active craft that, unlike a passive defense, signaled the immediate presence of craftspeople. Instead, looking above the ridgeline, he found the mountain spirits, high in the air like dozens of arctic auroras, blood red forms with blue halos glowing in his preternatural eyesight.

Such dead subversives of his theology still bothered him, but these ones seemed easier to categorize than family ghosts. These spirits were older and stranger, distorted from their original human shapes like figures from the Tibetan Book of the Dead, or the jinn that some climbers saw and attributed to altitude sickness. In short, they were demons. Such power in the hills helped explain why Afghanistan could be a problem for invaders, even for craftspeople. But for now, these things weren't coming closer to Endicott's party.

Sudden pain on his shoulder, and Endicott stumbled. What was that? From a crouch, he peered with his powerful eye into the darkness. Rocks and chunks of ice were flying at them from higher up. "Skew only as necessary," he ordered. Morton and Grace appeared unharmed. Uncaring nature was bad enough up here, but this bit was actively trying to kill them.

Or maybe *actively* was the wrong word. Endicott saw the spiritual force behind the projectiles—it was a passive defense, so no one necessarily knew they were coming.

Yet Endicott kept looking for a possible attacker. Instead, in the distance, he saw someone else roaming the slope, a dot on the landscape, but with an aura like the grace of some deity making straight their path and a thread of spiritual force like a climbing line leading onward, though the person was alone. This stranger seemed unaffected by the rocks and ice.

"Major Morton," said Endicott. "Someone at two o'clock. Looks like one of the pilgrims to the Sanctuary."

Before Dale could reply, one of the demons flew down and, clawed hand outstretched, it touched a nearby sheet of ice. Dale said, "Move!" and they were off in a slightly different direction than before. The ice sheet cracked. No avalanche, no flying chunks. Had Dale overreacted?

But someone had taken the noise as their signal to unleash death. The first shots came in an extravagant burst, trying to catch them unawares before they could bring their craft defenses up. The bullets snapped by, but no hits—they were firing at invisible targets, and the climbers' defenses were already prepared for the rocks and ice.

Dale kept them moving, nonlinearly, crouched, and in shifts. Neither he nor Grace returned fire yet. Endicott expected nothing less in terms of discipline. Then the enemy fire slowed. They wouldn't have an infinite number of rounds up here. The hostile shots got better and more skewed toward them. Dale and Grace skewed some away, which might also reveal them.

Ice and snow scattered around Endicott. Near misses had punched holes in his clothes and burned a line across his shin, but his defenses were holding off a hit. In his scan of the situation, an unsurprising oddity—nobody was shooting at the pilgrim.

An explosion where they'd been moments before. So the Yetis had a few grenades. These snowmen may have known they'd be coming.

Had Pandava set them up? Seemed excessive. Maybe Omar Khan of Pakistan had gotten close enough at the wedding to extrapolate that their path was hooked to Pandava.

The pattern of fire indicated two groups attacking from different positions—one more toward the Pakistani line, the other toward the Chinese. Endicott's eye detected their separate massed glows. The two sides were triangulating their fire on them.

"Morton, stop altering the bloody air," said Grace. "I think they're tracking it." Abruptly, it became even colder and harder to breathe.

Endicott signaled with two tugs on the rope and a hand gesture to draw up together. He pointed to the rough locations of the enemy for Grace and Dale. "Return fire."

They separated again. Grace held a weapon in each hand. "*Omnes viae Romam ducunt*," she said, and fired both at once. A scream pierced the thin cold air. One down. Endicott and Morton also fired, curving the paths of their shots sideways to make tracking more difficult and downward to hit people firing from cover or prone on the ground, but with no clear success. Grace's next shots also seemed less lethal. Status quo gave advantage to the enemy, who even if they failed to hit anything, only had to keep the party pinned down for it to fail. Or maybe someone would create an avalanche just to wind things up before dawn.

A flicker in the stealth bubble—Grace couldn't keep that up forever either. "Time to let out your inner fascist," Morton said to Endicott. "Order them to stop."

"If they know it's us," said Endicott, "they'll have precautions."

"Against the old you," said Dale. An enemy would know about the Endicott power of command, but wouldn't know its new extent in him.

"I won't be able to stop," he blurted. Ah hell, was it really that bad?

"Nobody else is here," said Grace. "It's the safest place to try."

They were right. Endicott readied his prayer, tapping into that transnational power. The easiest command, requiring the least subordination of their wills, would be to have them stop doing something.

"We move fast the moment you pray," said Morton, though the echo of the prayer would make tracking the sound difficult.

"In God's name, hold your fire!" They moved in a crouched clamber, arms working with legs. For a moment, silence—no shooting. But it was only a hesitation. Soon, more potshots. Was another will active against them?

"Not through their ears," Morton said. "You can speak to them soul to soul."

How had Dale come up with that? "I won't possess them." Hell, that sounded like an old accusation.

"Understood," said Morton, blandly. "But you can order them."

"Dangerous," said Endicott. Dangerous to him, to them, to the world.

"You have the gift for a reason," said Grace.

"Do the Pakistanis first," said Morton. "Still a little curse residue on me regarding Muslims. I can help you better with the Chinese. I can see their sins peeping out."

"Agreed," said Endicott.

Morton unhooked, leaving Endicott bound to Grace, and began his run for the Chinese, showing no doubt that Endicott's spirit would be there on time.

Endicott had not attempted to leave his body since the showdown with Roderick in the bunker. Something profane in such a practice—it was the theological equivalent of deserting one's post. Then, he'd been hacked at and on his way to bleeding out, and leaving had just been letting go. Harder now, when he felt so fiercely alive, here in combat at the top of the world.

He faced his first objective and pushed out of himself, letting his body fall away into Grace's arms. Spiritual winds, the equivalent of the physical polar weather, buffeted him. The demon spirits now appeared as solid as the mountains. They leered as he passed, but did not approach him.

First, to the fur-clad Pakistani Yetis—their souls were like beacons, radiating with their powers, save for the spirit that stood above the cooling body of Grace's kill. As quick as thought, he was on them. Their orders from Omar Khan still lay on the surface of their brains— ignore the pilgrims, but stop any party from India. Their minds, a bit dimmed by conditions, now lit up with adrenaline fear, as one by one they felt his spectral fingers grip their skulls. *Lord, put them to sleep,* he said. He probably could kill them, command their hearts to stop beating. But that seemed like a line not to be crossed except in a more dire necessity.

As Endicott flew on to the Chinese, he saw Dale's embodied soul as his friend ran up the mountain. The soul blurred with its physical speed as Morton dodged and skewed sparks that would be craft-guided bullets. Magnificent really. But a darkness, separate, black-lit, had its hooks in Morton's spirit. Endicott would have preferred to think that this was just the sin of Dale's unbelief, but no, it was the spiritual presence of the Left Hand. Not good, though Endicott also had that presence, and Dale was containing his demons.

The Chinese snowmen were more ready for him than their Pakistani allies. What kind of experience did they have with Left-Hand techniques? But then Morton was running up at them, and Grace was firing two guns at once again, and this broke their concentration against Endicott's spirit. *Lord, put them to sleep,* he commanded again, one by one at the speed of thought. In quick succession, the Chinese collapsed, a pile of endangered animal furs.

Time to return—Endicott's abandoned body wouldn't fare well under these conditions. But it was then, at his most vulnerable, that the Lords of the High Places struck. They came at him, battering and buffeting him with their spiritual fists like a leaf in a gale. *In God's name, back off!* They laughed at him; his disembodied power of command did not extend to these dead. With punches and kicks, he hit back. The demons backed off, but they now flew in a sphere about him. He couldn't see any forms or lights but theirs.

Only then did Endicott realize that, by disorienting him and now blocking his sight, they had killed him without his knowing. He couldn't see the thin silver line that had connected his spirit to his body. He couldn't find his way back.

Despair was tempting—having died once before, he didn't fear the end, but to lose Grace right now seemed unbearable, worse than damnation itself. *Lord, please, not yet.*

In reply, a whisper, like the quiet sound that had spoken to Elijah in the wilderness. *Thy will be done.* He followed the sound, punching through the demons in his way.

There, ahead in the distance, like a flaming sword, like Excalibur itself, stood Grace's embodied soul. She was a mix of colors all her own. He was guided by her light back to his body. The blows of demons were like the bites of gnats. He found his spiritless body in his wife's arms, and flew back into it.

His first physical awareness was Grace whispering in his ear. "... *love, come back to me, my love.*"

With his gloved hands, numb with cold, he reached up to hold her. They had sworn not to part until death, when scripture said all marriages ceased. But Grace had now called him back from the grave twice, and he could no longer imagine heaven without her, nor could any place be hell with her in it. His mind fuzzy from his spiritual trauma, he thought something he otherwise wouldn't have dared: *God forgive me, but I love my wife more than salvation itself.*

D ale didn't pause to check on the Chinese. He ran down from the ridge at a dangerous pace even by his standards. He wanted that pilgrim Endicott had spotted.

But the stranger was gone. Damn, Dale had wanted to see the moment of disappearance. But it was enough to confirm what he'd suspected. The enemy had been waiting for them here, meaning they knew that anyone seeking the Sanctuary from the Indian side would come this way. That, and the pilgrim's route, meant the crossing to the Sanctuary must be near.

The intensity of his earlier scrambling dash uphill over rocks and ice had chewed up the skin on Dale's hands even through his gloves. He'd deal with that later. Meanwhile, the Left-Hand voices in his skull were still reciting the instructions for astral transference that had given him the idea for Endicott's spiritual attack. Endicott and Marlow hadn't been perfectly clear about that part of the Virginia bunker showdown, but Dale had guessed much. The helpfulness of the Left-Hand voices didn't comfort him.

Dale returned to the other two. Marlow had dropped her stealth, and their sins helped Dale find his way.

Endicott, still wobbly, kept a hand on Marlow's shoulder, as if trying to tie himself down to the world to keep his soul from blowing off this mountaintop into the cold outer beyond. He was mumbling something to himself. "I shall not. I shall not."

Hearing this, Dale felt a horrible desire to ask Endicott whether there was something that he shouldn't do too, just for the pleasure of obeying. Oh, for a Morton, that desire was indeed evil, and vaguely apocalyptic besides. Instead, he asked, "Shall not what?"

"The spirits want me to come back and play."

"Bad idea," agreed Dale, rehooking to the climbing party. Nature continued to act against them with a random rock and the normal polar cold. Other fighters would come to replace those they'd subdued. The sun was coming up, exposing them all the more. As for craft protections, everyone now knew they were in the area, and that combined with the combat drain on her craft meant that Marlow's stealth was visibly faltering. Depending on the Sanctuary's awareness, that might effectively negate one of the reasons for this mission:

Dale's protection against farsight. Hell, even satellites would see them.

"This way," said Dale, trying to recoup the mindset that allowed him to find the uncertain location of the Sanctuary. They continued in the direction of high Sia Kangri. Dale felt some tension on the line. For the first time in weeks, Endicott was limping. No convenient footprints from the pilgrim greeted them, of course. That would make this too easy for the uninvited.

About to take another step, Dale felt death grabbing his ankle. He stepped back, nearly falling, but catching himself. He squatted down and reached out with his ice axe. It swung through, and Dale saw not a narrow, shallow crevasse, but the craft-hidden, huge fucking chasm that had awaited the party. The boundary to American Sanctuary had been a mild discouragement compared to this fall into the netherworld and beyond. Its size wasn't completely uncomforting. A Sanctuary border grew with time and loss, and the world had lost much. They must be near the right place.

They moved along the chasm, and Dale searched for the transitional space that would be the bridge. After many false phantom sensations, he finally felt the familiar uncertainty of a crossing. He went a little farther. The feeling weakened.

Shit, time to act. For Dale, entering the American Sanctuary hadn't been a leap of faith—as a Morton, he knew the way there in his bones. He didn't like this leap of faith one bit.

Finally, he said, "Here's where I pull my weight." He handed his weapons to Grace. "If the way opens, toss 'em. Those, and all of yours. Even the knives." Mostly it'd been craft that'd saved them anyway. "Also, send these coordinates. Whether anyone actually gets them, maybe it'll pin things here for a time." That trick might have helped with the American Sanctuary, but this behemoth would probably break such a quantum thread with ease.

Dale stepped up to the spot of strongest feeling. He'd have to step with authority, which meant that if nothing was there, he was going down. He might be able to glide for a moment, but he felt the desire of this abyss to drag him into its darkness. As inevitably as Wile E. Coyote, he'd fall. He was still roped though. No, that was wrong—the chasm would drag the rest down too.

He unhooked again from the rest of the party.

"Major?" said Grace.

"Has to be this way," said Dale. He closed his eyes, and walked the edge of the abyss until it felt like the path of the Sanctuary he knew.

Words sometimes helped. "We seek asylum. I claim the right as a defender of the American Sanctuary."

Dale's leg trembled. Would his ghost be the one to see his child born? With abrupt will, he brought his right foot forward, his weight on it. He felt himself falling forward . . .

His foot landed hard, right on the edge of a bridge of stone. This place was playing with him.

The bridge began with a broad stairway to a level path across the abyss. The bridge path was supported below by an arch of stone whose incredible length would have appalled any mundane engineer assessing it, and whose supports emerged far below from the chasm walls. The stone path continued straight for a hundred meters until it hit a mountain, or rather, hit a landing for a stairway carved into the rock. The carved stairway went up and up in long shallow switchbacks across the towering sheer mountain face for perhaps a vertical one thousand meters until it reached something level-looking that could be the high plateau of the Sanctuary. Dale knew of few occult constructions so grand, and this whole mountain and stairway would move with the Sanctuary.

He still couldn't see the damned pilgrim. "Let's go," he said. "Before it changes its mind for spite."

———

Back in Leh, Pandava received a report: after inserting the mission, Hima had radioed that he'd developed multiple mechanical failures of "probable craft origin." He'd made it halfway to the Siachen Glacier Helipad when his copter crashed and Hima was killed.

Pandava asked Prithvi, "What should we do?"

"Nothing," said Prithvi. "We wait and see. Everyone is where they need to be."

Even dying, I couldn't catch a break. Endicott had seen his mother in heaven. I saw somebody else, backlit by the massive flames she had set: a teenage girl, black haired and olive complexioned with just a hint of copper, her Persian eyes like mine but exaggerated with kohl. She might have fit fine in any suburban mall, but she had something feral in her stare and an automatic rifle in her hands. She rolled her eyes at me. "This would have been a shitty day to die." A roar of thunder at her words, and then stabbing pain. Was the villa chewing on me?

I came back enough to see what was causing the winter thunder and the sudden pain. The kitchen door had exploded open, and its wooden splinters had stabbed me into consciousness, though I was already going down again for the last time.

An older man above me tucked what looked like lopsided nunchucks into his belt. He fluoresced with green craft as if I were viewing him in night vision. He grabbed me under my arms. I made some moan of protest as my fingers fumbled futilely for the doll at my side. "Not all at bloody once, now," he said gently, as he dragged me with less care outside into the cold moonlight of the front driveway.

"That'll do," said the man. "Old house can't reach its dinner here."

My head lolled to the side, where the lifeless eyes of the housekeeper stared back at me. Was this good or bad news? I didn't care—at least, not about me. I felt for my child's life, and it still glowed within. The rest of me was twilight, though some little sparks of life now entered instead of exiting my soul. The man, grimacing, was going back to the kitchen door. "The dog too," I croaked.

"You're feckin joking," said the man.

"Psycho. Pomp," I managed.

"Oh. Probably should then," he said with sad eyes and a broken smile.

He came back, winded, with Rabu and the doll piled into his arms. His smile was gone; his blue-eyed gaze was piercing. "What happened to the priest?" he asked.

I shook my head.

"Shite. We'd best stay here." His Irish-accented voice quavered. "They'll be wanting to talk to you."

"Who?"

"The *Oikumene*," he said. "And their friends."

"I need to leave." Oh, good, I'd regained enough life for a whole sentence.

He didn't seem to notice. "This is a bitter paradox. They hoped to save you and your child. But when they see this . . ."

I wasn't thinking clearly. I didn't want to talk to the Pythia or the *Oikumene*. This Irish guy had to listen. "I need to leave!"

In a combat craft blur, his gun was out and pointed at me, like he was afraid. His trigger finger seemed a little short, but his gun didn't bother me—I was still out of it, with only one clear thought. "I need to leave," I repeated, quiet and calm.

"Right. I've got that. Where would you be going?"

"Rome. Airport."

"Right then. Let's make a deal. We take the road toward Rome. You recover and explain all of this horror to me. If I don't appreciate your story, we drive to meet the *Oikumene*, and you can tell them about it. No matter what happens, you swear not to do to me what you did to the fella in there."

"I . . ." The horror of what I'd done to Cornaro was coming back to me. "I would never . . ." But I had. "I swear it."

"Grand. We're off."

He helped me to my feet, and he caught me when all those incoming life sparks rushed down from my head. He supported my shuffle to the passenger side of his mini Europcar rental, and I leaned against the car to wait for my friends. The man was too busy keeping his eyes on me to retrieve Rabu and Madeline, so the dog got up with a shake and a wobble and, with some more awkwardness, picked up the doll in his mouth, as if he had fetched some joker's idea of a stick.

"You're good," said Madeline from his mouth, her voice frightening in its weakness. "But this is undignified. Kill you. Later."

Rabu's hang-dog eyes seemed to agree that someone should get killed for this. Feeling better by the minute, I managed to put my seat up and help them into the back. Madeline looked like the sorriest ventriloquist's dummy in the world.

The car was already moving out of the driveway when I shut the passenger door. I slumped in the shotgun seat and assessed my damage. Now that I was recharging with life, I'd need some first aid, but I'd have to talk this Irishman into that and everything else. He'd relied on my oath, so I suspected he had some sort of blarney detection craft. Blood on my clothes, and bloody handprints under my arms, but those weren't mine or Cornaro's. That was where my rescuer had grabbed me. I looked at his hands on the steering wheel—blood, and stained shirtsleeves.

"The housekeeper?" I asked.

"The old signora who ambushed me at the door? She blew poison darts at me. She must have thought I was her husband." He chuckled at his own little joke, then stopped. "She didn't bugger off when I told her to, so I got my hands dirty with her."

She had been the one to feed Rabu. "She tried to kill the dog," I said.

"T'anks," he said. "Feel better about the mess already."

Easiest thing would have been to close my eyes again. I was desperate for sleep, but this man demanded convincing, so I should know my audience. "Who are you?"

"Ossian MacCool."

"MacCool? As in Finn MacCool?" This wasn't helping with my dreamlike sense of things. I knew this Family's name from folklore and fantasy.

"Call me Oz." He laid his gun between the seats. I stared at this seemingly careless gesture.

"You'd be wondering about the gun. That was just for show. I could hurt you with just a word, and kill you with a poem . . . unless you're a very stubborn housekeeper. One of my Family's gifts."

"You're with the *Oikumene*?"

"Not a formal member, no, just doing them a favor. They sent out a general call for help, and I was closest. I'd been retrieving some of my things. The Greeks thought you'd be at the Vatican, but I sorted that quick enough with the doolally Cardinal of Craft. Found out where the priest's family house was. The house tried to hide, but I heard the screams. It must have had a chink in its stealth."

The cracked window—that was why Madeline had made so much noise.

Oz continued. "I have no doubt Cornaro was an evil fecker. But by the look of it, one of the great offenses was committed against him. Do you understand what I'm saying? Even if I let you go, the Furies will come after you. They don't spare anyone."

Furies. Endicott had invoked them in his vow of death. The *Oikumene* had threatened the dogs of Istanbul with their Furies, and the name alone had been enough to make that pack of well-armed killers back off from me. Then memory of what I'd done to Cornaro shook through me again. They'd kill me for that. The only way to avoid it would be to do what I'd done to the priest over and over again. As I'd already told Oz, I couldn't do that.

Of course, they wouldn't have to come after me if Oz were delivering me to them, but I'd watched his choice of turns down the back roads, and I'd checked the sky. From such stars as I could see, we seemed to be heading roughly in the direction for Rome—south and west, not north and east to round the Adriatic into Greece.

I'd kept my eyes on the horizon and avoided looking at his rearview mirrors. I did not dare even a glance at my face; I couldn't bear the letter for my unforgivable sin.

Oz was driving faster than sanity, taking turns on two wheels, barreling down the middle of one lane roads with two lanes of traffic, crazier than the locals, crazier than Pandava in India. Some craft in it, but that just gave him more boundary to push. "Are they that close?" I asked.

"Wouldn't want our little *craic* interrupted. Try beginning at the beginning," he suggested, "and give me the short version first."

How to convince him? I could apologize, but that implied what I'd done was forgivable, and it wasn't. I could play the baby card, but he already knew that, and my sin wasn't justifiable either. The only necessities that might matter enough were the ones in the future.

"My husband and my friends are going on a mission. They're important. If I'm not there, I think they're going to die." Grasping at straws, I said this only to gain his sympathy, but once out, it rang with the oracular gong.

Oz let out a breath. "Feckin hell. Morton, Endicott, and Her Majesty's bloody Marlow. I wouldn't mind that last one going missing, but seems a bit unlikely that anything in this world could kill those three, with or without you. Unless they're going someplace very special."

I decided to trust this man who had, at least temporarily, saved my life. I had no choice. "They're going to the Sanctuarium Mundi."

He nearly didn't make the oncoming turn; I grabbed the "oh shit" handle. "Joking Jesus Christ," he said. "They would be, wouldn't they? Latin is too young a language to name that place." He closed his eyes for just a moment. "You're very sure they've waited for you?"

Now it was my turn to swear. English, Farsi, and some new Japanese profanities tumbled out, sparking a little craft. Rabu growled at me, though no ghosts were about besides the trapped Madeline. It had taken outsider Oz to see it for me: no way would Dale and my putative friends wait for pregnant me. I was surprised how furious I was with all of them, not just Dale, for this betrayal.

I ran the math of the mission in my head. Depending on how long they spent at the Sanctuary, I might still have time to catch up with them, even if only to assist their evac. But that might not be enough to convince Oz that the craft world needed me just now. My head was clearing. I could think again. I needed to think harder.

Consciously or unconsciously, Oz was slowing the car back to Italian norms. He was already deciding to give me to the *Oikumene*.

Maybe I was thinking about this the wrong way. It wasn't my importance to the world; it was my importance to Oz.

"Wait," I said. "I've trusted you. Now, trust me for just a few questions. The *Oikumene* uses the natives of various countries to accomplish their will, but you're not from here. Why are you here, and where are you going?"

"That's not your—"

"I have a supersonic aircraft waiting for me. It can get you anywhere in the world quicker than any nonmilitary can follow, and you won't have any border hassles."

"Why or where, the answer is the same. I don't think we'd be going in the same direction. I'm looking for the end of the world."

Oh shit. Unthinking, I grabbed the handle again, though it wasn't the driving that bothered me. "Cornaro also said it was coming—a Left-Hand end times. But he didn't say where. Just soon."

In the backseat, the soft laughter of a destroyed woman. Only now did I realize that Madeline hadn't spoken a word since we'd gotten in the car. "I was going to leave without saying good-bye," she said, "but you two are just so precious."

"Forgive my rudeness," I said. "I forgot introductions. Oz, this is Madeline Morton."

"I assumed as much," said Oz with coolness he surely didn't feel. "She's not helpful to your story."

"Apocalypses were our hobby," she said, ignoring Oz's barb. "Planning them was something we did instead of playing the piano and reading novels. Something we looked forward to for different reasons. And one of our favorite apocalypses involved the World Sanctuary and forcing the end of this age in fire and ice."

Our hobby. Madeline had only one playmate worth mentioning. But naming him, dead in another universe, wouldn't help my story either.

Oz smiled. "That's feckin brilliant. But my interests and your apocalypses aren't necessarily the same. Tell me more details."

"Such a smooth bluff," said Madeline, with the silkiness of a Vegas sex kitten, "but with such an enormous tell in your pocket, you're just flailing and failing."

So, the nunchucks hanging from his belt were a flail? I didn't know what that could mean, but Madeline seemed to, and Oz seemed to understand what she meant. "I'm not a rash man," he said, "and I don't make a final decision until necessary. Why don't we see if your plane is even there? Then you can tell me what I need to know to decide."

"My knowledge is exclusively for family friends and traveling companions," said Madeline.

"In the stories, you aren't the most honest of God's creatures," noted Oz.

"Right now," I said, "I think she's most trustworthy of the three of us."

Oz hit the gas, and again we were roaring down the road at speeds that only craft allowed, rushing toward a Schrödinger's plane on which my life hinged. "You should see to yourself," said Oz. "First-aid kit and blanket are in the back."

I reached back, but Madeline said, "No. I've done enough to keep you alive. No more delay. Get me out of this thing, now."

"OK." That sounded like the old Madeline, only after all that had happened it seemed off-key. I pulled the doll from the back and, like a practice child from a prenatal class, I placed it in my lap. "What did you mean when you said you were about to leave?"

"Nothing," said Madeline. "A bad joke. I'm trapped here. Examine the back of my head."

I turned on the overhead light in the car. Oz just grunted something about "*night sight*," and pushed harder on the gas.

The fit was good, but I found the thin line in the wooden head. "There's a panel."

"Good. Wait—when you open the panel, you should see a box inside. Don't touch the box. Once you move it, I won't be able to talk to you."

"Can I just break the box?"

"No. You'll need your knife."

I still had a small blade tucked away. "I'm drawing my knife, Oz."

"Good on ya," said Oz. God, he was a confident bastard. Or maybe he didn't give an Irish feck about his life.

I slid open the panel and saw a finely engraved square face of what I assumed was a cube. "Touch one of the lines in the center of the square with the point of your knife," said Madeline. "Not there. Touch another. Again, another." The pattern was so confusing that I couldn't tell if each was a different line or the same one in a different segment.

"Follow that line," she said. I drew my knife along the engraving. Too fine, too easy to lose myself in the faint overhead light. The vibration of the car alone would put me off track, and the bumps on this old road had me flying up against the seat belt. "I'm not sure . . ."

"Go into combat mode," Madeline suggested. "It'll give you the necessary obsessive-compulsive eye."

"I'm a little tired right now." But before Madeline could point out how she must feel, I added, "I'll try that."

"The cube has some energy and some temporal craft. Try to call on it through the knife."

I shifted into combat mode, and at the same time I reached into the cube as if reaching into the land for energy. Suddenly, the trench of the line seemed larger and clearer, and the tip of the knife followed the groove without threatening to jump at every bump. Also, the wood seemed resistant to further carving or scratches. That might be a problem later.

The engraved line wound like the path of a maze, intersecting other lines as it went. Other areas had whorls as if this were a huge fingerprint. It seemed to have more length than the area of the square face could hold. A fork in the path led me to a dead end.

"Trace the line back," she said. "Take the other way."

Finally, the line reached the top edge of the cube, and stopped. I kept the point of the knife resting on that spot. "The line goes over to a hidden face here," I said.

"Which face?" she said.

"The upper one."

Madeline spoke with a sharp military precision, reminding me that she had been a Gideon. "Mentally—not with your knife—mentally mark the position of the line. Then remove the box. Follow the line on it with your knife to a six-line nexus. It should be on the upper face, so you won't be mapping the entire cube. Don't just skip to any nexus; it has to be the one connected to this line. Press the point of the knife into the nexus. Make it penetrate. Use craft if necessary."

"What if that doesn't work?" What if I couldn't find it, or took the wrong way in the maze?

"Try to put the box back in. If that fails, you can try what you like. Don't fail."

I took in some deep breaths for more calm and focus. They didn't help much. I memorized where the line ended, counting the other lines between it and nearby whorls and other distinctive features, then took away the knife. On the left and right edges of the box were two shallow indents for fingers to get a grip on it. I turned the doll's head up to get the assistance of gravity, and with finger tips pressed in the indents, I pulled on the box. It didn't want to give. I dried the cold moisture from my hands and pressed harder. I lost a bit of nail and skin, but the box came loose.

I followed the line on the top face, focusing further and further in, until I had the illusion that I was in an empty tunnel of fading twilight with no beginning or end. *Madeline, I had no idea.* After what seemed an eternity, I came to a round chamber with a choice of five new ways. In the middle of this bare intersection lay a black feather, and nothing more. I was at the nexus. Now to get the fuck out.

An illusion, I remembered. I left combat mode, and that snapped me out of the prison of the dead. After a moment of near panic, I saw my knife was at a nexus. I pressed the knife in, stabbing the cube. The wood didn't give. I worked the knife. Nothing.

Couldn't try conventionally any harder—I might let the blade slip. I'd need craft. All my relevant spell images and words involved flesh instead of wood. Hell, it wouldn't be a modern adventure without graphic surgery on the conscious hero, and though I wouldn't really be cutting into flesh, it still seemed awful.

"*Wound it*," I said. I pressed in. The surface broke, and the black static of the Left-Hand way jolted up my arm.

Then, nothing.

"Madeline?" I called. Had I destroyed her too, or had I trapped her in her own nightmare, back in the box forever? I shoved the wooden cube back into the doll. "Madeline?" Nothing, but I couldn't tell if it even connected. I'd gotten a little blood on the cube—had I short circuited it? I wanted to scream like Orpheus at my failure.

Rabu gave a soft bark. I took the cube out again, and it came easier this time. I examined it for new lines of attack. Maybe the bottom where the neck had been. I aligned my blade with it.

"Scherie, don't." I almost didn't recognize the voice, so faint and without manifestation. "I'm free. But I have been hurt."

"I can help," I said, not sure I could.

"No," she said. "I've spent spiritual centuries in there, and I've faded.

In real world time, I would have departed long ago, but I've been stuck here. I'm so tired of all these greater and lesser hells."

I felt a spiritual breeze whirling, ready to disperse the last of Madeline. Of course she'd lied about leaving; that was the only reason she'd wanted to get free.

"Going now."

"The fuck you are," I said, surprising myself.

"Going . . ."

"You're staying right here. I am utterly damned because of you, and we need you."

"Maybe you should . . ." suggested Oz.

"Mind the fucking road," I said. I could call spirits, but I'd always been better at expulsion. Someone else would be a better shepherd. "Rabu, make her stay!"

The dog whined.

"Do it!"

Rabu barked and growled. Madeline responded in some terrible tongue that sounded pure Left-Hand, and the spiritual wind rose in defiance, smelling of blood and ozone.

"Not another word of that!" said Oz.

Rabu bared his teeth and barked once more. The wind calmed, and a black-lit aura settled around the box, as if bound to it, but not within it.

Silence.

Then, from the aura, a voice strong and cruel: "I shall not forgive you for this, Rezvani."

"Add it to my list of unforgivable sins," I said.

After a minute of the most unpleasant silence in my life, I returned to my non-Madeline concerns. "I need to charge my phone."

Oz gave me a dubious glance.

"To call the pilot." Just to have her ready, not to see if she'd already returned to India.

"Right then. Use my cord in the glove box."

My phone was the same I'd had in Istanbul—rated for extreme environments—so it had survived the combat with just a single crack across the screen. With the phone hooked to the charger, I called the pilot. The phone functioned fine, but no answer. I left a message, and prayed she hadn't deserted me.

I didn't try the other calls I wanted to make—to Dale, to Pandava. I wasn't stealthy, so Oz would know.

I grabbed the first-aid kit. I seemed to have some craft for healing. "Rabu?"

The dog turned up his nose at me like I was bad dog food, then went back to licking where Cornaro had hurt him. Was he still pissed at me about Madeline? Maybe he could heal himself. I couldn't see him ever going to a vet, even if Kaguya-san had tried to get him to one.

I kept Madeline's cube close. I put the blanket over my legs, and began to clean and heal my more serious cuts.

"You cannot keep me here," said Madeline.

"I know," I said. I'd known it when I'd done it. I didn't care.

"I'll regain my strength and depart soon. The dog's *geas* will fade, and I will finally leave."

"Fine." I wasn't going to apologize. "You'll have had some time at least to think about it. What's a few more minutes, after what you've been through?"

More silence. I continued to treat myself.

"You're shaking," Madeline said, softly. "Tell the Irish savage to turn up the heat."

"Mind your arse on the way out," said Oz.

The heat was blasting; I wasn't shivering from the cold. My act of soul destruction gave me the shakes in ways that physical killing never had. Everyone died, but most spirits survived. "Was his soul really destroyed?"

"Didn't it feel that way?" said Madeline. She would know; she'd done it before.

"This has to stop," I said. "This corruption. What I did . . ."

As if Rezvani had thrown the cube into the fire, Madeline's rage flamed within her again. "You would have let him keep both of us, and the fucking dog. You would have let him kill your child."

"No, I . . . Madeline, it's horrible."

Another tectonic shift in Madeline's soul. She saw the act as Scherie must have—the abomination of desolation. She also remembered the House of Morton's gentleness to her despite what had been done to it. What would the House have said to her now, if she were Scherie? And then the words were there, like a recording from so long ago. "Oh my dear, dear girl. You are right. Horror is my job. If there had been a way, I would have spared you."

"Madeline?" Scherie stared at her, looking as incredulous as Madeline felt.

Oh, surely that wasn't what she'd meant. The shame of such feeling. She should leave right now. But she couldn't depart without knowing one thing. "You came for me. I was in the box, and you came. Why?"

Scherie reflected. "How many times have you helped me, Madeline? How many times have you saved my life?"

This was almost too easily dismissed. "That was for my own designs. I wished to be an ancestor deity. For that I needed descendants. It wasn't kindness. It was artful cruelty. And I'm done with it."

"Bullshit," said Scherie. "We become what we pretend to be."

"The dead don't become anything," spat Madeline. "We're dead."

"Do you now think you're an ordinary spirit?" said Scherie, throwing Madeline's own words in Istanbul back at her. "You're family. My family. I could never leave you in hell."

Stunned by the statement's truth, Madeline had nothing to say to it. But, if only for a moment, it gave her something to think about instead of pain and leaving, or instead of the look Oz had given Scherie, as if Rezvani had spoken an oracle, or an epitaph.

PART IV

FROM ARMAGEDDON'S SIDE

But, beloved, be not ignorant of this one thing, that one day is with the Lord as a thousand years, and a thousand years as one day.
—2 Peter 3:8 (KJV)

To see a World in a Grain of Sand
And a Heaven in a Wild Flower
Hold Infinity in the palm of your hand
And Eternity in an hour

—William Blake

TWELVE

When the call came, the young woman known as Meg was in Amsterdam. She was not in the red light district, De Wallen, that relative Disneyland of domesticated and regulated sex trade (though she still could have done plenty of her work there). Instead, she stood in the dark corner of a moldy room in an abandoned warehouse overlooking the IJ lake north of city center. Blond, blue-eyed, petite, a living doll, she appeared to belong there. No one saw her as a threat.

A small film crew prepared to capture some very unpleasant things for a discerning audience that found such acts sexually exciting. The unpleasantness was going to be done to a man brought here from Nigeria. It would be available only on a film of extremely limited distribution—uploading it would cause a great deal of trouble.

The man, though terrified (that was part of the thrill for this audience), was not resisting or trying to escape. He merely shook now and then with bed-rattling violence. One might compare him to an animal strapped on a vet's cold metal table, but this was a human being, with a human's full awareness of what was going to happen next. To the extent mundane Europeans were cognizant of this form of compulsion, they called it voodoo, though it was no such thing. This was craft suasion and an abuse of the power of command.

Two men armed with FAMAS assault rifles kept the area secure, while a woman with straight bangs and dark short hair worked the suasion craft. The Dutch were sloppy about keeping their craftspeople busy. Idle hands were the Left Hand's workshop, and a workshop was literally what this little movie was funding: an alchemical lab dedicated to the Left-Hand secrets. The film's purpose gave Meg another claim of jurisdiction, should the locals squawk.

Having mentally sketched her judgment upon all present, Meg was just about to go on to the next part of her work when she heard the call: *Come and see.* Did she have time to finish here? Yes, the necessary few seconds would not be the hinge of fate.

Afterwards, a forensic profiler would call the work Meg did "disorganized." Meg called it "Starry Night" in tribute to her favorite Dutch painter. The profiler would note that the rifles remained unfired, and that the wounds were all from knives.

Meg left the scene of the filmmakers' crime with the Nigerian man, the only survivor, who was now shaking so hard that she had to support his weight. He was still suggestible, so she suggested he forget the whole thing (like she would when she had time) and go to the *Oikumene*'s safe house near the Anne Frank museum, where his return to the mundane world would be the Pythia's problem.

Despite her usual excess of bloody enthusiasm, her response had been just and appropriate. This group had done the same and would do the same to dozens of men. A traditionalist, Meg preferred to liberate women from such situations, but her principles were universal and absolute. She held the office of Megaera, and when not taking furious vengeance on the high sins of the Left Hand, she stood against all sexual subjugation by craft.

Now to hop a helicopter to the air force base at Leeuwarden and borrow a jet and pilot for the first leg of her ride. She would not be returning as usual to her mundane artist's life and shedding her office (and most of her consciousness and memory of it—just too disturbing for day-to-day life), for the call had been for the highest of Left-Hand sins, and she had many miles to go if she was to be there on time for her next commission.

Ali was with her children in Madrid before the call came. Her children included her biological ones, the craft children they played with in this park, and all craft fledglings everywhere. Her dark eyes and sad smile were as gentle as a Spanish Madonna's, even when she saw the couple wearing American shoes who had come to steal the children from her.

Children were supposed to be sacred and inviolable in the craft—the Earth itself seemed to hide and protect young craftspeople. But they were a temptation to the evil minded.

The American couple didn't look evil. Like all Americans, they just seemed too earnest and needy. But what they earnestly needed were her little ones.

Sometimes the Left-Hand crimes against children also fell into Meg's sphere, but this wasn't one of those. This couple planned to misuse these niños like batteries in series for their tiny sparks of craft. The end result, however, would be the same as with the victims of conventional child predators: a lonely grave for little bones.

The couple assessed her with a glance. They would only see a woman in her thirties carrying a few extra pounds in her curves, and not a threat. They reached out to grab a child.

"Go home," said Ali. Without hesitation, all the children ran off, one just escaping the snatch of the American woman's hand. The couple looked about as their victims ran off, then approached Ali, intending violence. *For shame*, thought Ali.

Then Ali truly spoke. One voice gave infants their first commands. It resided so deep in this couple that they would not be able to resist it. It was their mothers' voice, and Ali spoke with it. She told them, "*It's nap time. Lie down*," and with the same lack of hesitation as the playing children, the couple obeyed her, lying down with smiles on their faces at the long-lost call to rest.

"*Sleep, my little ones.*" Then Ali sang them a lullaby that brought their hearts to rest as well.

Ali's office, Alecto, was gentle in its unceasing anger. Her office was her obsession: the protection of the fledglings. But that also meant protecting the world from the great Left-Hand sins, lest practitioners or mundanes cease to need or want children.

She returned to her apartment and, even as her son and daughter ran into her open arms for a hug, the call came: *Ven y ve. Come and see.*

She phoned home to let her parents know that they'd need to take care of her biological children for the next few days. Her family only knew about the clerical job she held for the craft section of Spain's Centro Nacional de Inteligencia. "Working late," said Ali. "I'll be back soon. Love you." She then departed for the east.

When the call came for Tess, it was after midnight, and she was digging in the backyard of a house in darkness and steady rain. Her wet hair was the color of bone. Her old but unbowed, lean frame meshed its skeletal features with thin hard cords of muscle that stretched against her skin as she heaved spade after spade of muddy dirt and clay from the ground.

The house's owner came out, a middle-aged man in tank top and boxers. "What in hell's name are you doing?"

"Digging for the men and women you killed," she said, as mildly as commenting on the bad weather.

"You're crazy. Get off of my land."

"I'm the law," she said, a slight Scandinavian sing-song creeping into her words.

"Then get a warrant."

"Not that law," she said. She bent down and retrieved a long bone, which she pointed at him in accusation. "They were your guests."

She stared at him and allowed her face to flicker between its Teiresian forms: man, woman, skull. It wasn't all craft; she'd had to make some medical changes to assume this office.

The man sat down hard. "For God's sake, it's been twenty years."

"That too was part of your punishment." She didn't add that she preferred the cold case, unsolved by mundane authorities and ignored by local craft. This desperate practitioner had imprisoned and tortured his guests until they'd given up their secrets and hidden assets, and then he'd killed them. But he hadn't been able to enjoy what he'd gained or to sleep at all well for two decades. He'd lived alone in guilt and continual fear.

She knew all this with the certainty of powerful farsight. More than helping her find her quarry, it enabled her to precisely tailor her justice.

The man closed his eyes and opened his arms wide. Having kept him waiting so long in self-torture, Tess spared him any further delay, and left him with his victims. Her office was Tisiphone, and in her own time, she had avenged.

Come and see, said the call. Roll up and see the greatest fucking show on earth. But the ineluctable ire of Tess would not be rushed. Though she might be last to get the call, she had made her plans days ago; the office of Tisiphone had its own farsight apart from the summons. With her two fellow Furies, she'd be there in time.

Grace Marlow hadn't tossed their weapons down the abyss, though Morton might have meant for her to do that. Assuming some steadiness in the Sanctuary's position, they'd be coming back nearly this way. Despite the urgency, she worked methodically, wrapping and anchoring their weapons in a camo tent, then activating the tent's rescue chip for locating later. If the gateway closed before she could follow, so be it—she'd stand guard here as long as needed.

Survival wasn't just short-term decisions.

Finally, Michael said, "That's good enough," and she agreed. She stepped onto the ascending stairs that began the bridge.

When she'd crossed the flat bridge path over the chasm, her radio crackled with static. "Morton, Michael," she said, in normal voice. Nothing. No visible threat, so now was the time to call aloud. "Radio out."

A moment passed, and the other two repeated, "Radio out." So this Sanctuary very much preferred electronic silence. They tightened the distances between them, and Grace dropped her stealth. They were going to be on this long stairway for a while. She'd heard that the Sanctuary of Albion was a roving set of gentle green hills in the Cotswolds or the Lake Country, depending on its mood. It wouldn't do for a servant of the Crown to be daunted by this different scale, but a Sanctuary was in the end a place built by losses, so she wondered at how much the earth must have lost, and what that might mean.

She also marveled at the strange sky. Neither sun nor stars were visible; instead, the heavens were gently illuminated with a pale, yellow-golden light that did not change. Nor did it seem to warm anything.

They continued on the stone path until it reached the bottom landing on the side of the mountain. There they stopped to confer. From the landing, the stairway turned right to hug the mountain's face and ran up to a half landing and the first switchback.

The Sanctuary's border sheltered them from the gales outside, but the profound, windless cold felt like they had crossed into outer space, and neither craft nor mental discipline could compensate. She was more concerned for her husband. He had kept pace, but that wasn't what worried her. Michael always had the look of Peter O'Toole with an eye patch and some meat on him, but now he was O'Toole's Lawrence of Arabia, pale and a little lost.

Another consequence of his spirit leaving his body was that he'd been motionless with a very low heart rate, and that meant possible hypoxia and frostbite. It didn't help that Morton's air bubble had been absent at the same time.

Something carnal might help his return to his body, and only one such activity would be appropriate here. "Major, you should drink something." One of the self-heating broth packs might help him both physically and spiritually.

"Yeah," said Morton, "this is a good position for a short break."

Grace helped Michael with his pack. Shoved between his pack and its frame was a long and narrow tube enlarged at one end, as if it held a bridge cue for a pool player. She had nothing like it in her equipment, but the length and shape were extremely familiar. She pulled it free and held it out before Michael. "What's this?"

"Ah, shit," said Morton, "is that what I think it is?"

Michael stared at it, uncomprehending. "I didn't pack it."

Grace opened the tube at the enlarged end. It was the Endicott sword.

"God damn it," said Morton. "No weapons."

"I thought I'd left it at Leh," said Michael.

No deception in his voice, but that only made the situation worse. Michael was mentally out of it, and Morton didn't seem much better. He hadn't been this short with his nominal senior since Grace had known him, and out of respect for her and Michael he hadn't generally used the Lord's name in vain.

Rule of thumb: if everyone else seemed off their heads, look in a mirror. She had helped Michael secure his pack, so why hadn't she noticed this tube before?

"Major Morton, I think we may all be subject to external stresses."

Morton flashed his angry eyes at her, then comprehension seemed to dawn. "I was packing gear with you."

"Exactly," she said. "In any case, we're too late. If this place wished to bar the sword, it would have hit us by now." She felt the power all around them, and knew it could attack them if it wanted. "It doesn't seem concerned about this." She brandished her ice axe, which she hadn't dumped with her weapons. After all, it was just a tool, even if every tool was a weapon.

"Still, that's weird," said Morton.

"Yes," she agreed. Whether some preternatural force was trying to help or hinder them, this sword legerdemain still ate at her. But the craft was full of such mysteries, and the worst mistake on this climb would be paralysis.

"From here on out, defensive spells only," said Michael, seeming to recover himself and his usual authority. "Maybe hostile intent is the real problem." Well, they'd find out.

They started up again. Though easier than climbing in the open, going by stair was still a workout. At least Michael's leg seemed to be doing better, falling into a more natural rhythm. The individual stairs usually had several paces between them, making the ascent less steep but longer. They would pause at the switchback landings to assess and catch their breath, and perhaps rehydrate or eat something. The air seemed to be getting less thin and warmer as they rose, which made absolutely no sense scientifically.

They reached the last long flight of stairs, which was fortunately more of a shallow rising, curving path than the steeper inclines that had come before. Ahead was a final landing, and nearly perpendicular to it, an elaborate, Tibetan-looking gate with high stone walls to either side of it. As they approached, something was coming into view on the landing; she and Dale drew monoculars to get a better look, while Michael merely stared intently.

Guardian statues stood at the sides of the gate, acting as its caryatids. They were not the usual demons of the compass points, but two stone skeletons, whose skull grins in profile gave them an absurdly happy look. One held up a wooden sword, and the other a wooden flower. "Lord and Lady Death," she whispered.

The skeleton statues glowed in craftsight, and their power seemed more than the usual threatening illusion, for below them on the landing were real human bodies. No obvious wards in place though.

"I count four down," said Michael. "Not obvious what killed them. Probably spiritual."

"Their hostile intent?" asked Morton.

"Perhaps," said Michael.

"Were they trying to get in, or out?" asked Grace.

Michael looked at her, then back at the bodies. "Unclear," he said. "Let's go."

Grace summoned her stealth again, and the three of them double-timed up the remaining stairs. Despite lacking firearms, they stacked on the gateway automatically, lined up against the stone wall from where the nearest of the guardian statues marked its end. This entrance had already demonstrated its potential as a fatal funnel, and they'd treat it as such.

Up close through the fish-eyed view of stealth, Grace saw that the bodies on the landing were poorly frozen and had gone bad, like meat in her cheap freezer at university. They wore simple clothing, probably homemade, that wouldn't work even as effective undergarments for these conditions. Not very combat ready—maybe they'd been stripped. But if her team tried to investigate the corpses in detail, they would be vulnerable out here in the open, and these bodies indicated that might be a very bad plan.

Morton reached the palm of his hand out and, without touching the statue, ran it up and down along its height. No response. He gave a bump to Grace and she bumped Michael, and Michael bumped back indicating readiness, which she passed on to Morton. Then, Morton was around the statue and through the gate, protective spells ready, heading to the right. She swung around and went inside to the left, feeling only a little static as she passed the line of the statues. Michael pulled security in the entryway to cover them, probably with a prayer of command at ready. All this was performed with preternatural speed and intensity.

The Monastery complex stood before them in sharp, hyper-real clarity, a hodgepodge of structures built with money for knowledge, and whatever Family estate funds these prospective monks brought. Most importantly, no visible hostiles.

"Status," said Michael.

"Clear," said Morton.

"Clear," she said, scanning her perimeter again.

Though they were now at a higher altitude, the temperature was considerably warmer than it had been outside or on the bottom of the stairs—perhaps just a little below freezing. In the far distance to the left and right were the points where the gates to the Pakistani and Chinese sides should be, though those areas were obscured, hazy with wards, as if arriving from the Indian side closed those other routes to them.

Closer in, the smaller buildings, averaging about twice a person's height, were an architectural history lesson. They included a beehive-shaped stone hut of an early Irish monk, a small Classical Greek treasury shrine, a modern geodesic dome, and a Gothic cathedral in miniature with walls of crystal and semiprecious stones. Also, the Monastery grounds had several modern storage sheds for whatever supplies sustained it.

But all were unlit with either mundane or craft power. "I'm seeing nothing out here," said Michael. "Follow me."

He went straight ahead to the largest building, the one whose colorful front and curved roofs resembled a Chinese or Japanese temple. He was moving again as if untroubled by injury. By mundane standards, it may not have been tactically sound to leave all the structures between the gate and this monastic hall uncleared, but since his injury, Michael's craftsight had become incredibly powerful, and the information they wanted was almost certainly in that central hall. Still, she and Morton carefully screened the right and left flanks, spells at ready.

Despite Michael's apparent confidence, he had the sense to stop at the entrance on the side of the building facing them, a red double doorway, again with statues of Mr. and Mrs. Death. Again, they stacked on the entrance, this time with Michael taking point. Breaking down the doors might be perceived as hostile, so Michael tried one of the lever handles. On three, he swung the door in, and they rushed across the threshold, Morton pulling security. No one greeted them.

The first room was a small foyer. Now that they were inside, the monastic hall had the distinct, inviting feel of a semi-sentient dwelling. The boards of the wooden walls and ceiling seemed translucent with golden light, as if the world outside were warm sunshine. The very air resonated with a low *aum* of energy.

This power felt like the opposite of that dead world she'd glimpsed in that bunker in Virginia. If this craft came from another place, that place so overflowed with life and beneficent power that some sloshed through to here. Perhaps it was a place where such generosity was itself power, and this monastery's way was followed by a whole world.

All very tempting—Grace felt a sudden strong desire to rest and warm herself. She ignored it. On the wall nearest her was a wooden grid like the letter boxes in an old post office, nearly full of shoes. Many of the shoes seemed both roughly handmade and faded old, and generally ill-suited for the climb.

"Boots off," she said. This was probably a temple space. Her gentlemen colleagues weren't idiots, but they could take the lazy route unless reminded, and she knew the demands of the world's sacred spaces better than they did.

"We may have a ways still to go," said Morton.

"Don't leave them here," she said. "Bring them tied to packs."

Having removed his boots, Michael looked down at his prosthetic foot.

"Don't be an ass," she said.

The foyer opened onto the intersection of two corridors, one running straight ahead and the other perpendicular to it. The one straight ahead led to another red doorway, with sliding *shoji* doors lining the corridor's sides. They slid open and cleared each *shoji* on the long straight corridor, searching for someone to tell them what was going on, saving what lay beyond the grand door for last. They mostly found living quarters suitable for monastics: one cot, one small table. All the rooms were tidy to the point of seeming unused. A few had round bulging crystal windows that looked out on the plateau as if the Monastery were an alien ship. Nobody appeared to be at home.

They finally reached the red entrance, which had things like golden bolt heads arrayed in a regular grid across both of the double doors. Craft energy flowed between the bolts. They did not stack on the doorway; instinct told them that even such "defensive" precautions would not be welcome here. Together, they pushed open both of the doors at once and went in.

Golden light, more intense than the foyer and corridor, streamed down through the hardwood walls, forming swirls and making the knots and rings look like the veins in an insect wing. The room was set up in the pattern of a meditation hall, familiar to Grace from her own training in meditational prayer. However, instead of cushions, shaped white stones apparently served as seats. The stones appeared to go down through the floor, perhaps all the way into the ground. Grace counted them: a double row of places on each side of the central aisle, making four rows of fifteen each, sixty total—the traditional number of hidden masters, though at the head of the hall on a dais were an additional three seats. In back of those, a large mandala hung on the wall, consisting of concentric colored circles which contained a six-pointed star, which in turn contained more concentric circles that grew smaller until reaching the vanishing point.

The shapes of the stones were all slightly different from each other, but all were empty. After all they'd gone through to get here, was no one left alive?

Dale saw the trick. It was one his grandfather used to pull with House to avoid unpleasant guests. He gave a signal to the others for readiness. "Hello, Monastery," he said. "We're guests, and it's not very polite to play dead."

As if the building were responding, the seats were suddenly

occupied—men and women representing the full spectrum of humanity, heads shaved in the manner of monks and nuns.

Dale whispered, "Thank you, Monastery."

The monastics wore loose black robes, dark as if to soak up even the energy of light, loose to accommodate absolute stillness in meditation. And these monks and nuns were absolutely still in their meditational poses, giving no obvious signs of life.

In the near-total silence, Dale whispered across the room to the others. "I don't see any sins. I mean, no sins whatsoever. Either they're dead, or whatever they've done, it must have been long ago. But then, where are the more recent pilgrims?" Also, he hadn't realized that sins could fade like this—comforting, though it was a limit on the Morton ability.

Another thing was comforting: here, his Left-Hand voices had stopped their incessant recitation of their damned way.

They waited for someone to stir in response to their presence. Endicott stared at the monks and nuns, then at the walls, then back again. "It's all in synch, the Monastery's energy, the breaths and heartbeats of the monks . . ."

"They're breathing?" asked Dale.

"About once a minute, in, another minute, out," said Endicott. "Very faint."

"When do they move?" he asked.

"As little as possible," said Grace.

"Eating? Shaving their heads again?"

"At their metabolic rate," she said, "they would need very little food, and their hair and nails would grow very slowly."

So these were the hidden masters. As Pandava had said, didn't seem to be doing much mastering. It was said that their farsight could plumb the depths of Lubyanka, but they had not intervened in the World Wars or the cold conflicts that followed. They must have known about Roderick too, and had done nothing. They had a peace that surpassed his understanding or remote desire. On death, would even an echo of their spirits remain? Probably not—they would make the final departure completely and at once, in their version of nirvana's dissolution.

No time for judgments. At the head of the hall, on a dais reserved for a monastery's head, sat a nun flanked by two attendants, all as still as the rest. The nun's robes, with their mix of dark and light brown, marked her as distinct from the black-robed others.

Marlow took point approaching this head nun, or abbess, while he and Endicott flanked her. The abbess's old face wasn't weathered (she'd come here young) but pale (the sun a distant memory for it). She had Han Chinese, not Tibetan, features, so she was probably no more native here than most of her monastics.

To the abbess's immediate right between her and an attendant was a ceramic bowl, painted like a stylized skull with its cap removed. The bowl's cranium-shaped interior was filled with crystal-like rice, with a golden handle protruding from the top. The emoting faces of some deity decorated the end of the handle. Dale didn't need to consult Marlow about this; he had seen something similar in his family's collection. It was a phurba, a ritual dagger used in Tibetan Buddhist meditation. Interesting—unlike the ones his Left-Hand relatives had used, this one was probably dull-edged, but it was another blade that this place didn't seem to mind.

As with the others, the abbess's eyes were half-lidded, unfocused on a point a few feet in front of her. Her skin was thin, but the bones seemed to glow beneath it with the same light that suffused the building.

"No sign that she even breathes once a minute," said Endicott. "Suggestions?"

Dale went over to the abbess and bent down to speak directly into her ear. Endicott and Marlow were waving him off, but Dale said, "I think I'll give one of these monks a good shake and see what happens."

The abbess's mouth gaped like a fish. "Do not disturb them!" she croaked, almost airlessly, moving nothing but her jaw. Then, eyes wide open and darting about, she whispered: "Where is your fourth?"

The question stung like an accusation. Where was Scherie now?

But the abbess spared him further consideration of this. "Pardon," she said. "First, greetings. It took me a moment to return to normal time."

Bullheaded Endicott plowed ahead. "Ma'am, what's been going on here?"

"Next, introductions." The abbess's voice now seemed to come from everywhere; she spoke in a panglossic out of the Monastery's structure itself. "I know who you are, of course. My name is something that I meditate on, and try to forget. My title is Eldest, so I have the duty of communication and leadership, though these may speed me to my end."

Marlow had more diplomacy than her husband. "How long have you been here, Eldest?"

The abbess smiled. "I was already here when Thomas Morton and John Endicott feuded, and Faust Marlow was trying to live up to his namesake." Holy shit, she was claiming to be over four hundred years old. In comparison, Roderick and Madeline had been children.

But good old Endicott wouldn't be distracted by wonders. "Ma'am, you have a stack of bodies at your door."

"And you've brought a sword to this place of peace," she replied, again finding the just right accusation. "The Monastery takes care of us. We don't interfere."

"The Sanctuary proper," said Dale. "Which way is it?"

But instead of answering, she said, "I cannot deny you access to the heart of the Sanctuary—this outer sanctum only is ours—but you're on a fool's errand. This thing will happen."

"What will happen?" asked Endicott.

"She didn't tell you." A flat statement. "This is Armageddon."

"We get that a lot," said Dale.

But Marlow asked, "The Armageddon of the Bible?"

"Yes," said the abbess. "Or the change of ages of Hinduism—all the same from our perspective."

"The pilgrims," said Marlow. "They've gone into the Sanctuary for Armageddon."

"Yes, very good," said the abbess. "The Sanctuary wants this Armageddon. Whichever way the pilgrims come, they have to pass through here to get to there. May I return to my meditations now?"

Marlow turned to address Endicott. "We've found what we need. Let's go."

Dale wasn't sure why Marlow was calling retreat, but her plan sounded right. They had surely eaten up nearly half of the forty-eight hours to the first possible rendezvous. They'd need to figure out a plan to get back to the extraction point, and they'd probably face combat.

"Agreed," said Endicott, seeming unduly relieved. "Time to extract?"

Dale checked his craft chronometer. *That couldn't be right.* It had taken them all night to reach the chasm, but since crossing the bridge and climbing up at least three hundred stories' worth of stairs along a long trail, only minutes had passed in the external world. Pandava's warning hadn't prepared him for this. It was like they were in a sustained combat acceleration. Not trusting himself, he showed his watch to his colleagues and saw their shocked faces as they compared it to their own.

The abbess smiled. "Perhaps you thought time would slow here, that this place would give us more life by skipping every other second that passes in the outside world. By cheating. But the Sanctuary has greater concerns then our span of years. As the end of the age approaches, time in the outside world will seem to crawl. Where the pilgrims have gone, the temporal flow is even faster. Armageddon will have all the time it needs."

No stops on our Italian road trip, not even for a minute, but we had to straighten ourselves up for FBO airport security. I had enough healing craft to stop any remaining bleeding. But to clean my face properly, I needed to look in a mirror, because I didn't want to ask for Oz's feedback in case he guessed that I was afraid to see my sin. Better to see it now; my crime's name could only be worse in the light of day. Maybe I wouldn't see it.

Using antiseptic wipes from the first-aid kit, I attacked my face with an economy of swift strokes, but the sin was already there, glowing at me, neither angry nor beneficent, but impassive and alien. It was shaped like two chevroned arrowheads, or two bodies of flying V guitars, pointing up and down and overlapping each other at their two base tips to form a stretched six-pointed star, with a five-petaled flower added at its center. All the other sin letters I'd seen seemed to speak their full names to me, but this sigil said nothing. Worse, it did not seem completely ugly, which frightened me more. Carved into me, I knew it would never fade. *Dale will see this.* What would it say to him?

I passed some wipes to Oz for his bloody hands. He had his travel bags in the back as well. He offered me a white Irish sweater, so I got rid of my damaged, bloody blouse. He changed his shirt. Pants could wait.

As Madeline wasn't expressing her current needs and I was uncomfortable with her spirit box out in the open, I put the box back in the doll, then put the doll in one of Oz's bags. I'd try to talk with her more in the plane. I shoved our torn and bloody garments under the seat. "We'll abandon the car at the FBO," said Oz. "The only people who'll connect us to it have other methods of tracking."

It was still nighttime as we approached Leonardo da Vinci Airport. Without any reference to the GPS or directions, Oz drove to the FBO area and right up to the security gate.

One of the two guards raised his eyebrows and wagged a finger at Oz. "There is peace now in Ireland."

"Not the old business," said Oz.

"Promise?" asked the guard with a rolled Italian *r*.

"And hope to die," said Oz.

"*Bene.*" The guard glanced over at me.

"Is her plane still here?" said Oz. The guard gestured, but I could see across the tarmac that the plane was there. Did that include the pilot? A little luck now would be nice.

We drove to the plane and got out of the car. My only baggage was Madeline, so I carried the bag with the doll in it. Rabu trotted two steps ahead, then stopped, sniffing the air dubiously.

Out of seeming thin air in the stealthiest style appeared a man and a woman, tall and continentally slim in Euro-cut suits, like missionaries for the Church of La Dolce Vita. The man smiled, while the woman smoked a cigarette despite nearby jet fuel.

Keeping my face as relaxed as possible, I looked to Oz, raising my eyebrows with a question. Oz gave the tiniest shake of his head, indicating I should take no action. So they weren't the Furies, I hoped.

"Signor MacCool?" said the woman. "You found her."

"Yes," said Oz, with a nod toward me. The *Oikumene* had been looking for me, so these two must be *Oikumene* agents. By their demeanor, they didn't know about the villa yet, but they'd be getting the word soon. Then all smiles would cease.

"*Grazie mille,*" said the woman. "Signora Rezvani?"

"Yes," I said. I couldn't insist on my rank, not with my current status.

"The Pythia has invited you . . ."

"Not now," I said, interrupting. "I have a mission. Maybe after that."

"She insists. Your safety, and the safety of your child."

I was tired of these vague notes of prophecy. "What exactly does my future daughter have to do with anything?"

"Daughter? You are certain? It is a girl?" Their smiles had gone tense. The auras around their heads took on a sickly hue, like something was giving them headaches. Was it Oz, or was Madeline still on the job from within the bag?

Of those two, it was Oz who joined the argument. "Tell the Pythia I'm going with her," he said. "I'll be responsible for her protection."

"We cannot permit it. She is very important."

"So ya say," said Oz. "*But please, oh please,* macushlas, *my darlings, let us go, let us go.*"

"Ossian, you shouldn't try to charm us."

All sorts of intentions flashed from them as they readied craft to catch me, maybe hurt Oz. Worse still, every instant we waited was another chance for their phones to ring and inform them of what had happened at the villa. Time for me to take the initiative. "Let us go or he's going to hurt the child," I said.

Oz's face made a transition that should have won an Academy Award. No longer the easy-going Irishman, he had the stony face and icy eyes of an assassin. "You shouldn't have been blabbing our business about like that. But I'll forgive you if it saves us words and time." He turned his gunman eyes on the *Oikumene*. "You heard her. One word from me and your precious girl child is with its evil ancestors."

Rabu was growling at them. I held up my free hand to keep them from trying something stupid. "We'll be fine," I said. "We have a deal."

The plane's pilot had opened the door. The pair of *Oikumene* looked up at her for possible assistance, but she shook her head at them. She had her orders, and the *Oikumene* had little presence in India.

"The Kindly Ones, for this they may come for you, Ossian."

"The thought crossed my mind," said Oz. "But they'll have to get in the queue." He signaled me up the stairs.

I n the plane, Oz's killer eyes were smiling again. "Well played."
     "But the Furies will be coming for you, too."

"Oh sure, the *Oikumene* will, once they tease out the true story. Deciding to go with you was always going to mean trouble with them. But the feckin Kindly Ones? I think not. Helping you is a much lesser offense than being you."

Oz went serious again. "By the by, don't use the F-word for your pursuers anymore. It may be shite, but the lore is that the sound of their name will help them track you."

We took off with all the haste our pilot could inspire in air traffic control. Oz gave me the courtesy of the bedroom cabin, and well, it was my plane. I tried calling India—Dale, Pandava, anyone. No answers. With a morbid compulsion, I kept checking on the silent form of Madeline's doll, which I'd left on the end of the bed, wondering if she had gone on to oblivion already. Rabu in turn was keeping a watch on me.

I was exhausted. Being passed out while the villa drank my energy was not the equivalent of sleep. I drifted . . .

"Perhaps I do not need to kill you."

I jerked awake, heart pounding. Madeline stood above me, not the doll, but her full manifestation, though a little transparent in parts, dressed in a simple white robe with the look of linen. A fine silver chord connected her ankle to the poppet. I couldn't guess why she maintained the connection—a swift spiritual kick surely would break it. I readied some invective in case her substitute for killing me was something worse.

"I have another solution," she said. She raised her left hand. "*Come witch, come wizard, come Indian powwow, come Left-Hand Mortons all.*"

As if they'd been lurking on the wing of the plane, the Left-Hand spirits appeared in their black-lit glory, wailing in some distress.

"Take me back," said Madeline, head bowed, arms open in supplication. "Swallow me whole. Leave nothing of me. Leave no memory."

More wailing as the dark mass dashed against the bedroom cabin walls like ocean waves in the land of the dead, and the airplane shuddered as if in turbulence while Rabu growled low in warning.

Madeline raised her head, lightning in her eyes. "Take me back. Or I will destroy you."

"We cannot," cried the Left-Hand ghosts. "Please, don't force us! You are abhorrent to our substance."

She jabbed her left hand out at the spirits, as if to call down their doom. With her lore, I thought she might be capable of it. Then, mouth open for some blast of exorcism, she paused, and for the first time since I'd met her, Madeline's eyes widened with doubt and wonder. She brought her left hand closer to her face, studying it intently. Only then did I realize that, unlike the spirits of the evil dead, she no longer had the black-lit glow of the Left-Hand way.

Oz rushed through the cabin door, his flail ready in his hand. "No!" I said, to whatever he wanted to do.

Madeline's eyes hadn't left her hand. "What am I?"

"Not us," said the spirits.

"I am not a good little dead girl," she said.

"Yes, not good," repeated the spirits, calmer, sterner. "But not us."

The Left-Hand spirits departed, leaving Madeline in quieter contemplation of herself. Oz went back to the main cabin, Rabu lay down on the floor, and I went properly to sleep. When I woke again, Madeline was still in self-study, peering at herself in a small mirror, something I didn't know a ghost could do. Freakish—I'd never seen her so obsessed. The silver thread remained connected from the head of the doll to her foot. I'd forgotten about that box. It and its gem were nearly as horrible as what I'd done. They could fulfill desires of eternal torture, and evil shouldn't have such easy tools. I pulled the box out of the doll; it came easily this time. "I'll destroy it," I said, not expecting a reply.

"No," Madeline said, breaking from her reverie. "Without the knife in it, it should still work. Bring it with us."

"You'd use this on someone else?"

"Perhaps," she said, with some of her old coyness. My hands gripped the box so tightly they went gray. Madeline sighed, a theatrical gesture for the unbreathing. "Only for the most deserving, and only for a short time. Not forever. Satisfied?"

"No." But I let go of the box.

Madeline stared intently at my face, then smiled with all her former malice. "Nice sigil. *In hoc signo,* destroy."

She was trying to piss me off. "I won't assist your destruction."

"Your lips say no, but your sin says yes."

Enough. I went into the main cabin, Rabu at my heels. Oz was awake. I checked my phone—still nothing from Pandava or Dale. I hit the intercom. "Pilot, have you heard from Colonel Pandava?"

"No."

"Do you know where she is?"

"No." I detected no deceit, but not my strength. But Oz said, "She's telling the truth."

"OK," I said to the pilot. "Where's the nearest airbase to the tripoint?"

"Leh, ma'am."

Wherever that is. "Take us there."

In an overhead luggage bin on Scherie's plane, the forgotten *Oikumene* sculpture beeped out a steady pulse to its craft-tied twin at Delphi. Scherie's one communication had left it in homing mode.

D ale, Marlow, and Endicott moved to confer at the entrance to the meditation hall, away from the abbess. The room distorted with Marlow's stealth, and the soft light smeared around their bubble like the outlines of a golden eye. Dale heard Marlow echo his own thought in a low voice: "We have a problem of too much time. Leaving the Sanctuary now will expose us to our pursuers and the elements for too long. We should wait this out in one of the smaller buildings."

Endicott pointed a finger toward the back of the hall. "If this is even a minor Armageddon, then it's what we've been looking for. This is where we should be. We should go farther in."

"Not without Scherie," said Dale. *Not without at least saying goodbye.* Their separation suddenly seemed profoundly, mortally foolish.

Marlow jumped on this with surprising eagerness. "Morton is right. We will need her for a ghost fight of that scale." They'd also be facing unknown enemy and friendly forces, and perhaps those who'd gone before had weapons, but no need to quibble about details. "If she has found the proper craft in Italy, we can return here with her later."

"I don't like the idea of just resting up here until we retreat," said Endicott.

I don't like the influence on us of these immortal lotus eaters and their home, thought Dale. Aloud, he said, "That leaves one area of further forward reconnaissance. I think I can find the gate to the heart of the Sanctuary. Then, maybe we can look through, see if a later return with Scherie is worth it. There's some risk, but if the abbess isn't full of shit, Pandava has already guessed what we know so far."

"We'll talk to the abbess and try to distract her while you look," said Marlow, giving Dale a fully loaded glance. Dale hoped that meant that she'd also distract Endicott from his quest for Armageddon in the Sanctuary's heart while Dale peered ahead.

"If we see something urgent, we head back down the stairs now, whatever the risk," said Dale, trying to preempt a decision by Endicott to jump into whatever battle he saw.

"Otherwise, we can rest and recharge before leaving," said Marlow.

Caught up in their momentum, Endicott nodded. "OK. Let's go."

Marlow waved away their stealth, and they marched down the center of the hall back to the abbess. This time, Dale noticed that a few of the meditational stone seats were empty, which troubled him, but he didn't have the time now to work out why.

Endicott immediately took up the role of inquisitor. "Ma'am, why do you want—"

"We want nothing, Major," said the abbess.

"Why does the Sanctuary want Armageddon?"

"Certain fundamental questions need to be answered again. Those answers will determine the shape of the next age."

During this discussion, Dale sidled to the left and raised his battered, bruised, and somewhat skin-stripped hands, feeling for a boundary of further uncertainty, a gateway into the deeper Sanctuary, the place where all those pilgrims must be going. As he turned about, he spared a quick look at Endicott, who looked a little sickened at the abbess's New Ager talk mixed with his precious Armageddon.

Dale needed to focus more on unfocusing. He closed his eyes for a moment and disconnected all his senses from the immediate, then opened his eyes again. He now felt the path with a sharp sureness. The heart of this Sanctuary was behind the abbess, behind the bull's-eye-like mandala on the back wall. He crept steadily forward, up the steps of the dais to the left of one of the abbess's acolytes. The ancient bell to the monk's right was tarnished, but not dusty. Neither the abbess nor her acolytes reacted to Dale's movement; the abbess was talking about the Tao of craft, while the acolytes had never left their stillness.

Dale reached out and touched the mandala wall hanging. Here, definitely here.

"You don't want to look there," said the abbess, not even turning to look at Dale, but no deception in her voice.

"Why not?" asked Dale.

"The sight disturbs peacefulness, and calls one to action," she said.

Taking that as permission, Dale's fingers found the invisible seam in the wall hanging, and pulled it apart. The mandala divided like a theater curtain on rungs hidden in the ceiling, the design breaking into two semicircles as it opened on an enormous round hole in the hall's rear wall.

The hole didn't open onto the outside of a Himalayan plateau. Instead, before him was a vast green valley, viewed from a height, as if the inner gate were on an overhanging precipice. It was cinemascope with a round frame. "I've seen this before," he said, keeping his friends posted while he tried to assess the situation. "It's like one of California's farming areas. No, that's not it." He'd been on duty somewhere, probably in the Middle East.

Dale took out his monocular. This much of what the abbess had said was true: in the nearest part of the green valley below, a great craft battle was lining up, the greatest he had ever seen or even heard of. To his right and left glowed the craft of hundreds of living practitioners and thousands upon thousands of ghost soldiers, dwarfing the scale of the conflict in the American Sanctuary. The outline of wooden-walled camps marked the core ground of each side. An ectoplasmic metal glint of sunshine struck his eye, which meant some of the spirits wore armor and that they were therefore impossibly old.

He could not identify any individuals with certainty, but the forces to his left (was that the west?) had a black-lit glow—they were Left-Hand path.

The abbess seemed to speak louder, though Dale couldn't tell whether she was answering Endicott or reading his own thoughts. "What did you think this battle was about? The Left-Hand way is the great question of the age. All sides are welcome here."

Too welcome. He was dangerously tempted to step through and join the cause. But the armies of living and dead weren't yet fighting—

there might be time. As if to confirm Dale's instincts, the view shifted slightly. The entrance wasn't constant, and he couldn't see the area immediately on the other side of this gate. No, not a good idea to cross through unless they meant serious business.

The shift of view brought some ancient-looking ruins to his attention, below and to the far right on a small hill. He focused in. It reminded him of the archeological tell where he'd killed the Persian sorcerer and had been cursed in return, starting the chain of events that had led him to Scherie. Like that tell, these ruins below were a place of power, and they had a distinctive though faded craft signature, radiating in white, black, red, and pale green. He remembered seeing this odd pattern before, in Israel, passing through the Jezreel Valley on the way north to the border, only the place below him had no sign of modern road or dwelling.

Then it finally clicked. Oh shit, these ruins were an echo of the tell of Megiddo, the place of Armageddon. He wasn't going to say that to Endicott, not just yet.

"Behold," said the abbess, "the Kurukshetra, the plains of Ilium, the Tain's last battlefield." *Shit.* She'd left out Armageddon this time, but Endicott would get the idea.

Dale turned to advise immediate departure, but not fast enough: Endicott had come up onto the platform and was approaching the gate. Dale moved to stand between Endicott and his goal.

"You're blocking my view, Major," said Endicott.

Grace caught up to her husband. "Michael," she said, seeming to grip Endicott's hand with more combat intensity than affection.

Endicott hesitated, then turned to face his wife, a pleading look on his face.

Then, the voices in the dungeon of Dale's mind exploded in unison: *Gotcha!*

A dozen hands, cold and bloodless and black-lit with Left-Hand craft had reached out from the seeming thin air, catching Dale as he spun in the gate's direction to face the threat. The hands gripped him like steel bands by his ankles, wrists, torso, and neck. The world smelled of human rot, and the shouting mental voices were too loud to think over: *Call witch, call wizard!* they urged him, drowning his flailing efforts at craft. It was the fear that had haunted him since childhood. His own personal monsters had finally come for him.

Scherie! he thought, but in less than a heartbeat, they pulled his consciousness into blackness and his body across the gate's boundary into the heart of the Sanctuarium Mundi.

G race and Endicott didn't hesitate. Not caring what the Monastery threatened, Endicott drew his sword as he ran after Dale, shouting a prayer of command: "*In Christ's name, stop!*" Grace raised her ice axe and yelled, "*Zombies delendi sunt.*" They went through the gate. They had good justifications, but they'd acted on that often fatal instinct and principle: leave no one behind.

The last thing they heard from the meditation hall was the voice of the abbess: "We do not interfere."

W hen the intruders had all gone through, the only sound in the hall was the high cruel laugh of the small abbess. Part of her delight came from how she had won. The choreography had gone perfectly. She had not lied, but she had completely deceived. Detecting no deception and with no time to lose in pursuit, they didn't stop to further investigate.

But her greater joy was in anticipation of when the other gateway would open, and her beloved would spring forth again in full to embrace her.

Left alone in the private cabin, Madeline again pondered the mystery of her missing Left-Hand glow. *I'd like to talk to someone about this disturbing abomination, but who?* She was fiercely proud, but sometimes, she reflected, pride wasn't even a decent vice. It was simply the knowledge that no one else could help.

No one? Among the dead who might have such knowledge, most were part of the Morton Left-Hand spirit creature of which she had been the dominant will. They wouldn't share with her now, so to hell with them. Bits of her father's thoughts had been in there with her, and she'd avoided them then. Lest he should come back together, she wouldn't now seek his memories.

One memory of his she would like to have, about one ghost whom Madeline had never seen, within the collective creature or alone: her mother. She still assumed that Mother had been destroyed by her father or consumed beyond recognition by the Left-Hand revenants. But she had never tried to summon her. In her life at the House, she'd felt too much shame to let Mother see her. Or, when she'd felt better, she didn't want Mother to return to that place of pain. Later, she'd tried to forget her mother a little more with each new body.

No such excuses now. She stood before the cabin's mirror, and manifested as she'd been in her first body, in that simple high-waisted black gown of her teens. *Mother, I summon thee. Come witch, I am your daughter true.* Nothing. *I must be crazier than they say.*

No matter. Mother's wasn't the spirit that would give her a reason for continued existence. Cornaro's and Ossian's apocalyptic expectations, the Sanctuarium Mundi, and the practitioners involved—the style was all too familiar. If she was correct, then her descendants were in terrible jeopardy, worse even than the world's peril, but she didn't fool herself: pure hate alone would be driving her forward. The mundanes liked to think that spirits only stayed for unfinished business, and like every stupid idea, it was right when it most annoyed her. *Just as long as I don't have to admit to Rezvani that I've changed my mind.* She would protect, but mostly, she would revenge.

B efore landing, when we'd again have Pandava listening to every word, I conferred with Oz about the things I'd rather not share with the Indians. (When shut, the cockpit was designed for passenger privacy.) I remembered not to use the F-word. "The ones who are after me. I need to know about them."

"They don't advertise on the telly. That's part of their dubious charm—they're a mystery." He poured himself a whiskey from the bar and sat next to me. "But here's what I know, for all the good it will do. One's the young maiden. She's got a young one's taste for absolutes plus a nasty bit of psychopathology. One's the matron, meaning she can command like a parent, but her kills are gentler than the maiden's. The last is an old one, with an old one's experience and patience."

"Which one will come for me?"

"If you're lucky, the matron," he said. "If not, well, it's a rare thing, but they may all three be after you."

"Is there any way I can change their minds?"

"No one ever does."

I remembered how the *Oikumene* had used their name as a threat. "Can't we call the Pythia?"

"That's a common misapprehension," he said, drawing out the long word. "For sure, the Pythia can invoke them, but she doesn't control them. She can't call them off. I suspect it's because their extreme power comes with a price of extreme dedication to narrow and rigid rules of retribution. In a way, it's like the Church's craft. It doesn't come from Family, and doesn't pass down to family. Given their duties, it could only be so."

I'd gotten his talk going, but he was avoiding the real question. "Any way I can stop them?"

"If for some reason you killed those three, another three would rise up against you. It's an office, and it never quits."

But what if I only want a little more time, to save my husband, my friends, my child? Then killing the current trio of Kindly Ones might make sense, if I had the stomach for it. Oz didn't need to know these thoughts. We were a long ways now from Europe and the *Oikumene's* home ground. Maybe that would do for now. I had something else to think about: what to do when I got to Leh.

W e landed at Leh in the late afternoon and stepped out into the cool highland air. Pandava was on the tarmac to greet me, Oz, and Rabu. She stood apart from her staff, probably shielding them from whatever undiplomatic language would be used. She frowned with anger, which made me angrier. This woman had certainly set things up so the mission could leave without me.

"Ms. Rezvani, you were supposed to return to Delhi," said Pandava.

"Where is my husband?" I started quiet; my rage would need room.

"He and your colleagues have proceeded with the mission."

I think she expected me to be surprised and befuddled by this. God, she didn't think much of me. "Take me to their position. Now."

"We cannot do that."

"You can, and you will," I said.

"You have no authority . . ."

"I have the only authority that matters to you." *I can kill you and everyone here, and destroy your souls besides.* Despite my previous reluctance, my anger made it seem very possible. How could I be more damned than I already was?

After a silence that was a second too long, I said, "I have someone you want." Only I wasn't sure I did.

But with her usual sense of the dramatic, Madeline appeared, standing at my left. "This communication failure is getting me excited."

"You survived!" cried Pandava.

Seeing her unrestrained joy softened me, but only for a moment. "When can we leave?"

"If you want me," said Madeline, "you'll have to do what she says."

"You don't understand," said Pandava. "The helicopter that inserted them was destroyed."

"Destroyed how?" I said. "I can control the weather." Or at least I thought I could now, thanks to my baby. "We cannot wait." No need to tell her the other reason for urgency—that I suspected pursuit, even here, and I needed to help Dale before dealing with the F-troop.

"You still can't ascend the mountains."

"I have help." Easier to say that than to mention my own new knowledge.

"Her presence changes everything," agreed Pandava. "But if we fly too close, either the Sanctuary will destroy us, or the Chinese and Pakistanis will."

"Not your problem," Madeline said. "I can pilot."

"You can?" I said. Then, I remembered her as the red-haired Gideon, Sakakawea, back when she was trying to kill me. "Oh, right."

"You should go forward to Siachen base though," Madeline said to Pandava.

"Why?" asked Pandava, in a tone that said a glacier above twenty thousand feet would not be a pleasant place to be.

"Because I say so," said Madeline. "Because I may need you in your Family's role—yes, I know about that. Because you'll have to get closer if you expect to bring force to bear on this wannabe apocalypse."

"I assure you," said Pandava, "this is quite serious."

"Serious? Sure, a change of ages is a serious power grab. Don't complain. This is the true mission you wanted in the first place. Once the personal vessel you've promised me is at the Sanctuary with Rezvani, I can report back to you, real-time intel. Move what forces you can up to Siachen now. I'm sure you're prepared to clean up this time."

Pandava stared at Madeline, then me. Oz and Rabu had remained completely silent, unprepared for this, and I wondered what they'd do now. But after her face went blank in one of her little "checked out" moments, Pandava nodded her assent.

In the western sky, unseasonably heavy clouds were threatening. A storm was coming. *Great, as if we need another bad omen.* I had a sudden dread that we were going to be too late, not only to save my friends, but to stop some vast awful thing from happening.

However great my dread, some delay for preparations was inevitable. We huddled by a space heater in a deserted, cold office reserved for those not officially present. Oz and Rabu still seemed to be along for this ride. As Madeline had predicted, Pandava already had planes and supplies lined up to intervene in force if possible, so our small needs weren't very difficult. I got some new knives.

Madeline was arguing again with Pandava. "Yes, we will be bringing weapons."

"That place has just killed Hima for coming too close with a helicopter," said Pandava.

"So what's it going to do to me?" said Madeline. Then, more seriously. "We'll be moving in too fast for it to stop us, and I have some distractions in mind."

"We also have the personal vessel for you," said Pandava, skipping to the next item on her checklist. "Wood reinforced with alchemical alloy."

"Wood?" Madeline's face twisted in disgust. "I don't want another fucking poppet's cage just now, unless it's flesh. We'll need three bodies. Very fresh, or fresh frozen will do."

"You misunderstood the nature of our offer," said Pandava.

"No, you did," said Madeline. "I'm not like those others you have bottled up. You offered me physical mobility. Give it to me. It's part of the distraction. I know you have the materials here. Siachen is notorious."

"*Accha*," said Pandava.

"Keep the manikin in reserve, as I may need it despite your particular talent." Madeline turned to me and said, "Give Pandava the gem box we took from Cornaro."

"I don't think . . ."

But Madeline was again talking to Pandava. "So I'll be able to find you quickly. Be ready to drive my chariot."

When Pandava left, I asked Madeline, "Can you sustain three bodies?"

"As basic puppets, I could animate many, many more. But you will be working with one, because where we're going you'll need that skill."

Now it was my turn for disgust. But my first objection wasn't the visceral one. "It's Left-Hand craft!"

"As if that should make any difference to you now. Ask Pandava and the Irishman. Ask the damned dog."

Oz just shrugged. "Eh. No harm done." Rabu gave a bark.

I changed the topic. "Not my first concern, but how will we get back?"

"Like I told Pandava, I'm the only sort of communication that works up there. I can at any time arrange the rendezvous to get you off the mountain."

For the first time ever, I saw deception in Madeline's spectral eyes, which probably meant that she wanted me to see it. I'd already begun to wonder about how we'd get close enough to the spot, weather control or not. "We'll work out the details en route," I said.

"What do you make of this apocalypse?" said Madeline, in a seeming non sequitur.

"You don't seem to think much of it," I said.

"Any Left-Hand con job usually has an apocalypse in it, if only as a diversion. My family had a taste for plans that involved using an enemy Family's nature against itself, and Armageddon sounds like Endicott bait. That's the real hurry—we need to be up there before an Endicott does something stupid."

"Not much time then," I quipped, feeling slightly disloyal to Michael.

While Pandava was seeing to the last preparations, her subordinates brought us the bodies from the morgue. Madeline claimed hers first. Her choice wasn't surprising. The corpse had been a Sikh, turban still wrapped about his head, tall, thin, and relatively fair, though now darkened with the freezer burn of the glacier.

In a moment, she'd ceased to manifest next to me and was in the body. I'd thought I'd seen Madeline in every terrifying aspect, but this was a new chill. While she possessed it, its conventional decay would slow to a crawl, but she didn't bring the corpus as close to the space heater as Oz and I were. She'd left me a woman's body. "Easier that way the first time."

The uniform had been deracinated, but I guessed that this was a practitioner from Pakistan, probably killed in an infiltration. Something very sad about her, even in death.

Two ghosts of the fallen hovered protectively over their bodies, and one stood menacingly next to Madeline. Rabu growled at them, and they disappeared. *I am sorry, but we are desperate.*

"Think of it as a drone," said Madeline. But that only made it worse.

"I'm trusting you about the baby," I said.

"She'll tether you," said Madeline. She paused, raising a finger for silence. "Hmm. A moment of déjà vu there. But not oracular. So go ahead, do it."

Remaining seated, and with the will and words that I'd learned from Madeline, I reached out into the corpse. It was the most horrific sensation I'd ever felt. I was wrapped in rotting meat, senses deadened, and the lungs in my own body felt smothered.

"Farther in!" said Madeline.

I pushed my will, my spirit, into the body. Though I'd viewed its cloudy eyes from the outside, I could see out of them clearly now.

"Good," said Madeline. "Move an arm."

Slowly, with inexplicable pain, I moved her right arm.

"Outstanding," said Madeline. "You can leave her now."

The abbreviation of my practice was strange, but I didn't question it, and I rushed back into my spirit's natural home. "That's it?" I said.

"For now," said Madeline. Again, her unconcealed deceit radiated even from the corpse. No practice walking? Something besides the bodies was rotten.

"Oz," said Madeline, "this isn't in your family's skill set, correct?"

"No. In those stories with the corpses, we're the other fellas."

"What stories with corpses?" I said.

"There's a set of stories common to both India and Ireland about a man hauling a big possessed corpse from glen to glen. The man ends up with important knowledge." So that's why he didn't have a problem with this. What then did Pandava expect from dealing with Madeline?

But Madeline interrupted my thoughts. She abruptly sprang at Oz and gripped his sweater in her dead hands. "What the fuck is your business here, MacCool?"

"I'm—"

"Stop," said Madeline. "You were about to blarney blather."

"I wouldn't—"

"Ah," said Madeline, raising a blackened finger. "Remember—I know your Family's history, and its gifts. Take a deep breath. Now, the truth please. And you might as well explain the details to Rezvani. The price of your ride is the truth. We don't need you anymore."

Oz smiled joylessly. "Well, as you put it so nicely." Madeline let him go.

But he just kept smiling, as if he hoped I'd change the subject. I'd just assumed Oz's helpfulness; Madeline had been sharper. "The MacCools have been craft fighters since ancient times," I prompted, guessing from Irish myth.

"That's right, for starters. We were fighting the Celtic version of the Left Hand. Their dead were thought demons, their living were called giants. But most of all, people whispered of the Left Hand as Serpents." He gave me a wink.

"I get it," I said. "So Saint Patrick . . ."

"A very powerful Christian craftsman from the continent. My namesake, Ossian MacCool, joined forces with Paddy and drove out the Left-Hand Snakes."

"The gifts," said Madeline, impatiently.

"The gifts," said Oz. "You see, we MacCools, we're gatekeepers."

"What gates?" I said, dreading his answer.

He nodded at Madeline. "Gates like the one herself's brother opened a few months ago. Gates to other worlds, most of which have become hells."

I went cold at his words, thinking of how close we'd come to a disaster in Virginia. "You open those gates?"

"Ah, no, generally that's a bad idea. I'm sorry for being too late to help you against Roderick. A breach is usually a slower thing, coming with all kinds of screaming precognitive notice."

"Spilt milk," said Madeline. "Please continue."

"My family has certain tools," he said. "Patrick brought them with him to Ireland from the *Oikumene*, which was falling apart, and gave them to my family for safe keeping. We use them to fight whatever comes through those gates. The *Oikumene* lets us keep them in return for the occasional favor. That's how I had the pleasure of your acquaintance—another favor for the Greeks."

"Tools," repeated Madeline. "One would be the flail that never fails. Explain it."

"It fights the spiritual masses, like what herself used to be," he said, nodding again at Madeline, "or the Yasukuni doomsday machine that you picked apart. For a time, the flail can even hold off the full spiritual weight of a dead world."

"What about the green sand?" said Madeline.

Oz sighed, as if he regretted having all his tools revealed. "Yes, I have that too. Retrieving some more of that was what brought me to Italy. It'll keep a specific area clear of spiritual intrusion."

"Our friend Oz here apparently thinks something is trying to get through. Why would you think such a nasty thing, Oz?" she sneered.

"Recently there's been interest in all my gifts."

"Meaning not just the flail and the sand," I said.

"Meaning also my Family's talent for opening a gate."

"You just said . . ."

"Yes, it's a very bad idea. But these are very bad folk. Roderick has inspired them, and my touch of farsight is screaming that some wee bit of hell is knocking at a gate, giving them an opportunity. With me and my tools, they think they could let just the right amount of demon in."

"But they don't have you," I said.

"There's still the knocking, and a gate to be fixed. The signs point to where you're going, and every third word you say rings like an oracle. I'm with you to the Sanctuary."

"Thank you, Ossian," said Madeline. "That'll do for now." She must have been distracted to be even dismissively polite.

But now I had a question for the last member of our team. "Rabu, what about you? Do you really want to go with us?"

Damned if he didn't seem to think about it. He looked at me, then at Oz, then at the door, then at me. He barked, once and low, and moved closer to me.

"In that case, dog," said Madeline, placing her dead hand on Rabu's head. "It would be best if you controlled the third body."

Perhaps she conveyed her meaning spirit to spirit, for Rabu growled, but then barked again, once and low. Then, we planned our mission, while Madeline spoke to the rest of us in ghostly privacy and explained why we didn't need to worry about our return.

We flew the small, slow-flying Dornier Do 228 utility plane out of Leh, leveling off at nine thousand meters. Oz and I were supercharging with oxygen for what was to come. We were outfitted with all the equipment we'd need, including full face helmets and gloves, so no skin exposed. Instead of protective clothes, Rabu had a pressurized dog crate.

With Rabu resting in his box and Oz reading a book of Yeats, I joined Madeline in the cockpit. Hands on the stick, she grinned like Death itself. "You look horrible," I told her.

"Shannon was a great pilot," she said, and I guessed she was referring to Sakakawea's real name. "Shame to waste those skills on these dead nerves. I'm beginning to see the advantages of artificial materials."

Thinking of Sakakawea reminded me that I hadn't seen Madeline in field combat since she'd tried to kill us in the American Sanctuary. Then, she'd been skilled enough to command elite Gideons. Now that she wasn't mixed in with the older Left-Hand revenants, she seemed to be more of that person again.

Oz joined us up front. "You should know one thing, a decision I've made. I won't be entering the monastery hall with you. I'll cover the door and the approaches."

"What?" I didn't want to question Oz's courage out loud, but I wondered why he'd stop when I would need him most.

"My business isn't yours, but it is feckin important. Also, we may have company a-calling."

The Furies? "You think they're still following us?" It seemed absurd.

"I told you. They never stop," said Oz.

"Good on you," said Madeline. "One less mortal coil to worry about."

I looked again at our coordinates. We were now above where Dale had been dropped, moving in the direction of the tripoint. Below us all around for hundreds of miles was the ground of Shiva, god of yogis and cemeteries. I had a strong, sickening sense of foreboding.

"Feel that?" said the Madeline corpse. "It's time."

I used words like those Dale had used in the Appalachians, projecting them out with a touch of power. *"I am Scherezade Rezvani of the House of Morton, protector of the American Sanctuary. I invoke that compact. Let us see you. Let us in."* Oz and Rabu were doing the same, trying to access this place through their respective Sanctuary privileges enough at least to see our target. Madeline remained silent—the dead's access was different.

Someone's invocation worked, at least in part. Just ahead on our flight path, the plateau of the Sanctuarium Mundi flashed into visibility.

The next minute, the plane blew up.

Endicott ran through the gate and found himself in midair, falling. Trained instincts and spiritual practice took over, and he hit the ground after a short drop in a three-point crouch, sword still out at ready. Some further flash awareness of his situation kept him from rolling with the fall. He was on the knife's edge of a precipice, all his weight forward, rocks and dusty soil giving way beneath him.

A hand snatched his pack and hauled him back from the edge. As usual, Grace had done better in matters of coordination and situational awareness. In the game of saving each other's life, she was too far ahead, but he wouldn't have it the other way, lest he ever fail.

No time for a thank you. Grace was already on the move. Long trails to the left and right sloped down to a series of switchbacks and finally ended in different parts of the valley. Grace was loping down the leftward trail with Endicott sprinting to catch up.

They did not have far to go. A triple line of the dead—not ghosts, but more meat-puppet zombies, blocked their way along the path. Others were farther ahead, moving with the artificial rhythm of craft-controlled things. They carried Dale above them strapped to a ladder, like a sacrificial offering to a god of decay, moving down toward the Left-Hand army. But he was still alive; Endicott's penetrating eye could see it.

Endicott shouted commands, invoking the Father, Son, and Holy Spirit, aiming particularly at the zombies holding Dale. But the meat puppets hesitated only briefly; they were powered by other wills. He reached for those wills, as he'd reached across Germany after the train bombing, but the practitioners were veiled. He felt the urge to reach farther, and farther, but with an effort of will, he stopped himself. The spiritual risk was too great. The temptation to dominate all had nearly overwhelmed him in Germany, and in this place of power, that temptation seemed as dangerous as ever.

No time in any case—they were nearly upon the lines of standing dead. Cutting around below or above to chase Dale was not an option; the slope was too rough and steep, and they'd be turning their flanks to the immediate threat. Grace wasn't waiting for other ideas. With sword and ice axe, they fell on their opponents.

The true folly of coming here without Scherie was brought home to him. Rezvani could have disanimated these nine corpses instantly, could have stopped the six carrying Dale before they'd gotten through the inner gate. And yet, for the first time, even more than in Tokyo, Endicott felt unleashed. Fighting here with Grace was absolutely wonderful.

The narrow path which delayed Endicott and Grace's advance also meant the enemy could not bring his nine corpses to bear on them at once without a lot of climbing. But despite their success in hacking off dead limbs, Endicott soon saw the futility of their own position. A quick glance ahead and below showed that the marching dead had delivered Dale to a larger force of zombies, living practitioners, and ghosts that had rushed up to meet them. Even as he hacked at the last line of zombies immediately blocking their way, he yelled down at those living practitioners, "*In God's name, let him go.*"

Nothing. His one eye saw a craft barrier against his words, as if they'd prepared for him. He could crack that barrier. As the last of the nine zombies fell, Endicott reached for the primal, irresistible power.

"Stop," said Grace, gripping his arm. "Michael, it's too much. You might not stop."

The power burned in him to be used, whatever Grace said. But then, from their rear, the thunder of horses, and the compulsion to command loosened. Grace and Endicott turned, weapons and prayers ready, and found themselves facing armored ghosts riding on spectral horses. These ghosts were the most substantial he'd ever seen, though their spiritual glow still marked them as the dead. They wore seventeenth-century clothes, with leather jerkins and lobster pot helmets.

The lead horseman drew in his reins and raised a bare hand, halting those behind him. "Hold, sir, madam. The armies of the godly stand ready below to aid you in retrieving your friend."

"We need to pursue now," said Endicott.

"Fear not. They have not slain him. But they will easily block your way on this path."

Of course, ghosts would know whether Dale was still alive, yet they were notoriously iffy on tactics. But Grace gave Endicott a nod, and he could see that pursuit down this path was hopeless. "What are they going to do to him?" he said.

"They may hope to corrupt him," said the horseman. "That will take time. Please, sir, madam, come with us."

They ascended the brief way back to the top, and Endicott had time for a better look at the place of their arrival. The entrance gate from the Monastery floated just out of standing reach above the protruding ledge where the two paths met. A higher ridgeline ran up to the ledge, and made a semicircular curve around it and the gate before continuing in its previous direction.

With the zombies gone, no other human forces were up here or anywhere above the plain besides themselves. But a pair of great saber-toothed cats, long extinct in the outside world, watched their progress from the ridgeline. Whatever weapons the armies below had, they seemed unconcerned with holding high ground. "Why isn't this place guarded?"

"Because this is where the pilgrims choose their way, Left or Right."

"But they came up here. And now you're here."

"You've been expected, Major." Farsight again. Endicott hated farsight, and the presence of the other side's meat puppets meant this time Left-Hand farsight had also been involved—a gruesome business. Sure there were natural talents like Roderick, but natural limits weren't respected by those evil practitioners. The freelance farsight of the Left Hand used psychoactive drugs despite the damage they did to a craftsperson. Endicott had heard of their blue lips, dilated pupils, and psychotic mental anguish.

They descended the Right-Hand path. Unlike the outer Sanctuary, the sun was visible here, warm and friendly. As they walked and the ghosts rode, the spirits sang, "O praise the Lord, all ye nations: praise him, all ye people. For his merciful kindness is great toward us: and the truth of the Lord endureth for ever. Praise ye the Lord."

Psalm 117. Then it clicked for Endicott. "You're New Model Army, Cromwell's men."

This seemed to make them uncomfortable. "He is not here. But yes, we served in Parliament's dragoons. Now we hope to serve another."

"What is your name, sir?"

"Colonel Henry Lambert, at your service." He introduced the other horsemen as well. The wonder of it. A year ago, he'd never spoken to ghosts. Now he was talking to men who'd been in the army of his childhood heroes. These spirits were old. The rules must be different here.

"Nice weather we're having," said Grace. Meaning that she wouldn't be talking about her High Church beliefs and her devotion to the Crown with these particular regicidal spirits.

In contrast to the bareness of the canyon-like wall of the valley and their path down it, the land below was green with farmers' fields, grass, and trees. Nearest them on the valley floor, banners flew and the troops not on the front line marched in the patterns of drill before the wooden palisade.

Grace discretely nodded a finger toward the rear of these forces. In the distance, a mammoth slowly lumbered across the plain. Endicott focused his preternatural eye. The beast was ridden by some body-painted cave shaman—a Neanderthal? That scene fit better with his understanding of Sanctuaries than the large gathering of living modern humans below.

Then Endicott noticed the details of the ruins in that direction, and recognized their four-colored pattern of radiating craft. He pointed excitedly at the site. "That's Megiddo! Or an echo at least."

Grace took his hand, calming him with her touch. "We should be cautious."

"Yes," he agreed. That made his neck prickle with the sense of pursuit, and he looked behind them. Someone was coming through the gate. Like the pilgrim they'd seen outside the Sanctuary, he was bathed in a protective aura, and instead of falling hard to the ground, he floated down along the guiding thread of craft. Pilgrims got a nicer welcome. Endicott turned away, not wanting to watch this pilgrim's intimate decision.

The gate itself seemed to have shifted slightly higher and to the left. That couldn't be good.

When they finally reached the bottom end of the trail, many of the living and the dead broke ranks to throng around them, while officers shouted at the front to "hold the damned line!"

The Endicotts, Marlows, and (to his surprise) Mortons took pride of place nearest them, with ghosts going back all the way to the late sixteenth century. Joshua Morton saluted him, and John Endicott stood at Joshua's side, armed with a different-looking sword than the one his living descendant wielded, as using the spiritual echo of Michael's sword might affect its material use as well. His father, mother, and grandparents on his father's side mixed with Grace's ancestors, Marlows going back perhaps to Kit Marlowe and Tituba. All Family hostilities were apparently forgotten here, and they all greeted Endicott and Grace with real warmth and delight.

The permanently dispelled Richard Morton was of course absent, but Endicott also didn't see Dale's father and grandfather. That was disturbing. Perhaps they were trying to help Dale. Among the living were lots of young practitioners, the residual glow of their pilgrim status still on them.

"So many," said Grace. "So much power in one place."

"And no one fighting," said Endicott. He turned to Lambert. "What are you waiting for?"

"Our commanders," said Lambert. "You."

Endicott's shock didn't stop his response; he needed to squash this idea right now. "I'm not pure. I'm riddled with Left-Hand craft."

Grace's eyes gave him a cut that said, *You're not leaving me alone in this job.* "I'd prefer to be on the front lines without other responsibilities," was all she said.

"All the signs point to you," said Lambert. "And it is you that the evil ones fear. You are the two witnesses of Revelation."

According to the Book of Revelation, during the End Times the two witnesses would oppose the Beast, aka the Antichrist. The Antichrist would kill them, and then God would call them up to heaven, dealing with the Antichrist at the Second Coming. The witnesses were roles that various people had pretended to in recent times.

In response to this conversation, Endicott's father, the general, had come closer. Endicott leaned in toward him until he nearly touched the ghost's desert camo and felt his disturbing chill. "This is cult nonsense," Endicott whispered.

"And a bit blasphemous," agreed Grace in a low voice.

"That's just what some of our fellow believers call you," said his father. "This is an international force, and these soldiers have plenty of different names for you, depending on their apocalypse."

"I look like the other fellow." Endicott remembered the conversation with his mother's true soul. Coming back to life after a head injury was right out of Revelation's description of the Antichrist.

"Hush, darling," said Grace. "That isn't very flattering to me." He was pretty sure she was teasing him; the only female figure associated with the Antichrist was the Whore of Babylon.

His father shook his head. "I told them you'd react this way to prophecy, but this just confirms it for them. And I suspect they want someone with your particular gifts."

"I don't like to use it," said Endicott, referring to his power of command. "Tried it, with restraint, on those zombies. Didn't work."

Lambert was now speaking loudly, presenting them to the crowd. "Two candlesticks standing before the God of the earth." He opened a hand toward Endicott. "You've seen the gates of heaven and returned. And you," turning to Grace, "saw him die and called him back. Have you seen your souls? They are very bright."

How had the story of his resurrection become so widespread? The dead must see a great deal. His father continued speaking to him and Grace in a low voice, and what he was saying wasn't helpful. "Maybe you aren't *the* two witnesses; maybe you're just the equivalent for spiritual practitioners. But if this is our Armageddon, you'd better hope you're something special."

"We aren't," said Endicott, thinking mostly of his own moral flaws.

"Right," said Grace. "But maybe it's worth taking command if we can get Morton back."

With that, the last door of a reasonable exit slammed shut. They would have to take command to save their friend. Endicott looked up to the heavens. *Please help us, Lord.* But instead of receiving an answer, he saw that the sun hadn't noticeably moved since their arrival. The miracle of Joshua at Gibeon was here, giving them all the time they'd need for battle.

The troops didn't wait for their acceptance. With wild enthusiasm and head gear tossed in the air, they hailed them with a roar of many names: Kalki and Kali, Maitreya and Kannon, Fisher King and Morgen, Death and Morrigan, Conquest and War, Good Emperor and Empress. They brought him a white stallion, and her a chestnut mare.

All spiritual special ops had basic horsemanship (never knew when it might come in handy in remote places), but Endicott sat particularly tall in the saddle, and the Marlows had hundreds of years of tradition in riding.

The crazed cheers only redoubled when they mounted their horses. Endicott spoke under the noise. "Grace, if they were waiting for us, what is the other side waiting for?"

Her mouth pursed in an O. "Nothing good," she said.

E ndicott rode with Grace slowly through the cheering troops, with his father striding close behind on foot. Beyond the crowd, the faded form of a woman in medieval armor raised her sword toward the riders. They worked their way to just behind the front of the line. There, from their mounted vantage, Endicott scanned the opposition, praying for his preternatural remaining eye to *see farther*, while Grace viewed the field through a monocular.

"I see certain traitors from MI13 and the Renfield that tried to kill us," said Grace. "And you?"

It took Endicott a moment to spot Dale, not because he was hidden, but because he was in plain sight. Then he spoke to his father. "General, is there a chain of command here?"

"Sorted, but I'm not one of the commanders."

"You're on my staff then," said Endicott.

His father gave him an insubordinate look, but said, "Yes, sir."

"Call a council of war to meet ASAP." With the sun standing still and watches not working, synchronizing action was going to be more difficult than for even premodern warriors.

"Yes sir," said his father. "There's a tent within our palisade."

"Good," said Endicott. He turned to Grace as his dismissed father trotted off. "Let's talk in private."

First, they ditched the outer layers of their climbing gear. They handed these excess clothes and their packs off to practitioners eager to make themselves useful, who took the gear back to the Right-Hand palisade.

Endicott and Grace then rode farther back behind the line to a copse of olive trees well out of earshot and, horses side by side, Grace threw up a bubble of stealth around them. Endicott asked, "That armored woman, that was Joan of Arc?"

"I expect so," said Grace, drily as ever. They both admired the Maid, but when it came down to it, a Catholic saint and Frenchwoman could not be their greatest hero.

Endicott finally told Grace what he'd seen. "They have Dale tied to the front and center of their palisade. Doesn't appear to be conscious."

"Laid out like bait," said Grace.

"We're like an ancient army, so I'm thinking of attempting a Gaugamela." That battle was Alexander the Great's crowning victory over a numerically superior Persian force. "With some adjustments of course," added Endicott.

Grace smiled at him. "You were paying attention in school. But you must know what that means. I have to play Alexander." Meaning that, like Alexander the Great, Grace would lead the main cavalry arm in the assault. He'd prefer her to play Roxanna, but no time for that. His urge to protect her was outweighed by her obvious qualifications: she had far greater horse experience.

"OK," he said. "But you're getting more than you bargained for. In council, we'll do things by consensus, but in the field, you're in overall command." He raised a hand to stop her protest. "Communications are going to be crap, so we probably won't even have a chance for con-flicting orders, but if we do, one person's orders have to have prece-dence. And I may need the restraint." *In case I try to command the whole world again.*

Grace nodded her assent. It might be their last moment of privacy prior to battle. So, though it wasn't professional, they reached across from their saddles and kissed, each with one arm about the other, not wanting to let go.

As Endicott's father had said, they found a silken tent behind the palisade, rectangular with rounded ends and as loudly colorful as any from a Renaissance fair. Inside it, the only illumination came from soft, flickering lamp light, so unless Endicott focused, he couldn't distinguish the material objects from the spiritual, as the spectral glow bled into everything.

Between the two support poles, the council gathered around a central table where a young woman dressed in the British uniform of a World War II air force auxiliary would position and move colored blocks indicating various units across a spectral map. As with the objects they handled, Endicott noted again how very substantial his father and the other dead were. Dale had told him that this was a sign of mortal danger, but perhaps here it was different.

It was good the officers had sorted themselves out in a chain of command, because as practitioners most everyone in this force had officer rank. That still left about two dozen commanding officers in attendance, which was too many for this space and for efficiency. The living commanders included an Egyptian colonel, a Brazilian general, a Canadian admiral, and a man that Endicott wanted to kill on sight: an infamous extremist practitioner whose nom de guerre translated as the Wrath of God, and who had aided several terrorist operations against the West. Yet here he was, on their side against the Left Hand. "What they do is against God's will," he said, as if sensing Endicott's need for an explanation.

Grace kept her eyes on Endicott to make sure he didn't act on impulse, but he'd been somewhat prepared for this. Dale had tried to explain this about the American Sanctuary: that the sides the dead took in its conflicts were in continual flux and often at odds with their actions in life. In the Sanctuarium Mundi, this contradiction was also apparently true for the living.

Endicott's natural panglossic made him the joint speaker for the co-command. The subordinate commanders all confirmed what the abbess had said about the signs indicating that this was a practitioners' Armageddon.

"We can't assume this is the Bible's Armageddon," replied Endicott. "That one won't depend on tactics; this battle may."

The command staff nodded their agreement, but Endicott's father said, "Sir, with all respect to his family, this focus on one person who may have gone over to the enemy is tactically unsound."

The Union-blue wearing ghost of Joshua Morton, official representative of the North American dead, gave Endicott's father a stern look, but Endicott preempted any disagreement. "That is why we will attack in force," he said. "Their ambush will fail along with their whole position. The best way to save Dale Morton is to win the battle as a whole."

Endicott laid out their plan, which consisted of something practitioners only did in legend—large formation tactics. Given the absence of non-spectral modern arms, Endicott and Grace thought in terms of the classics. They didn't have the numbers to chase the mirage of a double envelopment à la Cannae, and saving Dale remained an objective, so they proposed a variation on Alexander's tactics at Gaugamela. Their flanks would be bent back, inviting attack. The main body would keep the enemy's front pinned while Grace would lead a cavalry thrust from the near right wing to hammer the heart of the enemy formation and rescue Dale at the palisade (or knowing Dale, give him a chance to break out to Grace's cavalry).

When the council commenced working out the troop dispositions, Grace asked, "What can the dead do here against the living? What can the living do to the dead?"

The solidity of these ghosts had troubled Endicott as a harbinger of personal danger, but Grace had seen the tactical problem. The council confirmed that, in some earlier small skirmishes, the dead had demonstrated their liveliness. Their ghostly rifles and other projectile weapons remained more ectoplasmic than substantial, and a single shot would just give a living person a nasty burn. However, these spirits were substantial enough to hold material blades and strike with them. In turn, the ghosts here could be struck down by blades or fists, and if sufficiently hurt they would vanish and not return to the field.

Due to the Sanctuary's hostility to material weapons, the upcoming fight would be at least as much a test of preternatural power as mundane blows, so after finalizing their plans, Endicott brought them back to an urgent spiritual problem. "Though clocks don't work here, Left-Hand magic makes time a factor. We should start feeling their vampiric force soon, and the longer we delay, the weaker we'll get. Order your commands into these new formations. We attack on my signal, ASAP."

Dale woke up, seated in the dirt, wrists bound tightly behind him and tied to a stake in a wooden wall. *I suppose they could burn me as a witch, but that would be a bit hypocritical.*

His head had the muzziness of a tequila hangover, and his skin still crawled where the zombies' cold hands had gripped him. On the one hand, the Left-Hand forces had been waiting to catch him—a bad sign. On the other, though they'd injured him with some rough handling, he was still alive. They'd stripped off his pack and climbing outerwear, but they'd put his boots back on his feet. Now they seemed otherwise uninterested in him. What kind of trouble did that mean?

A living, middle-aged man approached Dale, pale and thin with a face like a predatory bird. The man's sins were legion; kidnapping, murder and attempted murder, and aiding in the destruction of spirits glowed with relative freshness. Dale had some guesses who this man might be.

"You're awake," said the man, and Dale heard clues of a London accent. So Dale's first guess was probably correct: a Renfield, perhaps the same Renfield who had tried to kill Marlow and Endicott and who had violated the Tomb of the Unknowns.

"I'm awake," agreed Dale.

"I am Mr. Cushlee."

As in Peter Cushing and Christopher Lee? All Renfields had taken pseudonyms since Stoker had outed them, but this was too much. Instead of commenting on Cushlee's name, Dale asked the obvious question: "Why have I been left so conspicuously alive?"

"Right," said Cushlee. "Can't kill you. Your ghost might snitch on us."

Yes, thought Dale, *I might snitch to my friends who you once tried to kill, and they won't pursue me here if I'm already dead.* Aloud, he said, "You aren't here for some change of ages, are you?"

"The new age doesn't pay in advance," admitted Cushlee.

"So what for?"

"Bit of this and that. Leading charter tours here from the Chinese and Pakistani sides. Also, had to get away from our customers. Your remote uncle's life-lengthening serum went bad with his untimely departure from this world, and his other secrets 'aven't been much use. You wouldn't be able to 'elp us with that, would you Major Morton?"

"I don't know anything," said Dale.

Cushlee laughed unpleasantly. "Deception, and poorly done."

"Back at ya. You've come for something bigger than guided tours, and it involves my friends."

"No matter," said Cushlee. "Just 'ere to offer advice. Some of our actives 'ave insisted you be treated with respect." He waggled his finger in the general direction of Dale's boots. "But don't get ideas. You're not the one we really wanted, and your face isn't worth a milli'elen, so don't be a bother. Be seeing you."

Cushlee strode away, issuing orders to the living and the dead that sounded more like suggestions amid the chaos of Left-Hand activity, leaving Dale to his unspoken true fear. This Renfield had been working directly for one man. If Cushlee was here, then some revenant of Roderick might be close behind.

Driven by this fear, Dale desperately started working on his bindings to free himself. The bindings felt like leather, and their knots would have pockets of air, very close to his skin. He started telling that air what to do, trying to make the knot breathe a little deeper and loosen a little more with each effort. The leather was just one of many obstacles between him and his friends, but it was the one he could address now, and his other craft skills wouldn't be very useful unless he was mobile.

No one paid particular attention to him; they were already forming up for battle. The numbers of living and particularly newcomers choosing the Left-Hand way disappointed him—the kids today. Seemed all the regions of the world were represented. Among the Americans were a man and woman from H-ring: Johnson of ENCOM and Van Winkle of PRECOG, the traitorous bastards who had messed up House's courtyard. Representatives of all the factions of the Mideast conflicts seemed willing to cooperate for Left-Hand power, along with a proportional number of Europeans, sub-Saharan Africans, and South Americans. But only China seemed to be on the Left-Hand side in a semi-official way, with numbers among the living that might match all the other regions combined.

As always, dead celebrities stole the show. Dale knew all too well that keeping the Left-Hand ghosts in line was like herding psychopathic cats. Napoleon was trying to form up a surly group of French and Italian practitioners, and those damned Nazi occult bastards, the Teutonic Knights, were gathering whatever Germans they could with less resistance. But Dale was drawn more to the Morton Family. Here, for the first time he saw the Left-Hand Morton spiritual mass individualized. They stood together, a disciplined-looking wedge with Joseph Curwen Morton at their point. Other Left-Hand dead had lined up to follow the Mortons, as they always had. No sign of Roderick though, and for once Dale would have preferred to see him here, just for certainty's sake.

Behind him and the wooden wall, Left-Hand farsight filled every spare moment with strangled cries and laughter, and with insane predictions: "probability the sun turns into a giant clown-faced wolf at ten to the minus tenth percent." Those blue-lipped wackos creeped him out. Also, he wondered where the bodies for the zombies came from. An obvious source would be pilgrims who came their way, but that seemed profligate in the extreme—one live practitioner was worth many meat puppets. Why didn't the Left-Hand side want more living sorcerers? Again, he suspected that the battle here was covering some other scheme of the Renfields and others.

"All lost, lost utterly." Dale flinched at the nearby voice, but it was only the echo of his dead father. Captain Will Morton was wearing the same formal dress uniform that he'd worn when he'd visited Dale in the rest home for the craft insane.

"Hi, Dad. What are you doing on the Left-Hand side?"

"The Morton name is my pass," he spat. The ghost's eyes cut to Dale's loosening bonds. "You're an idiot until the end. Just stay put, and maybe you'll survive a little longer."

This was Dad at his cynical worst, and not at all like the version who'd said good-bye to him with Sphinx in Virginia. "Which echo are you?" asked Dale.

"I'm the one who remembers everything." Madness flared up in his eyes. "You should have let Roderick have his way in the bunker. He might have destroyed himself in the attempt. Either way, then there was a chance that both the world and you could survive. Now . . ."

Grandpa manifested next to Dale's father. He was also in dress uniform, and it was odd to see him so formal. The older ghost said, "Dare is waiting for us." Strange that Dare Smith, codenamed Sphinx and Dale's biological mother, hadn't come herself. His grandfather had bloodshot, puffy eyes. Had the old ghost been crying? He'd seldom done that in life or death. "Grandpa?" asked Dale. "What's going on?"

But without another word, his grandfather led his father away.

Some subjective minutes after the war council, the army of the orthodox stood ready for action. Endicott had issued orders everywhere, but so far he hadn't felt the seductive temptation to use his power of command to speed things along. "I got it under control," he'd told Grace, before she'd taken her own position with her cavalry force.

Though most of the near valley was green with farmerless farms, the terrain directly between the armies was a reaped field, with stubbles of grain sticking out from the furrowed soil. The ground would not be a factor.

Their little army had nearly as many different uniforms as soldiers. With the primitive communications in a straight-up fight, commanding officers needed to be distinct and lead from the front, so Endicott and Grace rummaged through some of the bits of clothing and uniforms left by long-ago visitors to the Sanctuary, which appeared to be perfectly preserved despite the intervening years. Endicott wore a George Washington–style cocked hat and a bright blue sash over the clothes he'd been wearing, and Grace wore a bright red sash and a tall armored bearskin on her head.

As a child, Endicott had dreamed of fighting at the End of Days against the forces of Antichrist with someone like Grace. He'd been in better shape physically in those dreams, but his injuries seemed trivial compared to the blessing of being here, with her. Spiritually, he'd never looked better. He glowed like the pilgrim they'd seen. His sword was transfigured, shining like Excalibur, and instead of blending in, the chameleon material of his bared prosthetic foot gleamed in the stirrup. Even his eye patch made him look like Olivier's version of Lord Nelson, one of Grace's probable ancestors.

A wave of black-lit craft crashed on the orthodox line, and for a moment Endicott's heart stopped. This was what he'd feared—the enemy's first great parasitic tapping of their very lives. He tasted blood in his mouth. The Left Hand must have organized enough to coordinate certain dark spells. Countercraft spells worked to cut the connection, but the enemy would shell them again and again with this spell of attrition. As Endicott had told the council, this loss of energy put a premium on time.

The other commanders had assured Endicott that his mount and all the other horses were combat ready, but battle would be the true test. Grace was obscuring her part of the line in stealth until her charge, so Endicott gave the initial signal. "Forward!" he cried.

The center of the line moved ahead in perfect order at a stately pace. No crazed charge like the Highlanders at Culloden—they wanted to give the enemy time to come forward to meet them or to hit their flanks. To further motivate the enemy's charge, Endicott next signaled the start to his force's own spiritual warfare. Clouds gathered above the Left-Hand lines, obscuring the frozen sun, as weathermen brought winds, hail, and even lightning down on them. *Sorry, Dale*, thought Endicott. It wouldn't be fun to be hit with one's own spiritual gift.

Thunder roared like nature's cannonade. Left-Hand weathermen responded to the orthodox storms with bolts of cold and vacuum, causing some of the weakened advancing troops to topple over. Their deafening bolts cracked the air only inches from Endicott's head. Joining the general drain on life force were the more direct spells of black ops, which strove to split flesh from flesh and flesh from mind along the fine lines of being.

With the dull thud sounds of a punching bag, orthodox counter-craft spells and prayers deflected and diffused the worst Left-Hand damage, while the precog of both sides tried to penetrate each other's timelines, leading to a stalemate of uncertainty.

The orthodox would not use Left-Hand black-ops tactics here, which gave the Left-Hand an advantage. But that advantage would vanish when the two lines met, and enhanced combat craft came into full play. Then orthodox organization, discipline, and selflessness should overwhelm the chaos of the Left-Hand way.

As they advanced into battle, thousands of spirits were singing their war songs in a cacophony of fighting melody. The Americans under Joshua Morton bellowed the "Battle Hymn of the Republic," and some other peoples joined in that apocalyptic tune of righteous wrath. The Puritans were again singing Psalm 117, and bagpipers blared "Amazing Grace" with a touch of sonic craft warfare. Endicott briefly wondered what his wife thought of that. Cries of *"Allahu akbar!" "Bharat Mata ki jai!"* and *"Usuthu!"* roared out from up and down the line.

Astride his horse, front and center, shouting prayers at his opponents and repulsing their evil craft, Endicott thought, *God help me, but this is the most magnificent thing I've ever seen.* This battle was the way it was always supposed to have been—not the meat grinder of modern weaponry, but the spirit and the sword. He felt that some other spiritual force was protecting him, and like Patton and others, nothing seemed able to seriously harm him.

His father ran up to his side, firing his ectoplasmic M1. "Sir," the general shouted, "do you really have to be up there, such a plain target?"

"Yes, I do," said Endicott. "Report."

"There's enemy movement on the flanks, but they haven't engaged yet."

Before them the Left-Hand line remained quiet and still. Dragon banners with characters meaning "the two hundred million" and "the rulers of the East" marked the position of the living and dead Chinese contingent, the most organized force among the Left Hand. The references on the banners were from Revelation, and Endicott supposed they were designed to intimidate or confuse the Right-Hand Christians.

With fifty yards left, Endicott pointed his sword and ordered his line to charge. At the same moment, the Left-Hand center rushed forward to meet them. Good, thought Endicott. That should help open the way for Grace's hammer blow.

The lines came together with a clash of steel against steel, the screams of soldiers and horses, the smell of ozone and blood. The martial arts of the Chinese contingent were coordinated and often deadly. But the Left-Hand fighters were mostly young and inexperienced, barely trained though full of raw spiritual power that gave them a misguided courage. In twos and threes, Endicott struck them down with the power of the spirit, the cut of his sword, the kick of his bladed prosthetic toes, and his stallion's hooves. Those that could fled from his part of the field. His sense of the conflict's magnificence evaporated. This wasn't right; this was simple butchery, just more up close and personal than the usual.

Then, his eye found a familiar face—the Renfield, just ahead to his left and immediately behind the weakening Left-Hand line. No preternatural sight needed now to make him out clearly. Here was a worthwhile target who truly deserved his attention. Bastard probably wanted to be seen.

Endicott slashed his way toward the man who'd tried to kill Grace, who'd violated the sanctity of Arlington, and whose mercenary impulses had nearly destroyed the world. "I'm coming for you, Renfield!"

The Renfield stared back at him, jaw gaping open, arms outstretched and shaking as if trying to hold him off, a pantomime of absolute, uniform-soiling horror. Then, like a stage magician, he passed a hand over his face, and the show of terror vanished into a ghastly leer. He pointed his left arm emphatically toward Endicott's right, and shouted something worse than any spell. "Look after your missus, you bloody berk!"

From her stealth-obscured position, Grace Marlow's cavalry had a fish-eyed view of the center line's attack. Then, Left-Hand horsemen came out of their own stealth to hit her force on its far right, trying to turn the flank or get behind the orthodox lines. The visible portion of her force extended the flank, drawing the Left Hand still farther right. The combat sounded fierce, but Grace did not think the Left-Hand thrust had sufficient support to roll up the line.

"Wait for it," she said softly to herself. She wanted the perfect moment in the action, when her force could break the enemy into a rout, and they could achieve Morton's rescue and Right-Hand victory with the same stroke.

In an instant, the chaos of the battle crystallized, and she saw a weakness open up in the enemy's line. *Oh, I have you now.*

"Charge!" She and other practitioners dropped their stealth and all spurred their horses into a gallop. Hooves thundered. For half the distance to the enemy, they attacked straight forward, as if aiming for the opposing flank. Then, Grace signaled, and in a smooth evolution the living and dead horsemen wheeled forty-five degrees and dashed toward the gap in the line leading to the enemy's center-rear. There, from the red- and black-lit glows of their powerful, evil craft, the field commanders of the Left Hand seemed to be concentrated, and behind them, the palisade with Morton.

Cracks of craft and sizzles and snaps of ectoplasmic fire flew around them as their horses tore up the remaining ground before them. *Half a league, half a league, half a league onward.* Grace grinned fiercely. Where had this been all her life?

They hit the thin line of fighters that had been thrown up against them. She wielded her ice axe like a war hammer, like a tomahawk, like the scythe of Death itself.

Before her, the Left-Hand field command had dispersed. They were running away, just like Darius at Gaugamela. She could see Dale, arms bound behind him at the palisade. She yelled encouragement to her troop. "Forward, in the name of all that is good and holy!"

Then Dale's arms jerked out as if snapping some restraint, and he was waving them wildly. Waving her off, then signaling retreat.

In the same instant, all the dead and wounded bodies around her rose up from the ground. The surprise was total; no one had seen such a combined mass resurrection and possession during combat or even the necromantic power required for it. As one creature, the flesh puppets attacked her and her horse. Grace hit them again and again with axe, hands, and feet, but they were too many. She was flung from the saddle as the mare struggled, screaming in terror and pain as they killed it.

Grace sprang back to her feet, knocking away the encroaching bodies. To the rear, the other living horses had been struck with some panic and were bolting or throwing their riders. She heard words of exorcism chanted in some evil tongue, and many of the ghost riders that had been coming up to aid her faded away.

She swooped her weapon clockwise and widdershins, trying to keep her foes beyond arm's length. The living and dead enemy around her had formed a ring, and now they were drawing it in, weapons ready, roaring like animals at her, corpse throats as loud as the living flesh. The flesh puppets pulsed steadily with red craft. She parried a toying, trial thrust at her heart only to have a blade point slash her cheek and bloody her face. She might have been flattered. Against all tactical reason, much of the craft force of the Left Hand was focused here, on her alone. Her field authority was a mere improvisation; her husband could command alone with almost too much ease.

Then, in horror, she saw the unholy sense of it. Defying the noise around her, she shouted with all her preternatural strength. *"Michael, no!"*

Endicott forced his wavering eye to *see*. Grace was unhorsed and surrounded by meat puppets and living combatants. A wild mélange of spectral and material swords were raised against her. He could hardly distinguish friend from foe in the chaos. Her own dismounted horsemen were trying to break through to her, hacking at the enemy crowding around, but in the press of bodies they might hit her as well. Worse, all the death craft at the Left Hand's disposal was turning upon her, with sorcerers' hands stretched out toward her in gestures of power, their mouths opening to chant the first words of their evil spells.

No time to get to her. Endicott had to bring the fighting around her to a stop. He prayed a command. Nothing. He kicked an attacker away with the blades of his foot, then prayed again, in a louder, craft-infused voice. He thought he heard her calling his name.

They were going to kill his beloved. So he would have to go too far.

The urge to conquer the globe would take complete control of him, and he'd need to be put down like a rabid animal. But that seemed a trivial cost weighed against Grace's life.

He stretched out his arm, sword pointed toward Grace's battle, and reached for all the power this place would give him. As if it had been waiting for his call, the energy rushed up through him and into his command. "*In God's name, everyone stop!*"

There was a moment of absolute silence, as though he'd opened the Seventh Seal. Then a line, a rip in the fabric of all things, swept from his sword tip to Grace a hundred yards away, and exploded outward from her like stellar death. The ground beneath his feet shook, and the terrain broke as parts of the land thrust up and others collapsed.

Many soldiers fell to their knees. But everyone had stopped fighting, and those around Grace had frozen like statues, some mid-stroke with their swords.

Just a few paces away, the Renfield was still leering up at him, but with a new terrible joy. "You've done it now, my friend. You've broken the fucking free will of the world."

Cold dread cooled Endicott's need to kill this man—he had to get to Grace, or the thing he'd done would be totally in vain. He turned his mount and made his way as quickly as possible through the stilled fight. Even now, the soldiers on the flanks farthest away from Grace's melee were shaking off his command and resuming combat.

Oh God, what have I done? He had not repeated the sin of Moses he'd committed in Kiev. This was far worse, because he'd committed this horror in God's name. He had not lost himself to megalomania; the harm he'd done was far greater. In a way he didn't yet fully fathom, here in its spiritual heart, he had wounded the world to save Grace.

PART V

THE LIFTED VEIL

I'll be all aroun' in the dark. I'll be ever'where—wherever you look.
—John Steinbeck

For they are the spirits of devils, working miracles, which go forth
unto the kings of the earth and of the whole world, to gather them to
the battle of that great day of God Almighty.
And he gathered them together into a place called in the Hebrew
tongue Armageddon.
—Revelation 16:14, 16:16 (KJV)

The sharp edge of a razor is difficult to pass over; thus the wise say
the path to Salvation is hard.
—W. Somerset Maugham, taken from the Katha-Upanishad

CHAPTER

SEVENTEEN

As director of farsight at Langley, Eddy Edwards's business could be summed up by the framed Biblical verse on his wall: "For nothing is secret, that shall not be made manifest; neither *any thing* hid, that shall not be known and come abroad." But some places of power were meant to stay hidden from the mundanes, and the clear, high-resolution satellite images on his desk were a nightmare, the multiplied sum of all craft service fears. The Monastery of the Sanctuarium Mundi stood obscenely exposed before the world, its veil rolled back. That curtain needed to come down again, and soon. The three neighboring powers—India, Pakistan, China—would be rushing in, and the rest of the world would follow.

He and every person with the least bit of craft had felt the wrongness pass through the globe like a seismic wave. On his desktop computer, he viewed a security camera feed from the subbasement of the U.S. Capitol, confirming that George Washington's empty tomb had cracked.

From the Appalachian of the American Sanctuary came a rare message: "The nation's dead have ceased fire. Last time that happened was Pearl Harbor. Please inform if I should kiss my ass good-bye."

But according to the reports of his watchers, many governments apparently had taken the Sanctuary's revelation as an opportunity. Under the guise of eliminating the Left Hand, they were going after any practitioners who displeased them. In turn, craftspeople were breaking out from their holding pens, as some countries had never thought seriously about what control of practitioners entailed. Like last year in Kiev, open fighting had broken out within various craft services. In America, far too many colleagues were under supervision, house arrest, or confinement in craft-null zones cut off from any homeland, such as Chicago's Homan Square facility or Guantanamo.

Eddy didn't need watcher reports to know the last. With his abilities, he could directly see the suffering of each of his fellow practitioners. How much longer would he go along with this repression? If he wanted the odds, all he had to do was ask his own department.

Perhaps he would have already done something about it, but a subtler threat had him even more concerned. The repression was a symptom of a deadlier disease that, like many other invisible forces, was only observable in its effects. Since the revelation of the Sanctuarium Mundi, his watchers were reporting in terms of near certainties, 95 percents and higher, as if all the fuzziness was going out of the world. Some power was radiating out from the Monastery that they weren't seeing, and unless it was stopped, it would determine their future absolutely. Eddy could think of no greater tyranny.

The odds were as bad, the danger as great, as they had ever been. His only consolation: the four practitioners he'd saved for just such occasions all had trajectories that led to the World Sanctuary. But, even without resort to precog, he doubted he'd be consoled at the end of the day.

Fiery the corpses fell, and no shit, there we were, five bodies and one box with a dog. On precise cue, we had tumbled from our plane just a moment before surface-to-air missiles from both Pakistani and Chinese areas of control had blown it up. That was a surprise, as we'd expected the Sanctuary itself would destroy the Dornier.

The plane destruction part was what Madeline hadn't wanted to discuss in front of Pandava. Planes were expensive, and Madeline had never intended to return this one. Pandava had probably guessed that, but if she'd allowed herself to know it, she might have had to stop us.

Now we were in a HALO drop, or more like high altitude high opening, for we only had two thousand meters before we'd land on the mountain plateau. Oz, Madeline, and I were in wing suits in case we had to cover some horizontal distance to the plateau, but we were falling almost right on top of it, so we didn't deploy them. That was fortunate, because I doubted my capacity to have the wind move Rabu's box very far as it fell.

During our fall, I was spiritually present in a flaming corpse, in some ways more present there than in my own body. Rabu would be similarly tied to the other unoccupied and blazing human body, and Madeline didn't care if her meat puppet got a little cooked. Only Oz was fully resident in his own flesh. Anyone with craftsight would see the power, the flames, and the seeming death, and not bother to attack or pursue us further until it was too late.

Through deadened senses, I still felt the terrible pain of burning. "More than a karmic cost—a test of your bona fides," Madeline had said.

Though half of me was in flames, the cold cut through everything, doubling my agony. Worth it. We'd enter the Sanctuary by landing right on top of it, just like the Germans had taken Fort Eben-Emael in Belgium. But I had to concentrate, maintaining my presence in the corpse.

In a rainbow of craft colors, mountain spirits were flying up from below to assail us, apparently not deceived by our possession antics. But the ground was coming up faster. A triskelion pattern of paths led up to gates in the walled plateau. On the Indian side, dark spots resolved into bodies. Oh God, Dale's?

Seeing that on top of everything else made me lose myself, lose track of who I was in the fall. A living body (mine?) was heading right for the tip of a spired roof. Hard to care, except something inside was tugging at me to stay tethered. Oh right, baby. Sitrep: WTF, Mommy!

At the last possible moment, Madeline yelled, *"Now!"* reaching directly into my mind and snapping me back into myself. Oz and I deployed our chutes, and I triggered the chute on Rabu's box. I deserted my possessed corpse and summoned the winds to slow down and steer the living with preternatural precision while letting two of the bodies fall hard where they might. Madeline, with no chute, would invoke her own Morton control of the air, though this was somewhat experimental—the dead don't do normal craft.

We hit the frozen, barren ground with an impact as hard as we could endure without incapacitating injury; we had pushed everything to its preternatural limit. My baby? She was fine, despite my spiritual and physical strains. Was that her stirring? No, too early.

While we did the drill of stripping our parachute gear, I said, "Report. Those bodies at the gate."

"Not ours," said Madeline. That was a relief, but what followed wasn't. "My guess is they were trying to escape."

"Why?"

"We'll find out."

Great. "See anything else?"

"These small structures are craft cold. All the power is coming from the big building."

"Like a town meeting." I was reminded of that bit in *Aliens*, and shivered at the oracle.

Before I could get to him, Rabu had popped himself from his pressurized box. Not looking happy—he'd had a rough drop while spiritually leashed to human remains. But the dog stood at ready. In his box were weapons, ammo, and supplies. Madeline and I grabbed rifles and left the rest. Oz could keep an eye on it.

A rumble, not in the ground, but in the fabric of the craft that underlay the world, shook through my damned soul. Then silence.

"Did we do that?" But another, more terrible feeling had replaced the soulquake. I spoke the words of a small voice inside. "We're too late." Though I didn't know what we were too late for, the very air tasted bitter with the failure. *Too fucking late.*

We were off, double time for the big building's doorway, Oz falling into the military rhythm, Madeline straining the beat-up corpse to keep pace. Without me ordering it, Rabu had moved into point. A dog naturally wants to be the alpha in the pack, so I let his position stand.

We reached the front of the monastic hall. At the doors stood three robed figures, still as statues, faces lost in deep cowls. Remembering the bodies at the gate, I remained cautious, weapons ready, but the monks didn't make a hostile move. Must be the monastic greeting committee, though I was surprised they'd bothered to stop meditating just for us. They were blocking the doorway. I gave them some panglossic. "Seeking my husband. Please let me through."

No response. "Hello?" Perhaps this was a standing meditation. With her usual impatience, Madeline moved her corpse forward, Rabu at her heels.

A robed arm shot up, palm out, and an older woman's voice said "No farther." All three reached up and pulled back their cowls. Before us were three women variously European in features, lined up young to old exactly as Oz had said. "Scherezade Rezvani," said the Crone, "this is your day of judgment."

How the hell had they gotten here before us? No time to figure that out, because Madeline was getting angry. "Fucking Furies," she spat. "I'll give you judgment. Where were you when we were sacrificing to the elder gods? Where were you when Roderick . . ." She shook her head. "Move the fuck aside."

"We will not allow this thing to pass," said the Crone. "You have much to answer for, Madeline Morton, but you are dead, so beyond us."

"So lively though," said the Matron.

"Always exceptions," said the Maiden.

Without taking my eyes off the Furies, I grabbed Madeline's cold arm before she could move. "Drop this, and whatever else holds you back, and keep going. Rabu, you too, keep going if you can. Get Dale and the rest." I didn't know whether the Furies cared about dogs, but if Rabu stayed he might get himself hurt helping me.

Irritated, Madeline shook her arm loose from my grip, but then let her burden of a body fall like an empty dress. Rabu barked in a focused way at the door, then dashed between the Crone and the Matron. Though the Maiden belatedly lurched toward him, Rabu ran hard against the door, which opened at his impact. Good, they were on their way. That left one other person to position before things got rough.

"Oz?" Perhaps he could distract the Furies for a few moments with some preternatural bullshitting until my friends returned.

The Un-Kindly Ones' eyes went from me to him. They sniffed with disapproval. "Obstruction of our justice," said the Maiden, who smiled as if contemplating certain punishments.

"Still, you fall beneath the level of our jurisdiction. Or notice," said the Crone.

"No need to be insulting," said Oz.

"Beneath, for the moment," amended the Matron.

"That's better," said Oz.

"Stay out of this judgment," said the Crone.

"I have other business here," said Oz.

"Oz?" Surely he could see how desperate my situation was.

"If it's any consolation," he said to me, "I won't be leaving this place either."

The Maiden appeared disappointed at the lack of conflict, then smiled at a new thought. "We demand the *Oikumene*'s gifts."

"That's the business of which I was speaking. When it's finished today, I'll give them up."

"I see no deceit," said the Matron.

"Which from him is rare," said the Crone.

Oz didn't wait for his formal dismissal. I heard his footsteps as he moved briskly to some distance behind me, but I didn't look back; I wouldn't drop my guard for a moment with my executioners. My anger at Oz was tempered—at least he was safe, and I wouldn't be responsible for his fate.

I assessed my position. I had my usual three blades, one for each, but I wasn't sure my rifle would work. This place supposedly didn't like weapons, but we'd gotten them in anyway. No weapons in their hands, but hard to tell what was under those robes. One possibility of their craft concerned me—in legend, their mere presence could cause miscarriages, but that seemed more related to the fear they inspired. On my side, I could destroy their souls with a word, but no, I would keep to Right-Hand craft and mundane force. I would engage in the jihad of the spirit even if my soul was damned.

I trained my rifle on one Fury, then the other, then the other. "Stay back! Don't want anyone to get hurt. We can talk about my judgment later."

"Tempting," said the Crone. "But no." They rushed at me.

I fired. *Click*. Yep, this place disliked weapons, and I hated my luck. But I was already going to plan B, swinging my rifle around as a club. It broke against the Maiden's upraised arm. Damn, she didn't even flinch. But before they could surround me I was running across the Monastery grounds for the geodesic dome.

Madeline met some resistance from the guardian statues at the door. *Let me in, skullfuckers*, she said, but it was Rabu's passage that seemed to open the way for her. She remanifested within the foyer with Rabu at her side. Here she was again, extracting the young Morton from a damned Sanctuary, and this time, she had to keep him alive. She hated all Sanctuaries and their futile nostalgia. The world had moved on, and the consequences of humankind's sins were absolute. Magical zoo samples couldn't redeem us. Extinction was irredeemable.

But assuming this building held the gate to the particularly heinous inner Sanctuary, Madeline also had tactical reasons to stay on this side of the threshold, if she could. Paradoxically, in that place of ghosts she'd be more constrained. For the first time in months, she thought of her centuries-long partner in lust and intrigue, Abram Endicott. *Abram, are you in there with the other ghosts? I'd save you if I could. I was wrong. There is another way.*

Entering the meditation hall, Madeline saw through the stealth cloaking the monks. At the far end of the room sat the most useless person in history, the abbess of the Sanctuary. The stealth lifted, but Madeline couldn't see their souls or sins. Endicott's eye and the young Morton must have been distracted if they'd kept moving forward from here. The wrongness here was so pervasive, hard to see its source, but easy to spot the beginnings of mold-like rot in the golden flow of power down the walls. No sign of the young Morton though, so despite her own misgivings, she must go on to the inner gate. Where was it?

"Another disturbance," said the abbess.

"What kind of monastic screens their soul from sight?" asked Madeline, more than matching her tone.

"And an animal too," said the abbess. "Does a dog have a Buddha nature? *Mu.*"

Rabu ignored the human conversation, as the words had the falseness of an invitation to the vet. Instead, he sniffed in the direction of the abbess. He stepped back, growling, nose and body as straight as an arrow toward her. He had smelled many crimes, physical and spiritual, and nothing had smelled as bad as this.

The abbess didn't move, but her smell dared him: *come and die like a dog.*

Here it was, the razor claw's edge. He'd known it would come to this as sure as he knew when it was feeding time. Every "stay or go" the humans had given him had been a chance to skulk away; he'd stayed on the trail. But those noseless friends and this mixed-odored ghost weren't following fast enough. He must point the way, but his own body caged him. What would the good dog do?

With almost pack-like concern, Madeline was moving closer. "Dog, come here. She isn't your problem."

Rabu ignored the ghost. He stepped sidewise as if to circle around the dais, then in three bounds leapt up at the abbess.

Even by craft standards, the abbess was impossibly fast. One moment, she was as still as a waiting predator. The next, her hand grasped something in the bowl and threw it like a bolt of golden lightning. Rice flew everywhere, spilling. A three-bladed spike of metal drove into Rabu's chest. Rabu's growl turned to a whine as he fell back to the floor, heart bursting.

As the dog lay dying, the abbess drew another of her three-bladed phurba daggers, sharp beyond any ceremonial use. A force field of craft energy against physical menace sprang up around her. In that moment Madeline saw the abbess's tell. This nun was the source of all craft volition in this space, and no amount of screening could hide that moment of hatred, the hatred of her *recognition* of Madeline.

"I see you!" screamed Madeline, so that Rezvani might hear. Rational tactics would have her retreat to Scherie or advance to young Morton rather than square off against this still mysterious threat, but even the hint that she would find the vengeance whose prospect sustained her existence overwhelmed any restraint. In a mercurial blur, Madeline leapt right for the abbess's mind. "Kill them all!" she cried, then vanished from sight.

———

Most spirits had a gap of confusion between their death and their haunting return, but Rabu was a very good dog, and he hadn't a moment to lose in such a limbo. The dragon lurking behind the people scents of the Monastery reached for his ghost with all ten of its jaws wide like snakes and snapping like wolves, but Rabu dashed between its serpentine necks, too fast and wily to be eaten.

The building itself was a spectral kennel, but Rabu could track his way to the Outside anywhere on this plane of existence. Rabu knew what he should do next, what he'd helped so many others to do—go to the light and the bright call of his mistress's whistle. But his training didn't cover everything, and he hadn't sacrificed his body only to give up now. Scherie had told him to go fetch, and the scent of that task was on the trail of fate that had taken him this far. He wasn't an obedient dog, he was a loyal dog, like his ancestor Hachiko.

So he went farther in.

As Madeline dove into the mind of the abbess, the ease of her penetration confirmed this was no virgin to possession. Expecting trouble, she threw up her spiritual defenses, and readied the image of a simple weapon to manifest from the ectoplasmic stuff of her own being. What she saw supported her caution. She did not instantly inhabit the abbess's sensorium and perceive the meditation hall through her eyes. Instead, she wandered the woman's mental furniture and landscapes, mostly frozen in the China of four hundred years ago. *Plenty of room here*, she quipped to herself. *Not a lot of experiences.*

Walking the banks of a small river near a steeply arched wooden bridge, Madeline noticed an oddity—these scenic memories were like layers of photo realism over skeletons of monochromatic ink brush art. Though aesthetically interesting, these recollected scenes were another attempt to box her. But the river flowed with a real power that seeped through everything, moving downstream and perhaps down chakras, the same golden power with which the Monastery glowed.

The attack came in the form of a howling wind drawn from some remembered storm. The gale blew at her soul, trying to tear her in two or drive her back into some invisible ectoplasmic cage. But she let the wind blow through her, bending but not breaking, and not retreating. A Cornaro-style trick wouldn't work twice, and these magics seemed tailored to her former black-lit self.

The wind ceased, leaving the memory-world shrouded in rising mists. Surely she had forced a talk. She waited, and noticed her current manifestation for the first time. She wore the sweat, blood, excrement, and tear-stained robe of her burials. That would be his choice. Despite her skin crawling, she left it on. Her existence depended on playing each card in the proper order.

He still hadn't come forth, so she gave in. "You can come out now. I know you're here."

The reply was as if, instead of their throat, someone used all the waves of the ocean to speak. "Our dear sister. How good to see you again! Please, let's make love, just like we used to."

"Roderick. Why aren't you destroyed?"

"Destroyed? We are bigger than ever. We are Roderick the World." Before her, the mists cleared, and a dark lake bubbled. He rose from it as ten human faces on the long necks of a serpentine dragon's body that seemed appropriate for this landscape. His billions of scales each shimmered with its own color, and each shimmer was a consumed soul. He was now more plural than she'd ever been.

"Very dark lord, brother. You're almost pious with your biblical details."

"The shoe fits," he said, ten mouths speaking, twenty eyes boring red light into hers.

"What are you now, really?" she asked. "You were never very human."

"Sister, you've changed, too."

"My aura?" she said as if noticing it for the first time. "It's the latest fashion."

"We don't like it."

"Not thin enough for you?" Then some frankness born of perverse pride slipped through. "I've been through hell."

"Why, so have we! Still so much in common."

"So, you're doing Papa's Armageddon plan? I thought you said it was impossible."

"We said it would take a world of craft to pull it off. And voilà!"

"You found another hole."

"Yes. It would have been easier to reuse the portal we were thrown through, but that only led back to northern Virginia." At that place's name, all ten faces grimaced with utter disdain. "So we focused ourself at the ruins of that world's Sanctuary, and drilled through to here, with all its amoral power coming through from the other place."

"Your vessel, screen, way station, whatever you call her . . ."

"Shh," he said. "She loves us very much, and is murderously jealous of you."

"She can have you," said Madeline.

"You think you're over us? How charming!"

"I felt the wound to the world," she said. "You've broken the craft that sustains free will." *Or got Endicott to do it.*

"As you've seen, we have hollowed out the monks in this place." *Except for those at the gate who tried to flee,* thought Madeline. "Now we can direct the will of every soul in the world."

You cannot have them, thought Madeline. *You cannot have Scherie, and you cannot have her child.* She wondered at her own vehemence, but kept the thoughts locked deep within. He might not yet know about Rezvani and her baby; they were obscured in most farsight.

Instead, she said, "Brother, I swore that you would have no afterlife in this world. I meant to destroy you utterly, but I'm going to give you this last chance allowed by my oath. You should go back to your dead world. Find a new world to conquer. This one is mine."

The Roderick-Beast laughed across several octaves of tone. "Father said it might come to this if we weren't very strict with you."

"Have you ever thought about our mother? Even once?"

"You think we have been unjust. We will tell you what we told House: we made you what you are. Furthermore, you had centuries to torment us. We had mere decades to sculpt you."

"I was young." *That time was more important.*

An image of the abbess appeared, marked with the usual flatteries and anxieties of self-image. "She is still here?" said the nun.

"You are correct as always, my beloved," said Roderick. "It is time for her to go." He flickered between the dragon and the last body he'd worn on earth, the form he must take for the abbess's delight. "Good-bye, sister."

She did not wait for those jaws to open, revealing fangs and obscene tongues. She flew at him, aflame with the new light of her being, the ectoplasmic sword she'd prepared manifesting in her hands. "One head!" she screamed. "One fucking head!"

She didn't pause to see how badly she'd wounded one of his heads; she flew on, spinning to dive into the river that flowed through everything, gambling with insane abandon that it led down the abbess's spine and out of this box. But she did glimpse one other thing in her assault: at the dragon's tail, a mote radiating the dark energy from Roderick's hell. That was why no one had seen the portal; desperately restrained, it was hidden in the abbess herself.

Thank you, brother, she thought, even as she felt herself drowning in the river's power. *Your destruction is the sweetest reason to continue to exist.*

When the battle began, Dale's shitty seat had an obstructed view, well behind the lines with nothing but the backs of the Left Hand before him. But to his right front, he could make out a cluster of large flashing *N*s coming from six enemy practitioners. Their sins made their specialty obvious: necromancy. These practitioners must have operated the meat puppets that had seized him, though he didn't know the number they'd used for that op.

He didn't want to break his bonds yet—then his captors would be on him, and he was still trying to recover and recharge from whatever had knocked him out. His head had mostly cleared, but it was as if much of the craft inside him was as tied up in knots as his hands. So instead, he shimmied the loosening leather straps up the post so he could get a better look, but it was slow going, and splinters bit into his wrists.

From far across the lines of battle, Endicott's bellow of "Forward!" carried with a preternatural power that echoed in Dale's bones. So his friends were coming for him, and in force. That might be more than the Renfield had bargained for. If not, and they were all marching into a farsight-plotted trap, his friends would have to do better than expected, as always.

Heralded by a crack of thunder, the Right-Hand weathermen went to work. Gale force winds, some of which might be from Gale Family practitioners, buffeted Dale with bullet-like hail. *Goddammit, Endicott, you'd better not think this is funny.*

Endicott bellowed again, and the armies roared as they slammed together, drowning out individual noises in their cries and shouts. Though Dale felt hidden eyes still on him and doubted his own steadiness, the moment had come to join the attack from behind the enemy's lines. He looked for vulnerable spots as he prepared to free his hands. As if in answer, approaching hooves thundered to his left front and Marlow yelled encouragement like a queen out of Shakespeare. So she would be the rescuer, once her cavalry broke the line near him.

But before Dale could assist Marlow, the very air lit up with the familiar blood-red, steady pulse of death magic, craft that could animate corpses even as it fixed a living target to its fate. Here was the trap, and perhaps the signature of the dreadful power behind all this. In one heave, Dale broke the weakened straps binding him and tried to wave Marlow off.

But he was too slow. The dead and possessed wounded rose up and unhorsed her. Even though Dale saw it coming, the numbers and suddenness of the attack were shocking. Dale's "move air" spell flickered in his mind, but denying Marlow's attackers air wouldn't work, as too many were already dead. Breaking their bones might help. The odds were hopeless, but he wouldn't be able to face Endicott if he didn't fight.

One of the dead knocked Marlow's bearskin hat off. Other friendlies were trying to reach her, but the corpses were a physical barrier of blade, tooth, and the clawing of nails and bared bone. In a flash, Dale realized where he could best aid Marlow, and he ran toward the six necromancers. Though their extraordinary power was coming from elsewhere, the necromancers were the local conduit and the key point of attack. Dale's hands tingled with the craft to do what he did best.

But blurs in the corner of his vision warned him that the enemy had anticipated him. He stopped short just in time to avoid a sword slash as three practitioners dropped out of stealth between him and the necromancers. On the left and right stood the two traitors from H-ring, Johnson and Van Winkle, craft ready, blades drawn. Standing between them was a third fighter, the one who'd nearly cut him down. He was a dark-haired, mustached man of uncertain nationality with Arabic letters stitched into his clothes, and Dale recognized the prominent "Allah." *The Annotated Man*, thought Dale.

No need to see the glow of their sins to know that they'd intended to murder their prisoner whether he had tried to escape or not. Dale had served his purpose of drawing Marlow in, so now they would dispose of him.

In a blink, Dale assessed his opponents as they spread out, trying to surround him. Up close, Van Winkle bore the blue lips of attempting Left-Hand precog. Those crazy twitchy lips were smiling, as she would see no future for him, but Dale had been conceived to evade farsight. Johnson also seemed to have traded some sanity for whatever combat enhancements he'd adopted from his new pals—his wide eyes had the look of psychotic epiphany. Annotated Man's mien was the most relaxed and formidable, deadly in its coldness. Van Winkle would struggle to anticipate Dale's moves. Johnson would want to close and bring his direct physical power to bear. The Annotated Man might be able to do anything at leisure if the Persian sorcerer's blood-guilt-powered curse still restrained Dale's hands against a probable Muslim.

"Come on," said Dale, pivoting to face left, right, center. "What the fuck are you waiting for?" He lunged for Van Winkle—the obvious first move. Given time, she'd realize that she couldn't track Dale's future attacks.

But even as Dale began the spell and the blow, Endicott spoke his dreadful command. The force of it punched Dale simultaneously in the head, gut, and groin. A roaring filled his ears, like a firestorm or a woman exhaling all her pain.

Goddamn it, Mike. You knew it was a bad idea. But what if it were Scherie in mortal peril? Despite his promise to her, he would have done worse.

Dale recovered his will quickly; Endicotts could never tell a Morton what to do for very long. He let his momentum carry him forward and completed the spell he had readied: "*Short sharp shock.*" The still-frozen Van Winkle tumbled to the ground as Dale fell in a roll toward her fallen blade. *Bet she didn't see that coming.* If the electrical pulse through Van Winkle's brain wasn't killing her, perhaps it would be therapeutic.

Snagging Van Winkle's blade, Dale sprang back up and rushed at Johnson, who hadn't yet moved. *Dale had to reduce the fight to one-on-one while they were stopped.*

With an amazing economy of movement, Johnson parried Dale's oncoming blow. A nearby voice—the Annotated Man—said something in Arabic, and Dale remembered the Persian sorcerer's "*Feel it, Ferengi,*" and backed away. He had to avoid even a moment's paralysis at close quarters with these two.

Then, diverting everyone's attention, Endicott rode up in a gallop to Marlow's position, reigned in, and pulled her up onto his horse. Her face was covered with fresh blood, and the glow of her sins was fading. She must have been badly hurt.

To keep them from delaying Endicott, Dale yelled at Johnson and Annotated, "Come for me!" He made quick motions toward them with his blade outstretched. As Endicott turned his horse to dash back to friendly lines, he looked over toward Dale's noise and activity. Too many recovering hostiles between them, and Marlow needed healing now. Dale waved him off, broken straps still dangling from his torn-up wrist. "Get her to safety!" he yelled. "I'll join you when I can!" *Idiot, get going and save your wife.*

With a "yah!" and the stallion's haunches straining with the initial push, Endicott was off with Marlow, ectoplasmic projectiles now flying around them. *Good,* thought Dale. *Though very bad for me.*

Seeing that they wouldn't have to deal with Endicott, Annotated and Johnson returned their full attention to Dale. They'd all shaken off Endicott's command now. Annotated was moving his lips with some unheard spell, and he and Johnson had again split apart to hit him from two sides at once. Damn, Dale felt weak after just one bit of craft. Another man was approaching. It was one of the Russian Oprichniki who'd imprisoned him in the Moscow skyscraper. "Tsar of Bone sends regards," he said.

So the thing from the Lubyanka subbasement wanted him dead too. "Tell him to get in line," said Dale.

A loud, wolflike howl pierced the sounds of resuming battle, followed by an angry, approaching growl. A dog leapt at the oncoming Oprichniki. Holy hell, it was Rabu. As if both combatants were canines, they rolled together on the ground, jaws snapping.

Rabu was with Scherie, so she must be near. Dale couldn't let these fuckers have her. He needed to survive for her, to protect her and their child.

But his will meant squat; Annotated Man's words sapped at his already low strength. The ENCOM Johnson leapt into a flying, spinning kick that defied physics and connected with the side of Dale's thigh. Contact slammed an explosion of craft damage into Dale's hip muscles. With his weight all on his other side, he'd be going nowhere fast.

Subjective time slowed as the ENCOM closed in to slice Dale's throat. Dale needed to break his curse completely and now. The best external cure had always been Scherie, but despite Rabu's presence he couldn't feel her nearby. Within himself, he had only one untapped force antagonistic to the curse. It was time to let the Left-Hand part of his mind go.

Well past time, if you ask us, said those voices.

Do as you will, he thought. The balance of his mind shifted, and the internal scream of the curse changed from terrifying to terrified. He felt a dizzying lightness. Suddenly, Annotated's words seemed funny. Bloodguilt? Meaningless to the vampiric Left Hand.

Oh, someone was still coming at him with a sword. Time to try his new Left-Hand craft. *"Shatter all bonds,"* he told the ENCOM, as he parried his opponent's blade and, like smashing a windshield, sent fractures throughout Johnson's body along molecular fault lines.

As Dale well knew, it was very painful but very effective craft. "For every craftsman who's had to live in fear because of your treachery," he said, as his enemy fell dead at his feet.

That left the fan of Quranic-verse fashion. Dale stared him down, putting all the ancient terror he could into his gaze. "I can kill you now." The Annotated Man seemed to believe him; he sprinted away into stealth.

Nice to know that I won't be killing everyone I meet, thought Dale. *Despite my current compromised state.*

Dale turned to help Rabu. Damn, his leg was in bad shape. Rabu had his jaws around the Oprichniki's throat, shaking it like a chew toy. But the dog wasn't drawing blood. Instead, in an explosion of craft energy, Rabu jerked the Russian's spirit out of his dying body and flung it away into the ether.

Their part of the battlefield was strangely quiet. The zombies had collapsed in a corpse heap, and the six necromancers had vanished, with their craft expended and mission accomplished. OK, then Dale wouldn't rush to hack off Johnson's head to preempt resurrection.

The dead and wounded of both sides lay everywhere in small heaps, and bleeding men and women screamed and yelled for help. A dying practitioner was just like any other young soldier, crying for their parents in the end.

Further afield, much of the continued fighting appeared to be spectral. Many of the living Left Hand had bolted for the palisade or fled farther back down the valley toward the mammoths and cavemen, or they were flowing up the path toward the gateway to the Monastery.

Rabu trotted up to Dale, tongue out and tail wagging. "Good dog," said Dale, reaching down to pat him. But instead of warm fur, Dale felt the disturbing chill of a ghost meet his palm. "Ah hell, I'm sorry, boy." Rabu looked up at him. For a moment, a great fear stopped Dale's heart: was Scherie dead too? He searched about again—no sign of her spirit, so perhaps not. "Where's Scherie?" said Dale, without much hope of communication.

More like a pointer than an Akita, Rabu made an arrow of his body directed up and to the right, back up toward the gateway. Scherie must have followed them to the Monastery. Rabu's condition meant something was even more wrong there than Dale had noticed. Knowing that clarified what he was seeing on the battlefield. Those Left-Hand soldiers on the path to the Monastery gate were moving in good order to the top and effectively blocking Dale's way. Ghosts were providing covering fire for them with a selflessness they'd never shown in life. Dale was going to need help to get through such opposition.

But would anybody help him in his current ambiguous state? Dale found a polished knife, wiped it clean of dirt and blood, and peered at his reflection to assess his moral harm. Hmm. Some more ks from killing in combat, but no new sins of intention bubbling up from his subconscious. After a lifetime of resisting, apparently he wasn't going to start on a career of human sacrifice and possession for kicks. But as he tucked the knife away, he saw his hands together. They formed a sharp contrast. His left hand was distinctly black-lit, which seemed oddly literal, while his right still had its former glow of orthodox craft. He was a walking yin-yang symbol. Endicott wasn't going to like this. Then again, Endicott had been ahead of him in owning this part of himself.

A mad shriek spun Dale around, wrenching his hurt leg. From behind their palisade, Left-Hand precogs were screaming together their latest prediction: "Ninety-nine percent that we'll be out of a job!"

Another voice sneered, "One hundred percent that I don't care!"

Precogs out of a job? Then it was as he'd suspected—Endicott's command had damaged the free will of the world. That was a very old Left-Hand daydream; it would allow a sufficiently powerful practitioner to subtly pull the strings of all of humanity. Who could benefit from such a thing? Again, not these Renfields. They hadn't learned enough to be the real bosses here, much less become the triumphant will in an unfree world.

With greater care for his leg, Dale turned back around. A Left-Hand horseman rode listlessly toward him, either not recovered from Endicott's command or without a clue of what to do next. Due to the bad history of his family with animals, Dale was averse to riding, but he wouldn't be getting far on foot with this bad hip. The horseman seemed suggestible. "*Dismount and leave*," said Dale. With apparent relief, the horseman obeyed.

As if the horse were some oversized sheep, Rabu encouraged it on as Dale limped toward it. With more nasty pain, Dale mounted. Where to? Amidst his father's usual doom and gloom, he'd been telling Dale something important: "The Morton name is my pass." Dale's Family had been on the outs with the orthodox for so long that he'd forgotten: the Morton name still meant something to the global Left Hand. Hell, for them, Dale was aristocracy. One particular segment might have the most respect for him, and if they followed, others might join.

Dale galloped toward the American Left-Hand spirits. Sporadic ectoplasmic fire was wilting the remaining stubble on the battlefield. Many of the living orthodox seemed as demoralized or confused as the practitioner that he'd relieved of his horse, but one coherent group of Right-Hand horsemen was riding in parallel with him along the now disorganized lines of the battle. "Major Morton! We're here to assist your return!"

"I'm busy!" said Dale. "Tell Endicott I'll see him soon enough!" He turned his head long enough to give them the glare he'd hit the Annotated Man with, and they peeled away.

Dale came at the wedge of the American ghosts from their flank. Amidst the chaos, they remained in tight formation, though they stood as fixed in place as dead soldiers were supposed to be. They fired sporadically at any orthodox who approached them, but did not pursue. The head of the formation, the great patriarch of the evil Morton line, appeared to be sipping at the energy of those practitioners who remained—Left or Right Hand, living or dead, probably didn't matter. Though in the midst of battle, he wore Chinoise-style robes in which a wealthy Providence merchant might have relaxed within his study.

"Joseph Curwen Morton! I conjure you!"

"You do not need to shout, boy," said Curwen's ghost, dabbing his lips with a lace handkerchief as the flow of power toward him ceased.

"I am Dale Morton, last scion of our House."

"Ah, the argument from authority—a very thin reed. Did you ever consider that despite everything, we served you because we in part wished to do so?"

"I need help. My wife's in trouble."

"Go then. We never liked her much, but we will not restrain you. We are under another command. Unlike the living, we are truly here for the great cause."

"That battle has been subverted. Help me set it right."

"'Has been subverted.' Passive language. You don't wish to speak the name of the likely suspect."

"You know?" asked Dale.

"My son is dead and destroyed," said Curwen contemptuously, as if that were the greatest of failures.

"Then help me against whatever thing has taken his place," said Dale.

Curwen sighed. "Again, you fail to understand us. If we assist your return, it will not aid our Family. Quite the opposite."

"I have to save her," Dale said, hands open, beseeching. If Scherie was up there with Roderick, he'd find out that she was pregnant, and in his hands that was the worst thing to be.

Curwen closed his eyes, and the wedge of Left-Hand spirits behind him did the same. Some silent communication seemed to pass among them, for when Curwen opened his eyes again, he said, "Whatever your weak emotions and mistaken intentions, you are correct in one thing: the battle for the new age needs to be put right. We will follow you."

"Good," said Dale. "But you won't like where we have to go first."

D ale fell into his role as a Left-Hand leader with the natural authority of a man who'd kept such revenants confined for decades. Other living and dead practitioners followed in his train, as if sensing the purpose that they'd abruptly lost with Endicott's command and the scattering of forces.

He flew a white T-shirt on a stick, and the orthodox made way for his procession under this flag of truce. *Weird*, he thought. But both sides seemed more nervous about what had just happened than they were about the enemy.

Or perhaps they were all just stunned by his new sartorial splendor. Without any intentional craft, his clothes had the ghostly overlay of a steampunk mortician. Oh yes, Endicott was going to hate this.

B ehind the palisade walls of their little Right-Hand Ilium, no one was singing of the rage of Endicott. He was suffering the all-too-familiar sensation of being deceived by the enemy. He didn't feel any temptation to further commands, only anger. More than anything, he didn't want to look again at the battlefield and the stagey quality of it all that echoed the sword-and-sandal epics he'd loved too much. Nor did he wish to see once more the all-too-real bodies left behind by his crusade.

The only thing that interrupted Endicott's rage was the overwhelming sense that he'd disappointed Grace. The command tent was now part of the field hospital. Plain surgical stitching and cutting mixed with spiritual approaches, and healers used much of their energy as anesthetic, silencing with painful slowness the howls and groans of the wounded. Endicott sat by Grace's cot as two healers worked on her, halting the internal bleeding that would otherwise kill her. At the foot of the cot was a muddy bloody mess of her tattered clothes.

"You're in charge." Endicott's father had entered without his awareness, and he sounded nearly as angry as his son. "Get back out there."

Endicott didn't take his eyes off of Grace. "We've been played, sir." *Again.* "If you want to keep at this, go ahead. You're in field command now. Choose someone living instead if you like. Or let the Maid of Orleans do it. She's good at that sort of thing."

"But you've been chosen by God," said his father, sounding shocked.

Endicott turned to stare at him. "Chosen by God" was the kind of sinful and stupid thinking that had destroyed H-ring. Endicott barely controlled his fury. "You're dismissed, sir."

His father's eyes cut toward Grace, then back toward Endicott. "Yes, sir." He turned sharply and marched out.

A movement from the cot—Grace had stirred from her spiritually-induced slumber. She brought a hand up to her face. If she kept it, she'd have a scar on her left profile to match the one on her right. "Ouch. That's what I get for turning the other cheek."

Churchy humor—he couldn't help but smile at it, but just as quickly he realized that he didn't have much to smile about. "Can you forgive me?"

"For saving my life again?" She took his hand and gave it the lightest of pressure. "Darling, it's what we do." How could anyone have believed that they were the two witnesses? Willing martyrdom wasn't their style. "But you've really stuck your foot in it this time."

Her understatement charmed him, even as it tore at his heart. "The Renfield said that I broke the free will of the world. How the hell could I have done that?"

A mask of Oxbridge reserve descended over her face as she assumed a tutor's tone. "We're believers. We know that free will exists and that it doesn't come from physics, not even New Agey quantum physics. In theory, free will is the gap in deterministic physics allowed by spiritual power. Our will directs the power, and the spirit allows for our will."

She paused, closing her eyes, and her reserve cracked. "It is possible . . ." Anger and terrible sadness broke through, and a single tear rolled down her cheek. "I was supposed to save you from this. But it is probable that your command overriding the free will of the people here and now, in this special place and time, damaged that connection of will and power everywhere, for everyone."

Some share of her anger and sadness was directed at him, and it hurt terribly, but he'd have to remedy that later. "Why did they want free will damaged?" It seemed like a form of spiritual suicide.

"A powerful enough being could then manipulate the whole world."

"Not a Renfield then," he said.

"No."

Did she mean him? "I don't feel tempted at all."

"No, not you dear."

That left the other possibility that had been hovering over their heads for months. He gripped her hand tighter. "If that's the case, I need you up and spiritually strong ASAP." He could do for her that which she'd always done for him. "Please, take that strength from me, all that you can."

"But . . ."

"I clearly have more power than is good for anyone. Please."

He prayed, and the power flowed out from him. He willed the Left-Hand nanites in his system to assist the transfer. But the flow wasn't as strong as it had been. What he'd done to wound the world had also affected the source of his transnational power, which made very ominous sense.

A soldier interrupted his efforts: "Major Morton is approaching the fort, sir."

"So? Let him in."

"He's got a lot of the enemy with him. He's holding a white flag, and he's asking for you. He looks . . . really strange, sir."

"You'd better have a peek," said Grace. "I'll wait here." She was still recovering and renewing her spiritual power.

What was Morton's role in this disaster? Dale had waved off the rescuers Endicott had sent for him, and their report of his appearance had also been disturbing. Had his friend betrayed him, betrayed all of them?

Endicott went up the ladder to a firing platform and, standing tall without betraying concern for his own safety, looked down over the wall. There was Morton, mounted at the head of an army of the evil living and dead, like some vision from a nightmare bedtime story told by Endicott's father. The white T-shirt of truce was the least interesting color about him. Morton's left side was as black-lit as his Family's revenants, and his right glowed with clean spiritual power—in other words, he was a mess. His mountaineering clothing was covered by spectrally translucent, gothic garb out of Poe, as if Roderick himself had returned for some evil vengeance.

Morton raised a hand in salute. "Major Endicott! We need to talk!"

"Are your friends surrendering?"

"To you? They wouldn't like that."

"Come in, then. You alone."

"And Rabu?"

"That dog's here?" Even as Endicott found him moving around the horse into clearer view, Rabu gave a bark. That at least was a good sign. "Yes, of course, both of you."

Dale trotted his horse around the wall and entered the opened gate of the orthodox fort, Rabu at his heels. A cordon of the orthodox living and dead surrounded them as the gate shut behind them. As if showing off, the black-lit glow of Dale's left hand was intense enough to decorate a stoner's bedroom.

"In rode the Lord of the Nazgûl," said Endicott, shaking his head in disgust.

"It's not how it looks," Dale said, relieved that Endicott saw some humor in this, no matter how grim.

"Really?" said Endicott. "You've got a very bad color to you. And, other than the dog, you're keeping very bad company."

"I know. We can talk about it later." He dismounted, slowly and painfully, and Endicott motioned as if to help him. "I'll be fine," said Dale. Then, he pointed toward the ridge. "But Scherie's up there. Back in the Monastery, where someone killed Rabu."

Frowning in surprise, Endicott looked more closely at Rabu's ghost. "Who the hell kills a dog?"

"I have some suspicions—don't you? It would explain a lot about this trap."

"The fight here is more than a trap."

"Still isn't ours," said Dale. "This place may have another meaning for the pilgrims, but for us, it's a pitcher-plant trap."

Endicott looked back at the festive-colored tent. Did he need more persuading? Dale tried another tack. "It's not your fault for believing this set-up. This place is like Jerusalem Syndrome on steroids."

Endicott's head swung back around, anger flashing in his eyes, and Dale verbally back-treaded as fast as he could. "Everyone was fooled. Maybe if this had gone differently, we could have had a real nice fight, a clean one, and all would have been settled here and in the world."

Endicott stood silently for two long breaths, then asked, "What should we do?"

"We have to get back to the Monastery now with as many of both sides as will follow."

"And which side are you?"

Now it was Dale's own patience that was running short. "Hey, I could ask the same question, Mr. Free Will No More. But I won't, because I understand. I'm on the same side as always. The one that saves Scherie and the world, in that order." He pointed at his left hand with his right. "You need to trust me on this. I've always treated this like addiction, where one taste is one too many, but I'm strong enough now, and I can handle it."

"You always have," said Endicott, allowing a grim smile to crack his stony features. "I saw your soul on the mountain. You aren't so different now." He indicated the cordon of soldiers around them. "But these other practitioners might not be as trusting."

Oh well, Dale thought, *one other thing I can do.* He'd have to do it eventually anyway. "At three score and ten, I vow to let myself die, whatever my condition, Furies as enforcers, etcetera, etcetera."

"Right," said Endicott. "As if we'll be so lucky to see seventy."

But everyone had turned to look at another practitioner who was being carried out on her cot—Marlow. She stood up, waving off the attendants' efforts to either aid her or keep her down. "Morton's oath," she said, with an economy of words. "Truth."

As if in confirmation, a clap of thunder from a clearing sky echoed across the plain. That sure didn't happen at the wedding.

"I need volunteers for a breakout," said Endicott.

CHAPTER

NINETEEN

I ran for the geodesic dome, which was actually a hollow Tinkertoy set of struts; the synthetic canvas they'd held in tension within had collapsed to the ground. When I reached the dome, I ran up from strut to strut on the balls of my feet, then at the top readied one of my knives for my pursuers. My gymnastics were again good for something. The Furies hesitated at the structure's base. Good—every moment of hesitation was a moment for the cavalry to arrive.

The Furies made their opening moves. "*Rest, now, my dear,*" said the Matron. A wave of fatigue washed over me, as profound as mono on a winter's day. But I remained conscious, and the elevator-drop feeling passed, leaving only an ache in my muscles and head. The Matron's eyes went a little wide with almost maternal concern and surprise at my persistence. Something was blocking her particular craft—probably my own maternity.

The Maiden didn't seem to care whether the Matron's craft worked or not. In two bounding leaps, her feet just touching the struts, she was in knife's reach below me. Despite having the higher position, I couldn't force her back down with my craft-enhanced kicks. Her blade was a blur as she spiraled up and in for attacks, joining me on the topmost struts.

I was trying to stay focused on the combat at hand, but a question kept nagging me: how had the Furies pursued me to the Sanctuarium Mundi so quickly? Had Oz tipped them off? No, he hadn't wanted them here. Then I remembered the damned *Oikumene*'s sculpture, but something was wrong with that too. I'd gotten here from Cornaro's about as fast as humanly possible, craft or no. They shouldn't have been able to beat me to the Monastery.

We danced from metal bar to bar of the dome. The Maiden was never close in enough to drive her blade home or slash anything vital. With little lightning lunges and retreats, she gave a small, shallow cut, then another, then another, slashing clothes but just breaking skin. I answered in kind when I could, though I still looked for a crippling blow. Her style of strikes seemed a waste of time, so should have been exactly what I wanted, but the little pains seemed to drain my energy and distracted me despite my discipline.

I couldn't afford distraction; against three opponents, I needed clear situational awareness at all times. The Matron had moved inside the dome, looking for an opportunity from below while she avoided presenting a straightforward target for a knife throw. The Crone had disappeared.

The Matron was swinging around and up the bars from the inside. They were solving this spherical puzzle of two against one, and I still needed more time. Summoning a local wind to give me an extra push, I sprang off and hit the ground running, going next for the mini-Gothic cathedral.

Using a bell tower as a ladder, I sprang to the top of the church. I thought I could keep them from ascending the roof's steep tilt, but I was too exposed here to attacks from below. So I leapt for it, and the winds held me for a moment in midair as I made a preternatural spin toward the Maiden. I was trying to hit her from above, but she was again too fast.

What followed was an ever-moving, weaving combat of two on one. The martial style seemed to flow from kung fu to conventional boxing to kickboxing and back. The small, scale-model buildings made our fight around them seem like Godzilla versus Megatron and Gamera.

The one thing I couldn't do despite every impulse was get defensive about my baby and guard my abdomen at the expense of other parts of my body. To fight as if I were vulnerable would make it so, and we'd both die. I had to rely on nature's craft protections and otherwise use the best tactics available.

But other craft defenses began to fail and real damage got done. My foot caught the Matron with linebacker force in the knee, her furious counterpunch to my chest did something bad to a rib. I traded more cuts with the Maiden, but when the Matron joined in, I had to block a pommel blow from the Maiden barehanded, and with a crunch and mind-killing pain something in my wrist gave way. Shit. *Stop hurting and start healing, motherfucker.*

Despite the Matron's new difficulty moving, they were always able to contain and flank me, forcing me farther back. If they drove me too far from the monastic hall, help would never reach me. No Oz either. As we passed the beehive hut, Oz was just sitting next to it on the ground, staring into space. What could be so fucking important?

The little blood draws and the bone damage were taking their toll, and I was using too much energy just to heal myself enough to keep going. Fighting for time, but they were three chthonic forces of nature, with the third not yet in the game. I couldn't hope to outlast them alone. Where the hell were Dale and my friends?

OK, enough was far too much. Part of my problem was numbers, but I knew where to get some more. With no telegraphing of my intention, I spun into a sprint toward the mountain stairway's entrance.

"Coward!" yelled the Maiden. She didn't get it yet.

My running feet broke through the icy crust into the shallow snow on the plateau's edge until I was at the pile of bodies I'd seen from the air. I stopped, each breath painful against my poorly craft-patched ribs. The bodies were in simple homespun garments not fit for this plateau's cold.

I reached into the four corpses, not with my full self (I couldn't leave myself so vulnerable), but like sticking my fingers into meat pies. I pulled their puppet strings of sinew and bone, and they were up around me, just in time. The Matron and the Maiden had run up to the entrance, ready to give me a push off this landing into the void. But some force seemed to be making them slow up and hesitate, a force radiating from the strange skeletal statues at the gateway.

So I pushed first. Finely tuned combat wasn't possible for me—I just had the bodies walk into the Furies, two on each, lumbering on against their blows and cuts. With outstretched arms, I made the corpses give the Furies big dead hugs.

"Abomination!" screamed the Maiden.

For the moment, the Furies were fully occupied. This would give me time to get into the monastic hall myself. If Dale couldn't come to me, I'd go to him. I ran through the dead men's scrum, back to the hall's door where this fight had started.

But I'd forgotten something. Out of some stealth bubble, the Crone was in front of me, calmly waiting.

I would have kept running right on through her, but some instinct stopped me cold. Then I saw why. Her intention was a glowing letter— her executions were no more free from sin than combat kills. Her intention was a bright *SK*, a suicide-kill by craft. That was the sort of spell that Dale had been prepared to use on Sphinx—if, going for the door, I closed with the Crone in combat, she'd sync our hearts, then stop them both, along with my child's. I was a little overawed. She was willing to die to make sure I did as well.

Sorry Dale, but past time for me to call back whatever support might be near. *"Madeline, Rabu, help me!"*

As if in response, a faint smell came from the entrance, synesthetically colored like blood and sounding like a growl. "Oh God, no."

The Crone knew it too. "A dead dog is beneath our jurisdictional notice."

"Goddamn you. He followed me into hell."

Then, a distant echo of Madeline's voice rang in my head in crimson and scarlet letters: "Kill them all." *Not helpful, you old witch*. But, real or not, it just confirmed that the cavalry wasn't coming anytime soon.

The other two Furies had joined the Crone, all standing between me and the doorway. The Maiden and I were both red from head to boots with our collective blood. The sweating, panting Matron was moving slowly with her wrecked knee—but she had less blood on display. Her face resembled my mom's at the end of her tether with high-school me.

The Crone remained completely unruffled, unchanged. "No one is coming for you. Will you not end this?"

She was right. Time to face the choice—destroy their souls or die.

No, that was bullshit. Damn them and their absolutes, and damn me—I was as caught up in binaries as they were. Perhaps I could use my new power without destroying or even killing them.

As gently as I could, I blew on their flickering souls with the words of annihilation. I watched the letters of their sins grow pale. They were tougher than Cornaro; they'd have to be for their jobs, but they'd never faced anything like me.

The mouths of the Furies gaped at me, their eyes wild. For perhaps the first time, they knew real fear.

But they hesitated only a moment. The Crone stepped toward me, hands outstretched.

"Wait," I pleaded. "Let me say something." All of them were shifting around me, death in their eyes, and not caring whose. "For one second, just fucking wait." The Matron and the Maiden were readying craft to clear the Crone's way. I touched my forehead near the spot of my mark. "For God's sake, don't make me do this again."

The Crone lifted her hand, and they halted. "Confession is good for the soul," she said.

Not confession, but arguments, and for one of those, I needed to know something. "First, how can you already be here? I didn't do anything . . . anything interesting, until last night European time."

"We heard the call two fucking days ago," said the Maiden. "Two days too long for judgment."

"Then it wasn't my sin that called you." At least if precog wasn't involved, which given the absolute focus of these three seemed likely. "Why don't we find out what else is going on here before you execute judgment on me?"

The Matron and the Crone's faces remained oddly blank. "Blah fucking blah. Is that all?" asked the Maiden, impatience edging her tone.

No, that wasn't fucking all. I knew some words. Before my pregnancy, I'd always disliked women who played the mommy card, but now I turned to the Matron and spoke the old legal language: "I plead my belly."

Her face remained emotionless. "Let's get on with it!" said the Maiden.

I held up a hand and made my next plea to the Maiden. "I plead for just vengeance."

The Maiden never broke her sneer. "I'm so looking forward to killing you."

Without much hope, I addressed the Crone. "I plead for time." She just continued to stare through me.

This was justice? They had not only rejected my pleas; it was as if they weren't hearing them. I put the full force of my craft into my question. *"What the fuck is wrong with you?"*

It was like getting new glasses after not seeing well for months. The image of the monastic hall went crystal sharp, and I saw tendrils of dark power leading from its doorway into the backs of their necks. Like puppet strings, like the threads with which I'd controlled the corpses, but so subtle I doubted even other practitioners would notice.

"Goddamn you gravy fucking swine, get out of them."

The dark strings broke. The Furies blinked like owls in sunlight. "Were you saying something?" asked the Matron.

"Let's try this again," I said. "I ask to be allowed to bring my child into the world before my punishment."

The Matron's attention snapped to my midriff, and she took a step back. "*Si*, she is pregnant. I agree to a stay of execution."

But blondie's big eyes bulged with deeper insanity. "I don't give a flying fuck about her fetus."

"I plead for just vengeance."

"Vengeance. Justice. What would you know about those, you marked bitch?"

"Something here has taken my husband. It may have something to do with his Family. I want a just and bloody revenge before I die."

The Maiden stopped sneering. "Bloody?"

"Very," I assured her.

She waggled her open hand. "Hard to choose. What do you say, grandma?"

The Crone's eyes were steely young in an ancient face, and they hadn't left me for a moment. "I'm not so easily moved, dearie. You cannot contest our sentence. It's written on your soul."

"Weren't you listening? I do not contest the sentence." There were things one could not do. "I beg only for time. When I've had my revenge, when I've had my child, I swear to submit to your judgment."

"And what if we don't agree," said the Crone.

I had to believe this. "Or I kill you, probably destroy your souls, and then wait for another three to assume your office. I think my way is better. Besides, once I've had the child, my power will diminish. I'll be an easier task."

The Crone smiled dreadfully, with dreadful teeth. "Well said, and without deception. We will suspend sentence until the child is born. Your vengeance best be settled by then."

"You can help with that. Like I said, I don't think you came all the way here just for me. Let's go in there and take a look."

I didn't mean immediately; I was going to suggest some healing first, and I'd offer my own power for that as a good will gesture. Also, I had some doubts: would the Furies lie to execute me? Cops deceived all the time to get confessions, arrests, and these women were like cops.

But then my clarified sight saw a nightmare, and all other concerns vanished. "Get away from the building! It's reaching out for you again."

"What the fuck, did we drive one crazy again?" said the Maiden.

"Do it now," said the Crone. "I see it too."

We backed away fast. No longer radiating mere fingers of control, the monastic hall was completely covered in a black-lit glow of massed revenant power, like the Left-Hand Morton collective, only larger and denser, like Yasukuni. It was sprouting more tendrils, many more. A few reached for us or spread out radially from the building, but a massive coiling rope of them was winding its way across the plateau to the stairway entrance.

I yelled invective, f-bombing the revenant-thing with my usual abandon, but the moment a way forward cleared, more dark power filled in, sealing off the building again. I thought of drawing my full power against this thing, but an image of struggling in quicksand made me pause. *No, can't exhaust myself.*

I asked the Furies. "Can you do anything about this?"

"No," said the Crone, calm face now creased with uncertainty and worry. "This thing was swaying us, yes? Then we cannot even risk getting closer."

Either a whole Yasukuni was in there, or it was the leakage of a hellworld like I'd seen in the Virginian bunker. My research at Cornaro's had given me some new tricks, but invective exorcism by main force remained my primary skill. That would take far too long against another Yasukuni. Along with my foul language emotionally charged with craft, we needed the tools to make and maintain a path into the monastic hall.

It didn't seem to be an accident that those tools were at hand. "Let's get Oz."

———

W e found Oz still seated near the beehive hut, still staring up into space. No, he was staring at something. We circled around to his point of view. Images of horror I hadn't glimpsed since Virginia, now on full view. He had opened a fucking portal.

I readied a knife. "Oz, stop this now!"

As quick as moonlight, the Maiden was between me and Oz. "And who will shut it once you've killed him?" asked the Crone. "Let him work."

"What the fuck?" I said. Dale's father went mad looking through a portal into such a world.

Once again, the Crone anticipated me. "Take a pinch of the sand," she said, pointing at the pouch at Oz's feet. "Among its powers, it is an aegis for the mind, so we can remain sane."

We each reached over to the pouch, careful not to obstruct Oz's view. Following the Furies' lead, I put a bit of sand in my jacket pocket. Then I dared another look at what Oz was seeing in front of him: many scenes of what must have been many worlds, mostly dead.

Then Oz started singing, raising and lowering his quavering tones like a theremin, and the scenes seemed to move along with his voice. "Gordievsky, Andropov, ABLE ARCHER 83, VRYAN," he sang. "November 2, 1983. November 11. Pray for us, O Mary! Save us from the black star of the hellworld. Mystical rose, star of the vast sea of probabilities, where is the world-line? Ah! So many dead ones now. So many!"

With an inarticulate yell of frustration, Oz made the sign of the seal that was Solomon's, and the portal vanished. "The images in my mind. Can't fecking find it." He shook his head as if clearing it, then looked about at me and the Furies. "You've decided on a stay of execution. Happy I was able to assist."

"Going some elsewhere?" asked the Crone, pointedly.

"If need be," he said.

"I don't understand," I said.

"Oz creates portals that people can use," said the Crone.

"Why would anyone want to go through?" What lay on the other side in one of those hellworlds was beyond horror.

"Bad idea or not, his Family has gone through before," said the Crone.

Oz took a deep gulp of air, and seemed to further recover himself. "A demon world has breached into ours. We need to halt it now, and the best defense is a good offense. The demon's power and attention are focused on its own portal, so the best way is to open another portal away from its breach, but into the same world."

I pointed at where the portal used to be. "What can anyone do against that?"

"The power of hellworlds is based on having no other probabilities," said Oz. "Meaning the probabilities that free sentient beings create with their choices. The presence of a living practitioner even for a moment on a dead world can seriously undermine its negative craft."

"You have very little life left, Oz," said the Crone, in a cold and even tone. "In one bite, it'll swallow you whole, and chew your soul down to mere animal need."

I saw another angle on the problem. "Oz, weren't the Fianna a group? You're one man." *You'll never make it.*

"One man, going one way," he said. "Only need to breathe long enough, long enough to cause the beast to draw back into its lair. Danu, the Earth, will do the rest and seal the breach. This is how the Irish save civilization, again and again. But I can't feckin find the way there. Something is blocking me. Need to stop it now."

He hadn't seen what was coming from the monastic hall. "If you were closer to the existing breach, would that help? Cause it's in there."

We prepared to enter the black-lit building. The Matron and I dealt with such injuries as we could. My left wrist still wasn't great, but punching wouldn't do much good against what I had to face next. I called up the serviceable corpses again to use as an advance screen against the demon. The Maiden had completely broken one of the bodies from the landing, but the one Madeline had been wearing was still intact and had been ignored by the thing in the building, so I still had four to play with. The Furies were of course unhappy about this. "Add it to my sentence," I said.

With two corpses screening the front and two in the rear, the Maiden took the living point, while the Crone watched our backs. In the center, the Matron and I were shielding Oz, as he'd become the most valuable and vulnerable asset. But the truth was that, to be in range of Oz's tools, we were all crammed so close that it wasn't much of a formation. We were going into the belly of the beast, with the Furies literally breathing down my neck.

In the quiet after the intrusions, within a part of her mind untouched by time, Roderick and the abbess made love in the warm and soft neon green grass on the banks of the ever-flowing river of power. At the same time, Roderick monitored the abbess's thoughts for feedback on his performance. One might think their congress, being all in her head, was somehow less real to her, but that would be a mistake. As the abbess knew from centuries of meditation, all reality was at bottom a mental phenomenon, and thus all reality was illusion. The abbess had become quite good at cutting through the veil of Maya. Part of extending life was, paradoxically, perceiving its illusory basis.

Though he was simultaneously active elsewhere—feeding hostility against Rezvani into the Furies, piping power to his allies in the deeper Sanctuary, confusing Ossian MacCool's search for the right world—Roderick brought his A-game to this carnal illusion with the abbess. The abbess was his linchpin between the worlds and within his plans, so making her mind moan with transcendental pleasure was essential, no matter how busy he might be.

Some of this pleasure was higher-order tantric union stuff—it was with those psychic delights that he'd lured the abbess with that first infinitesimal tendril of his returning presence. But after he'd shown her how to more effectively mainline the otherworldly power that pervaded the Monastery, she no longer needed to be so fastidious about her life-extension disciplines, and she could get plain down and dirty and demanding. Should his own vast imagination falter, he had the experiences of billions of lives to draw upon.

After their lovemaking, they lay together in an absolute quiet disturbed only by the infrequent, distant heartbeats and breaths of the abbess's body. He was confident that it was better for her than it was for him. He was using her, but it should be enough that he wanted her for her mind. Through the abbess, he got more than a gateway to this world. She controlled the Monastery's large endowment, of which Roderick redirected a substantial part. First, he had to pay the Renfields in advance. Yes, he could give the usual promises upon success, but a Renfield wouldn't care. Roderick also had to re-earn their good will after their unused life-extension serum went bad—an unforeseen consequence of his own demise.

Roderick's larger mind was also busy with many other things. With delightful irony, his agents, mundane and magical, were using the Left-Hand threat to initiate the slaughter of all craftspeople, or their greater confinement in countries where such genocide was not yet an option. Alone of the world's powers, the craft militant could have resisted him for a time, and he hated to waste time.

All was coming to pass, and sooner than he'd dared to hope. He had not been sure that his favorite four craftspeople would come to him for their punishment; his farsight wasn't so sharp in this world anymore, and they had eluded it at its best.

Reading this thought, the abbess stirred next to him. "Why do you care about them so, beloved?" For someone who'd supposedly mastered detachment, she seemed remarkably jealous.

"Only for their usefulness, my love." This time, he hadn't wanted his fab four present for vanity's sake. He had concrete uses for each of them: Endicott to break the world, Grace to break Endicott, Dale to draw in Rezvani, and Rezvani to end her life here so that she couldn't warn the world of his presence and fight against his control.

Though the free will of the world was broken, he wasn't able to control the people in the heart of the Sanctuary—his puppet strings could only reach outward. But he had helped power the valley's zombies so certain important tasks would be done—the Left Hand wasn't great at volunteering. Endicott had already done his part. The wound he'd dealt the world would normally have healed, but Roderick wouldn't let it.

"You caught them in an epic," she said.

"Who can resist that?" he said.

Soon he could reenter the world outside this preserve for the useless and lost. He had spread out from the abbess as easily as water from an overflowing bathtub. The other monks were already so in synch, so nearly linked, that he was in them all before they knew it. He gave them the only true nirvana—dissolution. To call them puppets implied some separate existence which they no longer had. They were more like meat suits.

He wasn't worried about intruders. Called by the abbess's great sin, the Furies had come, but he'd stayed hidden within the abbess while she'd given them some dead monks' robes and put them off the scent long enough for Rezvani to arrive and for him to sink his subtle hooks into their wills. He'd farseen that Rezvani carried some distracting sin of her own toward which he could sway the vengeful impulses of the Furies. As for the Chinese, the Pakistanis, the Indians, hell, the whole globe, he wanted them to show up. An international incident would cover his further spread, and the survivors of the Sanctuary's battle royale would help carry him to the world outside.

He would not hollow out every human being, not like these monks.

He would only inject a piece of himself into everyone, everywhere, and watch them think themselves free. Then he'd pull the strings, and the world would dance to his tune, and speak with his voice. That priest, Cornaro, from that place of the puppets, he could see it coming.

So hungry. If the former Roderick acted as the cerebral cortex of this Beast, then the rest was all reptilian brain of animal appetite, and such thoughts made him ravenous. Nothing to fear—this incursion home was fun, but he/they could retreat anytime. Why did he/they feel a chill, or why didn't he/they feel at complete ease? Maybe because he wanted it all so much.

"Tell me about the future again, beloved." Ah, she knew just what to say to make him feel better.

He said, "We'll be the voice of the schizophrenic, the grandpa screaming at the television, the madness of crowds, a mob beating a helpless woman who resembles my sister. We'll be in the smarter machines too. Roderick the World, and you at my side. Until, after a thousand years, more or less, when we've done everything else, experienced all the permutations of human existence, we'll just become everyone and then have the world commit suicide."

He was perhaps being a tad deceptive; due to the energies required, he did not expect her to survive long after he extended his dominion to the whole planet.

"Poor world," she said.

"Our thousand-year reign will be nine hundred more than humankind has otherwise." That part was all too true: he saw about 90 percent probability of extinction by 2100.

"Then what will we do?" she asked.

"Then we'll talk with others of our kind alone, forever." He still had one secret fantasy. Though all would be his puppets, one would be his avatar among them, the Christ of his glorious thousand years. Not this abbess, but a true Abomination of Desolation, perhaps even an incarnation in utero. But where could he find the perfect child to ensoul?

Adrift in this daydream, something stirred his collective spirit, like a dentist's drill working toward the nerve. The Furies had somehow failed him; Rezvani would be coming in soon. He felt a moment of the old rage, but it quickly transformed to delight. He had one last deception to ensure her isolation. Then he would kill her and seal the world's fate.

"My love," he said to the abbess. "I have a wonderful new experience to show you."

PART VI

DULCE ET DECORUM EST

Death is a dignitary who when he comes announced is to be received with formal manifestations of respect, even by those most familiar with him. In the code of military etiquette silence and fixity are forms of deference.

—Ambrose Bierce

It is no question of living, but of setting out.

—Marshal Maurice de Saxe

I am not resigned to the shutting away of loving hearts in the hard ground.

—Edna St. Vincent Millay

TWENTY

As quickly as they could, Dale and the others prepared for their march up the boundary slope to the gate. Endicott rallied the orthodox volunteers, and Marlow was soon recharged enough to help. An already exhausted healer worked briefly on Dale's leg. "You may have trouble with this for the rest of your life."

Endicott scrawled a note and left it with a Civil War ghost. "For my father," he said. Then, turning to Dale, "May I borrow Rabu for something?"

"Ask him," said Dale.

They decided to approach the gate from different sides; it was tactically sound and would avoid incidents on the march. Dale rode again at the head of his column up the Left-Hand path. They seemed to suck the warmth from the very air. *Don't worry, Endicott,* he thought. *They're still not my preferred company.*

As they moved up their respective paths on the barren slope, signalers below communicated between Dale's column and Endicott's to coordinate timing. Farther away, the now mostly spiritual forces continued their fight.

Ahead of Dale's march, the Left Hand held the high ground, and across the path they'd thrown up a barricade made from camp detritus and spectral props. Revenants stared down ectoplasmic rifle barrels.

Dale still bore his T-shirt of truce, and he was just wondering how much closer to the barricade he should go when, at fifty yards, some Left-Hand leader shouted, "That's close enough!"

Dale raised his left hand in salute, and he almost thought he could hear the surprise of those behind the barricade. He wasn't sure exactly what he should say, but in a voice that boomed along the wall of the precipice, he began to speak anyway.

"I am Dale Morton, last scion of my House. I am Roderick Morton's heir. Roderick is dead, and whatever thing he's part of now is no longer human, or Morton. Let me tell you one lesson my Family knows well: the Left-Hand way is not self-destruction. And that's what you're doing. If you're up here, you must know that you're fighting for him, and not for any change of ages. But why do you think my ancestor, or the thing he's become, will share anything with you? Are you ever so generous? I offer you nothing but your own continued existence and freedom."

"We were paid in advance!" yelled someone from behind the barricade.

"Spoken like a Renfield. You then especially have no reason to stay. But some of you might believe that some prize awaits you for your service, that you only have to claim it. I say, remember Kiev. The Baba Yagas thought a prize awaited them, and they are dead. For those already deceased, you may believe that new bodies await you. The ghosts in Kiev believed the same thing, yet bodiless they remain."

He was cheating a bit in his rhetoric by using some suasion, and Left-Hand suasion is pretty slick stuff. But whatever his means, he must have been getting through to those at the barricade, because the Left-Hand leader yelled, "Open fire!" *Shit, here it comes.*

But no ghost fired, no living practitioner cast a spell against him. Someone else from behind the barricade jeered at the would-be leader: "Who put you in charge? That's a fucking Morton out there!"

Trying to hide his relief, Dale said, "We're going out through that gate to restore the free will of the world."

"Never thought much of free will," someone new shouted. "Don't think we'll notice the difference."

"Then don't come with us. But let us pass. I ask for a cease-fire, not because I doubt the outcome, but because I think part of Roderick's scheme is the destruction of as many practitioners as possible, clearing the way for his one will alone."

"OK," said the jeering voice. "One condition. Can you get us out of this chickenshit valley too? We can't reach that damned gate."

M r. Cushlee hadn't expected the barricades to give way so quickly, but he hadn't expected them to hold forever either. Up on the ridge, he was preparing his last little surprise. True, he hadn't been paid in advance for this extra service, but he viewed it as a matter of acute self-interest. If Endicott survived, he was not likely to forget or forgive what Cushlee had done today.

So, shielded by that stealth he did so well, Cushlee had assembled a compound bow. Each component had been brought in by a different Renfield, and this had been sufficient to fool whatever force screened the Sanctuary for weapons above the quality of edged tools.

With the barricade shoved over the edge of the path, Endicott and his orthodox were riding up to meet Morton on the shelf under the gate. Cushlee had Endicott lined up in his sights. A little craft assist, and the arrow would be in Endicott's heart before he could raise a defense.

Perhaps Cushlee was too focused on his work, because he never saw the enormous paw coming until its weight was crushing him against the ground. The great saber-toothed cat roared, and a little ways away, a spectral dog barked.

In a moment, Endicott had ridden up a narrow path to Cushlee's perch along the ridge. *"In God's name, show yourself, Cushlee."*

Cushlee felt his stealth fail. Fuck it anyway, it hadn't kept his scent concealed.

"Huh," said Endicott. "Didn't see that coming—I asked the dog to find you, and he got a cat to do it. I would have taken care of this before, in a proper fight during the battle, but I was so drained and you were so stealthy. Then I figured that once you had a moment to think about it, you'd regret leaving me alive. Nice to get one right."

With an effort of ribs against paw to speak, Cushlee tried one last throw. "We could still 'ave a go, if you've got the stones for it."

"No, that wouldn't be fair," said Endicott. "After all, I wasn't the one to catch you." Then, echoing the favorite words of the Gabble Ratchets, he said, "Supper's ready."

The dog barked at the great cat, and Mr. Cushlee had a unique if painful experience, unknown by humankind for thousands of years.

As with the portal in the Virginia bunker, Endicott and Marlow had some command of the gate to the Monastery, but not enough to bring it all the way down to ground level. So Dale directed the formation of a human pyramid from spectral bodies. "As always, we'll get there on the backs of the dead," he said. Then, addressing all the living practitioners of both sides, he added, "You might want to wait before following us. It's not going to be pretty in there."

Some of them followed up the pile of ghosts anyway, enduring the uncanny cold discomfort of spiritual contact. They were approaching the gate from directly below, so perhaps whatever was in the Monastery would be unable to observe their activity. Endicott was holding Marlow's hand, giving her more of his energy so she could cover them in stealth as they climbed and continue to do so when the first wave went through. But to complete the surprise, Dale had another trick in mind. At the top of the pyramid, he summoned a whirlwind. "Why walk, when we can just glide on in? On three, hold your breath and jump."

Madeline was drowning, suffocating in the wonderful river's light that called for her surrender and promised to end all pain in nirvana. She could let herself dissolve here; a shame that she now needed to destroy her brother first, as even that one desire would ensure her continued suffering. She went over the cerebral edge and down the spiraling spinal falls, through bright suns of the abbess's chakras, growing darker and more grossly material. She continued to follow the river down through the ground, seeking depths where Roderick couldn't follow, caverns measureless to man, as if only Hell's bottomless pit and its angel could save her.

A distant laser swept through her dimming awareness; it was Cornaro's gem calling to her like a lighthouse that hungered for her to wreck on its rocks. With etheric speed she followed the neural network of ley lines that crammed this part of the world. Station to station she caromed, the returning thin pale revenant.

As she flew up through earth and ice at Siachen Heliport, she veered at the last to avoid the siren call of the gem for the quieter lights of the Indian colonel's mind. "I require your talents," she commanded, and leapt into Pandava. It was rudeness to the point of violation, but she'd warned the colonel to expect this.

Only one protesting thought from Pandava: *You may not like what you find here.* But what she found in Pandava's mind was an exquisitely appointed chariot from India's classical age. In the outside world, Colonel Pandava was clad for the arctic conditions of Siachen and armed with an AK-47, but her mental chariot bore her avatar in traditional sari and armed with a bow. "Let's go," said Madeline, boarding the chariot next to Pandava. "Now. We're ten minutes out. Reinforcements can follow. It's Roderick, and hell follows with him."

"The helicopter is already spinning up," said Pandava.

Surprising, but no time to ask about it. "Outstanding. Keep the gem with you, at all costs. Bring the poppet too, and bring my manikin—the light-weight one. Bring a wing suit. Bring more weapons—the place is sickening so fast it won't matter what we bring. I think I can keep you alive."

Pandava actually smiled at this. "You alone against 'hell'?"

"He has the power of a world behind him," said Madeline. "I have my rage." Pandava was still smiling as if to deliberately annoy her. "You're taking the End of Days with suspicious calm."

"I've had a visit from an old friend," said Pandava. "She was wounded in the recent fighting, and she told me that you'd be needing support. You should speak with her."

"I don't have time for India's national concerns."

"It's more important than that," said Pandava.

This was also very suspect. From what Madeline knew of her Family's background, nothing was ever more important to a modern Pandava than her country. But again, no time for questions, and Madeline certainly wasn't going to sit still for any wounded friend. "The copter has radio. I will speak with your friend on the way."

"Yes, you will," said Pandava, with an Indian head shake. "Now excuse me, I will focus outside."

Pandava's avatar stepped off the chariot and disappeared, as her consciousness directed her body into action, picking up her remaining gear and running for the copter. Madeline had access to Pandava's sensorium, but at arm's length, more like a virtual version than the thing itself.

But like the sudden flash of a dying sun, another spectral being manifested next to Madeline on the chariot. At the speed of thought, Madeline's sword sprang into her hand, and she attacked, throwing everything into her first blow, knowing she'd never get a second against such power.

As fast and skilled as Madeline was, the new being snatched the blade from her hand as if it were a child's dangerous toy, and the sword blazed with sudden fire at her touch. Though this female being seemed so powerful, Madeline readied craft against her. Madeline could see this woman in all her many dimensions beyond the usual three, and it was too much—Madeline couldn't even bear to look at herself too long in that cosmic way.

Even as Madeline readied some exorcism, the multidimensional being collapsed into a more conventional spiritual form. *Hell, is this mind a hotel?* But this wasn't just any guest. Her astral body fluctuated in dress and appearance. Virgin Mary blue robes changed to the blue skin of a Hindu divinity and then altered to the many breasts of the Artemis of Ephesus, each form embroidered or tattooed with the intertwining goddess symbols of a thousand cultures. Her face morphed with the features and complexions of all the world's peoples, though her closed-lipped smile was a constant promise of terrible mercies. Another constant was a Christlike wound in her side—a wound that, despite her best effort, Madeline hadn't delivered. Though hurt, this spirit was radiant with enormous power, power that would have dwarfed Madeline even when she'd been plural.

The would-be divinity smiled at Madeline. Madeline had an idea of what was coming, but that didn't make it any more tolerable when the spirit said, "Hello, daughter."

Oh no, none of this. "You're not my mother. My mother was destroyed. And don't give me that crap about being everyone's mother. I'm not going to be your good little girl."

The spirit laughed like desert sunshine. "Good? I'm neither good nor evil. Like you, I survive." She shrugged. "You may call me Prithvi—it's a regional name that fits."

Madeline knew this iconography. "Bullshit. Who were you?"

"I was someone like you."

The spirit's repeated use of "I" surprised Madeline into a question. "You're not plural?" The singular didn't fit such power, so it must be a deception.

"I am one," said Prithvi, "though my power comes from many. Much of the energy of the truly departed eventually flows to me, but not their personalities."

The copter had taken off, so time was short. "What do you want?"

"I want to help you destroy Roderick and drive back his demon."
Madeline pointed at her wound. "He do that to you?"

"He caused it," said Prithvi.

There would still be a catch. "What's the price for your help?"

"You become my enforcer."

Oh this was far too much. "You must be fucking desperate," said
Madeline.

"Desperate times," said Prithvi. "The first law is death. Who better
to enforce it than you?"

"If you think you can give centuries of hell and torture meaning,
you are insanely mistaken." Madeline had given and received oceans
of pain, and it all felt the same now.

"I didn't think you were a whiner," said Prithvi. "Choose."

"I choose my vengeance," said Madeline, unwilling to concede more.

"Close enough," said Prithvi. She examined Madeline's sword. "This
isn't a recording from your life experience. It's from your own substance, meaning that something of you is like this blade." Before
Madeline could respond, Prithvi etched the shaft in Sanskrit characters with a long, clawlike fingernail. As she finished the final letter, the
sword flamed again, but with the fires of black-lit and pure craft, al-
ternating, contesting, blending.

Prithvi handed the transformed weapon back to Madeline. "This
blade has had many names. Call it Nandaka, which means 'source of
joy.' Goes with your new look. Don't do anything I wouldn't do."

"But you'd do anything," said Madeline, grimly flourishing the hy-
brid sword as proof.

Prithvi's answering smile was terrifying in its love.

Prithvi disappeared, and Madeline looked out again on the world
through Pandava's eyes on the high mountains. She prepared to
work. In a living body, Madeline could perform better weather craft

than in a corpse. But they experienced no rough conditions, though they were conspicuously armed—two automatic rifles, a satchel charge, and grenades. The manikin for Madeline was an ultralight, almost stick-figure version: a body of wood with alchemical metal rods through it like the lead of a pencil, and a smaller than life wood-encased metal sphere for a skull, with a heinous smiley face carved into it. Also, a couple of little boxes and straps to hold things where the organs should have been. Pandava would carry the manikin folded up and hung from her pack. Once in possession, Madeline would provide all its motive force.

On the radio, Madeline heard the same updates as Pandava: the Sanctuary was now clearly visible by satellite, and the Chinese and Pakistani air forces had scrambled.

As they approached, Madeline saw the reason for crisis. Tendrils of Roderick's invasion were reaching out down the Siachen Glacier into the wider living world, unveiling the Sanctuary's plateau. But that might have one favorable consequence—something she'd been going to try anyway might actually work. "Take the copter all the way in."

If they made it, that would signal the other nations that intervention on the ground was possible. She should have found that upcoming international chaos delightful, but now it was an annoying distraction from her revenge.

Madeline would not announce her arrival to Roderick. Two could play at the hiding game, and Pandava's spirit chariot provided the same sort of stealth that Roderick had enjoyed within the abbess's mind. Madeline would stay deep within this mind until she was in shooting range.

Perhaps she should have brought the gem box the first time, but no, this order of things felt necessary, because she wasn't sure the gem would have worked then. Cornaro had successfully sliced Madeline out of the Left-Hand collective and trapped her, but Roderick's Beast was far vaster than Madeline's old plural self, and Roderick's will might be far more scattered. She or someone else would have to help the gem pull Roderick the individual together before amputating him from the world-devouring thing he'd become.

She would do her best to antagonize Roderick in order to excise him, but Madeline was afraid she knew exactly what might draw him out far enough: Rezvani's unborn child. If he hadn't learned of it yet, he would when he saw Scherie.

The copter had reached the high plateau of the Sanctuary, and as the satellite surveillance had indicated, its structures were all clearly visible. No sign of movement, but the bodies at the outer gate had been moved, and the residual craft wasn't her brother's. *Good work, Rezvani.*

But as they descended near the monastic hall, approval gave way to dark concern. Madeline had left Rezvani with the Furies, but that wasn't what worried her now. *Please, don't be in that room with him. Not without me.*

TWENTY-ONE

Our living and dead group stepped forward into the shadow surrounding the monastic hall. Oz scattered the fine dust of the green sand with one hand like a sower, and with maybe the slightest motion of the fingers of the other hand, he kept the flail whirring around above him, reaping in a whirlwind. The flail created a general, clearing wave, though sometimes he had to skew it toward intrusive tendrils. I and the Furies still carried our little sand against their piercing efforts to suborn our wills or sanities.

Up close, the dark spiritual mass resolved to something like its individual elements. The flail knocked souls out of the collective, sending them off in a long-delayed harvest. They weren't just around us, but also above and maybe somewhere below us. We were in an all-too-flexible bubble.

While possessing the corpses, I completely relied on Oz for spiritual defense. I was somewhere close to exhaustion, but soon I would have to fight far more, and perhaps with fewer tools than I'd been using. In the company of the Furies, one of my weapons, my soul-destroying words, might be off the table. Probably for the best, but it would have been nice to discuss the rules of engagement.

The collective tide made a slithering animal noise as we drove it back, its malice groping for a gap through which to strike us. Call me paranoid, but I felt them reaching for my child. If they were, they were doing it with the simple yet coordinated will of a swarm of ants. This collective creature wasn't a Yasukuni—the individuals were more homogenized, the end result of billions of spirits being slowly chewed by their own vast totality, a worm ouroboros of souls. Also, unlike Yasukuni, it was growing, tendrils spreading fast out into the world.

We reached the entrance with its skeletal guardian statues and levered double doors. The one Rabu had used was shut again. We couldn't stack on them properly and keep our formation against the encroaching evil, but the doors opened easily with the dead hand's touch of one of my shield-corpses. Odd—so much spiritual force to keep people out, but no one locked the door. No, it was more than that. Those same guard statues had helped me at the outer gate. Despite this spiritual version of the thorn barrier to Sleeping Beauty's castle, the building itself felt like the House of Morton when it welcomed me, warming and comforting, only this semi-sentient building was terminally sick, and didn't seem to know that it was welcoming us to some fresh hell.

The foyer had a shoe rack. Fuck it—no time for the local customs. More importantly, no sign of the likely boots of my friends.

Exiting the foyer, we steered straight toward the red double doors at the end of the long corridor, which seemed to telescope out endlessly, like in *The Shining*. I wondered how my husband and friends, without my skills and Oz's tools, could still be alive in here, then banished the thought. I would know if they were dead, the same way wives and friends often knew such things. Also, this place had gotten a lot worse just in the time I'd been here, while they had arrived much earlier.

As we moved forward, careful to keep formation, the dark spiritual mass was less menacing and grabby in our personal space, as if it were concentrating on the borders for attack or defense. But we had new horrors trying to distract us. The sliding doors of the side rooms of the corridor were all open, and on the walls of the rooms and the panels of the doors silhouettes were doing nasty things to each other. This theatricality meant that, unlike the soul-mass outside, a malicious intelligence was at work here.

At the end of the corridor, I again directed one of my corpses to open the doors. As I expected and feared, it was a meditation hall and a hellscape combined. A hum filled my ears, like the world's largest microwave. Golden streaming power faded into leprous gray sickness on the walls. Like the side rooms of the corridor, shadow plays performed on the floor, ceiling, and walls, but they'd moved from conventional crimes to scenes from Hieronymus Bosch.

A scattering of monks and nuns were seated on stones, not moving. Were they still meditating? This seemed extreme even for their reputed uselessness. Madeline had said, "Kill them all," but I couldn't trust her rules of engagement against such as these.

In the center aisle, Rabu's body lay with no sign of his spirit. Rabu, but not Dale, Endicott, or Marlow, thank God. No sign of Madeline either.

At the front of the hall, the monastic-robed bodies of two women and a man lay at the foot of the dais. On the dais, a short nun in a distinct robe, probably the abbess, stood behind a seated monk. In her raised right hand was some ritual-looking blade, while her left rested on the shaved head of the monk. This was a clear provocation to break formation, and I didn't dare. Besides, I was going to give her one chance: give me Dale and my friends, and I'd leave it for others to punish her killings.

Killings. She had no *K*s or *M*s. "I don't see any sins," I said to anyone listening, though the place was manifestly wrong, and Cornaro's conscience had fooled me. No sign either of the distinct power of the person I half expected to be here at the center of things.

"Stay where you are," said the abbess. She fixed her gaze on me, then on the Crone, who'd moved up next to me. "You had one task."

"Yes," said the Crone. "And we're doing it."

The abbess pointed her blade at them in refutation. "My method is mundane, far from the West, and outside of your jurisdiction. This is none of your business." She pulled back the monk's head, and sliced his exposed throat from ear to ear. Blood spurted from the cut carotid with an unnatural sluggishness.

I briefly wondered about taking control of the now four bodies in addition to those I was running—but no, beyond my current skills and energy.

"To her," the Crone said. "Slow and steady." We moved down the hall toward the dais at a measured pace, approaching first Rabu's body. "KIA," said the Maiden. "Outstanding." Which, despite the seeming coldness, I realized was her way of honoring him as a fellow fighter. She took the dagger out of the dog's chest and gave me a look over her shoulder. "Bloody vengeance," she said, like Siri reminding me of a dentist appointment.

As we moved delicately around the dog, I and the Maiden kept alert for any attack from the front, while the others kept the rest of the room secured in their gaze. The abbess stood motionless, waiting—and why not, she had the high ground in the hall.

If we were going to fight, this might be my last chance to interrogate this bloody abbess. "Where's Dale Morton? Where are Endicott and Marlow?"

"Shush," said the Crone. "Do not speak to the accused."

On the wall was a circular opening to a valley vista that didn't belong in Siachen. Though I couldn't see the details, the view wasn't as horrific as it should have been. I asked Oz. "Is that the portal?"

"Not the hell portal. More likely, the gate to the heart of the Sanctuary. Your friends may have gone through it."

I thought to charge into it immediately, but then Oz started his crazy portal song, with its mantra of military operations and Russian names. Behind me, the Crone murmured as if to herself: "You don't have much time left for singing."

She'd said something similar outside about Oz. And something here was tugging me to stay—in the microwave hum, in the sickly golden-gray luminescence. I'd remain, at least for another moment.

At some silent signal, the Matron and the Maiden broke formation and leapt onto the dais. The abbess threw her bloodied blade like a

Jovian bolt, but the Maiden caught it in midair, adding one to her collection.

A flurry of kicks and punches ensued, too fast for me to follow. I'd fallen out of accelerated mode to save my energy, and the Crone had a hand on my arm to discourage joining the fray. The other two Furies confirmed her confidence, pinning the small abbess between them, though they were breathing heavily from the effort, and more than a few of the abbess's blows had landed hard and true.

The Crone stepped forward to face the restrained accused. "The Earth against Chu Jiang, Abbess of the Monastery of the Sanctuarium Mundi."

"No sins," I repeated weakly.

"You're not looking right," said the Crone, somewhat exasperated, but not wrathful. "The sins are in the land." She continued her indictment. "Count one: you have summoned one of the so-called Left-Hand gods into our world, putting all sentient beings at risk."

The abbess laughed madly. Still singing, Oz had taken an empty stone seat in the front right-hand corner of the hall, beyond the steps up to the dais on that side. He was spreading a circle of sand around him, and his flail was still out and whirring protection, so for the moment he was set. Good. Could I just jump through now? No, still something tugging me back, something about this whole bloody display.

"Count two," said the Crone. "You have destroyed, or have assisted in the destruction of, the souls of the men and women in your charge at this Monastery within the World's Sanctuary."

I looked again at the monks. "No souls?" That could be a problem. I readied my exorcistic invective.

"I think I'll make a pyramid of their skulls," said the abbess.

Oz sang louder and louder. "Still can't find the way. Some power in my way. We're so fecked, fecked, fecked, diddley-ay." Something in his high overtones was giving me a headache.

"Quiet!" said the Crone. "Count three: you have attempted to suborn the will of the agents of the *Oikumene* and obstruct the Earth's justice."

Oz kept at his song in a quieter mode, but it still crushed my head. The Crone reached her summation. "Any one of these offenses brings you within our jurisdiction. The very ground beneath our feet accuses you. I will now pronounce judgment."

Tactically ridiculous, this announcement of their intentions. But at least it gave me my cue for my final opportunity. "Wait, before judgment, I need to know. Where is Dale Morton?"

"Come closer and I'll tell you," said the abbess.

"Is he through there?" I pointed at the hole in the rear wall.

"Girl," cautioned the Crone. "You've long exhausted our patience." Then she nodded at the other two Furies. "Ready?"

"Something is wrong here," I said.

The Crone nodded her head again. With one of the strange daggers, the Maiden stabbed the abbess in the heart, then sliced her throat from ear to ear with the other blade.

The Matron, hand on the abbess's forehead, said "Go to your rest." The Crone and I watched as, with the usual explosion of craft at the death of a practitioner, the abbess's spirit left her body.

The Maiden's hands were red, and for the first time, her smile seemed truly happy to me.

"We'll mark the time of execution as approximate," said the Crone. "That concludes these proceedings." She nodded at me. "Your vengeance is also done. We appreciate your assistance in this matter. We'll see you in a few months."

Oz's song of frustration indicated he was still trying to find a portal. "We still have this invasion from hell to deal with," I said.

"Our jurisdiction is narrow," said the Crone. "That's the point."

I held up a hand. I still needed to find Dale and my friends, but the pull of this place had only gotten stronger with the abbess's demise. "This is still ongoing. Wait. Just one moment. Please."

I pushed this killing's associations through my mind, trying to find the one making me hesitate. In chess, to go the crooked way was as direct as straight ahead. No, not chess, but theater. The theatricality was familiar, the bloody sleight of hand of a stage magician from the Grand Guignol. "Kill them all," Madeline had said. Madeline—I'd seen this scene before, when I'd tried desperately to destroy that ancient witch in H-ring. How old was the abbess? Fuck the body, how old a spirit? Old spirits could come back, and these Furies were about to leave me alone with her.

With desperate déjà vu, I yelled, "Hack her body to pieces!"

In a synchronicity of major craft impossible for any one practitioner, the abbess was already attacking. Between her reanimation and action, she didn't hesitate. No chitchat, no monologuing, no fucking around. Her arm a preternatural blur, she pulled the dagger from her own chest and threw it, striking the Matron to give her a matching wound in the heart.

But I was only partially aware of this, because as the abbess rose into the air, glowing with power, she politely spoke the horrible words that I had used on Cornaro. As if standing in front of the blast of a moon rocket, I was hit with the soul-destroying craft.

Subjective time became eternity as my soul was slowly, painfully burned away from my flesh. Even with such pain, I had the space of thought to be so, so scared. Annihilation was coming. My only small comfort was that at least this time, I wasn't doing it to someone else.

Unbound, I fell into blackness. *Good-bye, world. God is great.*

At Leh, Vasilisa was yelling at an officer with a close-trimmed beard and mustache while other Indian soldiers nervously held Tavors at ready. "Is stupid! We need plane. Now." The Russian was at the head of a group of practitioners who'd received a farsight report of the coming crisis: Mama Suji, Dude, an anonymous Korean dressed in a suit appropriate for airport security, and several others. Their friends were in mortal trouble in the mountains, so they'd come from around the world to help any way they could. Of them, Vasilisa was the least constrained by social propriety or craft diplomacy, so she was hitting the Indians with their collective frustration, while Mama Suji and the others assessed the quickest way to steal one of Leh's aircraft.

That Vasilisa's greatest fear in the world, Roderick Morton, might be behind the danger in the mountains was a concern for later. Right now, their biggest enemy was time.

In the dark silence, a young woman's voice said, "Not quite yet."

With painful spiritual impact, arms caught my astral body, shocking my soul back into coherence. The arms spun me around; it was the kohl-eyed teenager I'd hallucinated at Cornaro's. "Fuck it, you're heavy." Then, hands under my astral armpits, she flung me back up through the void.

As I rose back into my body, I knew two things. I realized who the teenager was, or rather, who she would be, maybe. People said that having children was like living with your heart outside of your body. But my heart, my daughter, was still within me, saving me.

I also knew the enemy I faced. At the beginning of the terrible words, she, no, he, had said *"Please."* Perhaps the abbess was still in that body too, but Roderick Morton had always been my true adversary. One way or another, that fight had to end today.

Seeing again through my wide-open eyes, I remained absolutely still, not wanting to draw Roderick's attentions until I'd scanned the room, assessing the tactical situation. Perhaps I was now immune to easy soul-destruction, as if by antibodies passed from my child, or a mirror fashioned within my mind—but for how long?

The four corpses I'd brought in with us had been swiped from my control, and they were fighting along with the soulless monks and nuns against the Furies. I was probably too new to this skill to get them back, but I'd try.

Other former monks and nuns were rushing in, puppets all. But they weren't the poorly controlled meat puppets I'd seen before. Each fought with a different martial art, though they were all coordinated in their attacks. They were also preternaturally powerful, punching into the wall and kicking into the monks' seats as if stone were Japanese paper.

Dagger in her chest, the Matron remained up and fighting, weakly, as her heart's blood flowed out like some Catholic martyr's. Discarding the other ritual dagger for her own knives, the Maiden was leaping and fighting atop the stone seats in a slashing joy of fighting and blood. The Crone grimly moved from point to optimal point, giving the perfect blow at the perfect moment to disable one zombie, then another.

His initial onslaught accomplished, Roderick surveyed all through the abbess's body, still atop the dais, and spoke in free admiration of that body's mortal wounds. "Who needs blood when ichor flows through our veins?"

What was my priority here? The one thing that could threaten Roderick's otherworldly power was what Oz was doing, but if I moved closer to Oz to protect him, Roderick would focus on us both. I would protect Oz by keeping Roderick's attention on me. Me against Roderick—this was my impossible fate from the start. Impossible, because I was no St. George or al-Khadr. First, I'd try to get my corpses back.

But even as I decided this, the Roderick-abbess thing pointed down at me and said, "Liar. You're still in there. *Please be silent.*"

My craft died on my tongue as he, no, they continued to speak. "Silence means consent. We used to tell Madeline that." They leered at me. "Do you understand us? I see that you do. You understood us from the beginning."

Oh yes, you fucking mind rapist, I knew you from the first stink of your craft.

The merged things were talking faster now, loudly over the sounds of the Furies fighting, and differently than the Roderick I'd known before—short sentences merging multiple personalities. "The spell was supposed to be a nuclear weapon. Not possible. With this much power, should be instant destruction. We'll try again. Wait. *Please show me your sins.*"

My only consolation was that my soul's shame might distract them from my true secret.

"Oh, you have been very, very naughty," they said. "You bear the mark of the Great Beast, destroyer of worlds. But we are that world destroyer. You are merely damned. Or maybe . . ."

The Roderick-abbess's eyes went weird and black-lit, and I felt I was being looked through in all dimensions. Then they stole my remaining hope. "Ah, you're with child! No one told us your happy news. Well, suffer little children to come unto us, for this is the kingdom of heaven. Let's see, *Oikumene* prophecies, Morton blood, so much possibility . . . She'll be perfect. For unto us a child is given. Please hold still while we work on you. We shall call her Madeline."

Tendrils of dark power reached out from Roderick-abbess's fingertips down toward my womb. On the other side of the hall, the Maiden was roaring in pain, and the Matron had finally crumpled to the ground. No sign of the Crone. Oz was singing a nuclear winter rebel execution ballad. All was lost.

Then, the young woman's voice returned, not in my head, but standing next to me, opaquely spectral, and full of gothic teen outrage. "Madeline? That's not my fucking name, and never will be."

And with her words, I was free. Horrible obscenities spewed from me as I drove back the dark presence that reached for my body. I wanted to tell my little girl, *cover your ears!* Between invectives, I spared her another thought. *How can you be here, like this?*

She heard me. *In this god-awful shitty place and time, what I could be, or could have been, matters.*

I felt the very air change temperature as the Roderick-abbess brought most of their attention to bear on me. "Please, resist all you like. We will take your body and the girl at leisure. No help is coming. The world is ours."

My possible teenage daughter didn't respond with a roll of her eyes and a "whatever." She gave the Roderick-thing the finger and put a spike of exorcising craft on it. *Wonder where she'd get that from.*

In riposte, the tendrils moved around us instead of directly toward me, threatening to cocoon us for a dark metamorphosis. I should have despaired, but with a miracle fighting beside me, I was done insulting God. Instead, I insulted Roderick. *"Goddamned sister-raping mutant, get the fuck away from my daughter!"*

Reaching for obscenities that tapped the core of our minds' power, we fought to keep the weaving cocoon at a distance. We fought to move up the stairs to get my hands on that abbess's throat. We fought in the true jihad of the spirit, though damned I well might be.

Against our struggle, a burst of power pulsed through the abbess's small form. I hadn't seen such power since the bunker. The invading portal must be inside her. Good to know, but very bad news. They had barely begun to tap the energy I'd seen in that world, and I was already tiring. *A little more help would be nice,* I thought, or prayed.

As if in response, in the corner of my vision, a distortion of the air moved in an arc from the hole at the back of the hall over the dais and down to the floor. A feeling filled me, a presence, and attacking with renewed intensity, I tried to hide my emotion from the Roderick-thing or the surprise would be lost too soon.

But one of the stealth party wasn't briefed on tactics. A single bark broke the silence of their bubble. The Roderick-thing's cocoon wavered. Then, a whistling moved across the octaves as a pocket tornado took shape on the dais and slowly moved toward the enemy.

"Daddy's home," said my daughter, eyes rolling with mock exasperation. "About fucking time."

A fter using his favorite power to distract the abbess with hurricane winds, Dale surveyed the situation just long enough to see that Scherie was alive and fighting before he broke from his friends and moved toward her. He wanted to hold her close, but despite every emotion, he kept his tactical sense and kept a distance between himself and her. They would hit the enemy from all sides.

Dale took a swordsman's stance toward the threat, his black-lit left side to the rear, his left hand tucked behind him. He felt like a child hiding his mischief.

In rapid response, the abbess's face seemed to bud into five, blurring as if rapidly moving from one position to another. All five mouths seemed to speak at once. The one facing the whirlwind asked it to *"Please calm down,"* as if Dale needed further confirmation that it was Roderick in there. The face turned in Dale's direction called him out. "You again? You useless jism of Joshua's line. We are the true heir of the Morton Family. All of it."

Dale grinned like the trickster Coyote stealing the sun, and with a wave of his left hand, called forth the proof that he was the son and the heir of all Mortons.

Like a raptor made of night itself, the Left-Hand spirits rushed through the gate. In this space of the outer Sanctuary, those spirits were again massed in combined form, not as the naughty pet of the House of Morton, but the unrepentant killer revenants of their collective hearts' desire. But something of their recent individual manifestations survived, for Dale thought he saw Curwen's face at the front of their attacking mass.

The spirits attacked with the pent-up outrage of two centuries. Roderick was supposed to have saved them or joined them. He'd done neither, throwing away his legacy on his quixotic quest for apotheosis. They did not care if they burned up their remaining substance in this fight—when better, against what worthier opponent?

Instead of all joining the direct assault, some of them split off to contest the control of the bodies of the dead. The demon of this invading world had never needed to fight so sharply for its food of souls. Though the Left-Hand spirits couldn't face the direct power of a whole hellworld any more than Dale could himself, they could help to keep Roderick's force divided, giving them all time and possibility.

Even as Roderick fought the spirits of his former family, he whispered polite suasion at Dale. *"Please join me, and rule with me."* But Dale had a lifetime of resisting such promises, and his acceptance of Left-Hand power hadn't so skewed his moral compass. He continued to direct spirits and storm against this blight on his Family, grown beyond all scale of possible continuance in a living world. Though Dale fought in the Family's name, the Sanctuary's echoes of Joshua and Dale's father, grandfather, and real mother hadn't joined him, causing him a brief disappointment and a brief wonder why.

Concerned despite the necessity for absolute concentration, Dale spared another glance toward Scherie. Something was wrong with her forehead that he couldn't quite make out. He also saw the strange spectral young woman fighting with her. Strange, but familiar in a way that someone who'd lived with centuries of ancestral portraits instantly grasped. She was like a foreboding made manifest, driving Dale desperately on.

When Morton went toward Rezvani, Endicott moved the other way, taking the left-side steps up the dais in one bound. Disdaining modesty, his eye now saw through the shell of the abbess's body to the being within, and he knew that Dale was right: the many-headed dragon was Roderick returned.

To help the team keep Roderick occupied and unable to concentrate on any individual, Endicott would use his strongest spiritual force, despite the taint it now bore. As he rationalized it, though he was still in the Sanctuary, he wasn't in its heart, so his power of command was again on the table. Or at least he couldn't screw things up any worse.

So, in his prayerful way, Endicott told the evil spiritual mass to fuck off. "*In God's name, go back to your hellworld, Demon.*"

Other than the abbess appearing to sprout multiple faces, nothing seemed to change. He realized that he could have successfully repulsed the evil presence in this world only to have it instantly replaced by a different portion of the hellworld's collective spirit.

The abbess's face in his direction retaliated. "*My children. Please hold him still and silent and take his craft for yourselves.*" Those were Roderick's words from the fight in the bunker, and he was trying to take control again of the Left-Hand nanites in Endicott's system, and through them, Endicott himself. But as with forgiven sins, Endicott had long ago assimilated those nanites, and they remained his alone.

The spiritual strikes now came as fast as their thoughts. Both combatants wielded greater power than in their previous fight. He repeatedly commanded Roderick—*"In Christ's name, freeze"*—but each held for a shorter time than it took to say the words. *What now, God?*

His preternatural eye saw the tendrils reaching for him and his team. He waved his sword, now shining again. *"In God's name, back off!"* In a succession of such prayers, he wrestled Roderick for his own will and the will of his friends, keeping them all as free from compulsion as he could. He didn't try to save the free will of humanity; he couldn't protect the whole world at once, just this small part, and maybe not even that. Praying on, and on, Endicott's commands broke down into mantras, the mantras fused back into new prayers. *Father, Son, Holy Spirit, thy will be done.*

Then, he felt the spirit effervesce within him, and like his Puritan ancestors, he started singing the Psalms with his commands. Roaring, tuneless, singing. *Oh God, anything but this.*

Even as he drew from the deepest well of spirit for his tremendous authority, a truth tore at his soul. *This isn't a stalemate. She's dying.* The global presence who had first given him such unprecedented power was failing, and unless they found a way to win, he'd fail along with her.

With Rabu's bark, Grace Marlow dropped the stealth that had gotten them in close and sought the best tactical position for her talents while keeping the demon's attention divided. She knew it was Roderick in the abbess the same way she knew some puddings had raisins in them; once she knew where to look, she wasn't easy to deceive.

Then she saw Meg, the one they called the Maiden. She'd known Meg before she'd taken her office as Fury, when MI13 had thought that a kiss and a cuddle with an agent of the *Oikumene* might be helpful. But it was friendly spying, and before the assignment's end, Grace had actually come to care for this strange, broken, yet terribly strong and angry girl.

Meg was covered in blood, her own and that of the meat puppets that assailed her. Grace knew well the look on Meg's face: she was in ecstasy. She would not last much longer.

Grace knew how to fight zombies. In the recent battle, they had surprised her mid-charge. Now, she would surprise them.

Part of deception and stealth was appearing weak to an opponent. Well, Grace was still recovering from her hurts, so she was halfway there. With a Latin invocation, she exaggerated the appearance of her problems.

She cried out, "Meg! Help me!" At this ridiculous request, Meg spared her a glance and gave Grace's deception a broken-toothed smile that melted her heart. Like predators sensing the prey lagging behind the herd, some of the zombie monks turned their attention toward Grace. Excellent. As the royal head of British craft liked to say, "If God won't save the Queen and country, do it yourself."

D ale and my friends had spread out their attacks, and it was helping. The concentration of Left-Hand power on Dale disturbed me, but I couldn't help him with it except by continuing my own fight. I had my sensitive synesthesia of all the combats, so I didn't have to take my eyes off Roderick to have an idea of what was going on.

But I did look when I heard the bark again. It was Rabu's spirit. My heart didn't have time to break—later. The dog circled behind Dale and approached Roderick between us, hackles up, pointing himself at Roderick, growling, but not moving. If Rabu was waiting for some command, I didn't dare give it. He knew his business.

From outside, the sound of a copter. "Good," said the Roderick-thing. "That will be Colonel Pandava coming for her Kurukshetra War redux."

From my right, Oz sang, "He's blocking me."

Shut up, Oz, or he'll focus more on you. I was already doing everything I could to distract Roderick, but he apparently wasn't going to neglect Oz's efforts while he dealt with the rest of us and Pandava outside.

Hold it, there was one thing the dog could help with that I'd neglected for tactical reasons. "Rabu, protect Oz!"

"Feck that," sang Oz from his small bubble of power. "I'm grand. Working. The flail turning and turning in steady gyre, the center can hold and wait for things to come together, right now, over me. I just need one break."

Maybe he'd get one. The power radiating from the abbess seemed erratic, as if gaps were forming in Roderick's control. Perhaps all our efforts were stretching his multitasking to the limit.

I wouldn't use the terrible words where they might actually destroy a human soul, but here, even though Roderick could surely resist them, they might be the straw that broke the Beast's back.

With all my force, I spoke the words and did the craft. The blast hit the Roderick-thing like a slap, staggering him back.

He recovered, straightening, the abbess's eyes that faced me blazing with his inner rage. "You dare!"

"Oh shit," said my possible daughter. "You've pissed him off."

The abbess's five faces turned red with anger, then purple. Then, like grotesque balloons, they filled with otherworldy power, expanding, stretching, stretching . . .

"Oh shit, shit!" said my daughter, raising her arm over her immaterial face. "This is gonna be so gross."

With a wet pop of exploding power, the abbess's body burst. Bits of abbess flew everywhere. For a moment, the invasive portal stood revealed, naked, at the feet of the ten-headed spectral dragon that must be Roderick. Then, small tendrils reached out from the portal and, despite our continued attacks, grabbed the larger pieces of flesh. Without regard to human form, they morphed the pieces together as a large fleshy tentacle reaching out from the portal, with five smaller tentacles branching out from its end, the probing material aspect of the Beast in our world.

Each smaller polyp-like extrusion had a tiny mouth at its tip. As the mouths opened and closed like a fish's, I could see glimpses of the portal's hellworld-show within.

The five polyp-mouths of the Roderick-thing spoke at once in high, piping voices. "We were afraid this might happen. Our poor, dear abbess is gone, but what's done is done. We wish to warn you: we are fighting you with our many arms tied behind our back. Please do not force us to further exertion. We are difficult to restrain as it is. Continue to resist, and our greater self will break our bonds and devour all, and in the brief time before the end, humanity will despise you as the nightmare figures from their apocalypses. Delightful irony, yes?"

A doomsday threat, and something almost pathetic about Roderick trying not to destroy the world. But Roderick was a profound threat to human freedom, not in some political sense, but a threat to every choice. I'd seen what those reaching tendrils could do to powerful practitioners with strong natural resistance. Anyone less powerful would be absolutely enslaved.

"Live free or die," I said, with more craft invective following. None of us stopped fighting for a moment.

"Very amusing," said the Roderick-thing. The sound of jets passed over head. "Hear that? That will be the advance forces of China, Pakistan, and India. The other great powers will be here soon as well, all vectors for our disease."

Damn it, we were fighting so well, but we were giving all we had, and it wasn't enough. Time was running out.

My face must have betrayed my desperation, for even as she fended off Roderick's continual incursions, my possible daughter reached a spectral hand toward me and said, "The greatest of these, Mother, is hope."

Then, the doors to the hall exploded.

Madeline and Pandava landed in front of the monastic hall. Wearing a full pack of armament, Pandava moved through the dark spiritual mass like a deep ocean fish, but Madeline stood with her flaming sword on the ramparts of her mind, and nothing of that evil could truly touch either of them. Still no sign of Rezvani or the rest; damnation, she'd gone in without her.

Like fairytale breadcrumbs, bits of Oz's green sand on the ground outlined the path Rezvani had taken. The dark tendrils reached for Pandava, but Madeline deflected their advances with economical strokes, trying to keep her true power hidden. The tendrils weren't particularly aggressive. Why bother? If they thought about it at all, Pandava would appear to them to be the first of many to be assimilated and sent back out.

At the entrance, she again faced the guardians. They had resisted her before, but she had been alien and rude. *Please let us in*, she thought. *We're here to fix this.*

Just as the House of Morton had once allowed its Right-Hand invaders, the doors swung open. Roderick still hadn't learned to respect the land. Inside, only thin shafts of gold remained in the rotting, oozing ambient craft on the walls, while in the side rooms, the shadows dramatized Roderick's memories and fantasies of torture and killings. So, so sick, in such a short time. She thought again of her old home. *So very like you, House, in the last, bad days of my brother.*

Roderick's will seemed absent from this periphery; his focus must be totally elsewhere. That was very bad. "Hurry," she told Pandava.

Disregarding personal safety, Pandava ran down the corridor. The inner doors to the meditation hall were locked. They'd get one try, then Roderick would bar this way against them.

That was why they'd brought a twenty-pound satchel charge. *Sorry, Monastery, this is going to hurt. But you know it has to be done, or the rot will spread.*

Pandava set the charge and sheltered in one of the phantasmagoric side rooms. *Ready my manikin*, said Madeline. They laid it out on the floor. *Get down and stay down*, she told Pandava. The colonel had done her job without question or compensation, which was something even a Left-Hand Morton appreciated. Madeline jumped into the stick thing, put on the pack with the grenades, and slung the AK-47s over each of her shoulder bars. She stored the gem box in a wood-and-metal container around where her pelvis would have been.

"Keep Cornaro's poppet safe," she said. "Now, set off the charge." What did she care about shrapnel? With the rattle of wood-sheathed limbs, she ran out into the corridor even as the doorway exploded inward, percussing her stick form with its thunder and collapsing parts of the ceiling and lintel. No time to survey the damage, she was going in. She was a golem, but she needed no kabalistic word. She was the word of life, and death.

Bounding over and through the rubble, Madeline surveyed the hall. The good news was that Roderick was indeed highly focused. The horror was that, even as he fought all of the craftspeople, he was concentrating particularly on Rezvani and the spirit who fought with her. Like a grasping fist, his power was closing around Scherie and the strange spectral girl with her.

Madeline had to get his attention. "Roderick, I'm here. Come out and play, little brother." She had been first born of the twins, and in life he'd punished any reminder of that.

Other than a few probing tendrils, he was ignoring her. She'd always hated that. And the damned zombies everywhere. What the fuck was so hard to understand about "kill them all"? A rifle in each hand, she fired at the meat puppets. She pulped several of them into collapse with a storm of metal never seen in this place. "Death, death, death!" She laughed with the sheer joy of it, for she (and everyone she'd ever been) missed this carnage. *Whoops, watch my aim, nearly hit Marlow.*

But breaking Roderick's toys wasn't working today. As she'd expected, he was obsessive about Rezvani and her child. No sense in keeping anything in reserve—time to deploy the gem. She let go of the rifles, hanging like puppets on a puppet. With one hand, she pulled the gem box out of her container and held it toward the tentacle. With the other, she summoned her sword, Nandaka, and flourished it, mostly as defense against what she expected to follow.

"*Lazarus, come forth!*" she said. Invoking Roderick with a blasphemy would surely make him listen.

Roderick's dragon form manifested around the tentacle. A line of magnetic force seemed to have caught one of the dragon's ten heads, stretching it out toward her. But the thing's scrawny neck held.

"*Break, damn you!*" Perhaps it stretched another inch, but as she'd feared, Roderick's Beast was vast enough to resist the gem.

Beast. Didn't she have one of those around here? Yes, there he was, as always right where he should be.

"Rabu," she said. "Kill."

B ack where he'd died, Rabu was less substantial again, more like the normal spirits he'd herded all his life. He wasn't done yet. The souls of the long-sitting ones were long gone, but there remained one spirit here who was within his territory. He had gone to another world, but now he was back in Rabu's yard: the dragon that was once a man.

Rabu would help him move on.

The dragon's many heads looked the same, but Rabu could smell which one was the rotten soul who directed this rabid mess. He watched it, tracking it with his muzzle, waiting for the moment like he waited for scraps.

Then, the mixed-odored ghost said "kill." Not quite right, but he knew what she meant.

Rabu bounded into the air and clamped his spectral jaws on the rotten head's neck. Slowly, like gnawing a bone, he began to worry the rotten one out.

Good dog, he thought.

I'd sensed it as Madeline's stick woman had brought out the gem box and Rabu had attacked the dragon, going right for one of its throats. Whatever they were doing was working. The force directed against us abated, so I turned to see. Something spectral like Roderick's old decaying head was being stretched toward the box in Madeline's left hand, while in her right she wielded a flaming ectoplasmic sword. *I want one of those.*

"Come to me, brother," said Madeline. "I've such things to show you." She stepped toward him, and he screamed at her in some dead language of the Left Hand, blasting at her spirit with craft that should have destroyed even the memory of her existence, but she stood against him, shattering the shots of malice with the fiery blade.

The cocoon around me and my possible daughter drifted completely apart. Marlow had stumbled back to Endicott, and they were holding each other up and looking for the next threat. Dale was calling the Left-Hand spirits to heel.

I would go to Dale now, but a coldness on my arm stopped me. "Done with that bastard," said my possible girl, suddenly serious and stern beyond her apparent years. "You'll get your choice now."

"What?"

"You've seen the power of my potential," she said. "Now you know. Your choice." And with that oracle, this future child vanished.

I didn't want to think about her words. My hand went to my stomach. *Still here*, I thought.

My husband was studying the tentacle and its continued steady flow outward of dark spiritual power, seemingly oblivious to all else. "Dale!" I called.

He turned and held up his left hand to halt me mid-stride. "Wait a moment, love. Don't get too close to this. We're far from done here."

Oh God, his hand. The concentration of Left-Hand power hadn't been attacking him; it was him. He was black-lit with Left-Hand craft. Tears welled up. My damnation seemed nothing to his. What would we do?

The greatest of these, Mother, is hope.

No, it couldn't be. *See better.* Then I really saw it, felt it: he was only half Left Hand. The realization was like a thunderbolt. He simply was what he'd always been. My fears for him, his sanity, his moral destruction weren't gone, but his compromise wasn't so great a change, nor was it the final word. We had time.

I looked into his face. His mouth was gaping; he'd had his own shock. He pointed at me, then at his own forehead. He'd seen my sigil of damnation.

"I'm so sorry," I said. My tears fell.

He gave a ghastly smile and held up the three sign. Trinity, made with his black-lit left hand. "Nobody's perfect, love. It may not be what you think. Besides, it looks good on you. We'll talk later."

Damn him. I was going to hug him to death.

But then the levee failed, and the hellworld broke loose. The tentacle disintegrated in a ball of dark flame. Dale tumbled away from it.

The naked invasive portal floated freely in the air, a growing rip in the very fabric of existence, and like a monstrous snake of infinite length, the Beast pushed through, ripping the fabric further. Roderick hadn't lied; he was all that had restrained the Beast. The demon was pouring out in a peristaltic stream across the hall and through the doorway, ignoring us few of the living here. The dark stream seemed to obey gravity, as it would be flowing down these mountains for the bright juicy world. Yasukuni had been thousands of souls, and it nearly broke me. This thing might have billions behind it.

Faster and faster came the raging flood. Unchecked, it would devour all life and make our Earth a twin of its home.

Madeline was still dueling with Roderick. "Curwen!" called Dale. "Help us stop this." Marlow and Endicott rushed toward him. A dark river divided us, but I could cross it—I was the world's greatest exorcist.

But Oz was yelling for attention. "I've got it. Someone help me hold it."

Thank God, the other portal, finally. I entered Oz's sphere of protection, and saw what he saw. Toward the right wall of the hall stood his portal, right even with the floor, and big enough for a person to duck into. This portal felt, sounded, smelled the same as the other in this room, or the one back in the Virginian bunker. He'd done it.

"OK," I said. "What do you need me to do?" I was exhausted, but anything that could help his mission to save the world would be worth it.

"I need you to come with me. Now."

N o," I said. It was too much. Too much for him to ask. Too much after fighting so hard to survive, to save my child, to see Dale again. *This must be what Cornaro thought that no one would be willing to do.*

Yet, as sure as gravity, the craft had its own cold equations. To save the world, a living person had to step through the portal to give possibility to the zero world. When that person failed, as they eventually must, their body would be killed and soul consumed until nothing was left of self, until they were just a small piece of the overwhelming hunger.

But before dying, that person had to survive for long enough for the death to have meaning. Oz's sins were fading, his power and life sputtering. The flail was whirring slower and slower. Oz didn't have the strength both to hold the portal open and go through it.

"This is why you were born," he said.

"No." Dale and I and Endicott and Grace were supposed to fight and have adventures forever. Not this.

"Not everything can be justified for a child," Oz said.

"No." He wasn't helping, just pissing me off.

"But the world . . ."

"No," I said. "Not both of us. Just me. You need to hold the portal open." I explained it in his own language. "You're fecking useless."

I opened my hands. I didn't have to tell him again. Oz slapped the flail into one open palm and the pouch of green sand into my other. I ignored the pain from my damaged left wrist.

He resumed his portal song, his voice weak from singing and failing life. "Now," he said. "While it's nearly headless and looking another way."

I would make a choice while anyone still could. The world, my friends, and my love, weighed against me and my child. Everyone gets eaten, or just us. No real choice at all. If it came to it on the other side, I could destroy us both rather than be chewed down to nothing.

I looked over again at Dale, fighting hopelessly with the others against the oncoming tide. If I didn't do this, he would. I would never allow that—the Beast would have him as completely as it had Roderick.

So this is the funeral I promised—what Oz might call an American wake, a funeral in advance. One funeral for two, me and my unborn daughter within me, and everything she would have been. I don't feel that it's redemption, just necessity.

I raise my fist to my shoulder and thrust it forward, signaling action to my front. Knowing her sensitivity, I turn my head to Madeline and mouth one word: "remember."

A last surprise: Rabu's ghost has run up from dealing with Roderick to follow me, though I'm sure he's never seen the Mahabharata or *The Twilight Zone*. KIA, so his funeral too. I don't insult him by asking whether he means it. This dog has already twice followed me into hell.

A last look back at Dale, still fighting. *Good-bye, my love.*

"God is great." I go through.

CHAPTER

TWENTY-FOUR

Despite all her power, Madeline was tiring in her fight with her brother. *Can't let him beat me again.* But at this moment of her greatest need, Rabu let go of Roderick's neck, and like a deserter ran off toward Rezvani. She mouthed something at Madeline. *Remember? What the hell is she doing?*

Now, revenant! Strike now! It was the Crone, who'd at last dropped her stealth and was speaking in her thoughts. Roderick had turned his decaying eyes toward Scherie and Oz, and the Crone stood near him, silently pointing at a spot on his dark shimmering neck.

With no time to approach, Madeline made a desperate play, and threw her flaming sword where the Crone's long bony finger marked Roderick's doom.

At the moment her sword Nandaka plunged into her brother's neck, the tide of dark spirit abruptly pulled back, and as if a rope had snapped, she nearly fell as the gem finally ripped free that spectral head, the chunk of the Beast that was Roderick. Her brother was trapped.

"Rezvani!" cried Madeline, hoping to stop whatever madness Scherie intended. But she was gone. Madeline tossed the gem aside— it was her brother's turn to wait in the box. *Goddamn you, Scherie. I told you, the horror is my job.*

The portal was shrinking, closing off Rezvani's retreat. The living could better do the necessary. "Ossian, damn you, keep it open." But though Oz's eyes were fixed on the portal, he wouldn't be doing much of anything.

The others finally seemed to realize what had happened. "Endicott, command it to stay open."

"*Please, Lord,*" he prayed. "*Save our friend. Keep it open.*" His wife grasped his hand, and more power flowed through to him. For the moment, the portal held. But Scherie did not return.

"Dale Morton," said Madeline. "Call her back."

Dale looked at his hands, then at the rip in reality where the tentacle of abbess flesh had been. The Beast had resumed its forward flow, slower but steady. "As long as she survives there, she's fighting this, isn't she?"

Madeline saw his intent. "Don't."

With a running start and perfect control of the air, he leapt like a fish over the river of darkness, flipping midair to stick the landing near Oz and his portal, with a brief grimace as the impact registered on his bad leg. "I'm coming, Scherie. Wait for me!" Crouching, grinning with the pure madness of love, Dale, last of the Morton craftsmen, ran through.

Madeline's wooden frame was shaking with rage and something else. "Go, then, damn you, go and keep her alive for another minute."

Madeline had been berating the absent Dale, but it was Endicott and Grace who heard her. They stared at each other, looking for the answer in each other's eyes. This time they'd think about it.

But then, defying whatever attack it faced in its own world, the dark spiritual flow of the Beast poured faster through the rip Roderick had made.

With more measured steps than Dale's, they walked together around the rip and up close to Oz's portal. Risking madness, they followed with their eyes the line of Oz's unblinking gaze, peering through for Morton and Rezvani.

"They're still fighting," said Grace.

"Looks like they could use some help," said Endicott, trying to match his wife's usual dry understatement.

Again, they looked at each other. Instinct and principle were still sound.

"Queen and country?" asked Endicott, raising his sword.

"Against all enemies," said Grace.

"Bring them back!" called Madeline.

But they didn't acknowledge her. With a prayer and holding hands, they went through after their friends.

*I*n the name of all the dark powers, stay open!" Madeline threw her own remaining strength into holding the portal. She ran directly through the river of the Beast's attacking spiritual mass, her outrage carrying her past its effort to consume her. At Oz's portal, the view of the other side was now obscured by a black-lit whirlwind. She thrust her wooden arm through the portal, reaching into the wind. Nothing but fiery pain.

She had her own instinct and principles. She would risk everything and go all the way through to grab Scherie and pull her back. But even as she thought this, some force restrained her, halting both her stick-man and her spirit, pulling her and her arm back.

She found Pandava's hands on her, but it was Prithvi's will. With mass murder in her words, Madeline said, "*Let me go.*"

Pandava-Prithvi simply pointed at Madeline's arm. Its wood, made by a living thing, had decayed off, leaving only the dead metal rods.

"Oz!" she cried.

But instead of keeping the way open, Oz's fingers made a small, twitching gesture, and with a groan and a rattle of breath, his portal closed.

Madeline felt everything empty from her, and she greatly feared what would fill that emptiness. She had one small consolation: she was in a body that could not weep. She also had her brother in her power at last. But it was another who would have to answer for what had happened here—though not yet, not today, not when she was so, so weak.

The Beast contracted again, so fast that it left some soul bits of itself behind in the room as it flooded back through the rip to its world. Pandava-Prithvi stood in front of the invasive portal and sang her own song at it, not of operations and cryptonyms, but of the life that sprung from seed and egg, and slowly, stitch by stitch, the invasive portal shut.

Madeline didn't aid her. She didn't even want to be near her, lest she do something suicidally stupid but which right now seemed like the best idea in the world.

Instead, Madeline found distraction in the surviving Fury. The Crone stood before Oz, rendering her judgment. "You gave Rezvani our gifts. They are gone from this world forever." But Oz just seemed to stare where the portal had been, for his body was already cold, and his spirit was well beyond the Crone's jurisdiction and justice.

The Maiden lay dead and buried in a flesh cairn of her own making. Madeline was jealous. Fighting to the end, the Matron had reached a dying arm toward her young colleague. "*Dulce et decorum est*," spat Madeline.

The slow breathing of the few intact zombie monks and nuns stopped. The other, beneficent world's power flowed again through the hall, and the residual dark bits of the Beast were washing away in that golden light. Madeline tried not to listen as Prithvi gave thanks to the light from that world of generous, unconditional love—"a world we will one day wish to be." Prithvi then turned to Madeline, compelling her attention. "I'm off to end the hostilities of the three powers. But we'll see each other again, soon."

"Yes, we will," said Madeline. It was as much as she trusted herself to say, but only Pandava was now there to hear it.

A ragged line of living practitioners, Left-Hand and Right, was stumbling through the gate into the hall. These veterans of the battle in the valley were all nerves and spells, ready for combat, so the ones who came in earlier had to talk the later ones down in a continual chain of responsibility. Pandava promised assistance for those who wanted to descend on the Indian side, as no one knew whether the Sanctuary would be as helpful in departure as it was in arrival.

Like night birds fleeing the sun, the Left-Hand spirits passed through the gate in the other direction, to the inner Sanctuary, becoming individuals again as they did so. Madeline caught a brief glimpse of her father Curwen staring back through the hole. Staring at her. He silently nodded. Damn him, it was more acknowledgment than he'd ever given her in life. Then he turned away, back to whatever twisted Valhalla he had going on in there. So maybe he'd been a true believer in the Left-Hand cause after all, and not just a selfish old man.

She had only one cause and consolation now. She picked up her sword from where she'd struck the dragon and the gem from where she'd thrown it aside. She had promises to keep.

At Leh, Vasilisa stopped yelling at the Indian officer mid-obscenity. Tears began to stream down her face. *Too late.* The Dude closed his eyes in confirmation. "They're gone."

At Langley, Eddy saw what had happened even before his watchers did. *It can't be true. Sphinx would have known.* He ordered the Peepshow to search for the possibility of survivors and their return.

In Providence, the House of Morton had known many losses over the centuries. But Dale and Scherie were its rebuilders and renewers, and unlike most of the Morton dead, they would not be returning to it. Along with its sentience, the House had absorbed other bits of Morton magic over the centuries, but it could not cry with tears.

Rain, it said. For several days, a cold, steady rain fell in Rhode Island.

Madeline returned to Leh in time to see the practitioners from around the world as they departed. "Go, you useless things, before I make you truly weep," she said, but without much conviction.

She took possession of the heavier artificial body that Pandava had prepared for her; it had brass-colored alchemical alloy overlaying her form of fine-grained oak as well as within it, and ruby eyes set in mother-of-pearl. Then Madeline placed the gem box containing Roderick in the ugly hunk of wood that was Cornaro's poppet. Roderick's old decayed face flashed briefly through the poppet's head.

"Brother, you are there?"

"Ah, finally," he said. "I knew you'd come. Now we can talk." His voice was unsteady, a little desperate. The gem and poppet did that to one.

"Yes, talk, but not for long. You remember our last conversation by the river. I warned you that I would destroy you utterly."

"Oh yes," he said, too quickly. "Very dramatic. I approve."

"We Mortons do not make idle threats," she said. "We're more inclined to understatement."

"Oh dear," he said with a weak little laugh. "What torture do you have for me now?"

"Good-bye, brother. I may have a new vocation soon. I shall be the enforcer of the law of death. And you have cost me someone I cared about." Loved? Maybe words didn't matter.

"Not the first time I've taken someone from you," said Roderick, with some of his former nerve back in his tone.

He seemed to have some hidden meaning that he wanted her to pursue, an old game of his. She didn't care. "It's the last time."

She began her new vocation with him. She wasn't an exorcist, so it took her days. When she was finally done, she taught her new mechanical body to smile.

EPILOGUE

OF THESE, HOPE

You will never hear anything more about Oz, because we are now cut off forever from all the rest of the world. But Toto and I will always love you and all the other children who love us.

—L. Frank Baum

Any attempt at recovering the bodies was absolutely hopeless, and there, deep down in that dreadful caldron of swirling water and seething foam, will lie for all time the most dangerous criminal and the foremost champion of the law of their generation.

—Arthur Conan Doyle

And now abideth faith, hope, charity, these three.

—1 Corinthians 13:13 (KJV)

Distracted by the fight to save the world from Roderick and the hell that followed with him, the outside world never knew the outcome of the battle in the heart of the Sanctuarium Mundi between the orthodox and the Left Hand. All anyone knew was that in a moment in the Earth's precession, a new age had begun and the world would change.

In other craft news, Scottish practitioners threatened to secede from the UK and take Scotland with them. World craft energy levels, which had risen steadily, now fell dramatically. Some of the newest practitioners found themselves powerless, and some of those joined the ranks of the homeless insane. Knowledge without power is a brutal thing.

At least two unknown persons found themselves with far greater power when they were selected for the offices of Maiden and Matron.

In her cabin within the American Sanctuary, the Appalachian drank a toast of moonshine and shed some tears for the last Mortons of the Compact. She felt so damned old. Perhaps it was time to find a successor as guardian of this place.

In her house on leg-like stilts within Ukraine's Sanctuary, Lara's face remained as impassive as ever as spirits brought her news of the Sanctuarium Mundi disaster. But within her cool heart she mourned the craftspeople who'd helped her stop Roderick's abuse of her dead. She could have used their help again: no one in the West seemed to care that, in Russia, that thing from Lubyanka's subbasement was in charge at the Kremlin. Invoking the power of her land, she raised her arms against the fall of the night.

Mama Suji returned to Japan and, after reporting what had happened at the Sanctuarium Mundi to the Japanese craft service, she pointedly insisted on Kaguya's release and promotion. Suji had to push hard, with politely stated threats, as Kaguya's assistance in saving those who saved the world, though apparently necessary, had still been embarrassing. Upon her release, Kaguya went with Suji to Shibuya to visit the statue of Hachiko, Rabu's ancestor. Amid the crowds that orbited about that traditional place of rendezvous, the two craftspeople each placed a single rose at the statue's cold forepaws. "For Love of Hachiko," said Kaguya.

General Attucks himself delivered the message to the Rezvanis at their home in Cranston: *your daughter missing in action, along with her husband, presumed dead.* Scherie's father took the news as stoically as he could, but Mrs. Rezvani's rage threatened harm to self and others. "You don't think I know what you are?" she cried. "What they were?"

On a cold, windy night in Arlington National Cemetery, the

342   TOM DOYLEghosts of Endicott's parents and grandparents gathered together with those of Dale's father and grandfather. The dead do not often mourn, for that in the end would be a form of useless self-pity. But these ghosts, former enemies brought together by the friendship of Dale Morton and Michael Endicott, cried bitterly for the spirits of loved ones now utterly lost to them. The wind carried their mourning across the Pentagon, and Langley, and the astral plane of America.

But the spirit of Dare Smith, who was the oracle known as Sphinx and Dale's biological mother, did not mourn with them.

Hundreds of miles from the tripoint, an earthquake shook Nepal. For some synchronistic reason at Langley that same day, Eddy Edward's precog viewers gave him their latest verdict: probability of death for Rezvani, Morton, Endicott, and Marlow greater than five sigma and asymptotically growing toward certainty. Between the lines, their message was actually that he'd kept them on this task for far too long. He gave in. "Stop the surveillance. Close their files."

The rest of the world had gone back to the fuzziness that meant freedom of choice to those who wanted to believe in such. Working with Sphinx had made such beliefs complicated for Eddy. Closing the files made him feel like a Norn wrapping things up at the end of a Wagnerian opera in which all the characters had perished from cosmic necessity.

Not for the first time, Eddy despaired of his life's work. He had changed nothing. He finally understood Sphinx at her end, when she had complained that for all her farsight, the universe just didn't care. "It just doesn't fucking budge."

At this, one of the lowest moments of his life, his old government BlackBerry buzzed with a text message that he would lately discover had bounced stochastically around the world for years. The message was three words from Sphinx: "Of these, Hope."

Shortly after this, Eddy was called to testify about "the recent unpleasantness" before the ultra-secret craft oversight committee. Other nations were blaming the U.S. for Roderick, and they wanted answers.

Some of the committee members seemed to believe the growing rumors that the four deceased craftspeople had assumed the evil roles of Antichrist and Co. in the apocalyptic drama. They had plenty of supporting evidence: use of Left-Hand life extension was a case per se, and the four had again freed the Left-Hand Morton dead.

In the committee room, Eddy put aside his notes. "Let me tell you a story," he said, "about the bravest men and women I've ever known."

L ife went on in the craft world, and that world's secret continued to leak. In Widener Library at Harvard University, an under-graduate dressed in the perennial grunge style of that place was researching the American Revolution, and found the documents of the formal magical split from England. In Michigan, the ones they called Ozma and the Patchwork Girl were fighting against a different world of magic and malevolence that L. Frank Baum had glimpsed a hundred years before.

In India stood a temple of Kali-Durga made of sculptured female forms. There, seated in contemplation in her new manikin, Madeline spoke wordlessly with the world. She was not ready to go home yet or assume her global duties; she was awaiting answers, and she would not leave without them.

Her duties were not the problem. Whatever had happened on the battle plain of the Sanctuarium Mundi, she knew what her fight going forward would be, assuming she survived this meeting. Death must have dominion, and significant life extension may come but not through craft. Ironic—the Left-Hand way of long life and artificial bodies would eventually win, but only by its magics becoming mundane science.

She'd need a new cryptonym for her work; her birth name of Madeline Ligeia Morton had too much baggage at home, and not enough weight abroad. She knew she was no goddess (her delusions were of a different sort), but the people here were a bit looser on what it meant to partake of the divine, and goddesses had the best names. Kali was a goddess of many aspects and avatars. Madeline could be Matangi—the Left-Hand Kali.

Finally, having meditated for forty days and nights, Madeline raised her eyes to see Prithvi standing before her. "Congratulation," said Prithvi. "You've slain the would-be king of the dead. You are this world's champion against all comers. What else could you desire?"

"Desire is attachment," said Madeline. "Your wound seems to have healed nicely."

"Yes, thank you," said Prithvi. "You didn't answer my question. I didn't think you were the passive-aggressive type."

Madeline glared up at her. "I think I would have liked to continue as an ancestor-deity. Only, part of being an ancestor-deity is having fucking descendants!"

Shit, shit, shit. All this meditation had been to keep from doing something stupid at this meeting with a very powerful being. But Madeline's anger wouldn't be denied, and Prithvi seemed to be deliberately provoking her.

"You believe I am at fault," said Prithvi.

"You set them up. You gave Endicott the extra power he needed to wound you, and you let him break the will of the world. You knew Roderick would try to take Scherie's child. You set me on him personally. Yet you stayed hidden behind the scenes until the last. All to bring Roderick out into the open and bring matters to a head while there was still a chance to defeat him, but only through their sacrifice." She wouldn't call them her friends for the shame of failing them. "Did you also bind them together with the sense of destined love? Doesn't matter. If I had the strength, I would destroy you now."

Prithvi finally stopped smiling. "Careful, my dear, that is how this office passes: combat. Do not challenge me until you are able and ready. Able to win, ready to do my job. Believe me, no one is more anxious for that day than I."

Then Prithvi was gone. But Madeline remained in meditation a while longer, pursuing a lost memory through her many lifetimes back to the self of her original body. What had made Roderick so angry? What had he taken from her? Why had it made her so sad?

Madeline was still away when a stranger came to the House of Morton. She had hitchhiked from Taos to Providence. Small and thin with skin touched by Native American copper and dark hair bleached by the southwestern sun, she could have been any age from eighteen to forty-eight. People called her many hateful things: gypsy, whore, skinny slut, thief, grifter. She was none of these things, though some of their arrows of meaning pointed toward the truth. The world bent around her, and people saw that she was rewarded beyond her apparent merits, and that made them angry.

The House, godmother of all the Mortons, was angry too; only its silent, mournful hate greeted the stranger at its door.

The stranger looked up at House's highest windows. "Gonna make me be formal about claiming you?"

House groaned in its foundations. *Usurper.*

"Don't worry, House. I'll take care of you. I am Melissa Morton, descendant of Morella, the stolen child of Madeline Ligeia Morton, and I've come home at last."

As always before, many writers and artists were given farsight of these events, through a glass darkly. One saw the high mountains and the Sanctuarium Mundi during a performance of the Fantastické Scherzo by the Vienna Radio Symphony Orchestra, another wept in the middle of a comic movie for the world's loss of magic, and another saw these battles in a confused series of dreams induced by the chemo and radiation treatment for cancer. Open an uncanny book, and you will find the craftspeople remembered there, the fragments of their ruin scattered across thousands of pages.

Shanti shanti shanti

APPENDIX

FOOTNOTES TO THE CRAFT WORLD

PART 1: THE DOG WHO WAS DHARMA

As told in the Indian classic epic, the Mahabharata, after the end of the Kurukshetra War, King Yudhishthira of the Pandava family made his last journey across a great desert toward the mountains and the afterlife. He was joined by a dog, who stayed with the king for the whole arduous way. At last, the Lord of the Gods came down in his chariot to carry Yudhishthira to heaven. The god said that the king could not bring the dog along with him, but Yudhishthira refused to enter paradise without the loyal animal.

On hearing this decision, the dog changed into his real form. He was Yudhishthira's father, the god Dharma, and he praised his son for passing this great test. For this version of the story, I referred to *Mahabharata*, retold by William Buck (University of California, 1981).

In a later variation on the Indian story, *The Twilight Zone* episode "The Hunt" changed the setting to Appalachia. While chasing a raccoon, a hunter and his dog drowned. Their spirits wandered a path along a fence until they came to a gate. A smiling gatekeeper dressed as a rural civil servant informed the hunter that he had reached heaven, but he could only enter if he left behind his hound. The hunter refused to part from his beloved dog.

The two roamed farther along the path until they encountered a young man dressed in the same mountain-man style as the hunter. The young man told the hunter that he'd arrived in the real heaven, and that the gated place had actually been hell. The devil hadn't wanted the hound to come in because the dog would have smelled the brimstone and warned the hunter.

Both the original and later versions of the story illustrate the principles of loyalty and compassion for all beings, but they also thereby highlight an opposing truth about the Left Hand: its utter disregard for the lives of even loyal animals as it pursued its goals. Hence, the Indian officer used Rabu as a test.

A postscript: as I was creating this appendix note, the writer of "The Hunt," Earl Hamner, Jr., passed away. Perhaps at the end he saw his boyhood dog coming to guide him home.

PART 2: THE CROWLEY SANCTION

Aleister Crowley embodied one of the paradoxes of the craft: if, despite all the traditions of secrecy and its sometimes brutal enforcement, a craftsperson went public, it was as cover to their true power and work. Crowley was a very public and notorious mage, but he hid much of his skill, and he was also a covert assassin in the service of the British Crown.

In 1905, the Sanctuarium Mundi was in the Himalayan range near Kangchenjunga, the third highest mountain in the world. Crowley led an expedition nominally to climb the mountain, but with a covert purpose of visiting the Sanctuary. But within that covert purpose was another, still more secret mission: the elimination of a Swiss craftsman and his minion who had joined the expedition. The mountain was treacherous, but Crowley was more so. Crowley drew on the usually beneficent power of the Sanctuary to make the killings look like a climbing accident, an accident that was solely the fault of the victims. While disposing of his two targets, Crowley also murdered two innocent porters and nearly killed two other fellow climbers. The British Crown viewed this amount of collateral damage for a simple assassination as excessive, and the infamous incident became known as the Crowley Sanction.

Crowley knew all too well the karmic Law of Return. Due to his profanation of the Sanctuarium Mundi, he never dared to approach it again. By the end of his life he could no longer separate his fictional identities from his real one, and neither could anyone else. Other practitioners found the style of his many killings both absurdly baroque and steely cold, and the misinformed adulation of heavy-metal enthusiasts made those with knowledge a little sick to their stomachs. Crowley's writings reputedly influenced the music of Led Zeppelin, and that was why Scherie's reference to their song "Kashmir" so appalled her colleagues who'd grown up in the craft.